THE EGYPTIAN HEIR

JANELLE FILTEAU

FriesenPress

One Printers Way
Altona, MB R0G0B0,
Canada

www.friesenpress.com

This book contains sensitive material relating to violence, sexual assault, and physical abuse

Illustrator: Rebecca Romphf

ISBN
978-1-03-911027-4 (Hardcover)
978-1-03-911026-7 (Paperback)
978-1-03-911028-1 (eBook)

1. YOUNG ADULT FICTION, ACTION & ADVENTURE

Distributed to the trade by The Ingram Book Company

Five Millennia ago, an Egyptian kingdom flourished under the careful guidance of the Pharaoh Obeko. Droughts and floods were non-existent, and the people maintained full bellies with lush, prosperous farmland. Wars raged around them, yet no invaders broke through Egypt's borders and the inhabitants were lulled into peace.

Obeko reigned by commanding the power of seven diamonds that controlled otherworldly abilities. He was a just and fair man, and he used his extraordinary gifts to benefit his country. The diamonds were a well-entrusted secret that few knew of. He long foresaw that the elitists of Egypt would demand for unnecessary wants rather than care for their low-status freedmen. He, instead, sought to bring happiness to his entire country, as to not fall victim to man's natural greed.

Many questioned his abilities and wondered how the good fortune was obtained, but Obeko entrusted the secret of the diamonds to only a handful of people, including his wife, Haeibba. Obeko married Haeibba after disregarding his advisors' warnings and removing her from her bondage of slavery and bringing her into the world of riches and royalty. Obeko was so enthralled with his undying love for her that within months of marriage, Haeibba was told all the secrets of the diamonds. He would regret this in the following years.

Years of magnificent harvests fed his people and lessened the need for raising arms. Egypt found itself in a pensive state, but it would not last once Haeibba mistakenly informed the slaves of Obeko's fantastic feats.

During a visit at her family's poor village, she celebrated their reunion by drinking red wines and chattering the night away of how her husband had provided for his people. Unaware of her betrayal, Haeibba awoke to find a rampaging crowd of unpleased slaves. They demanded for the Queen to retell the story of Obeko's magical diamonds. Each word was stuttered as Haeibba explained Obeko's secrets.

An uproar of shouts disturbed the lands when the news travelled throughout all regions of Egypt. A rift had been created when the slaves began to believe Obeko used the diamonds to unnaturally control the lands and promote the elites rather than sparing anything for the slaves. They misunderstood Haeibba's fondness towards the man who sacrificed his own pleasures to better the rest of Egypt.

Haeibba scurried home to alert Obeko of the disaster soon to arrive. The Pharaoh of old was disappointed with the obvious betrayal of his wife and subjects. In desperation to make peace, he came before his people, and explained that the reason for their lack of poverty or malicious war mongrels was the diamonds. With the outrage already thick in their veins, none listened to the Pharaoh's honest words. Instead, a great war erupted, spilling the blood of his suddenly disloyal people.

Obeko's most devoted fought bravely, but the slaves made up for their untrained skills with numbers. The war split the land into two. Egypt collapsed into turmoil and all of Obeko's precise calculations to avoid civil war had suddenly become a volcano of hatred.

The war ended with Obeko making a final push to eliminate the leaders of the faction which corrupted his ideals. The state of his land, by the end of it, brought tears to the Pharaoh's eyes as the death count had risen higher than ever before in all his years as ruler. Without mercy, he executed the punishable, and when the time came for Haeibba's final verdict, she pleaded and begged for her husband to spare her life and allow her to explain her accidental betrayal. Without a sign of remorse, Obeko banished her from Egypt to live out her days as a slave. She lost the grip of her son's clutching fingers and heard her daughter's cries as she was hauled away. Obeko beckoned his children to his side, explaining the reasons for her dismissal and then led them into the caverns of his temple. Their first sight of the glistening, mystical diamonds brought a longing to their innocent eyes. Obeko denied them any involvement with the diamonds. Instead, he forced them to swear to bury all seven diamonds inside his tomb with him when he passed. Holding their small palms, he described the curse he wished for them to place on the tomb:

Whoever enters this tomb, and is not heir to the diamonds' powers, will surely die. When the heir is revealed, they will be able to control the diamonds as they wish.

IV

The Pharaoh passed into the everlasting three years later, and as they promised, Obeko's children dutifully placed the curse upon the enclosed tomb. Alone with his sacred diamonds, Obeko still awaits his heir.

•　　•　　•

Cassandra was enthralled in the story her elderly grandfather told in her floral printed bed. The old man bowed his greying head, smiling whenever the youth yearned for more. Being his only granddaughter, on each birthday, he sat her down, and retold the peculiar story. With his deep, gravelly voice, he enthusiastically threaded Obeko's curse into a fantasy world of amazement. The small, brunette, hazel-eyed child had just turned five, and grand fondness brightened her grandfather's glance when he admired her bundled up in her blanket, anticipating each word. She patiently clung to the blankets with her small fingers and refrained from blurting out questions until the end of the story. He always threatened to stop if she interrupted. She leaned against the fluffy pillow, full of awe.

The story ended with Cassandra teeming with chirping queries. "Did the heir ever come get the diamonds?"

"Not yet, but someday, they will." The man's wrinkled face burst into laughter.

Excitement caused Cassandra's tiny frame to bounce on the bed and reach for the plaid sleeve of her grandfather's button-down shirt. "Do you know who the heir is? Come on, grandpa! Tell me," she demanded excitedly.

Grandpa shied away when his daughter strolled in. Cassandra's gorgeous mother, with straight mahogany hair flicking off her shoulder and freckled cheeks, grinned with rosy lips that blossomed into a full-on laugh when her daughter gave her a wispy, dreamy glance. A butterfly kiss fell onto Cassandra's cheek.

"Dad!" her mother jokingly accused. "My little girl is in a dream world and you're helping her mind wander. That silly story is always on her mind for weeks after you leave."

Large hands patted Cassandra's head when the old man tilted his in appreciation. "Cassy's a smart little girl, Marilyn. Her mind wandering is not a terrible thing. She will be a brilliant young lady one day and prove to the world that she is someone special."

Marilyn's brows rose, curious of her father's special affection towards his granddaughter.

"Well, that's enough wandering for now," Cassy's mother sang. "Let's get you to sleep, Cassy. You've had a long day of activities."

Marilyn's thin hand patted the pillow to encourage the child to rest. Cassy stopped her hyperactivity and admired her mother as she finally lied back. Marilyn's hair teased Cassy as it waved in front of her, and two sets of hazel eyes connected as the two glanced upon one another. Her mother's eyes were all knowing, predicting that Cassy's naughty brothers snuck from their beds to cause mischief in another room. Cassy sadly blinked as she wished to look like her mother did. Most of her features were her handsome father's. Dark brown, lightly wavy hair was knotty atop of Cassy's head. Her mother sank beside her and tried to untie a straggly braid.

Her grandfather leaned in to kiss Cassy goodnight on the forehead. His lips whispered, "One day, when you're older, I'll tell you who the heir is."

He straightened, grinning wildly. Leaving his daughter and grand-daughter, he hummed his way out of the small, shared bedroom, filled with cluttered toys and schoolbooks.

"Don't forget, Grandpa! I'll be waiting," she called back.

Shifting her butt back and forth, Cassy snuggled into the blankets once more as her mother bent to pick up part of the clutter inside the bedroom shared by the oldest and youngest children. Cassy rethought through the fascinating story. Bobbing her head, her eyes landed upon her mother's once the woman halted in her never-ending battle to maintain a bit of cleanliness.

"Mum, is Grandpa's story real?"

Marilyn bit her lip and paused before she replied. "I believe that there was probably an ancient pharaoh who once saved his people. I'm not sure how he may have done it. All I can say, Cassy, is that your grandfather is fond of you, and he is always proud to share this story. Whether it is true or not doesn't matter."

Cassy accepted the words and swung her arms around her mother's neck. "If I were the heir, Mum, I would make sure that you, Dad, Michael, Brant, and Vince were all happy and super rich!"

"Cassy, I am glad you're not this heir. The story sounds like Obeko sacrificed a lot to make his people happy. Besides, I have all the happiness I would ever want because I know my children are happy. I bet your father would say the same thing. Money cannot buy happiness. It will only make people greedy. Remember that." Her mother's smooth hands straightened her hair before releasing her grip. "Now, it is time for sleep, my little birthday girl. Have a good night."

Releasing the child, she stretched her thin arms above her head, shuffled to the beige door, and flicked off the single light. Hoots and shouts were heard when Cassy's two brothers were scolded for leaving their bedrooms. The eldest brother came barrelling in. Cassy heard his cackles in the darkness as he ridiculed the punishment about to be had towards the other two. He hurried to change into pajamas and then bent at the waist to kiss her cheek. His long legs and leanly muscled chest showed off his soon-to-be-teenage figure.

Cassy rubbed flaky sleep from her drooping eyes.

"Grandpa told you that stupid story again, huh?" her brother queried.

"It's not stupid!" she defended. "Didn't you like it when Grandpa told you it, Michael?"

Michael silently crossed the carpeted floor to reach his bed as he thought of a response. Once he settled between the sheets, he replied, "He never told that story to me. Up until you were born, we never heard it. None of it is real, though."

Cassy frowned in a huff, and responded, "I like it!" With a wishful glance upon the rough ceiling, she whispered, "Isn't it neat that one man made all those people happy? To be the heir to the diamonds would let you do whatever you wanted!"

Michael's bed creaked under his weight in the darkness. His recently changing voice cracked out, "To be honest, that does sound neat."

Silence filled the bedroom with their final goodnights and Cassy's hyperactive world entered a short hibernation of relaxation.

Chapter 1

Cassy jolted in a cold sweat from the night terror. The sweat dripped along her spine and bristled her arm hairs as she shivered at the realistic dream. Her chest stung into a clenching heartache, leaving behind the dreadful nightmares she had night after night. Salty tears dripped through her guarded emotions. Angrily, she swiped them back with her trembling palms and curled into a hunched ball against the backseat door of Brant's vehicle to protect herself of the reality of her soon-to-be circumstances. Each time her eyes squeezed shut, the newspaper picture of the car wreck showed a reel of destruction.

In her dreams, her father drove, speaking to her mother on the passenger side. Their car halted at a blinding red light, where they held each other's hands. Shifting forward, as soon as the lights changed, there was no time to react before a speeding vehicle drove straight through the intersection. Cassy could only imagine the thoughts that crossed their minds in the split second before the truck struck her mother's side, rolling them into the ditch. A sudden calmness after the debris settled caused an eerie silence drifting into the unknown.

If only she hadn't looked at the newspaper clipping, this horrendous scene may never have been etched into her inner eye. She could have been oblivious to her parents' last moments. Combined with the description from the police officer's sensitive explanation, her mind wandered each night to the act of rotten luck.

The vehicle's cold window left Cassy dreading the move from her family home to live with Michael, who had two days ago gained legal guardianship over his three younger siblings. Now that he had permission to take in the siblings, they were uprooted from their pleasant memories in Edmonton to live in a new province and city.

"How're you doing?" Brant pondered aloud from the driver's seat to whoever would listen. He noticed Cassy's heavy breathing. "We just crossed the border. We will be in Saskatoon in less than three hours."

Cassy banged her head against the glass, miserable to even consider where they were headed.

"We can definitely take longer..." she whispered.

Brant clicked his tongue and sucked in his square jawline. "Eventually, we will have to face him."

"Why couldn't we go live with other relatives?"

Vince reclined the passenger seat to be in a lying position once he heard the disdain towards Michael.

"Mum has no family anymore and Dad's brother isn't in a good place to take in three teenagers, especially a troublemaker like you," Vince joked lightly. "Auntie is still in London."

Brant continued the explanation, "Michael is given the first opportunity to gain guardianship over us."

"Why couldn't we stay at home and have you as our legal guardian, Brant?" Cassy debated. "You're seventeen! You even graduate soon."

"That may be, but I'm still in high school and have no means of taking care of you guys. Michael owns his house, he has a stable job, and he's more mature than I am right now."

"Yeah right," she spat.

Brant maintained his cool by swiping a hand through his shortly cropped, brunette hair. Vince's narrow, elongated face pointed towards his younger sister curled in the backseat. The fourteen-year-old sister pressed her knees tighter into her developing chest and whimpered away at the changes occurring so abruptly. The youngest brother reached out to give condolences to her, while he also held a strong face at the current situation.

"He could've moved to Edmonton... He's making us move, when he should be considerate and move so we can stay in *our* home."

Brant shook his head, unpleased with the depression she portrayed.

"Michael's in the middle of a term for his schooling. If he ups and leaves, that's a waste of his money and time. It's easier for us to move."

Huffing out in adolescent rage, Cassy folded her arms across her chest and slammed her head once more against the windowsill. Vince rolled his eyes at the frustrated sister. Even when he found her pouting intolerable, he understood her anger.

"Why is his schooling more important than ours? You're supposed to graduate this year, Brant. It's barely three months away. Why couldn't we wait until at least the end of school for this year?" Cassy grunted.

Brant's dark, brown eyes leered at her.

"Cassy," he layered his voice with a strict tone, "we explained this four days ago…"

"Yeah, yeah…"

He continued, "Michael can't afford to take care of both houses while he's working hardly full time and doing school."

"Didn't Mum and Dad leave money for us?" she quipped back quickly.

"They did, but only Michael has access to it while we are still underage, and he wants to save it for us to be able to go to university. That's what our parents would have wanted."

Pained tears brimmed her eyelids as she was forced to listen to Brant's rational thinking. He hardly seemed affected by this entire event that shifted their lives into an abyss of agony.

"It's not fair!" she hollered, fed up with both brothers in the cramped vehicle. As she continued to speak, her head swung around to watch the truck driver pulling their things behind them. "I'm leaving all of my friends… so are you! I don't want to live with that traitor, and I definitely don't want to leave our home!" Her clenched fingers bit into her skin. "I hardly got to say goodbye to Tanya before leaving!"

Vince defended, "You visited with her all last night. Besides," he countered, "it's not like we won't ever be back there. Just wait, we will see our friends again. You guys will be texting and calling one another all the time."

Cassy patted her silent cell phone, which had not received one message since she sent a final farewell to her friends.

Brant prodded with a joke, "That's the most sense I've ever heard from Vince."

With a toothy smile and flashy wink, Vince chuckled, half defensive. "Hey now, I can have my moments more often than you think."

3

Cassy allowed them to continue their mockery of one another while she stressed over living with Michael in a strange city.

"Cassy," Brant hooted, "we will all be able to make new friends quickly."

Direct eye contact lingered on the road as she commented, "Don't try to play it up as a good thing. You're leaving behind your friends and hometown just before graduation to a place where the people you know are your siblings and one of those siblings abandoned us."

Vince punched Brant playfully, wincing at the sister's bluntness. "Wow, that was a fail in consoling on all degrees."

• • •

Cassy exclaimed loudly, "Holy shit, that's Michael's house!" while she plastered her face into the rear window. "How did he afford this!"

After half an hour of hunting for Michael's home with no luck, Brant snatched his phone and dialled with nimble fingers to figure out his whereabouts as he U-turned in the middle of a crescent. This unfamiliar city proved difficult to navigate, and the brother shamefully bowed his head when Michael laughed with snorts during his explanation. On the driveway, Brant reluctantly admitted that he had passed it four times.

"It's been a while since we visited here," Brant said, awed. "You don't remember Grandpa's house?"

"This used to be Grandpa's?" Cassy remembered nothing from her childhood visits with her grandfather. "I thought Michael was living in a small apartment."

"He was, but last year, he was able to put enough down to buy it from Mum and Dad. They wanted to keep it in the family."

A towering, two storey home loomed above them with a dark, chocolate brown exterior that reflected the glistening sun nicely. A veranda stretched along the length of the house to the front, barren grass where spring crept from its dormant state after a frosty winter in the prairie lands grew nearby. The front lawn was brown with small patches of snow still lingering underneath the large trees that swayed, naked in the winds. March brought warmer weather, but the transition from cold to warm brought an ugliness that soon would be full of magnificent life.

Despite her best attempts, Cassy admired the home. Above the two-car, attached garage, a large bay window was closed off by swaying curtains in a room which would be one of the siblings' very soon. Even with the opportunity to enjoy a home so unlike her parents' smaller one, Cassy lost all insight when, through the solid wooden entrance, a tall, slightly built young man strode from the porch and hopped from the steps with his arms wide open. Each time Cassy looked upon the brother that looked identical to her father, she squirmed with unpleasantness. Broad shoulders swayed with each step forward as Michael ruffled back his hair to figure out what should be said about this trying situation.

Vince, without even a friendly hello, loaded Michael's arms with a suitcase and large backpack filled to the brim. Michael accepted the items willingly, offering a welcoming, award-winning smile that spread across his shaven, square cheeks.

"How was the trip?" Michael inquired.

Michael shuffled the bags from arm to arm to allow himself to at least offer hugs for their safe arrival.

Brant huffed while he struggled with a box cluttered with photo albums. "Fine. Pretty uneventful. Unfortunately, in either province, the scenery is boring."

Michael accepted the ounce of a conversation starter. "Did you guys sleep a bit?"

He hunted for the youngest sibling, who snuck behind the vehicle in hopes of not being pinpointed.

Bluntly, she ignored the question and replied with, "Where's my room?"

"Oh… um." The distain filled him with disappointment. "It's not quite ready, but it's that one above the garage. Upstairs and three doors to the right. The movers can get most of the big stuff. Let's fit in the smaller items and then catch up. I haven't seen Cassandra in a few months."

"My name is *Cassy!*"

Without a second to correct his mistake, Michael gaped as she stormed up the porch, headed through the entrance, and slammed it shut behind her. Unsure why she suddenly snapped like that, Michael focused on the other two, who redirected their attention to the filled car.

"What did I do this time?" Michael bellowed.

"Well, other than her thinking you abandoned her, given the fact she just lost both her parents in a horrific way without being able to say goodbye, which caused her to move from everything she knows, and that you called her Cassandra… that's a typical reaction for her in the last few weeks," Brant stated.

"I moved three years ago…" he half-heartedly defended. Not all those issues were his fault, but he understood the frustration that all three siblings carried with moving. "I never abandoned her. I left for school."

Shouting over his shoulder, Vince strolled up the unfamiliar steps, "That's how she views it. Trust us, that's all we've been hearing."

"The name thing isn't my fault. I assumed she grew out of it."

Fits of laughter exploded from the younger two brothers.

"If she ever grew out of that name, I think she would die. Mum and Grandpa called her that."

Brant, shuffling by the eldest, who still stood with the heavy load of a suitcase and backpack, briefly whispered, "I recommend being happy. She just started talking a couple days ago. Today, she even made a joke while we were in the vehicle. It's been hell just to get three words from her. You got four in five seconds."

With that, they began unloading the bulk of the packed away items.

•　•　•

Cassy escaped the empty, modernly painted bedroom after dreading going to sit for dinner with all of her surviving family members. From the bedroom exit, the room across from hers in an offset position had Vince scattering boxes around in frustration about where to put all his clutter. Without a spoken word to him, she strolled down the hallway towards the steps. She passed the simply set up bathroom before she stepped down the wooden staircase leading to the open concept living room. Cassy's hand ran down the railing during the many steps to the main level of the house. The steps curved slightly to face the living room. A cream suede loveseat faced the television above a low bookshelf, and a matching couch was pushed against the window on the same wall as the front door. It faced the rocking chair and the doorframe where the kitchen and dining room were. An office broke up the open concept in the living room.

Cassy controlled her chin from wobbling as she passed the office and entered the kitchen. Brant and Michael talked in a monotone as they worked to place kitchenware away before starting to cook.

"Can I help with cooking?"

Michael flicked his wrist to tell her to sit and relax. Cassy slammed a hand down on the counter and argued about not being allowed to do anything.

"You have a lot of unpacking to do. Brant and I can do it. Cooking shouldn't be your priority. If you want to help, either set the table or work on unpacking."

Handing over plates from the top shelf, Michael set them next to her. Enraged she was being treated like a child, Cassy angrily crashed the plates against the table. Cassy leaned against the island once she finished and distastefully examined the unknown house. The kitchen itself was a decent size, with a rectangular island breaking up the open space. A small breakfast nook settled in the corner, with a rounded booth and small table. Vince had relinquished all frustrations and reclined across the bench while answering Michael's questions about the trip. He tapped his long fingers against the table, anticipating food without assisting.

Perfectly matched kitchen appliances cluttered the dazzling, dark marble countertops and the cupboards, which were situated in a long L-shape. The simplicity of the kitchen made it convenient as well as appeasing for a family atmosphere. Cooling tiles soothed the tension around them when she twisted her feet over the smooth floor in boredom.

Michael stirred the food, patiently holding his tongue from drilling Cassy with questions. He expected it would end poorly. Instead, he turned his back on his three siblings and contemplated how to approach the issues without having an explosion of emotions.

Brant took the opportunity of quiet to hand cutlery to Cassy so she could continue setting the table. Rolling her hazel eyes, she snarled and stuck out her tongue at the older brothers. Again, slamming occurred once she crossed the kitchen, passed Michael's arrogant cooking, and went into the attached dining room. Brant tilted his head with disapproval at her behaviour. Cassy flung each utensil down in defiance. Just as she finished, Brant handed over more items to keep her busy. Cassy swung an annoyed arm towards Vince, who lounged teasingly. Brant silenced any snarky comments from arising with the raise of an eyebrow. Cassy sank at the dining table and huffed in exasperation once Brant lost things to hand over.

Michael gave an appreciative smile as Brant gave a nod to encourage him to say something. Instead, Michael lost the nerve and poured the gravy into a bowl to be served. Brant struck his own head, thinking the broken bond between the youngest and eldest proved too damaged to mend.

As all the siblings gathered at the table, they began eating the large, welcoming meal. Cassy, even though she was hungry, only nibbled and played with the delicious dinner that she had hoped to help with. Michael tapped his fork against his plate, making it clang loudly.

"So... how have you guys been?"

"If you had been there, you would already know how we've been..." Cassy snarled.

"Cas-" Brant started to warn.

"No! He asked, I'm answering!" she shouted. "Do you want to know how we've been, Michael? Well, first off, three weeks ago, our parents died. I hope you got that memo! Vince was recently kicked out of school for drinking and Brant's been having to deal with all the paperwork that you couldn't do because *you* were too *busy* to come to Edmonton to deal with it." Food splattered when she flung her fork down and solemnly held her defensive wall high. "Does that sum it up for you?"

"Unfortunately, Cassy," Michael attempted at a calm tone, "we've got to figure out how we can live together without being at each other's throats all the time."

Infuriated with his words, she stood abruptly, saying while she rushed from the kitchen, "I didn't want any of this to happen! I just want to be home! I hate you for everything that you did when we needed you, and I hate that I couldn't stay where I'm happier."

Brant hopped up from the table to halt her scurrying feet. His large, burly arms pressed her weeping face into his chest as she buried her chin deep inside.

"Cassy..." Brant whispered, "It's alright. It's been a long day."

"I just want it back to how it used to be... I want them back."

Michael examined his family. Finally, he realized the pain they all had suffered, as Vince shied away from inhaling his food and bowed his head. Brant never wept a single tear, though his overbearing protectiveness wavered as Cassy trembled in his arms. Michael released a deep exhale.

"I'm sorry," Michael stated. "Please, eat something."

Brant shifted Cassy back to her seat. Embarrassed for her explosion of emotion, Cassy streaked the tears away from her eyes and hid her puffy face. Michael reached out a sensitive hand, one that she once clung to so tightly whenever she feared something inside their small, shared bedroom. This time, she was forced to recoil.

Silence shrouded the table except for forks and chewing. The newly-moved siblings searched the house, calculating how to make this arrangement work. The tension between the eldest and the youngest seemed to grow with every second. Vince and Brant feared that one might explode. Michael chewed thoughtfully, trying to lighten the mood by explaining the high schools the siblings would be attending, but their savoury meal had been soured by Cassy's overreaction.

"So, you know how I mentioned I have a friend next door?" Michael asked, announcing it to any siblings who listened, yet truly intending it for Cassy. "He has a younger sister the same age as you. I've mentioned that you're moving in. She goes to the same school as you. Whenever you're ready, I think you should go introduce yourself this weekend before you start school. Because it's the middle of the school year, I couldn't get all three of you in the same high school. If you want, we can transfer you guys next year, but until then, you'll be separated."

Vince clapped happily, "Excellent! No pestering siblings anywhere! I can go nuts now!"

Michael ended the clapping with a chuckle, "Brant's at your school. Cassy's the one separated, unfortunately."

"Ha!" Cassy stuck out her tongue, "No siblings for me!"

A loud ringing interrupted the breakthrough conversation between the four as Cassy's pocket chimed and brightened. Reaching into her jeans, she pulled out the cell phone and went to answer it. Michael's dexterous fingers snatched the device, which he put onto silent and placed on the opposite side of him.

"We need to establish some ground rules. First, no phones at the dinner table. It's family time."

"Yeah, some family," she mumbled.

Eyebrows rose high on Michael's forehead, "What was that?" Sealed lips retorted nothing back. Pleased to find no snarky comments, Michael continued, "Once everything is unpacked, we will have to create a cooking and cleaning routine so it's fair for everyone to do daily chores. Homework and catch up is expected to be priority."

"Fine." Cassy pushed back her chair. "I'm done. May I go unpack my shit?"

"Language, Cassy."

Rolling her eyes, she stormed from the dining room to avoid any other confrontation. Heading through the now disorganized home filled with boxes, Cassy crept across the living room and dug her hands deep into her pockets in frustration. Brushing up against the loveseat, she found herself thinking, *Michael was lucky to afford this house. It fits us perfectly.* She clung to the railing of the stairs and glanced over it to leer down in the basement. Since Michael hardly ever went to the basement, Brant claimed the entire space. Michael's master bedroom was on the main level down the small hallway, right before the living room cut into the kitchen. The master bedroom had its own joined bathroom, thus providing all the siblings, except for the two upstairs, their own private bathrooms.

Upstairs, Cassy headed down the hallway to her bedroom entrance on the right-hand side, entered, and flung the door solidly shut before freezing in step. The first day was almost finished, but emotional turmoil riled her up. Collapsing to the floor, she took a minute to breathe in several times before wrenching out her cell phone and dialling her friend.

"Hello?" Tanya responded on the other line.

"Hey, Tanya. I forgot to call once I got here."

Shifting of the phone occurred as Tanya was busy scribbling away at homework.

"That's fine. Was the trip alright?"

"I guess so. I keep having that nightmare, and then, of course, I'm now living with Michael… I already hate it here."

Tanya cynically laughed aloud. "Oh you! Give it a chance. It might surprise you. How have you and Michael been doing so far?"

"Well, I think we've had at least six fights already, so I think it's starting off fine."

"That's not fine at all!" Tanya spoke as though she rolled her eyes. "You two should be supporting each other after what's been happening, not pushing one another away."

"How can you say that when you know what he did?" Cassy hollered.

"Cassy," Tanya strictly said, "he moved away to better his life. He didn't intend to abandon you."

"That's not the entire problem though! I would call him, and he was always too busy for me. He never even took a call from Mum or Dad. He moved here and then his family didn't matter anymore. I *needed* him and he just left me there to sort out everything…" Cassy bowed her head. "I was dependent on my big brother because he had always been there for me. When he left…"

"Cassy, that's not fair. He left for school an—"

"But he blindsided everyone! He was supposed to go to school in Edmonton. Then he suddenly changes his mind two weeks before he's supposed to start, and changes his degree and city! He was gone within a week! Mum cried for days! She worried that they had done something to push him out. He caused all this pain when he moved, and now he hopes to fix it just because we're forced in his house. It's bullshit!"

Tanya hummed during the rant. When it ended, she agreed fully, yet gave her opinion on the matter. "Does he know that he did this?"

"I tried to call and talk about it."

"No… Does he *know* what he did to cause the tension? Maybe you should make him aware so he will apologize and both of you won't be so combative."

Cassy groaned, annoyed at the logical thinking. "I'm tired. I think I'm going to do some unpacking and then go to sleep. I miss you!"

"Hopefully it gets better, Cassy! I'll talk to you soon."

Now hung up, the phone bounced on the bedspread as Cassy sprawled across it herself. Looking about the room full of scattered, miscellaneous items, Cassy couldn't drag out the nerve to unpack the few boxes of her parents' things. Once she determined the perfect spot for them, she would be able to remove them from the cardboard darkness.

The old house creaked as her brothers moved about. The wind struck the siding from outside and caused the house to groan as it shifted slightly. The spacious bedroom held an eerie sensation that caused her to jump up and pace about several times until she settled on her knees to scour for a book to flip through. She widened a novel once she curled into her covers. None of the words registered. Silent tears dabbled her cheeks, filling her mouth with salty wetness. The past few weeks' changes consumed her, and she struggled to rid the fact that her parents had passed on.

It seemed as if the brothers had already dealt with the recent losses and continued their lives. Cassy dropped her head onto the open book and thought back to the funeral a mere two weeks previously. Michael refused to embrace Cassy, and while they sat in the pews of the church, stiff as boards, he intently listened to the eulogies of their young parents without any effort at consoling his other siblings. His hands were neatly folded across his lap and his jaw was tightened. Cassy curled into Brant's quivering arms and clutched Vince's chilled fingers. Afterwards, Michael stood, accepting condolences for their losses. Cassy had rushed towards him, wrapping her weak arms around his waist, and hoped for pleasant words to ease her pain. He redirected his attention to other people, proving how severed their bond had become. He released her grip, handed over his cell number to Brant, and surrendered into the bright sunlight to collect his items before heading back home.

He walked away from me, just as he did when he moved.

Falling asleep, Cassy dreamt of mournful things. The long, drastic day of changes wore her down.

• • •

"Morning!" Vince twittered, eating his cereal in the kitchen. "Sleep well?"
"Where's Brant?"

"He and Michael went to get groceries and other things that we seem to be missing."

Cassy tapped a nail against the countertop on the island. "Oh."

Vince halted the spoon from entering his gaping lips. Cassy's anxious movements had him searching for reasons she needed to talk to Brant.

"Did you have another bad night?"

Rubbing the top of her eyelid, Cassy shook her head before disappearing to sit outside in the cool late morning air. The recently melted snow left small patches of ice in the shade. Cassy sank onto the stairs. The smaller city had less hustle and bustle than Edmonton. The old crescent horseshoed around, bringing about a quiet air compared to the noise of rushing people found in Edmonton. As Michael had explained the night previously, her high school was within walking distance, while the other two had to drive or catch the city bus. Anticipating learning the route to the mysterious school, Cassy wondered if wandering around would be a good idea when she only knew a small section of the city.

A slamming metal door to the right of her caught her attention as a girl her age hopped from a vehicle pulled over near the neighbours' driveway and waved goodbye. Red hair, tightly braided behind her back, waved back and forth as the lean, lanky female hefted a large duffel bag over her shoulder, hurrying towards the front entrance. Large blue eyes, perfectly framed by eyeshadow and mascara, flared brightly when she noticed the unfamiliar girl sitting on the porch.

"Hello!" she waved and giggled. "You must be Cassandra. Michael mentioned you were coming sometime this week." Crossing the slowly greening grass, the girl went to greet Cassy. "I'm Rebecca. My brother, Mark, and Michael have been best friends since Michael moved in."

"You go to the same high school as I will be?"

"Yes, the same grade too! Dolesia is a decent school. I think you'll like it there."

The bag dropped and Rebecca sank beside Cassy, crossing her long legs over one another. Rebecca's smile blinded Cassy with her perfect dental hygiene. Rebecca glanced over Cassy, making her feel self-conscious about her slightly larger hips and diamond shaped face compared to

Rebecca's sculpted, model-like features of lean figure and sleek, feline looking cheekbones.

Without intending to, Cassy instantly judged Rebecca. *Ugh, she's going to be an annoyance in my life.* Realizing she was being rude without Rebecca knowing, Cassy changed tactics and queried, "Whereabout is the school?"

Excited to gain a small ounce of conversation from someone her age, Rebecca said, "It's just down the street, about ten blocks. You leave from here, turn right, or go through the alleys, and then follow the street until you meet up with a winding path. The pathway meets up with the basketball court and student parking lot for the students who have their licenses."

"What's the school like?"

"It's alright. There's a few trouble students that always seem to be tormenting other people." Rebecca lowered her red head into her crossed arms. Turning it to face Cassy, she warned, "There's one crew that you should know about straight away. Zack Exacil is in the center of it. He's an intimidating prick whose main goal is to scare people so he doesn't have to deal with nuisances. He may try something towards you. The last new student, albeit a guy, had the shit kicked out of him."

"What's this guy's deal?"

Rebecca shrugged, unsure how to respond to that question. "Well, when we were younger, he used to be fun loving and happy all the time. I guess a lot of stuff went down in his life and then, when he returned to school, he was different. He's been in more than fifty fights in the past three years and rebels whenever possible. A lot of rumours suspect gangs, but nothing has been actually confirmed. The fights have never gone any further than him beating someone down before the cops intervene."

"How come he's not in a juvenile delinquent facility?"

"Nobody pressed charges."

"Weird." Cassy directed her attention to Rebecca's bag. "Which sport do you do?"

"I swim. Which sports do you do?"

Cassy grew embarrassed at her lack of hobbies. "Nothing really. I've learned a little taekwondo, but that wasn't professional. It was through Michael."

"Oh..."

As Cassy spoke of Michael, he appeared inside his vehicle with Brant as they drove up the driveway and into the garage. Rebecca continued speaking, yet Cassy heard none of it. She reverted towards disliking the fact that Michael had arrived home with the ridiculous grin he carried when he had bright conversations with Brant. The neighbour noticed Cassy's distracted attention and heaved her bag over her shoulder.

"We will chat on Tuesday. That's when you start classes, right?"

Cassy shook her head, realizing her rudeness. "Sorry." She returned her eyes to the redhead. "Yes, Tuesday…"

Rebecca began the march across the yard before turning and rushing to Cassy. She swung her arms around her neck.

"I'm sorry about your parents! Please call me if you ever need anything."

Stunned by the affection, Cassy returned the hug lightly. Rebecca released and scurried off before Cassy could find her words. Michael rounded the garage, lifting grocery bags in both arms.

"So, you met Rebecca?"

"Yeah…" Cassy turned her back on him, hurrying away.

"Did you want to visit some more?"

With a quick shake of her head, Cassy hurried away, back up the stairs and into her mayhem of a bedroom.

For the rest of the weekend, unpacking took up much of Cassy's time and patience. Brant and Michael searched through each box, deciding whether to store or give certain items away. Arguments between the oldest and youngest increased when he entered her room and attempted to toss out a few of their parents' trifling things that Cassy kept as mementos. Shoving him out of the door viciously, she slammed it and hid away for the next two days.

Chapter 2

Rebecca met up with Cassy outside the house early Tuesday morning. Cassy accepted the quick friendship since it stabilized a small ounce of her world. Filling the air with talking, Rebecca spouted out anything that came to her mind to dwindle the amount of dread that filled Cassy's.

Halfway down the block, they cut through a catwalk. It angled slightly to attach the next block, where they continued until they stepped onto a paved path along the slowly forming greenery of grass. Cassy concentrated on the route, figuring out the simplest ways to return home. The twenty-minute walk proved to be full of twists and turns. Cassy sighed in the morning dew as they strolled underneath towering trees. Rebecca questioned her a little, trying to learn a few things about the mourning girl who was hardly holding together. Up over a hill, a two-storey building reached out towards the two girls. Green tin rusted beneath red brick. Tarmac covered the grounds where a basketball court tempted the early risers to play a round before classes began. Grassy fields surrounded most of the school, connecting baseball fields and a running track together. Several vehicles were parked in the rectangular lot where older teenagers smoked or joked about with one another.

Rebecca waved at other students who welcomed her and called her over to join them. However, when they noticed the new girl, the group went on with their business, realizing that the strange teenager would be showed around beforehand. Rebecca took Cassy into the school, where tiled floors clicked as students bustled about to gather items from lockers and then await classes.

"Yesterday I asked where your locker would be for you and I got your class schedule. Unfortunately, our first class isn't together, but the rest of them will be!"

Cassy awed at the friend's prowess in assisting her.

"Thank you. When did Michael choose my classes?" Cassy wondered.

Rebecca led her up the steps and down a hallway to the right. They halted at a locker and Cassy struggled to widen the metal lock.

"I guess he would've done that once the school admitted you. Most of the classes are typical for our grade, but Michael also chose a cooking course for you. That's your first one."

Leading her down the steps in a tightly packed stairwell, she directed Cassy up another corridor. This one held large rooms, some with heavy practical applied arts equipment and others filled with stoves.

"This is your class." Rebecca announced as the first warning bell rang. "I will meet up with you here after class, alright? We will head to our science course together."

Nodding nervously, Cassy bowed her head when a stampede of students intruded on the solitary hallway. Cliques of students appeared, all halting in their conversations when they noticed the new student standing just outside, building the courage to enter. A group of boys arrived, strutting in their loose-fitting jeans and presenting an air of cockiness. The one directly in the center halted for a second and frightened Cassy into petrified stillness as his dark brown eyes grazed over the unfamiliar face. A sneer formed just as he encouraged the group to enter. Exhaling sharply, Cassy found herself unable to move and unsure if she was wanting to stay in this school.

A quick peak inside the loaded classroom found several rows of bench-like desks with two students at each. Tall stools held the students up as they prepared for a day of lectures. On the other end, kitchen stations were set up, enough for each bench to work as a pair with a single oven, counter space, and kitchen sink between them. She wearily realized that one of the people inside this room would be her partner for the rest of the semester.

"Hello there," an adult's voice spoke, "are you new to my class?"

Cassy jumped back, startled that she was found while wavering on the thought of ditching class for the day. Nodding and handing over the crumpled slip of paper with her schedule printed on it, the teacher wrapped an arm over her shoulders, beckoning her to enter.

"Alright, class!" he shouted over the chatter. "Sit down!"

The teacher clung securely to Cassy's shivering torso in front of the class.

"We have a new student today. Please make her feel welcome." He tilted his head, calculating on where to place her. "Whose bench is open for another body?"

The menacing boy rose a hand, twiddling his fingers about. The subtle muscles stretched from his forearm to his shoulders and tensed, showing off to the girls. Cassy shuffled towards him when the teacher praised him for being honest and then went on with his lecture. Her butt plopped onto the wooden stool, and she tucked her hands over one another.

The boy swivelled towards her with his long legs that easily reached the floor where Cassy's toes barely touched without stretching. He leaned in close, giving Cassy a cruel expression.

"What's your name, new girl?"

Cassy tilted backwards in avoidance to being too close.

"Screw off."

A menacing frown helped show his true colours. "Excuse me? I asked you a question."

The teacher rescued her from replying whence he snapped at the twosome to focus upon the lesson. Strictly ignoring the boy, she pulled out a notebook and began jotting down the food safety discussion. The boy sucked back his lips, chewing on them to show rebellion against the teacher's harsh tone towards him.

The bell rang fifty minutes later, the students' cramped hands from speedy writing unfurled from their pens. Hopping off the bench, Cassy shoved her books into her backpack and hurried from the kitchen-like classroom to meet with Rebecca. The friend wildly waved and hurried to Cassy to ask how her first class went. However, something caused her to falter. Twisting only her head, Cassy caught sight of the menacing boy's group hunkered in a corner, pointing and snickering at her.

"You met Zack!" Rebecca yelped.

Cassy, unsure of who she met, said, "He never introduced himself."

Rebecca towed Cassy far off into another hallway before they lingered too long to attract attention.

"This isn't good. What did you say to him?"

Nonchalantly, Cassy answered, "'Screw off'."

Ghostly white terror filled Rebecca's freckled cheeks. Realizing that what she had done was against protocol, Cassy apologized to her friend for being too hasty in making an enemy. She clutched Rebecca's palms and told her to relax and swiftly asked to be led to the next class. With a task at hand, Cassy hoped that Rebecca's anxiety would fade; however, it only increased when Rebecca found herself trapped in the middle of a grisly scenario as Zack appeared with four of his brutish companions. Cassy barricaded Rebecca from the boy while she herself attempted to clear her mind before she overreacted.

"You're exceptionally rude," Zack said. "All I asked was your name."

The teenage boys formed a circle to ensnare them in the barren hallway.

"I don't give my name out to pricks."

Zack stepped forward. Long legs were concealed inside baggy jeans that snuggly clung to his waistline with a black belt. Rebecca bowed her head, unsure of how to dissuade the aggression. Zack snapped out a hand and snatched Cassy's wrist. She stumbled back, startled by the brutality as she struck the wall and felt his hand tighten as his anger escalated further.

"Let go of me!"

Rebecca lost sight of Cassy. The foursome of boys shoved her from Cassy's side. Her shrilled voice caused a headache. Cassy wanted peace and quiet, not this loud, obnoxious school that already corrupted her peace.

"I asked you what your name was. Don't be stuck up." He leaned closer, intimidating her lightly. "I'll only ask one more time. This time I'm telling you give me your name, and this may end now."

Cassy snarled, "And I'm telling you to let go!"

Zack gazed down his straight and narrow nose upon Cassy. His brunette hair concealed the vicious eyes flaring towards her.

"You're such a stuck up, spoiled brat. When someone asks for your name, you give it."

Annoyed with his arrogant personality, she retorted sassily, "And you should really try to leave people alone when you have no inkling on what you're talking about."

Riled up to the point of uncontrollable behaviour, Zack rose his hand to strike Cassy's face. Rebecca shrieked loudly, unsure what to do. Cassy saw the scene in slow motion. His hand rose high above his head and curled into a firm fist. Behind him, his friends showed how fearful they were towards him as well. Rebecca begged them to stop their friend, all the while they pulled her away and restrained her flailing limbs. The fist became an open hand, yet the slap never reached her cheek; she ducked low, still restrained by his hand, and dodged his attack. Before he could comprehend that she dodged it, she countered with her own fist and struck him beneath the ribs with a direct hit to his gut. He wheezed as he doubled over. His grip loosened, though Cassy thought he seemed trained in some form of martial arts because he took the strike well. Instead of wasting time on checking if he was finished, she gripped his wrist, using his own unbalanced position against him, and manipulated her foot between both of his to trip him to the ground. Coughing at her feet, Zack rested his head on the cool tiles, knowing when to give up.

Without a threat from Zack's friends, Cassy gathered Rebecca and ushered her away from the attracting action.

"Holy shit!" Rebecca mumbled, stunned by the events. "You just beat up Zack!"

Cassy shrugged, searching through her class list for the next classes she would be forced to attend.

"Technically, I didn't beat him up. It was self-defence. He was going to hit me."

"Well, we better be careful. He's going to be in quite a few of our classes and he might retaliate."

Rebecca showed the way towards the stairs and where their science class would be held. No rumours spread about the girl who beat up the infamous Zack Exacil yet, but Cassy prepared for the repercussions when the gossip did spread. Up the steps, the hallway's walls changed from a blue to a red as they entered a significantly smaller corridor with three classes clustered within. Cassy halted at the first right hand entrance to calm her racing heart before entering with Rebecca. Since the classroom had unassigned seating, Cassy followed Rebecca to a far corner desk, and they sank next to one another in preparation for the beginning of class. Digging through her backpack, Cassy pulled out a notebook and pen as the teacher introduced the newly transferred student. An awkward silence followed, and the teacher spun and scribbled a chemical equation across the board. Leering eyes penetrated Cassy's skull, making her skin itch. She hunted for the source of the perturbing sensation. In dismay, she cringed at what she found. Zack had perfectly timed his entrance, framed by the door, to the introduction of her name. He filled with arrogant self-satisfaction by gaining an answer to his original question.

Great, now I need to deal with this guy… Mum, dad, why can't you just wake me up from this nightmare… Cassy thought to herself.

Nothing was said when he passed her to reach an empty desk. Her bravado left her the moment the adrenalin had dissipated. Removing her steady eye contact, Cassy ended up bowing her head low and intently listened to the lecture. The beige, dull classroom placed her into a lull of just wanting to run away from dealing with everything. Unfortunately, she had no such luxury.

She stretched her stiffened limbs at the end of class. Her legs straightened beneath the wooden and metal desk, too sore to even fully extend. She followed Rebecca once more to the next class, which turned out to be math, only three hallways down. Rebecca went into overdrive to hurry Cassy out of the classroom. She wanted to remove herself from another confrontation with Zack. It was, however, unavoidable when he came barreling down the aisle Cassy stood in and used his momentum to bulldoze her into a desk. She grunted back the pain before twisting to strike at him. He defeated her feeble attempt to retaliate with a simple block. Cassy stomped her feet when he winked to say goodbye and strolled from the room.

"You've got to stop reacting," Rebecca said, rolling her eyes in anguish. "He's trying to get a rise out of you. Let's go to class. He's not in our math class. If you keep your head down, he won't bother you."

With mockery in her voice, Cassy chuckled, "I'm already in his sights. I'm going to have to keep fighting until *he's* bored with this shit."

Without Zack's annoying grimace targeting her back for her fifty minutes of math, the class went without a single hitch. Cassy, relieved to finally enjoy a moment of peace, furiously took notes to keep up with the rest of the class. She now understood how much work would be needed to catch up with her classmates. *I'm going to be studying until midnight tonight just for this one class*, Cassy thought.

The class abruptly ended when an intercom speaker, above the chalk board on the far-left side, chimed in. "Excuse me for interrupting, but I need to see Cassandra Waters in the main office, please and thank you."

Encouraging Cassy to go, the teacher briefly described how to get to the office before returning to class. Unsure on the reasons for being called to the office, Cassy gathered her things and left. She followed the teacher's instructions and made her way to the main floor to a large hallway with several offices. Just as she made it halfway to her destination, an unwanted sight appeared.

Zack rounded another corridor, hands shoved deep inside his pockets, and he swaggered over to the startled girl. In an instant, the reason for being called down to the office dawned on Cassy.

"Shit!" she exhaled. Her hands folded across her chest, guarding her from the boy's smug approach.

"I'm glad you figured it out," Zack mocked. "Most times, princesses like you expect to be rewarded."

Cassy tried not to get riled up, but being called a princess and spoiled brat continued to irk her. "If you knew anything about me, you would know that I'm no princess." Cassy stepped forward, attempting to stay behind the boy who sneered. "This is your fault. You started this whole thing."

"And it proved to be an unexpected surprise."

Cassy's rolling hazel eyes lifted towards the ceiling. "What made you into such a prick?

"How come I'm suddenly the prick when you hit me?"

"You tried to strike me first! It was self-defence!"

Zack halted, expecting Cassy to catch up. When she walked next to him, he continued at a similar pace.

"You had no prior knowledge of me beforehand, so why did you have to be so defensive? If you had told me your name in the beginning, none of this would have happened."

Cassy stuttered when she realized he spoke the truth. She had instantly built up her guard and snapped at him.

"I, for one, do have a reputation," Zack announced, "but I have never hurt anyone who doesn't deserve it. Besides, half of the rumours are not real. People don't understand everything, and the rumours become more fictitious each time they're told."

With a frown, Cassy glared at the boy beside her. "Well, it is partially your fault that this all happened. You first gave me a snarky welcome and then you attacked me."

"I fully agree with the second part, but I don't think I gave any form of attitude at the beginning. I was even nice enough to allow you to sit with me when I typically work alone."

"Yeah, so nice..."

Brushing back his smooth, thick hair, styled in a longer Caesar cut, he curiously asked, "Where did you learn that tripping move anyways? It actually caught me off guard."

Cassy's jaw clenched, unsure if he would use anything about her past against her. "Well, my oldest brother taught me. Both of my parents wanted us to be able to defend ourselves, so when we were young, my brother, who's a high level in taekwondo, spent time teaching us younger ones."

"Mhmm, interesting," Zack mumbled, "I'd assumed you had learned from an actual instructor."

Unsure if he was mocking or praising her, Cassy intently stepped towards the office door.

"I must say, you moved flawlessly," Zack praised.

"Thank... you?"

Reaching into his pants pocket, Zack's next comment was cut short as he pulled out a vibrating cell phone. The caller ID forced him to groan as he struck the screen to answer the call. "Yes?... I can't at this time. I'm in class..." The person on the other end questioned him. "Well, okay, technically, I'm not right now, but I was. I'm heading to the office again... I got in a fight... NO!" he hollered defensively. "I didn't do anything... This time it was a girl. No, I didn't hit her. She punched me and knocked me down." Annoyed, he shouted, "Quit laughing. I wasn't rude. It's nothing like the last time. That bastard had it coming..." Zack searched Cassy's reactions while she listened intently to the conversation. "Give me a sec, I just reached the office."

Cassy spun with him to face the office. The receptionist sat in a swivel chair, comfortable when no students bothered her. Zack pressed the receiver of the cell phone against his chest when he approached the woman and announced their names and reason for their arrival. The woman briefly nodded before calling the principal out of his small office. Cassy and Zack followed the well-dressed man around the front desk and into a small hall further into the depths of the office space. They marched into a symmetrically perfect square office. Once the front entrance closed behind them, Zack shoved his phone in front of him, sick of the hassle caused by the day's events.

Taking the unpermitted device, the principal answered, "Hello? Ah, Mr. Exacil, I was about to inform you of today's events... Oh," he became concerned, "that's no good. Thank you for notifying me. I shall send Zack home straight away. Hopefully, everything is well. Give your wife my best wishes." Hanging up, the principal handed the phone back. "Zack, you have three hours' worth of detention, plus another two for having a cell phone on during class. I'll speak to you later. Your mother has been in an accident. Your father is not worried about her condition, but she is in the City Hospital. You may go; he will arrive soon to pick you up. Once her condition is determined stable and you've returned, come see me."

Zack quickly agreed and headed to the exit. To Cassy's utter astonishment, he grinned giddily once he rounded away from the principle's gaze. *How can he smile? His mom was in an accident.* Sorrow filled her stomach. *He doesn't understand what it's like to lose his parents.*

"Cassandra," the principal said softly, "I realize you have been through a tough time. However, when I learned of this fight between Zack and yourself, I could not slough it off. Your actions have consequences, and you will receive the same punishment as Zack: three hours of detention. This will be completed in increments of an hour after your final class."

"But..." she choked, "that's not fair! He was the one who started this! He grabbed me and was going to hit me!" Keeping her voice even and calm, she dug her nails into the palms of her hands during the argument.

"A witness to the situation explained this. However, I believe you should have found a method of resolving the situation without violence."

"I used self-defence."

"Instead of your body, you should've used your voice, called out to someone."

"The only people available to listen were his friends! Rebecca was there! She was calling for help the entire time!"

"Cassandra, I'm begging for you not to argue. You are old enough to realize your faults. By acting as you did, you created more violence. I'm sorry, but this is your punishment." Smoothing out crumpled papers on his desk, the principle awkwardly avoided watching her wobbling chin. "Now, should I call your brother, or would you like to?"

Cassy fought the rage when she said, "You, sir, if you'd please."

"Very well. You may leave." The principal sank to his plush chair before inserting, "Cassandra, understand, I must treat all students fairly, no matter their history." Cassy took several steps from the office as soon as he finished, "Let's finish your first day on a good note."

Dashing out of sight of the principal, Cassy found herself whimpering back her anguish during her search for Rebecca. The noon hour had begun, and with it, time for fresh air to clear her head appeared. Her new friend leaned against a chain link fence, facing the parking lot, eating a sandwich. Rebecca was disturbed by Cassy's distraught bustling. Infuriated, Cassy explained in grunts the punishment and all that was said in the hallway.

"I'm beyond grounded! I'm dead. I swore to Brant not to get in trouble at school anymore. I've got a bad record already... this is making it worse!"

Cassy munched down on her own sandwich without tasting it. She found herself dreading the following two hours, since once they finished, she was going to be at the mercy of Michael. The following two classes, which both would have had Zack in them, proved to be less torturous because he was nowhere to be seen. Without his menacing glare piercing her back, she was able to accomplish learning just how far she was behind the rest of the class. The school load would become a main priority soon enough. The final two classes, a history and an English course, flew by without accepting her pleas to slow down. The walk home was lonesome when Mark picked up Rebecca for a swim practise. Unsure on how to get home, Cassy took her sweet time to navigate her way. Her detention would begin the proceeding day.

Nothing seemed to go as planned that day, and Cassy found another prayer unanswered as she rounded the final corner to her home. Butterflies tickled her stomach. Michael's and Brant's cars sat in the driveway. Michael had obviously driven enraged since his park job was less than perfect, while Brant stayed calmer and neatly parked his small red vehicle next to Michael's black one. Creeping across the grass, Cassy pressed her ear to the door. Michael shouted from within, frustrated with Cassy's already troublesome actions. It soon muffled when he moved to a rear area of the house. Taking the chance to slip inside unnoticed, she opened the wooden entrance, kicked off her runners and rushed up the stairs. On the fifth step, Cassy's foot froze in midair, and her grip tightened against the railing. Michael's voice chilled each of her bones and caused their mobility to halt.

"Cassandra Nadine Waters! Get your ass down here!"

Cassy spun, her hands loosening on the railing to hide their trembling. She smiled weakly. "Before you get mad," Cassy began, even though Michael reached the boiling point hours ago, "that boy was harassing me."

Michael investigated, "Did he hit you?"

"No."

"Then you're the one who's in the wrong."

"No, I'm not! I defended myself! I warned him twice to release me."

Brant glowered at her shrills. "Cassy, you swore not to get in trouble."

"I had no choice! Should I have let him hit me?"

Michael crossed his arms. "That's not what I meant."

"Everyone makes it sound like that's what should've happened. I should've taken the hit and just been the victim of a bully. I stood up for myself and I'm being punished! This is bullshit!"

Standing his ground, Michael replied, "Cassy, you didn't think it through. What if he got seriously hurt? No matter if it was self-defence, and he may have started it, you still struck him. This is why they're punishing you: because you used violence to solve violence."

Cassy gave up on her stubbornness and begged both brothers for forgiveness. Tears threatened to stream down her defeated features. Preventing them, she wiped away the saltiness quickly.

"Cassy, you're going to apologize to this boy tomorrow at school, no ifs, ands, or buts. You need to be the bigger person and know when you are in the wrong."

"Just like when you accept you're in the wrong?" she snapped.

"This is not about me. Stop sidestepping the issue." Michael rubbed his forehead, glancing over at Brant as he picked his words carefully. "You're grounded for a week. No phone, computer, or television. That will give you ample time to think about what you did wrong while working on your homework."

Hitting the banister, Cassy hollered, "That's not fair!"

Michael roared back, "Life's not fair, Cassy! Give me your cell phone and go to your room."

She tossed the device at him without a care in the world and marched upstairs with harsh mumbles escaping her lips. The one Michael caught stung him.

"Maybe I shouldn't have ever moved here. Then your perfect little world wouldn't be destroyed by a pain in the ass!" Cassy stormed away. "I hate you!"

Tears escaped Cassy unchecked. Her defences dissipated and she hurried to seal herself into her bedroom. Kicking and punching the mattress, she yelled into the pillow about her despised situation.

● ● ●

Michael massaged his forehead in distress. "Great, now she *hates* me."

"Honestly," Brant commented, "the day you left, Cassy was never the same. She closed up, even to Mum, and secluded herself from school events and friends. With everything that's happened lately, I think you should be a little easier on her." Brant patted Michael's shoulder. "Her world keeps becoming a hole of despair. If we aren't there to support her, how is she ever going to dig her way out? Besides, I don't think she was in the wrong. She acted as she was always told to against bullies. You strike back if there are no other options. Why are we reprimanding her for that when we all have done the same thing at least once in the past?"

Michael confessed in an undertone, "I know, but I can't allow her to continue on this destructive path. I have responsibilities. If this type of issue becomes a trend, I'll lose custody over Vince and Cassy. Since you're almost of age, the courts agreed for you to come only if I sold the house in Edmonton or purchased it from the bank. I could never see them get dragged off to a stranger's house because I'm not able to sort out a bit of her anger. That's the whole reason why, when I had the choice, I took you guys in immediately. If either of you were placed in the foster system, you would be separated. How could I be expected to go to the funeral and say goodbye to my parents if I chose that route?" Michael shifted, moving to the windowpane and leaning his head on the cool glass. "I'm no longer just her brother. I can't spoil her."

"She doesn't need to be spoiled nor coddled. What she needs is her older brother, not her father. She already had one of those." Brant, unsure if the words penetrated Michael's thick skull, left to prepare supper.

Michael groaned in dismay. "It was easier when Mum and Dad were alive!"

•   •   •

Cassy committed to Michael's orders, and the following morning headed to school in search of Zack before classes. In the brown fields of early spring, Zack's friends fooled around with a soccer ball, swearing at one another whenever someone cheated. No cocky Zack showed off his prowess between them. Enraged, she folded her arms and grunted. *Why should I apologize?* She thought. Unable to find Zack after a brief search, she figured she would find him in their first class together. Entering the school, she searched out the library where she would attend her detention that following afternoon. A book fell from her bag as soon as she rounded a table between a couple of bookshelves. Flipping through a few pages, she became enthralled in studying for her history class.

A shadow disturbed the light above her. In a first glance, she noticed dirty sneakers shifting lightly, as though eager to dash away. Cassy focussed her gaze towards Zack's growling face directly behind her. Startled to have him find her so easily, Cassy slammed the book shut and stood to gain a small advantage in case he attacked her in the uninhabited library.

"Umm," he muttered, in obvious torture, "Cassandra, can I talk to you?"

"I need to talk to you as well..." she confessed.

His tone shifted, becoming its natural rudeness, "You start!"

Cheerfully, she obliged. "I'm sorry I hurt you yesterday. I overreacted."

"I'm not pathetic!" Zack snapped. "It never hurt. I was shocked, that's all." Clenching fists halted and he cleared his throat before he said, "I'm sorry too. Can we start over? I'm willing to make it up to you... Can I take you out?"

Cassy stumbled back, dumbfounded. His request echoed in her ears. This was most definitely unexpected.

"Take me out?" she repeated.

"Yeah, like a date."

Before her lips stammered in response, she realized how silly it was. Stomping a foot, Cassy accused, "Who put you up to this?"

This egotistic jerk! He really thinks I'll go out with him just because he smiles at me? Relieved for not falling for the prank, she gathered her items and shoved her way past the tall boy barricading her in. He reached out to grab her, then thought better of it. Instead, he bulldozed forward to trap her in the aisle of books.

"I got this from nowhere!" Zack exclaimed. "Maybe I just realized that we should get to know one another."

"With your reputation, I honestly doubt that. I don't like having my emotions toyed with, and you're beyond conceited to even believe that I forgot everything from yesterday."

Cassy placed her hand against his chest to move him out of the way. It lingered for a second longer than necessary when she felt his pectorals that were meticulously taken care of. Whipping her hand from him before he realized what she dwelled over, she dashed from his sight, filled with butterflies in her stomach. *Damn him! He always catches me off guard.* Concerned that he might follow her, she dodged into the women's washroom. She waited within it until the second bell rang. Sitting on the bathroom's vanity ledge, Cassy regretfully knew she couldn't skip any classes, and would have to endure an hour of sitting beside the boy who tormented her so.

Calculating each step to the classroom, she realized that Zack waited for her approach before entering himself. Cassy peeked her head around the doorframe to watch him sit and fold his hands under his sharp elbows when he crossed them. Ignoring his frown that twisted to a proud grin, she sank next to him, only to find herself having to force her attention on the teacher while Zack whispered that he wanted to court her. With his unconvincing antics increasing, Cassy half-turned away and scribbled in her notebook.

By the time the bell rang, Cassy was drained from Zack's pestering and wished to return home to bed. Instead, she strolled down the hallways, weary of Zack's creepy, watchful eyes that followed her even when he spent time together with his friends. Rebecca's appearance was a welcome sight. Cassy rushed to her and swung her arms around her.

"You will never believe the morning I've just had!" she shrilled.

Startled by the sudden embrace, Rebecca released her grip and thoughtfully considered Cassy's pale face.

"What happened?"

"Zack happened! Michael *commanded* me to go apologize to him, but when I did, he asked me out."

Rebecca's perfectly reddened mouth dropped open, stunned by this turn of events. She giggled, "No, he didn't. Don't joke like that." She softly punched Cassy's arm.

"I'm not kidding. All through first period he asked me."

"What did you do?"

"I asked who put him up to it. There's no way he would date me after everything."

Rebecca twiddled her thumbs, unsure how to react. "I'm glad you didn't fall for it. It sounds like he's going pretty far to make your life miserable."

"I suppose so," Cassy said absently.

Zack strolled by, flashing a look towards the girl. Even if he was joking, she couldn't believe how hard he was pushing for it while still trying to keep it secret from his friends. Her rejection obviously stung him. *It was as though he needed me to agree. What is going on? Ugh! I'm so confused.*

Rebecca towed Cassy into the classroom before the teacher scolded them for being late.

• • •

Detention landed her inside a dank library classroom. Cassy tediously studied her assignments to catch up on her classes. Zack sat diagonally behind her in the sealed room with six benches facing the white board. Every slight movement he made was caught in her peripheral vision and distracted her.

Her eyes awkwardly lingered on him occasionally, and a sweet, kind smile flashed back at her, encouraging her to feel safe around him. The shift in attitude hardly made her feel safe; instead, it made her terrified of what his true motives were. This gentler and adoring boy made Cassy consider what the following day would bring. Tucking her head low, she trudged on without sneaking another peak.

The walk home worsened the nerve-wracking sensations. The weaving path kicked up dust behind her with each step she took. Her feet dragged heavily, exhausted by the day and the nagging feeling of being stalked. Every couple of steps, Cassy turned to find no nearby walkers, yet she could not shake the chill. So, in anticipation of returning home to hide within her bedroom, Cassy quickened her pace. She avoided enclosed alleys to stay visible to any neighbours outside and prevent the mysterious stalker from pouncing. The rustling trees and swaying branches were caught in the light breeze around her. Cracking from every direction caused her to jump and hyperventilate, her mind filled with the unpleasant possibilities of what lurked in the depths. As she spun for the twelfth time, a shadowy figure along the trees caught her attention. She halted in mid-step. She was absolutely stunned by the false humble incline of Zack's head as he straightened and approached with his cocky swagger. Zack pretended that he had not been following her and fell into step.

"What the hell is your issue?"

Cassy jerked away when Zack reached out his hands in a form of surrender.

"You're seriously screwed in the head. Why can't you just leave me alone?"

No response snapped back at her, but he became uneasy with her accusations. She took off running through the catwalks and across several blocks to return home before he could explain himself. Zack lost whatever intention he had and escaped in the opposite direction, back towards the high school. Once she travelled far enough away from him, she slowed down. Her heavy feet became lead, and her shaking hands reached for the front entrance once she stepped upon the porch. She finally met the devil's face firsthand, and she feared him greatly.

Nobody shouted a 'hello' from another part of the house when she slammed the door. Assuming her brothers hadn't arrived yet, she sank down into Michael's large, fluffy beige chair in utter defeat and barricaded her head with her knees and arms. *That bastard! What was he doing, following me like that?* Wrenching at her braided hair, a great howl expressed her anguish.

Vince appeared from upstairs. Worried about the horrible noises coming from the main level, he swung from the banister and searched around like a maniac. Standing on the last step, he found Cassy as her depressed demeanour sank further into the abyss of unpleasantness.

"Hey, what's wrong?"

Lifting her head, she wiped off cold tears before her face worsened into a swollen, red mess. Vince crossed the living room to kneel next to her.

"Where's everybody else?"

Vince denied her a reply. "Answer *me* first."

Her lips sucked into her mouth while she nibbled at them. "You swear not to tell anyone else?"

Vince stuck out two fingers to commit to silence. Accepting the promise, Cassy explained the issues at her new school while curled up on the plush chair.

"I can't handle any more of this. Michael forced me into this school, and when I try to keep out of trouble, someone attacks me. When I defend myself, I get in more trouble. Now, that same guy is following me around and trying to convince me to go on a date with him…" She massaged her head. "I just want it to end, Vince. I'm sick of all this bullshit."

"This fellow sounds like a piece of work. Does the school know that he's still harassing you?"

Cassy sprang forward to tug at Vince's sleeve. She was fear-struck at the insinuation, and shook her head vigorously.

"No, and they *can't*! Zack's popular and if he keeps getting into trouble because of me, he'll ensure my life is worse than hell."

"Cassy, if you're having major issues, you can't hide it from Michael. He needs to know," Vince pushed the topic. "He may be able to change your school for you."

"You swore not to tell anyone! If you tell the school, I'll deny it. Besides, all Michael will do is intrude more into my life."

Vince's scrawny arms landed on her knees while his hands folded into a cupped praying formation. A deep, confused sigh escaped his lips, since he didn't have much advice on how to approach the issue without exposing too much to the others. Though all three brothers were protective, Michael reacted poorly to certain situations and Brant, being a logical person, would consider only the best option and fixate on that choice. Vince had to hide Cassy's troubles until she attempted it her way. Once it failed or succeeded, he would gain permission to tell their brothers.

Before a single word was spoken again, the quiet burst into loud chatter. Michael and Brant lugged in plastic bags of groceries, laughing at Brant's most recent comment. In midsentence, Michael caught sight of Cassy's tear-stricken cheeks. A bewildered expression showed honest concern towards her, and he dropped the groceries to rush over for consoling. He stumbled forward in his half-on shoes.

"What's wrong, Cassy?" he inquired, almost within reaching distance to snatch her into one of the brotherly hugs he once had given on a regular basis.

Cassy dodged the embrace, grabbed her school bag, and disappeared upstairs. A paralyzing glare froze Vince's tongue as a warning to not speak a word about their conversation. Once he was unfrozen, the youngest brother scurried to the kitchen to find a snack. Piling food into his mouth would slow his breakdown. Michael huffed in disappointment while his hands slammed against the loveseat's back. Brant hummed in a thoughtful manner as he strolled deep into the kitchen's tension with Vince shovelling chips into his mouth.

Chapter 3

New York City

The man tapped a pen distractedly, a flattering collared shirt wrapped around his dominant form. Dark, meticulously kept brown hair hung over his forehead, shadowing his chiseled face. Assembled behind a wooden desk in a cramped little office, he leaned back in a creaking chair and massaged his head. News came at a snail's pace while he waited for his companion to report his findings. It should have arrived days earlier, which made the man ripe with anger. He checked his watch, grunting at the late hour. *It's been too long...* A sip of amber alcohol filled his parched lips as he swigged back the last of his savoured drink.

The small hideaway in New York City groaned when the front entrance slammed shut, and a pair of heavy feet took barely five seconds to trek from the front to the tiny office. A knock echoed, bringing the relief of an arrival long past due. The man straightened his shirt, leaned forward, and pressed his pointed elbows onto the dark wood.

A bulky man overtook the small light that cowered in the left-hand corner near a research-filled filing cabinet. The new arrival brought his nasty demeanor scowling into the office. His dirty blonde hair was closely cut to his scalp, proving his past in the military still affected him. His large shoulders almost eclipsed his neck while the rest of his torso was shaped like a V, since the bulky man focused on upper body strength rather than the complete package, unlike the more balanced man sitting before him.

Nearing his boss in excitement, the bulky blonde man tossed two beige folders onto the desk. The brown-haired man sleepily flipped through them, unimpressed with the trivial contents in both.

"Jonathon, why do you waste my time with this garbage," the brown-haired man snapped, flicking a disgusted hand at both folders. "Is this really what you've been working on since you left three weeks ago? I sure hope your research hasn't started lacking."

"I gathered as much information on Ryan Anorld as you requested. However, it turns out he isn't the heir either. He comes from a whole different lineage of Egyptians. That damn group tricked us again." Jonathon leaned over and snatched the whiskey bottle to pour himself a strong one. "Something I did receive during my search of Anorld was a ping."

The brown-haired man became erect in his interest to hear more. His finger tapped against the wood in anticipation.

"It's been, what, almost a year, since we received info from any of the organizations?" the brown-haired man queried.

"Yes, sir."

Rolling eyes scoffed at the bulky man's strict military training peeking through.

"Sorry, Victor, I did it again." Jonathon swung back a shot, hiding, to the best of his ability, his excitement. "Bryce Éclair, who the group mentioned in the beginning as the Enlightened One, pinged in my system two and a half weeks ago. I have not seen any mention of him since I first put him in the system."

Victor tapped more aggressively, searching for his memories of the Enlightened One. "Ah," he said, "the Enlightened One will show the way to the Egyptian heir. That is what the first few members repeated in their dying breaths." He flicked a piece of fuzz off his shirt as he recalled aloud, "If my memory serves me correctly, Bryce Éclair died from a heart attack nine years ago."

"Correct!" Jonathon poured another and drank some more. "However, what we failed to catch, because those damn agencies are so good at erasing people, is that he left behind a single daughter."

"So, you assume his daughter is the heir?"

"I sure hope not. She's dead!" Jonathon chuckled half-heartedly. "That's why we were pinged. Her and her husband's obituary mentioned her father in it. No, I assume it is her teenage daughter. This woman left behind four kids, all related to the 'Enlightened One' and all erased from any systems that I could hack until I really dug deep. Three boys and one girl. It all fits perfectly into the massive puzzle that group wove for us."

"So, why do you assume it's the girl?"

"Remember that gurgled comment from one of the group members I mentioned? 'You will never find her!'? Well, I'm going to bet anything on this kid being the heir."

Victor frowned at the explanation. "When you say 'kid', how old are we talking?"

Unsure, Jonathon flipped through the thinner of the two folders. Pointing, the number fourteen landed beneath his pudgy fingers.

"Damn it, she really is a child, huh?" Victor massaged his weary temples. "She's also a female, which, could lead to some trouble." As he thumbed through the file, shallow hums reverberated in his throat. "There's not much here. How accurate is this?"

"As accurate as possible. From the moment I hacked in, I had five minutes to get what I got because they completely wiped the system. Obviously, they don't want us to learn about this family."

Victor gave a brief nod. "You did well for the time you had."

Jonathon puffed out his chest in pomp from the rare compliment.

"You even got information on the brothers, where they live, and the high school she's attending. And what about our other issue?"

"That problem is still in the works," Jonathon replied. "Unfortunately, he's gone off the grid, but since they've gone into high alert over her, he'll be brought in soon enough." Jonathon took one more shot before sinking into a chair. Shifting closer to his boss, he whispered, "By the way, this is the first time they've gone into high alert with any of the supposed heirs."

"So, we're getting close."

Victor calculated for a long moment in silence. Jonathon, used to this, relaxed with the whiskey bottle in his hands. Eventually, the boss tossed a neatly written scrap paper at him. Red ink marked down her name, the city name, and her address.

"Contact Austin. Tell him we're heading out in two days. Whatever he's doing, he's expected to drop it and come. We are to meet in that city."

Victor rose to pace across the creaking floor in anticipation of their unfolding plan. Jonathon planted his sturdy, small-muscled legs and hurried from the office to commit to his chores at hand. The boss leaned over the dark desk. The folder fell open once again, and his trained fingers flipped the papers over one another as he read the words, trying to catch anything that might dissipate their excitement. Nothing appeared. He reached the final paper and flipped it over to find a family photo with six family members. Picking it up gently, Victor caught sight of their prey, happily smiling with her parents and brothers. He unconsciously stroked the girl in the photo.

"You're going to be our lucky charm," Victor sneered.

Chapter 4

Saskatoon

Michael aggressively ripped off Cassy's blankets and shook her roughly as he shouted, "Cassy! You'll be late for school if you're not up in five minutes."

Stretching, she waved his dread away. *Missing school wouldn't be so bad... ugh, but I'm so behind already...* Her heart pounded just thinking of what day three at this school would bring. Groaning out a curse word, she sat up and commanded Michael out. Her feet caressed the chilled flooring as she slumped across to the haphazardly organized laundry hamper. Rummaging through it, she found a shirt and pair of jeans that seemed clean enough, and then shoved her schoolbooks into a bag. Lacking a chance to fully prepare herself for the day, she doused her face in the bathroom with warm water. She soon would be cooking some form of dish with Zack next to her. She struggled to predict what personality he might have. Dashing from the bathroom, she hurried to search for the lunch she'd prepared the night previously. At the kitchen entrance, Michael leaned against the frame, clutching it in his one hand while he sipped coffee.

"Would you like a ride?" he offered.

Refusing swiftly, Cassy snatched the bag from his grip and sprinted out to reach the school before classes started. Huffing and sweating in the morning breeze, she spotted Rebecca nearing the paths. She hollered to alert her friend that she was coming, and begged her to stop so she could slow down. Rebecca gave a small giggle before waving towards the speeding girl. Cassy caught up, heaving heavily as she cupped her knees and wiped away the salty droplets of sweat across her forehead.

"You woke up late too, huh?" Cassy asked.

"Not as late as you!" Rebecca mocked. "Michael answered the door and was stunned that you hadn't awoken yet."

Cassy fell into step, brushing back her ponytail. "Last night was kind of rough."

"Because of the Zack thing?"

Cassy only nodded.

Rebecca tilted her head. "Have you told Michael that you're getting bullied?"

"Hell no! The moment I tell him, I'd end up in worse fights at school. Zack definitely isn't backing down, and he has people backing him."

"Well, I sure hope he'll lose interest if you keep rejecting him," Rebecca mumbled.

Cassy did not tell Rebecca about the odd encounter after detention. Noticing her tension, Rebecca nudged her shoulder and started a new topic. The winding paths teased Cassy with each twist. The closer they got to the school, the more edgy she became.

The edginess was valid when both girls' thoughts snapped straight to Zack again. Cooing from behind caused them to halt and sharply turn.

"Hey!" the voice hooted.

In pure disbelief, Cassy gaped at the sprinting boy already halfway to them. Rebecca tugged Cassy forward, trying to evade the advancing bully before something harmful befell them. They saw none of his friends, so they anticipated that he planned something as a lone wolf. Cassy pressed on, unsure what to do if he kept this stalking up. *He came from the direction of my house.* Cassy thought. *Yesterday he headed back to the school grounds before I lost sight of him. Does he live near me, or is he a stalker?* The school grounds welcomed them with the busy bodies of students, and they tucked into the middle to reach their lockers and then head to class.

"What the hell does he want from me?" Cassy asked.

Cassy slammed her green locker shut. Her patience towards the boy was growing thin. If he wanted to harm her, she wished he would do it already. Rebecca leaned against two other lockers and folded her arms across her developed chest.

39

She muttered, "His intimidation tactics have never gone this far. You really perturbed him."

Scared to ask, but needing to know the answer, Cassy whispered, "The last person who got in his way, what happened to him?"

A shake of the head denied a response as Rebecca's red hair floated around. Unable to explain Zack's aggression, she said, "Nothing good came of Zack getting sights on you, Cassy." Lugging her backpack higher, she bowed her head. "Maybe you should let someone know what's been going on."

"That's out of the question."

Rebecca backed down and headed for her class while Cassy dawdled to hers. An hour with Zack would soon fill her with anguish. When she rounded the corner into the corridor, she found Zack with a couple of his friends, basking in front of the classroom. Fearful, she tucked her chin into her collarbone and marched past them as they hooted and mewled at her to return to the shit pile she crawled out of. Once the bell rang, she found herself staring at the stove with Zack next to her, prodding at pizza dough and trying to find a way to have a pleasant conversation.

"You're still going to deny my request?" Zack wondered softly.

Cassy slammed the knife down, unable to focus on cutting the vegetables while her annoyance grew at his question. "If it has anything to do with you, I will never agree to it."

His pestering hardly ceased before he tried his hand at a new tactic and started to add friendly conversation. Anytime someone came too close, he spewed out mockery. Once they were out of hearing distance, he reverted to a soft-spoken boy as they worked. Cassy's migraine of confusion increased. Eventually, he decided to add in a small tidbit that sent her into a spiral of nausea.

"Somehow the school caught wind of me tormenting you..."

Did Vince tell Michael?

He placed their pizza onto the metal pan and tossed it into the oven to bake for twenty minutes. "Since we were still on school property, I've received two more detentions because of you."

She sealed her lips from shouting aloud and altered her glance to the floor. Before she knew it, he was tight against her, with a hand creeping up her arm.

"Prepare yourself for some trouble."

Inhaling sharply, she gaped towards the boy who smirked menacingly each time she viewed him.

"Please," she begged, "I don't know how they found out. I didn't tell anyone."

"That's not true..." he stated matter-of-factly, "you told your brother."

"How did-"

Seconds to the words being spoken, Zack snatched the knife and sliced open his palm with it. A howl escaped as he whipped it upwards and blood dribbled down his arm. His unharmed hand wrenched her fingers around the blade's handle and forced her to take hold of it. The teacher hurried over to determine the cause of the excessive screams. Within a minute, Cassy was towed outside to the office while Zack was mended up inside the classroom, telling a fictitious story that she had broken into a rage and cut him. Sitting inside the office once more, she cowered at the sight of the principle's stern face, ready to expel the troublesome girl.

"Cassandra, why did you attack him?"

"I didn't..." she murmured.

"According to your story, he sliced himself on purpose. Why would he do that?"

Cassy shrugged her small shoulders, unsure how to answer. "I don't know, sir. He just did." *I rejected him... that's all I did.*

"Cassandra, for the following month, you are to attend detention every day after classes for an hour. We will chat with Mr. Waters to figure out a way to sort out your issues towards Zackary."

Cassy sobbed inside the women's washroom after being dismissed from the principal's office and being warned that she had one more chance, otherwise, she would be expelled. *Mum, Dad, I'm beyond tired of this nightmare,* Cassy thought. *Nothing is getting better.* She skipped her second and third period, and by the time the noon hour started, the rumours had spread about the new student stabbing Zack. She listened to girls gossip inside the washroom, hidden inside the cubical, and feared showing her face again. He had made her infamous by her third day, and now she was stuck with him until his detentions ended. According to the gossiping girls, however, Zack's detentions were increased when he began telling off their history teacher.

Cassy felt utterly defeated. *I just can't get away from him.* Rebecca barrelled into the washroom once she learned of Cassy's whereabouts, and hurried her out of the school and onto the pathway. Examining the weeping girl, Rebecca could only embrace her snugly between her bony arms.

"Cassy, tell me it's not true. Did you really stab Zack?"

"No, I swear, I didn't! He caught me off guard and cut himself."

Rebecca huffed out in exasperation. "He's getting out of hand."

"I think he only did it because someone called the school, and caused more detentions for him."

"But it still doesn't explain why he's doing this to you."

Cassy sank to the ground, pinning her knees into her small chest. "I'm in so much trouble. Michael's going to blow a fuse, Zack's getting so much worse, and now I have all his friends after me."

Rebecca was unable to deny the words. Sniffles were supressed as Cassy stood up and headed back to the school. Rebecca followed a couple paces behind, worried about what might occur.

● ● ●

In detention, Cassy's pencil tediously scribbled away on the lined paper inside a blue binder while she maintained her focus upon her homework. Zack continued the staring contest with himself, fiddling with his bandaged palm, showing obvious pain whenever he poked and prodded at it. Not only did she dread finishing the detention to only return home to Michael's wrath, but a sneaking suspicion of Zack being close behind her on the walk home caused her to hyperventilate more with each passing minute.

As she assumed, the walk home carried an air of tension as Zack followed her, not even attempting to stay hidden. He gave her several steps of space but was always within running distance. Luckily, nobody watched as she tolerated this form of bullying and took long strides to reach home as soon as possible. Michael's wrath would be thirty times better than Zack's unknown goal. He disappeared in the last alleyway before her home loomed over them both. As soon as he abandoned her, the teenage girl gained time to breathe in preparation for Michael's reprimanding.

She shut the front entrance gently, yet she was face to face with three brothers conversing in a serious manner on the living room furniture. Michael pointed to the couch before she could speak a word. Cassy dropped her bag, kicked off her shoes, and slumped to the awaiting cushion. Her knees bounced anxiously.

"Cassy, what the hell is wrong with you?" Michael started.

"I…" she muttered.

"You stabbed him!"

Brant, flabbergasted by Cassy's rash behaviour, said, "Do you understand that you could've had worse repercussions than what you got?"

She said nothing. Words would increase the emotional turmoil swarming her.

Michael clenched a fist onto the arm of the chair, unsure how to explain his sister's behaviour. "We need this all sorted out, Cassy. I was called by social services. If I can't get you under control, they'll remove you from my custody."

"I don't want that!" she cried. "No matter what we argue about, I don't want to go live with strangers!" The fear in her voice proved how sincere she was.

Brant patted her shoulder. "Tell us what we can do to prevent another problem. Michael has one more strike."

"I wish you guys hadn't gone to the school about Zack…" she whispered defiantly. "That's the reason why he acted out. I never stabbed him. He framed me. I can't prove it, but it's the truth. Since this happened, I'm a pariah. I'm going to keep my head down and get through this. I *need* you to stop intervening."

Vince yelped when she explained the reasons for Zack's retaliation. Michael swallowed a thick lump, realizing that he had caused this hazard by contacting the school.

Brant, remaining logical, spoke wisely. "What's done is done. What should we do to prove we're trying?"

Michael leaned back, sighing harshly, "We could get a counsellor. That was an option the principal offered."

"You want me to talk to some stranger?"

"Cassy, no arguments. You obviously need something. Whether you stabbed this boy or didn't, it's time for us to get some professional help. I'll start making some calls tomorrow. For now, go to your room. I'm so disgusted with what's happening."

"You're disgusted?" shouted Cassy. "I'm the one who's been harassed within three days of moving here! I hate this place! You don't care about anything except for saving face!" She burst from the seat and disappeared up the stairs.

The following week brought with it more fights at school and at home. Michael took her word as lies whenever she tried to deny stabbing Zack and searched far and wide for someone she might be willing to talk with. None proved a suitable match, which left Michael growing frustrated and desperate. Cassy bottled up her bubbling emotions, unable to break down the walls without feeling vulnerable. With no words of advice leaving the counsellors, Michael was left unsure on how to deal with the decisions surrounding his solemn sister. She arrived home usually drained from a trying day of schoolwork and combatting the bullies.

Zack upped his game. Friends were sent to follow and harass her. They found vulnerable times to ridicule her when nobody was around. Cassy bravely faced each day, unable to skip a day because it might show weakness. In the cooking class, she was removed as his partner and placed with a friendly guy who cheered her on, though, as Zack's glares deepened, the friendly boy's bravado faded, and he soon began staying far from her. At times, she purposely arrived late in the mornings and the other classes that Zack attended. She stayed behind to talk with teachers about assignments to avoid the group that would always be waiting outside to trick her into trouble or bully her into an unescapable corner. Throughout all of this, Zack's persistence in secretly asking her out became the most intolerable. His friends would find them together, and without even questioning it, they assumed she was the one bothering him. So, water bombs or smelly garbage was tossed at her as she headed into class, or nasty things were written across her desk in any classes with his friends in them.

The worst punishment for crossing Zack's path was after a long morning of everlasting lectures, and she was heading home for lunch. Zack's brute of a friend, who was abnormally tall and thick, pinned her against a tree trunk. If she screamed, he only clutched tighter on her throat as she gasped for an ounce of air. Whimpering at his pudgy fingers constricting her airway, she listened to his deep, grumbly laugh.

"Stay away from Zack, you whore. You're a real pain in his ass. If you're not careful, worse things will happen to you than some silly little pranks."

He released. He shifted his bulk, watching her cough, and then he strutted back to the school grounds.

Cassy steadied her breath, looking with terror at where the bully's form had stood. It took all her strength to end the trembling of her chin. If it quivered too much, the tears would run and drip onto her blouse. Hiding away in Michael's house, she wanted to stay in her covers, concealed from the boy making her life hell. The wooden frame of her bedroom door sealed her inside its shadow and protected her from the leering eyes that made her skin crawl. Everyone misunderstood.

A week and a half now spent at the new school, Cassy sat in detention, anticipating Zack would walk through the door, head to the back desk, and watch her every move. She felt relief when the group of girls trapped with her gossiped that family issues detained him. She smiled conceitedly when she realized that she finally had an hour to herself. Reading a history textbook, Cassy fiddled with her hair as a heavy weight lifted from her shoulders.

The peacefulness lasted a split moment, until one of the girls, part of Zack's network of friends, swayed her hips smoothly into the classroom and made a beeline to sit beside Cassy. Sensing trouble about to start, Cassy tensed and prepared for the worst. Poking Cassy with a pencil, the girl leaned over ever-so-often to whisper sharp-tongued words. Angrily, she wanted to stand and strike the girl. *Ignore, ignore, ignore.* She worked for the whole hour by breathing in her resentment. The hour proved to crawl slower than any others with Zack.

Afterwards, her legs dragged her from the wooden desk. She piled her books into a backpack and grudgingly shifted towards her locker. Staring into the dull green, Cassy's emotions had finally defeated her willpower. She wished to never set foot in these school walls again.

Cassy's mindless state was interrupted when manicured hands shoved her into the locker. The metal resounded in the empty hallways.

"What right do you have?"

Cassy swiped across her face to check for blood before retorting, "What the hell? What are you talking about?"

Turning around, Cassy saw her abuser was the girl who had sat next to her in detention. "You've wrecked Zack's reputation and stolen him right from under my nose!"

The abused shoved her abuser back and reached for her bag.

"I have no idea what I've done to become so notorious in this school, but I would never attempt to steal that jerk. Go ahead and take him back. Ever since I came here, he's become a pain in my ass."

Making the first move, Cassy left the girl to simmer in loathing rage and darted for the nearest exit. The blinding afternoon light slowed her reaction time at the sight of a couple more girls waiting along the wall. Comprehending that they were waiting for her to appear, Cassy watched them smirk, ready to jump her. The original tormentor shoved Cassy down three cement stairs to the ground.

"I've noticed," she said, rounding Cassy's crumpled body, "how Zack looks at you. His obvious obsession for you is disgusting. He's completely zoned out when he's around you." Tapping her chin, she wondered aloud, "I bet once I slice that pretty face of yours, he'll lose his attraction for you."

Cassy struggled up to her knees. She was small beneath the foursome. "He's not attracted to me. I'm not attracted to him!"

"Then why is he always around you?" she exclaimed. "Even during lunch breaks he's distracted with trying to find you."

Startled to hear this, Cassy answered, "That's a good question. Can you tell me? I have no idea!"

The foursome clenched their fists, refusing to listen to Cassy's logic, and struck her. Her lip split and she tasted the coppery blood in her mouth. The girls kicked, punched, and one even spat at her. They waited for her to cry for mercy. Cassy sealed her mouth to endure each strike without a single complaint. The moment she found an opening, Cassy swept her leg across and tripped one of the girls. She closed her own fist and struck a blonde that fell to her knees. Surprised by the retaliation, they backed away, leaving their one friend to gain a black eye.

"This is bullshit!" Cassy stood, enraged. "Zack only wants to make my life hell. I'm not after him. If you want him so badly, work on it yourself. I just want to find some peace while I live in this godforsaken place."

"You bitch, you stole him. You just waltz in and catch his attention."

"That's stupid. I didn't do anything. I'm minding my own business. Maybe Zack isn't interested in a slut. If Zack wanted you, you would have him. Leave me out of this stupid love-triangle you created."

Cassy grasped her dropped bag and began walking away, feeling her lip. *Shit, Michael's going to flip.* That was the least of her concerns, as Zack's wannabe girlfriend brandished a knife. Cassy fell against the brick wall as the girl warmed her cheek with her breath and pinned her. Absolutely defenceless, the blade swept close, almost slicing the skin on her right cheek. She felt the metal blade shaking; it wanted to be driven deep inside Cassy as her abuser became engrossed in jealousy. Cassy twisted her neck to the side and pinned her head as far back as possible. If she were cut, she would take it in stride. Cassy inhaled and took in the stale air, full of anticipation for searing pain.

A figure, far in the distance, darted from in between the trees and sprinted towards them. A leanly muscled boy bent low and rammed into the attacker's hip, knocking her down. The knife dropped. Kicking the gleaming weapon away from reach, Zack planted his runners down sturdily to determine the reason for this attack.

"Victoria, what the hell?" he said.

"She started this! She sliced your hand and is preventing us from going out!" she whined, shocked Zack defended the cause of all their frustrations.

"Vicky, I've never been interested in dating you. I've only ever viewed you as a friend. And..." he awkwardly looked at Cassy's swollen features, "she never cut me."

Victoria stuttered.

"I did it because she snitched to the school. If you hurt her, it would've meant more than detentions, trust me. None of this drama is worth it."

Victoria struggled up as the love of her life protected the girl she hated. Reddened eyes met Zack's serious glare. She'd never seen this side of him. He spoke honestly and bluntly. Howling into the skies, Victoria disappeared, embarrassed in front of the others. Once the other three trailed along with their friend, Zack spun, exhaling with his eyes closed.

Zack's presence was appreciated. However, Cassy lost her relief when he strolled closer, double-checking her battle wounds. When his fingers stroked the beaten skin, it stung, and she swatted the hand from her.

"Stop getting in the way, I can handle myself!"

"I can see that," he sneered, "and what were you going to do with that knife?"

"I, umm…" she shied away.

"Exactly. If I didn't show up, you would've been hurt."

Cassy thought about his comment. "Why did you show up? You never showed up for detention. Were you hiding out, waiting to follow me again?"

He plastered a hand across his face as gears grinded to find a convincing answer. "Yes, I was," he finally admitted.

"Why are you doing this to me?"

"Certain circumstances have forced me to."

"Quit being a smart ass and tell me!"

"I'm your protection…" he swiftly snapped.

Cassy backpedalled several times. "You're insane. Nothing you've done in the past week has been protecting me. You almost had me removed from my brother's custody. You framed me for cutting you!"

Zack nervously chuckled. "Yes, I did, and I will fix that to make it up to you."

"You've got something seriously wrong with you."

Raising both hands, Zack steadied his grounds. "No, I don't. You will, though, if you don't learn to trust someone."

"Am I supposed to trust you? You're the one who's been harassing me this entire time!"

"We started off on the wrong foot."

She grunted, yet she left her readied stance in curiosity of his statement. Zack sensed her barriers drop and took three shuffled steps closer, but the instant he did, she became startled and guarded.

"I can take care of myself. I don't need your bullshit protection. How is getting me detention for the rest of my school life protecting me?"

"It's the only time I can watch you without anyone else knowing. The moment people start to notice a shift in my personality, I'll end up alerting the people who are after you."

Cassy disliked his explanation. "You follow me anyways."

"Those are my orders: to never have you leave my sight unless you're safely at home."

Cold crept along her spine, chilling every limb into paralysis. *Cassy, run. He's part of the gangs.* Stumbling back several steps, she shook her head. She didn't want anything to do with his agenda. Zack realized her unravelling thoughts and reached out to snatch her. It struck thin air when she bolted down a secluded path towards an empty street. She heard his speedy steps seconds behind her. She wanted to flag down a car to stop Zack from hurting her. She never expected him to be so cruel. She was hidden by the trees as she wildly flailed her arms, yet Zack lengthened his strides and snatched her. His free hand wrapped around her lips to prevent her from screaming out for help. Cassy panicked as she realized that she was in danger. Squirming and bending, her torso thrashed to release his everlasting hold, but Zack stood his ground, trying to whisper into her ear with each grunt. Not hearing a word, she widened her lips the best she could, and chomped down onto his already injured hand. Wrenching away, Zack growled and clung to the throbbing, lightly bloodied palm.

"Shit, you bitch!" he snarled. "Will you just listen to me? I'm here to prevent some dangerous people from hurting you!"

Cassy halted her stumbling feet from dashing off. She was startled by the sincerity in his voice.

"You have no idea what's coming for you," Zack groaned, sucking back the ache and relinquishing the pain-stricken face. "Give me a bit of your time, without attacking me, to explain... please."

Cassy settled on preparing to fight or fly when he walked forward. Her black runners edgily prepared to run.

"I will start at the beginning," he said.

Both hands rose to swear he was not about to hurt her.

"Why would I be in any danger from anyone other than you?" Cassy demanded.

Zack's deep brown eyes veered off to the left; he anticipated the question. "Alright, well, Cassandra, I work for an organization called the Federal Undercover Agency, or FUA. My task as an agent is to protect civilians, such as yourself, or investigate criminals." He went onto a tangent as he thought aloud, "Actually, your case has been the weirdest the FUA has dealt with in history."

Cassy grew annoyed, "You're lying through your teeth. There's no such thing as the FUA."

"Nobody has heard of it, and that's what makes the FUA special for your case. We can deal with it in secret without having to involve protocols that regular organizations do."

Not accepting the lies, she wanted this conversation to finish so she could remove herself from this lunatic's rantings. "Alright, say I believe you. Why would anyone need to protect me or be searching for me?"

"Several years ago, a man named Bryce Éclair contacted several organizations to try to get help with protecting the Egyptian Heir. The only organization that believed him was the FUA because one of our agents from Egypt's branch was part of a group safeguarding the heir."

Cassy took several steps back when her grandfather's name was mentioned. The story from her childhood seemed to have made a full circle back into her life.

"What do you mean my Grandpa contacted someone?"

"This group called him the Enlightened One. He had a vision about the heir's existence and hunted for answers. Ever since then, the FUA has kept tabs on the Egyptian Heir Assignment, but, unfortunately, a group of men started a hunt for the heir as well."

Cassy gulped, comprehending what he was saying. "Who's the heir?"

Zack leaned in, surprised she hadn't clued in yet. "The heir is you."

Grandpa only ever told me the story, none of my brothers heard it. He mentioned that the heir could have been a she... Cassy ran a hand through her hair. Trembling fingers fell down her face. "You're lying..." Denial set in. *He's screwing with me.*

She dashed with her arms forward to shove his chest, demanding for the truth as to why he was stalking her. Zack reacted by gripping both of her wrists. Her arms bent and her face fell forward as he spoke to her.

"If I'm lying, how would I know what story your grandpa used to tell you about each birthday until his death after your fifth one? He was preparing you for this." Zack tightened his grip as she struggled harder.

"But... but," she found nothing snarky to reply with. "Why have people started hunting for me?"

Zack gave a sincere smile. He was pleased to hear that she was absorbing something. "This criminal group formed three years ago when two of the members located Obeko's tomb. Ever since Victor, the leader of this group, researched and became enthralled with the curse, their tirade for the Pharaoh's diamonds has become malicious and progressively obsessive."

"Why haven't they been arrested by this secret organization before it gets bad?"

Zack sighed. A frown creased his youthful, handsome features. "We lost their location a month ago when we were about to close in."

"Then how do you know they have found me?"

"Technically, we aren't a hundred percent sure on this yet."

Cassy laughed in his face. "Then I have nothing to worry about and you can leave me alone."

"We are ninety percent sure they found you."

He spoke with such ice; she was frozen in place.

"When your parents died, our Egyptian connection was pinged because of your mother's ties with your grandpa. If we were pinged, then so was Victor's group." Zack's lean torso smoothly twisted when he released Cassy's wrists and settled the urgency in his voice. "When your grandfather passed away, all his files, those about your family, his link with the diamonds, and your location, were completely sealed. Your mother's death brought it all to the surface because she, unknowingly, was supposed to be in hiding."

"So, my parents knew nothing about this?" she queried earnestly. Her hands rubbed the painful lip. Suddenly, she recognized how disconnected this entire story was. "You sick bastard! Using my parents' deaths to gain something from me."

"And what would I gain from telling you any of this?"

"I have no clue. By convincing me of this ridiculous lie, you're tricking me into something."

Zack tossed his hands into the air, infuriated by her stubbornness. "How can I convince you?"

"I doubt there's anyway for you to prove this stupidity."

"Will you let me take you out?"

"Excuse me? You just made my life miserable, and now that you're coming out with this garbage, you think I'd mindlessly follow you anywhere just to be beaten up again?"

"Alright, alright," Zack begged for mercy. Her untrusting nature shined brightly, giving him little leeway to settle this dispute civilly. "I get it. Instead of taking you out, let's call it me proving the truth about who you are."

"If you're going to start with the truth, maybe you should tell the school that I never cut you."

"I already have to do that. My boss wasn't impressed with that move at all," glowered Zack.

"Why did you cut yourself?"

"I needed you in detention to keep an eye on you. It was the first thing that I could think of. Unfortunately, I didn't think it would cause so many problems with your family. It wasn't my intention. I told the principle not to expel you because I was irking you. I've been trying to resolve it without explaining everything."

Cassy's shoulders sank when she realized the reality of it. *If he's telling me the truth, then I'm in worse danger. If he's lying, I might be falling into a huge trap that could potentially be worse than this last fight.* Zack startled her when his hands caressed her swollen, blue lip with dried blood on it. She flinched as it stung sharply.

"Will you please trust me?" His brown eyes glistened in pleading. "I need you to understand the extent of your situation. I can't prepare you for this group's brutality if you don't listen. I swear on my life, my intention is solely to protect you. My reputation is so misunderstood, and it's only increasing because of our bickering. I swear to prove it to you tonight!"

Gaping, Cassy found herself truly wishing for the truth, so she accepted his pleas.

"Fine," she said, "where should I meet you?"

"I'll pick you up at seven!"

Zack hurried off with a flashy wave before anything else could be said.

Chapter 5

Jonathon whined in the backseat of the taxi while Victor scoped out their companion's whereabouts in the passenger seat up front. Their two days had turned into a week since contacting Austin was deemed impossible for several days. Once Jonathon reached him, Austin demanded answers before he would uproot himself again for a wild goose chase. The ex-military man exposed little, except for a brief, "You shall be greatly surprised." Intrigue exhilarated Austin, making him more willing to meet up, but the prairie landscape threw them all for a loop with its barren fields. Victor found the city to be a decent size, leaving them unsure where to start their hunt for the girl. First off, they required a place to set up shop while their prey remained safe and sound for a moment's time.

Victor groaned as Jonathon's complaints grew throughout the search for a mechanic's shop. It was the typical meeting place. Enraged as he watched the meter rising with each stop, Victor's agitation at Jonathon's complaints and wasting money became an untameable volcano about to explode on an unlucky victim.

"*Enough*, Jonathon," Victor snarled. A parking lot caught his attention when the driver headed towards the northern outskirts of town. "Stop!" Victor pointed to the parking lot's occupants. "There he is."

He noticed a second man standing with the expected one. The yellow cab pulled into a spot a few feet from the shivering twosome in nothing more than t-shirts in the early Saskatchewan spring air. Varied sizes of bulky muscles protruded as they crossed their arms over their chests to hide themselves from the brisk winds. Victor told the driver to park there for another fifteen minutes and then they would finally get to their destination. Jonathon and his boss exited the car to march over to the two, disliking the weather.

The familiar one, a dark-haired of average height with beefy shoulders, sighed, relieved to finally be in proximity of his boss once again. They had arrived a day earlier and sought out a location to settle until the final decision to abduct whoever they hunted was made.

Twenty minutes prior, Austin had threatened to leave the damned cold and return to his warmer climate homestead. He was captivated by Jonathon's call, though now it seemed a bit too good to be true. He flipped around a Swiss knife, wracking his brain with everything that they might have needed. This man's expertise was limited when he realized during their city tour that procuring the required drugs would be difficult without the usual contacts. He stumbled upon someone willing to introduce them, yet he remained unsure on the safety of it. They didn't want to murder whoever was the assumed heir until they reached Egypt. One thing for sure: Victor would be weaponless until they escorted him to the hideout. Knowing his boss's love for the pistol they had purchased, Austin confidently awaited appraisal from the approaching man.

As the leader ushered Jonathon closer, each member of the original group gave curt nods as a hello.

Victor hid his displeasure toward the group he had gathered for this important task. At the beginning, they had been replaceable pawns, then they demonstrated their skills and proven themselves handy tools. All the kidnappings and murders swiftly had been accomplished without much help from Victor, which left him rinsing his hands clean of the crimes. He disliked working in numbers, but for practical reasons, he long since decided that he would tolerate it for a short while until the diamonds were in hand, and then they would go on their separate ways.

The newest man stood erect across from Victor as the four men formed a circle to protect themselves from eavesdroppers. The scrawny man furrowed his brow, which slightly aged him and formed a shadow upon his green eyes. He was the youngest any of them had worked with, ten years Victor's junior. Wavy blonde hair covered his pale-skinned, angular face, while proud shoulders rolled back as Victor's deep brown eyes grazed over his body. This man had been the cause of their delayed arrival, and because of it, he felt under attack by all of them. As soon as they arrived in the chilly province, his travelling companion busied himself with tasks that needed to be accomplished. He was left with the miniscule task of gathering forgotten equipment, which unfortunately, still needed some time.

Victor raised his eyebrows high as he contemplated the youngster.

"Who's the brat, Austin?" he asked, pointing rudely with his index finger.

"Buddy," Austin explained. His English accent stuttered in the cold. "He heard me talking to Jonathon and wanted in. I gave the test and he passed with flying colours."

"Mhmm, interesting," Victor replied.

He shuffled, rummaging through a folder.

"So, what's this about?" Austin wondered. "Jonathon mentioned this one will surprise me."

Jonathon took the lead in explaining, "I was able to hack into the FBI data base with your system. Ryan Anorld was useless to us, but during the search, I got pinged."

Austin tilted his head, fully enticed by this news. "With which name?"

"Bryce Éclair."

"That old man!" Concern burst from Austin's lips as he realized what that meant. "Shit, hold on, don't tell me he was the heir?"

Victor almost laughed aloud when that ludicrous possibility was mentioned. "If that were true, I would've said fuck it."

Jonathon continued, "Nah, we believe that it is his only surviving granddaughter."

Victor handed over the family picture.

"This is Cassandra Waters. She is fourteen, almost fifteen. The parents died four weeks ago in a car accident, so she and her siblings moved here to live with their oldest brother, Michael." Jonathon pointed at the teenage boy next to a beautiful woman on the far right. "He's gained custody over all three younger siblings."

"Hell, Jonathon, you weren't joking about wanting to try a female," Austin chuckled.

"Go to hell," Jonathon grunted. "You heard it too when that prick died. He said, 'You'll never find her!'. He gave it away without intending to."

"Fine," Austin said, "why else, other than that, do we believe it's this kid?"

"She was the hardest to track down. There was mention of a granddaughter, but anything even vaguely mentioning her was masked behind a shit ton of firewall."

Austin scratched his head with both hands. "That does sound pretty convincing. They sure worked hard on hiding her, huh?" Austin left the circle to lean against the brick wall. His hands folded under his armpits to warm them up. "So, what's the plan? Have they sent him yet?"

Victor tapped a finger over his chin as he examined the newest group member. "That's something of which we're not sure. He's dropped off the face of the planet since our last meeting... that damn bastard."

A loud hum vibrated his mouth as Austin threw back his head in laughter. "Shit! Poor Eric! Learning that the heir might be a female was something he hoped for. Those poor bastards will miss all the fun!"

"Umm, excuse me," Buddy stammered, "who are you talking about? Who's Eric?"

Victor flipped his hand around to slough off the question. "I am going to finalize a plan once we get to this location you've moved into. However, I just realized that we may have an advantage here. Nobody has met or heard of you, kid," he said, half announcing, half plotting, "so we may be able to insert you into her life without anyone questioning it at all."

Piping up, Jonathon added new information. "I've actually been tracking her school file, since that was something they haven't been able to lock down. According to the most recent files, she's been getting into a shit ton of trouble. Her guardian has requested counsellors to talk to her to prevent losing custody over her. Everyone who's spoken to her was unable to get her to talk."

Victor slammed a hard fist into a cupped palm when he stated, "That's our in. If you're able to weasel into her life without anyone asking questions, we'll be able to do proper research."

The rest instantly agreed; however, Buddy was still confused. Unable to find answers in the brilliantly formed poker faces, he took to asking.

"Why don't you just kidnap the kid? Who makes you so cautious you'd take it as far as trying to hide out?"

Jonathon swatted Austin's head. "What the hell, dipshit? You let him join in without telling him how we work?"

Austin retorted confidently, "Victor needs to meet group members before they're told anything. You knew nothing for months. Don't get smart with me. We play it safe until Victor is introduced."

"That was a wise choice," Victor inserted. Appreciating the respect from the men, the boss massaged both temples as he worded things properly in his head. "Buddy, to work with me, you will need to learn quickly. We do not just abduct willy-nilly. That would be idiotic and get us caught. We have only ever taken a person to the tomb if we have compelling evidence on who they are. Kidnapping a child will increase charges exceptionally. First, we learn all we can about her and her family. If she knows anything, I want to know what she knows." Victor nonchalantly ordered, "The rest of you know what's to be done."

As if on cue, Austin handed the Swiss knife he had previously been playing with to Victor and nudged Buddy's shoulder to move along. Witnessing Victor at work made the men edgy. The boss familiarized himself with the blade by flipping it around as he strolled to the taxi where the driver sat unaware, texting on his phone. Jonathon followed suit, steps behind his boss. Before any actions were made, Victor halted.

"No slip ups this time, understood?"

He tapped the glass once before widening the unlocked door and driving the erect blade into the driver's throat. Blood spewed from his gushing wound and mouth as he gurgled a plea for help to the empty parking lot. Victor drove the knife thickly into the man's chest, insisting for him to die. Once the driver made no movements, Victor stepped back and wiped his hands clean of the innocent blood. Jonathon reached in, removed the body from the driver's seat, and tossed him onto the tarmac to be found when the mechanic shop opened. He took over the driver's seat in preparation to follow the other two.

"You shall lead the way?" Victor hooted as if nothing occurred.

Buddy paled, surprised the event had happened. The crimson blood flooded the street, making his sight woozy. A solid swack struck in-between his shoulders as he almost contemplated running. Austin teasingly shoved him.

"You wanted to join. No turning back now."

The younger one nodded. He'd decided this course of action the moment he approached the man entering the hotel in New York City. Witnessing them at work was either a saving grace that he was still alive or a death sentence if he ever attempted to flee. Shaking, Buddy listened to the ignition. With a bit of regret, they led the way to the outskirts of the city, passing an industrial area en route to their temporary home.

• • •

Ding, dong. Ding, dong, The doorbell chimed.

Cassy raced downstairs, hoping to answer the annoying doorway before any older brothers could. Zack proved to be punctual with their arranged "date".

After Zack's convincing conversation, Cassy snuck into the house to clean off her bloodied lip. Inside the upstairs' washroom, she had been rinsing out the dirty wounds, and plastering cover up onto the blueing bruises when Brant appeared, wondering how school went that day. The concern of making sure she stayed out of trouble had increased in him, and if no news appeared, he made apparent signs of relief. The half-finished cover job ended when Brant snatched her wrists and dragged her closer to examine the damage done. The busted lip was swollen beyond measure, the bruises and the small nicks from the blade startled him into a frenzy of lugging her to the kitchen, grabbing ice cubes for the swelling and a first aid kit to stop infection. Touching the lip delicately, Brant interrogated her.

"Did that boy do this?"

"NO!" she denied the allegation. Banishing Brant's mending hands, she tried to stand up. Brant used his weight to pin her to the chair. Cassy relented, and said, "I got caught in a weird, makeshift love triangle between him and this chick."

"So, technically, he did cause this, but just didn't physically hurt you?"

"When you say it like that..." she mumbled. "Zack's actually the one who helped me when she pulled a knife on me."

Brant angrily swore, blaming the boy for being the root of all their problems. He then disappeared to get more ice.

"I need to tell Michael," he shouted from the kitchen.

Cassy slumped into the dining room chair, huddled tightly together when the ointment he had rubbed on soothed the searing pain.

"Brant, if Michael finds out, he'll take me out of school, or worse, he'll go back to the school and then I'll just keep getting the butt end of the deal."

Brant despised this. "He's a bully, Cassy. This is what he wants. He'll push you into a corner to make you feel like you can't come to us because it'll get worse. It's bullshit. It will stop if I tell Michael and the school."

"Brant..." she pleaded.

Before anymore words influenced his opinion, a hand silenced her. Brant already decided the route to take. Michael would take matters into his own hands and potentially cause more damage than good.

"Hold that there," he said as the cool cloth pressed against her lower lip. "The swelling should go down before Michael gets home." A warning escaped before he disappeared to cool down in the basement, "If I notice any more bullshit, I'm going to make sure Michael and the school learns about this."

The swelling gradually lessened, and Cassy was able to cover up the cut with lip balm and gloss before anyone else noticed.

Reaching the last three steps facing the living room, Cassy stumbled forward to make it to the entrance. However, Brant emerged from his cavernous dungeon to reach it first. He found a youthful boy once he opened the heavy doorway. Both of the boy's hands dug deep within his jeans and he smiled sheepishly.

"Who are you?"

"Hi, I'm-"

Zack reached out a gentleman's hand to introduce himself. Cassy interrupted by budging between the two. Forcing his extended hand to lower, she clutched it tightly inside her fingers, rising with anxiety.

"Brant..."

Brant's nostrils flared just as he predicted what she was about to say. "This is the prick who's been harassing you?"

"Yes." Cassy slipped into her coat. "Brant, you guys all told me to sort this out. So, Zack and I have come to an agreement to settle our differences. We must talk about this in private. I realize that I'm grounded, but this was also part of Michael's orders."

Brant almost regressed into a state of shock. "What the hell! After everything he's done, he has the nerve to take you out? You even accepted!" His head shook around, waving his thick hair into dishevelled mayhem. "I don't care about your excuses. You just got the shit kicked out of you because of him!"

"I know, but I need to sort this out. I can't live like this if I'm always targeted by the bullies. I need peace in my life and Zack's promised to try to figure it out. If there's any problems, I'll call."

"I'm such a damn sucker!" he mumbled. "You owe me huge! Be home by ten at the latest. Michael finishes work at ten thirty." Ruffling aggressively in his pants, he pulled out his black cellphone. "Michael still has yours under lockdown. Take mine."

Brant disapproved with an incline of his head as she agreed and placed the phone into her front jean pocket. Cassy finished getting ready and headed out. Her stomach twisted in multiple knots, growing tighter anytime Zack glanced at her. The most nerve-wracking thing was when Zack escorted her to the black jeep parked across the street. Instead of entering the passenger side, he rounded the vehicle to sit in the driver's seat, clutched the wheel and revved the engine. Cassy's hand faltered with opening the handle. Perplexed, her palm dropped, squeezing her jeans in a clump.

"You aren't driving, are you?"

"Yeah." He shrugged indifferently. "I've had my license since last year." He smugly added, "The FUA puts older-looking, under-aged agents through their test for easier transportation. I am lucky enough that if I get pulled over, I won't be busted for being underage."

"I still don't believe you about this FUA thing." A glare shot at her when he huffed out exasperation. "*But*, I've decided to play along with this until I have proof. So, won't your boss mind if you're driving around town?"

Zack released the hot air before speaking. "Mr. Edwards invited you to the agency." Leaning over and opening the door, he said, "Just get in. We have a tight schedule. You don't need to get into more trouble."

Frustrated with his cockiness, Cassy hesitantly crossed her arms, thought for a moment, and then stepped inside. Zack drove off. He followed the road to the first turn and then went right. She watched tentatively to see where they travelled. If something suspicious popped up, she would call her brother straight away. The unknown streets blended together into one long street, which directed them downtown. They passed the large mall. The possibilities of their destination increased with every street they drove on.

As the drive progressed, seemingly in circles, she began to lull into relaxation. Zack drove effortlessly. She remained guarded, yet she snuck quick glances over towards him. Her sight glued onto the boy's face in the glinting sun. His handsome features put her in awe and ease. *He really is attractive.* Shaking her head, Cassy's throat cleared to stop the inner, drooling voice. The only thing he would gain would be her trust, if anything at all. The stories had to be proven true. Admiring his deceptive figure and personality was out of the question.

Near the river, underneath a decrepit building that once may have been a ten-storey office complex, the vehicle made a final stop. The building's windows were all smashed or boarded up. The roof sagged, buckling under its own weight, about to collapse any day. A dark alley led the path to other, busier buildings that seemed unfazed by this unsightly place. Even the entrance, which once held a readable sign telling what it was, contained a condemned notice across it.

Zack waited near the hood, tapping it impatiently as Cassy finished calculating whether she should enter or not. She had choices. *Go with him into the alley, where he probably has people waiting to jump me, or go home, and keep on believing he's deranged. I think I can deal with those men if they are real...* She slammed her head against the passenger window, hating herself for the choice she decided upon. Breathing thickly, she gave him the benefit of the doubt.

Stepping out to greet his welcoming wave, she watched him bound down the alley with a spring in his steps.

"Um, Zack, this place doesn't look safe... Can you just be honest? You're lying about this whole FUA thing." She stopped her quick paces. "Let's just settle the score now and go our separate ways?" Swift glances around had her consider her next course of action. "I can walk home from here. Please, I don't want anymore trouble."

Without a single reply, just raised eyebrows, Zack lost the spring in his step and made determined strides to lead her further in. The alley was dark and concealed in shadows from the little sun left. The cement was broken apart, unkempt by the city, like it had been completely abandoned. A large Loraas bin waited to be picked up near the entrance of the alley. It did not smell, so she assumed it had long since been forgotten. The building's side entrance was tucked in the background, covered in dull black paint and showing rusted metal beneath it. The S-shaped handle dared troublemakers to open it. Cassy gripped Brant's cell phone snuggly in her grasp. Zack's torso was tense as though he prepared for her to dart away. He returned to her side to take hold of her arm and held on tight, refusing to let her leave the alley.

"Stop overthinking this," he scolded. "You'll see the truth. I have no score to settle, and I swear that no one is waiting inside to hurt you."

Cassy almost snickered aloud while she reviewed all the abuse she already tolerated because of him. Shivers expressed her fear when he moved closer to the door that would prove whether people waited for her or he was telling the truth about her fate. Neither seemed like a positive outcome.

Checking around, he towed her forward, causing her to stagger over her clumsy feet. He knocked twice, stopped, and then knocked four extra times. Cassy jumped as far as Zack would allow when the iron door swung forward and a man, shaped meticulously into a bodybuilder, peaked out. He moved aside, allowing them access. This tanned man inclined his chin when Zack greeted him with a friendly hello. He was exceptionally large and stunted Cassy with his mountainous size. Cassy edged closer to Zack's chest when the guard with a round, bald head came into full view. Though both men beamed kindly at Cassy, she was petrified of the brand-new world that transformed before her eyes.

An open space, crowded by about twenty people, was well supported inside, with large pillars built with metal beams and light grey resin flooring. Glass and silver elevators stretched all the way to the highest floors to her left. Their glass refracted the light brightly, giving the people within a shimmer of wonder. Above her, the center of the floors were separated, allowing a view of a skylight that reflected the moon's blue glow. They passed the mountainous man's workspace, a large desk with three computer monitors and several folders scattered about the almost black wooden desktop. Off to the right, an office helped to support the floor above while also creating a small hallway for another area blocked from view by a wall.

Cassy's grin widened. The dumpy exterior hid such a beautiful building within. Zack clung to her wrist and towed her along. He commented to a few strolling agents before heading towards the singular office on this floor. Many of the agents eyed Cassy shadily while she glanced about. The boy who held her close was factual with his story. The building alone would be difficult to fake.

"Who's the man at the front?" she wondered aloud.

She strode quickly to stay next to Zack. The fearful adrenalin lifted to allow her to appreciate this secret world.

"He's a security agent. His job is to ensure no one enters without the proper code and that they have no restrictions. If discrepancies arrive, he is to deny them access."

Half hearing the response, Cassy heard whispers behind cupped hands from a passing twosome, "Who's she? Exacil's never had a partner."

Shying from the pair, Cassy comprehended how she still didn't understand the full extent of her predicament.

"Zack, all these people are agents, right?" He gave a brief nod. "Then, why do they keep staring at us? Am I not supposed to be here?"

An amused sparkle brightened his lovely eyes. "First off, it's probably because you're staring too." She jerked her attention to him. "And they probably assume you're a new agent. Most assignments aren't allowed in here."

"Why am I?"

"Because."

Her attempt to entice him to further explain ended. Zack absently waved at a man approaching them. He was a small, middle-aged man. Frown and worry lines creased his forehead with greying hair speckling the pitch blackness. He was shorter in height than the front entrance guard, as well as smaller in muscle, and Cassy lessened her fear while in this man's company rather than the other. He halted, briefly giving a curt incline of the head.

"Evening, sir," Zack welcomed.

The man acknowledged Cassy with a fatherly glance. "Cassandra Waters." Though his voice was stern it warmed her being. "I've been waiting to meet you for years! Ever since your grandfather reached out to us."

Zack formally introduced the man. "Cassandra, this is Mr. Edwards. He's the head of this FUA branch."

"He-hello, sir," she choked. Irritated that she stuttered, she clenched her fists and redirected her face. "Nice to meet you."

"Don't worry, Cassandra. You're safe inside this building."

Aging hands gripped her small ones tightly. Mr. Edwards held a deceiving short stature that didn't seem to have any physical prowess, yet his persona gave the impression of a man who would get things done as needed. She saw leadership in him.

"Um, Mr. Edwards?" Cassy nibbled her lips. "Did you ever meet my grandfather?" She leaned closer to the man. Her heart yearned to discover more about her grandfather.

"I personally did not. However, I've heard many stories about him and assure you he was an extraordinary man."

Cassy's disappointment was apparent when she said, "How come he never told me about this whole heir thing?"

Zack reacted by pulling her close to his chest and glanced around to find anyone in ear shot. Cassy inhaled deeply. Her heart pounded inside Zack's arms, pinned to his chest. Mr. Edwards edgily began moving from the vulnerable space towards the elevators.

"This is not a topic we should discuss in the open, Cassandra. Come along," Mr. Edwards whispered in an undertone.

En route to the double doors across from the elevator, they hurried her along. Cassy pushed to take larger steps. Zack used his free, outstretched hand to swing a single doorway wide and encouraged Mr. Edwards to enter first. Zack's chest remained Cassy's headrest while they entered this new space and turned right.

A wave of excitement crashed over her when a full view of this area was seen. The walls were ghostly white, half covered by clicking machines whirring as they worked. Vials of unknown substances were situated specifically upon rows of tables spread amongst the laboratory. Various vials bubbled and others steamed. People rushed about in the process of doing a study, dodging around one another, and carrying clipboards. The large space was not crowded with people, but inhabited by all the research done behind these walls. Cassy faltered, slowing her guardian down, to examine a couple experiments. Zack loosened his grip, yet still escorted her to avoid attention falling upon them.

Mr. Edwards had already crossed the lab, waiting at a wooden door in a diagonal wall. A woman unlocked it once he announced their arrival with a couple taps on the wood. She backpedalled several steps to permit them inside. Blonde curls flicked about as she fidgeted around and eventually settled to face them near a cluttered desk. Cassy curled into a wall once Zack released her, and they all were locked inside the smaller room where four desks and multiple filing cabinets were sealed away.

"Cassandra, your situation is unique. No other FUA or government affiliated agency has ever seen a case like this. You must remain a secret. If we can, we will prevent you from ever being taken to Egypt."

"I'm still confused. How come I wasn't told about any of this until now?"

Mr. Edwards leaned against a desk and stretched his shorter legs out in black slacks. "Your grandfather's final wish was to keep the secret of you from everyone until your eighteenth birthday. Once you were of age, we would notify you and then you would make the decision to enter the tomb and inform your family, if you felt it necessary."

"Then why tell me now? Can't you stop this group without involving me?"

Zack replied, "This group is not going to back down easily. Victor is clever and knows how to disappear in a flash. He could snatch you like that," he snapped his fingers. "We want to prepare you to be cautious of your surroundings."

"Why did you take such drastic actions to convince me? You could have told me when we first met."

Zack filled with embarrassment when he said, "That first day, I didn't know who you were. A team head called while we were heading to the office—" he interrupted himself to explain. "Nothing bad happened to my mother. When I arrived here, I was informed that a surveillance team had located you in the city. Then, I realized I needed to fix our first meeting. You're honestly impossible. I tried being nice, and when that didn't work, I needed to do everything possible to watch over you. I took the best measures I could think of."

Interjecting, Mr. Edwards layered a sarcastic tone, "Zack definitely took the *wrong* measures. He has been reprimanded, especially for that knife stunt. He will be admitting to the principal that he lied about you cutting him. Hopefully, the truth will stop any social worker issues. We do not want you taken away. You are safest at your brother's."

"Can I tell my brothers about this?"

"We prefer them left in the dark. The moment too many people learn about this, you will be publicizing to Victor where you are."

Cassy crossed her arms, disliking all the lies she would have to tell her brothers. "How sure are you of me? Out of how many people in this world, why is it me?"

"We cannot be *sure*, per se, unless we took you to the tomb and removed the diamonds, but our sources are fairly sure."

"Sources? What sources?"

Mr. Edwards leaned against the table and hummed. "During your grandfather's hunt for help, he came across the Sacred Chosen."

Cassy scoffed at the name. "Sacred Chosen?" Her lean eyebrows rose high onto her forehead.

"Obeko not only created an heir, but he also ensured that a group of people would be able to teach and protect you. This group is the Sacred Chosen. Since Obeko's death, they have been sharing the secret of the diamonds to their lineages and awaiting news on you. Your grandfather headed to Egypt to find someone to help. An FUA agent who was part of the Sacred Chosen explained the story and introduced your grandfather to other members. They tracked your whereabouts and kept your identity secret, even to us. We were only told that the heir was alive during this generation. We have assisted in keeping the Egyptian Heir Assignment safe."

"Why do you assume it's me?"

"In the beginning, your grandfather alerted the FUA saying that he was related to the heir. There's only ever been one note on this, which has been hidden by the Sacred Chosen. I was lucky to have found it when we received the case three years ago."

"I have an uncle on my mom's side, and three brothers, and what about my parents? What if they are…"

Mr. Edwards sighed. "At first, we assumed it was Michael, since he is the oldest. That is why this FUA Branch took on the assignment."

Cassy frowned in confusion.

"Since it was an FUA agent who originally brought the Egyptian Heir into the spotlight, the FUA Board gained full authority to this assignment. And being as your grandfather and brother lived in the vicinity of Saskatoon, our branch became the lead three years ago when this most recent threat came into play." Mr. Edwards sank onto a swivel chair, upset that he was breaking the silence. "When the group murdered a member who accidently blurted out 'her', we became horribly concerned for the safety of your mother. When she passed, the accident brought everything to light."

The silent woman shivered and rubbed her arms in the cool air conditioning of her office as she suddenly admitted, "We just recently learned about your existence. The Sacred Chosen hid you so well… far beyond your parents, uncle, or brothers. Bryce Éclair's secret granddaughter… it could only mean one thing."

Cassy gaped. "I didn't exist?"

Both adults pierced their lips. "We had no idea. Your grandfather passed and all the secrets he held disappeared as well. The Sacred Chosen lost their trust in us and have gone silent."

"What happened to them all?"

"Most have been murdered, while the rest went into hiding. Unfortunately, we have limited answers to your questions. They kept tight tongues to avoid exposing you. When your parents died, we learned that the Waters family was moving here, and that's when we figured out that you were most likely a target."

A thick gulp showed Cassy's fear. Cassy wavered in her spot. *Grandpa kept so many secrets...* "Did my parents know? Were they involved with these Sacred people?"

"No. Mr. Éclair wished to keep your entire family in the dark to keep everyone safe."

Cassy widened her gaping lips further to ask another question, but Mr. Edwards interrupted.

"This criminal group hunting for the heir has murdered most of the Sacred Chosen and is getting close to finding your location. Your mother's death brought trouble that we weren't expecting. We couldn't contain the secret any longer. We feel that to keep you safe, you knowing how to react and who's truly helping you will assist better than a surprise."

The woman cleared her throat. They needed to hurry the conversation along.

"Forgive me," Mr. Edwards apologized. "Cassandra, this is Mrs. Ember. She is our communication liaison, as well as one of six people who will know of your predicament."

The short, stout woman curtsied in a loosely fitting pencil skirt.

"Mrs. Ember, this is Cassandra Waters."

The woman raised a brow, twisting a curl around her left index finger as she examined the girl. "She definitely looks like her mother and grandfather."

Mr. Edwards looked on with a serious expression. "We need some way for them to communicate."

Mrs. Ember frowned.

Mr. Edwards continued. "She should be able to communicate with Zack whenever necessary."

"Sir!" she exclaimed. "Has that been permitted by the Board? I've never needed equipment for the assignment. Isn't the location system enough for them?"

"No. Communication will be key in preventing Cassandra's kidnapping."

Cassy's stomach sank, feeling nauseous at their bluntness. Zack recognized her edginess and scooted closer to hold her steady in an upright position. Her smooth, small fingers clung to his strong fist.

Wondering about this woman's concerns, she leaned closer to Zack and probed, "They really believe these men will get to me... What form of communication are they going to give me?"

"Give *us*," Zack corrected. "It will be a disguised telecommunication system that will give us the ability to speak anywhere. As well, I'll be able to find you anywhere in the world if it's on your person. It will tell us your wellbeing, and," he pointed towards a third entrance over in a corner, "will be connected to the FUA headquarters' system here."

Mrs. Ember grudgingly busied herself by looking through drawers. Three cabinets were searched through before she sang, "Perfect", and swivelled around, carrying small articles in her palm.

"Here you are, Cassandra."

A violet-coloured bracelet was securely strapped to her wrist. It flicked about, feeling odd, as Cassy's wrist was usually bare. A metal piece with a strange symbol scribbled across it embellished the simplistic jewelry.

"To contact Zack," Mrs. Ember began, "you tap the charm twice, and instantly Zack will be able to hear you. This is waterproof, so you may shower with it on. I recommend for you to never remove it from your wrist. Nobody, other than Zack, will be able to contact you by this means." Tossing Zack a black watch, she waited until his trained fingers strapped it to his wrist. "Zack, you know how this works, though I've recently updated our system. You should have been briefed on this, but if you hit this button here," she manipulated the button beneath the one that would have been for changing the time on a normal watch, and the screen scrolled through the options of equipment, "you will find storage for field tools."

Fiddling with the innovative watch, Zack tuned out any further conversation. Mr. Edwards wearily admired the teenage girl that absorbed upsetting news splendidly.

"Cassandra, I know you have a lot of questions. If you ever need to ask anything, you can ask Zack. However, if he has been instructed not to elaborate on some topics, do not become irate. Divulging certain things will be against the rules around some confidential files." Tapping the desk, Mr. Edwards contemplated about what he may have missed, then snapped his thumb and middle finger together. "Because of the advantage of being forewarned, if any trouble occurs and Zack is indisposed, you are to come here. Zack is a top martial arts student, yet compared to a couple of those men, he's out of his league. If you return home and the men have set their goals on kidnapping you, they will hurt, or even *murder*, your brothers. Do not give them a reason to hurt loved ones."

Mr. Edwards began the stroll back to the heavy wooden door from the communication ward. The laboratory was still busy with experiments, even when the researchers had all abandoned the room for their supper or to return home.

The boss's speech lengthened as he said, "It should be blatantly clear to you that this headquarters is a government secret. We want to prevent your brothers learning about any of this, unless necessary."

"Sir," Cassy piped in, "if this place is so secret, why am I allowed?"

Zack conked his head, becoming tired of her prying questions. "If you ever retrieve the diamonds, you are a potential weapon," Zack explained. "Keeping you nearby is safer than us failing and Victor digging his manipulative talons into you."

Cassy gulped a lump down. *I never considered that.* His comments, while blunt, explained it well. *I can never make it to Egypt, otherwise, I might do something horrible with those diamonds... but even they aren't sure if I'm the heir. What would those men do if I turned out to be the wrong person?* She mindlessly followed the two men from the double doors, past the elevators and closer to the front desk. The answer to that question would remain filed in her brain until she was able to bravely say it. If they were brutally honest, she worried about how she might handle the answer.

Halting at the guard, Mr. Edwards tugged Cassy into front view by the shoulders and picketed her.

"Greg, this is Cassandra Waters. She is Agent Exacil's primary assignment. No code for entry will be required. If you notice her at any time without him, she is permitted inside."

Greg jotted down a note in a beige folder and accepted the terms. With a final nod at the two teens, Mr. Edwards gave a quick farewell, then marched back to the only visible office located on this floor. Greg widened the main entrance, leading them out. Shaken by the reality striking her, she followed her protector towards the streets.

"I know I have a lot of questions, but I swear this will be the last one for tonight," Cassy said, interrupting Zack's quiet blissfulness. "How will that man know it's me without a code?"

Zack opened the passenger door and then rounded to the driver's seat.

"The entire building is monitored by cameras and other surveillance. Greg will have a picture of you, when you go to that door, you must stand beneath the light, and he'll be able to identify you. If you're not within the light's radius, it'll be harder for him to see you and he'll more than likely not open the door."

Cassy studied the new bracelet. Tapping the charm twice, she said, "Hi." Her voice spoke through Zack's watch as it lit up with the word swiftly darting across the face. Zack looked at it, raising an eyebrow.

"What are you doing, Cassandra?" his voice drawled.

She answered innocently, "Sorry, I just wanted to test it out." Her attention went into figuring out the device, as well as mentioning, "You can call me Cassy, by the way." She shrank small, depressed she couldn't figure out how to end the conversation that continued across Zack's watch. "Um, how is this turned off?"

"Tap the charm once more." He cleared the conversation with agile fingers. "Why call you Cassy?"

"It's shorter…" she sheepishly looked off, adding, "Friends and family call me that. Since we're on good terms, it makes sense that I allow you, too."

Zack said nothing. The trip was silent as the road crunched beneath the jeep's tires. His fingers clutched the wheel gently, giving slight adjustments to the vehicle. Cassy fiddled as Zack's eyes focused on the road, showing tiredness, which she attributed to her constant accusations of dishonesty.

"I owe you an apology. You didn't lie about the FUA and about me being this supposed heir. Your reputation… I get it now." Her head bowed into her collarbone. "You were catching the criminals that your assignments put you up against."

Zack flicked his attention towards her. He was startled when he found genuine sorrow filled her tone. With no words to express his thoughts, Cassy resorted to silence for the rest of the trip.

When they sat outside Michael's huge house, Zack parked the jeep further up the street to stay out of view of any leering brothers.

"Have a good night, *Cassy*."

Emphasizing her name, he grinned, revelling in the sound of it. Cassy liked the way he rolled the syllables off his tongue.

Twisting her torso, Cassy clung her hands together. "What are we now? I understand that I'm your... assignment?" He nodded at the title. "And you're my protection, but how should we act at school?"

Leaning back his head and moving his jaw back and forth, Zack sighed. "Well, let's start by being friends. I will protect you. We can get to know one another, and see where this assignment leads us."

Cassy agreed. "If anyone asks, we came to an understanding and have dealt with our problems."

Glad to hear she was not disappointed with the response, he brushed back her hair, giving her a final, friendly goodnight. Shifting from his tingling touch, Cassy hopped from the vehicle. She flashed furious waves at him as he sped off. She approached the porch just seconds before Michael rushed out and left the rustled curtains in disarray. Angry grumbles exposed his stressful worrying that had lasted two hours. He had arrived home early, surprising Brant and Vince with Chinese food. Brant had stuttered as he tried to find any excuse as to why Cassy would not join them for dinner. Michael soon realized something had been amiss and demanded for the truth.

Now with the truth in the open, Cassy was hauled to the couch once more by Michael's tense arms. His lecture about lying lengthened into a tangent of displaced anger before he even focused on her sneaking out while she was already grounded. Cassy hunched low, unable to dispute this fact. After Michael cooled down for a mere moment, a second round of eruptions twisted Cassy's stomach into a knot as he began a speech about dating.

"You're too young for boys... especially that boy," he grumbled. "Dating should be the least of your worries. Homework and keeping out of trouble should be your highest priorities."

She folded her arms cheekily when Michael demanded that she never go out with Zack again.

"You have no right to talk like Dad!" she rebutted. "I am capable of making my own choices, and maybe Zack's not a bad guy after all."

Her words broke Michael into a swearing hurricane, which caused her previous punishment to increase. The railing supported her to her bedroom and kept her sore body upright after the verbal assault given by the eldest.

There's nothing wrong with dating... she snapped within her inner thoughts. *You just don't like this specific guy.*

Locking herself away for days, her anger stewed into loathing. Every chance Michael got, he yelled. She couldn't believe how hypocritical all the brothers were. *They all had at least one girlfriend at my age. Why is this any different?*

Not even when her bracelet beeped and Zack apologized for being a hassle was she able to stop her bubble of happiness from shrinking. Venting to him was impossible. Zack may have changed from being a bully, but they hardly knew one another. Complaining to him might annoy him. The strain of having a secret bodyguard could've increased by tenfold if he was unpleased with who he had to protect.

Disheartened, she hugged her pillow and curled into a tight ball. She had no one to vent to.

Chapter 6

Monday afternoon brought the sunshine, gentle breezes, and a surprise knock on the door at the Waters' residence. Vince hurried from the kitchen, shovelling a half-eaten fruit into his mouth before he had to face whoever lurked outside. Answering the second doorbell, he became unsure of what to do with this stranger in casual clothes and carrying a giddy smile. He shouted out to Michael. They anticipated a surprise visit from social workers, but this blonde with broad shoulders stood tall and unnerved by what he was there for. Michael edged forward from the dining room, leaving his schoolwork on the table, to welcome someone who might have come to take his siblings away. A clenching, metaphorical fist struck Michael's stomach as he tried to figure out if he had done something to cause such a visit.

He swallowed all the worries and welcomed the young man into the household.

"Good afternoon, Mr. Waters." The man, who looked about the same age as Michael, extended his palm. "I'm Buddy Sisk from the City School Division. I'm a counsellor who's been sent to speak with Cassandra Waters."

Relief flooded Michael and a hospitable smile sprouted.

Vince rolled his eyes in annoyance since he'd rushed his afternoon snack for nothing. "Ha! You'll have better luck talking to the wall than her. She's not going to say a word." Stomping back to his bag of chips and cut fruit, Vince disappeared.

Buddy tilted his head to the side. His eyes darted around the house in casual curiosity. They briefly halted as Brant mounted the stairwell to meet the twosome in the foyer from the basement.

Buddy swiftly explained his theory on why she might talk to him. "I have a technique that is sure to open her up and resolve this situation," he explained in a matter-of-fact way.

"Cassy hasn't arrived yet. She has detention for an hour today. She'll be home around four thirty. You're welcome to wait or reschedule," explained Brant.

"I'll wait." Buddy glanced about, gaining his bearings in the unexpectedly large house.

Brant, intrigued to meet this unlikely counsellor, invited him to sit on the loveseat. The two oldest brothers and the counsellor chatted about Cassy's disruptive behaviour. Buddy jotted notes down in a thin notepad as Michael explained the reasons why she was so volatile towards him. Buddy's swift writing unnerved the brothers a bit before Buddy realized the social tension and set the pen down. Instead, he folded his hands together and asked about her parents.

Brant covered this question. "It was a shock for us, but Cassy spiralled into a depression. They were close. She completely shut herself off and has been a lot more emotional."

"Is that the reason she fought with that boy?" Buddy flipped through the empty notepad, pretending to be searching for names. "What was his name again?"

Michael and Brant both frowned, unsure on that subject as well.

"I really don't remember. We've been calling him the prick around here," Michael retorted harshly.

Brant nudged Michael's shoulder, astounded he said that in front of the school's employee. "Technically, she never fought with him. She was defending herself."

"And the knife incident?"

"He did it to himself." Brant objected with how stringent this man was with the queries.

Buddy plowed further. "Have these type of school disputes transpired before?"

Michael brushed back his hair, nodding apprehensively. The fluffy couch made him feel like he had fallen and was in a dream of never-ending questions about what was wrong with his family. His skin flushed and he inhaled deeply to calm down. He realized how troubled his sister really was.

"Michael, I don't mean to rile you up," Buddy said, ending the barrage of questions and softening his tone. "This is how I get information from people. By speaking bluntly and causing you to become emotional, usually people will get angry. When anger seeps in, a lot is said. Not many realize how much is told when someone is upset. With this, I'm able to calm them down and trust me more."

Brant fiddled with his fingers, noticing how much they had told when they normally were barricaded.

"I'm sorry I pulled it on you. I noticed how guarded this entire family is, so I thought I should try it out. Let's speak normally from now on," he raised his hands in forgiveness, "and I swear, no more of that technique. I'll wait for Cassandra."

The chat led into deep conversation about Buddy's past and the brothers laughed with the new acquaintance as though he were an old friend.

•　•　•

Cassy cheerily burst through the doors of her home. For once, no bullies bothered her throughout the day. During the detention, since it was her and Zack alone, they sat side by side, talking. They talked mostly about Victor's group, but it was a step in a better direction. Zack shrugged off anything that might lead her to learning about him unless it revolved around assignments and Victor.

Inside the usually noisy house, Michael and Brant chatted with a stranger. Cassy dropped her bag near the closet and started for the stairs. Their words were in a monotone. She sensed that they were not meant for her ears. She froze before her movements caught their attention and glanced upon the back of the unknown man's head. His blonde hair waved about as he chatted. Cassy noticed instantly that he was clamming up, on edge about something.

Michael halted her progress upstairs when he waved her nearer. Striding off the three steps beneath her, she rooted her feet on the main floor as the man rose to spin towards the troubled girl.

"Cassy, this is Mr. Sisk. He's a counsellor from your school."

As if on cue, Cassy built her walls so high that even welcoming the man became impossible. The blonde man towered above all the siblings, even stunting Michael's six-foot nothing height. Mr. Sisk was a skinny man, with little body mass. She noticed the slight muscles he did maintain were still strong enough to threaten her if necessary. Doubting everyone's intentions had become a habit of Cassy's since she learned of her spot as the supposed heir. Anyone new could potentially be out to snatch her. He carried little colour upon his complexion, and the dirty streaks of dark blonde dabbling his entire head did little to darken his skin tone. The man's large green eyes oddly swept over her person. He led with his right hand, hoping for a small handshake. A giddy grin crinkled his eyelids, aging him, but only enough to make him seem slightly more than an older teenager. When his hand gripped hers, Cassy trembled inside at how tightly he squeezed. Michael was her saving grace when he unintentionally plowed between them to do a proper introduction. Mr. Sisk straightened at the hips, as he had inclined slightly to lower his stature for Cassy, and glanced down upon Michael's square features in irritation, though none of the brothers witnessed the disgust.

"Cassy, why don't you take Mr. Sisk to your room," Brant encouraged. "He's here to talk about the incidents at school."

Awkwardly following the orders, she beckoned him with a flick of her wrist and climbed the steps. Michael pierced Brant with a worried glare when the man and his little sister disappeared. He should've prevented a grown man from entering Cassy's bedroom, especially if they would be by themselves. Being unsure of what he should be cautious of made Michael's head spin. Butterflies fluttered his stomach. Brant shrugged, also confused about policies around permitting this.

"They need privacy," Brant defended his decision.

Agreeing, Michael edgily headed into the kitchen, rummaging around for their dinner. Fidgeting in the pantry became his stress relief for the time being.

● ● ●

Mr. Sisk sank onto the desk chair and settled his notepad onto his lap, followed by a small camera. Cassy, fully aware of the conversation about to follow, remained standing so she might be able to pace.

"Cassandra, as your brothers said, I'm a counsellor from your school. I've come to figure out what happened on your first day and since to resolve any pent-up rage that might be causing your rebellion." A pen landed on the open page. "Shall we start at the beginning?"

A half shrug of acceptance was the only reply he gained.

"Who started this fight?" No response followed. "Cassandra, you won't get into trouble. Anything that we say will be confidential. I'm here to listen and guide you through anything that might be troubling you."

That's what they all say, she thought. Her folded arms tightened before her feet began to pace up and down the laminate flooring. As they moved from the window's bench seat to the wall with the door, Cassy's feet almost left a tread mark. *They all write those notes. If I say anything and somebody wanted into my file, nothing that I'd say would be private any longer.*

Mr. Sisk narrowed his green eyes, considering her body language. "Alright, I get it." He tossed the notepad and stretched out his legs. "You're not going to talk to me. Most people wouldn't talk to a counsellor. So, what should we do? Want to learn about me a bit?"

Cassy's pacing halted.

"Well, I'm from the US. I came here to study for my master's in architecture, but once I started getting into it, I fell in love with this place. I decided to transfer here. I even left architecture to pursue Sociology and Psychology Degrees. Once I graduated, I settled in the city and have been working here ever since." Mr. Sisk brushed back his hair. "My first name is Buddy. My parents named me after their huge English Mastiff when he passed away. That dog was as big as my dad. I guess when Buddy was around, little kids would ride him like a horse. He was a trusty steed that never faltered in his love for my parents. That's why I got the name. They wanted me to be like Buddy the mastiff. My parents were a little kooky, but I must admit I actually really enjoyed growing up with them." Clapping, he said, "I want you to call me Buddy. Let's not make any of our meetings formal. It'll be like two friends relaxing and chatting."

Cassy had never met a counsellor like this. He was wide open and trying to make her comfortable.

"Do you know why you're named Cassandra?"

She shook her brunette hair back and forth, depressed that she had never learned this.

"That's too bad. Your parents picked an awesome name, Cassandra." He bowed his head. "I want to sincerely give my condolences to you. You lost your parents too early. I don't know what I would've done had I ever lost my parents. From what I could tell from your brothers, they were bringing all four of you up right."

Cassy's lip wavered, wanting to release the pent-up emotions. "Thank you," she whimpered. "They were amazing people."

Buddy flashed an award-winning smile and burst into cheers, "Oh goodness, she speaks!"

Cassy was unable to hide an embarrassed grin from growing.

"You know, I like you better when you talk. My voice is an overused drawl, yours is still light and fresh."

Sinking onto her comfortable bed, Cassy found herself wanting Buddy to stick around longer. "You're really the nicest person I've met since moving here. Even Rebecca or Zack haven't been this kind."

Buddy slammed his elbows into his knees and leaned forward to cup his chin. "Rebecca?"

"She's my friend next door. She's been there through all the crap at school. I'm really lucky to have her tolerating such bullshit when I'm the one who started this."

"How did you start the fights?"

"Well, technically, it was both me and Zack..."

"Zack?"

"Zack Exacil. He's been the one tormenting me for the past two weeks."

Buddy tapped an index finger across his cheek as if he knew more than he wanted to expose; even so, he fell into deep contemplation.

"So," he continued, "Zack was the one you beat up?"

"I didn't beat him up," Cassy said in an undertone. "It was self defence. Zack and I *both* started it. I gave him attitude and then he tried to back me into a corner. I didn't back down, so I punched him when he went to strike me and then tripped him."

A loud laugh exploded from Buddy. "Wow, he's not proud about that, I bet!"

Cassy snickered along with him. "He definitely wasn't."

"I heard there was a knife incident. What happened there?"

Cassy recapped the few events leading to that miserable day, yet, for an odd reason, she carried a heavy burden of guilt. *If only I'd given him a chance to explain things, we would have made up then.*

Buddy drilled further into the school attacks. "You didn't seem too miserable today. Did something good happen?"

Cassy hummed loudly, loving how talking about Zack lifted her so high she might float away.

"Him and I have recently made up. We went out last Thursday. Zack's a decent guy, regrettably for Michael, who hopes that Zack walks off the face of the planet. We spent our detention today talking and making jokes."

"That's a good sign. How did you come to realize he was an alright guy?"

Cassy struggled to find an appropriate response when that topic was off limits to everyone. "I don't know. I guess I was fed up and wanted to regain some civil days at school. I'm going to be stuck at this school for the next three years. Zack and I are going to try being friends and see where it'll lead us."

Buddy bobbed his head. Checking the time casually, he stretched, yawned, and then stood.

"It's time for me to be going. I think we made some breakthroughs today. Would it be alright to meet with you next Monday?"

"Um, sir?"

"Cassandra, it's Buddy," he winked jokingly.

"Buddy," she shyly wondered, "why come again? Nothing's wrong anymore."

"We are going to make a sincere effort. I know that you won't fully open up to me for a while and I need to make sure your mental wellbeing is in a good place. Losing your parents was the toughest thing you've experienced in your life, and then having to move into a new city where people start to bully you… that all takes a toll, especially on a developing teenager. I want to make sure you're dealing with it properly."

Cassy considered the response. Opening up, even if some things were neglected, lifted the weight from her shoulders. Appreciating this odd man who seemed to connect so well with her, Cassy accepted the meeting for the following Monday.

"Excellent! I'm excited to talk more with you, *Cassandra*."

Buddy hopped from the swivel desk chair and headed for the door. As the metal handle kissed his skin with its cold, Cassy froze the intention to leave.

"Call me Cassy. I like that name better than Cassandra."

"Mhmm, both of them are pretty names, Cassy," Buddy grinned. Flipping the camera over, he waved it around, wondering, "Can I take your picture? It's fine if you're uncomfortable. I just want one for my file. I don't like looking at those impersonal folders unless there's a face looking at me. I get more in touch with my counselees."

Shrugging, Cassy allowed him. The camera pointed directly at her, carefully aiming to snap the most pristine photo. Glancing at her afterwards, he announced a final farewell, and abandoned her with a smirk smeared across his thin lips. He became exhilarated for the following Monday.

• • •

Victor waited alone on the top floor in the abandoned warehouse from old, industrial Saskatoon. He patiently killed the time until Buddy returned to report back from his first meeting with the supposed heir. If things had gone sour, Victor would deploy a second plan after disposing of the useless garbage the newbie was to the group. However, with the benefit of the doubt given for now, Victor hid away while hunting for news from any of the men. The others strolled freely around the city since their involvement was that of lackeys, and Victor would be implicated for any evidence gathered upon them.

Victor leaned back on the ratty furniture found in disarray in the warehouse. They assumed a furniture store once buzzed like a bee in this building. However, when times became difficult, things were left without a care.

He enjoyed the arrangement of the building. There were no annoyances from hotel concierges demanding money, nor was there a need to add another murder to their belt to settle into a house without notice. If his men remained low key and always watched for followers, he could tolerate the musty smells, the billowing dust, and low-lit living arrangement until the kidnapping was set.

Knocks vibrated the doorway, in response to which Victor cheerfully announced, "Come in."

Buddy sluggishly entered. Sleep wept from the corner of his green eyes as he lingered in dreary consciousness.

"Jesus, Buddy," Victor chuckled in mockery, "you look like hell."

Buddy ignored the jibe and said, "I've gained some interesting tidbits from her and a more recent picture."

The recently developed photo was tossed over to Victor. It skidded across an old, glass desk where a hand stopped its momentum. It remained upside down.

"What's this interesting *tidbit*?"

Buddy stroked his bristly chin, hoping for Victor to offer some of the amber alcohol on the table in a glass bottle. Without any hospitality given, he slumped against a clutter of boxes.

"There's not much. She was quite shy, and it took a lot of those tips you gave me to open her up. You were right about making them emotionally involved. Her brothers sang like little birds. She had to be taken another way. Being buddy-buddy with her was my best route. Even then, she was unwilling to talk about much."

Victor flicked his wrist around in hopes that the man would move along.

"So, the good news is I found out Zack Exacil's location."

"Damn it, she has met the bastard, huh?"

"Yes. Her first meeting went fairly sour since he was the one who's been bullying her and was the one who caused the knife drama. There's been a ton of tension between them. So, she may not have learned about us yet."

Victor glowered. This news meant the FUA had caught wind of their ping.

"The bad news is that she was forced to apologize." Buddy breathed in.

"How is that bad news?"

83

"When she apologized, Zack asked her out. I suppose it took her until last Thursday to agree, but they seem to be growing closer and bonding quickly. She's trusting him a bit more."

Buddy reflected on his first night meeting Victor, once they had moved into the large compound. The warehouse, with one large loading zone where they parked the murdered taxi driver's vehicle, connected to a large office area. On the main floor, several offices that led into the front entrance of a furniture store were claimed by each of the accomplices as their personal rooms. Down the hallway, up a set of thirteen stairs, an office overseeing the loading zone was taken up by Victor's equipment, including computers, priceless artifacts, and any form of weapon he may have needed.

The weapon with which Victor took the most time to familiarize himself was the Jericho 941 pistol, with its average barrel length, black colouration, and semi-automatic capabilities. This was Victor's favorite gun to use. He never once had issues with it. The way the grip and trigger melded to his touch, with its light weight and compact size, he finally felt whole. His nimble fingers fiddled with the safety and checked for any imperfections. Austin had done exceptionally well locating this pistol on such short notice. Victor had chosen the perfect weapon's specialist for the job. Though Austin was unsteady with firing weapons himself, he used his intelligence for exactly what they needed.

Victor soon lost his interest with the weapon when it was holstered to his hip. He exited his private quarters to check up on the rest completing their duties. Austin sprawled the drugs that might be handy in the next few weeks onto a table. Victor checked on the handy work of gaining possession over the potent paraphernalia. Austin then scurried off to assist Jonathon in setting up computers and loading his programs.

Buddy aimlessly wandered around, searching for tasks to accomplish without getting in the way. As Buddy rounded the office space Austin had claimed, Victor demanded that he follow his new boss. Into the rundown upstairs, Victor jabbed a finger towards a loveseat with hardly any springs left and encouraged him to relax. Victor sank onto a chair as Buddy anxiously collapsed to the appointed seat.

"So, you passed with flying colors, huh?"

Gulping, Buddy nodded.

"What did Austin test you with?"

Buddy focused upon the ground and tapped his foot. Victor snapped his fingers together to create eye contact.

"Come on, kid. I don't keep useless shit working for me. If you aren't worth my time, then I recommend you disappear before I feel an urge to expel my pent-up energy." The threat had Buddy leaning back in utter fear. "What did Austin get you to do? Why are you valuable to this group?"

"I'm an architect. While scoping out land my boss wanted in the city, I overheard Austin nearby a hotel. I heard the name Obeko before, so I did my research. Intrigued by what I found, I wanted to approach him." Buddy trembled at Victor's menacing glare. The boss swirled a drink around, navigating through Buddy's story as if he expected something incriminating to appear. Buddy continued. "He was staying at a high security penthouse suite…"

Victor rolled his eyes. "Of course he was…" he mumbled as though disagreeing with the flashiness of the man.

Buddy placed his elbows onto his knees. "I couldn't get to him, and I became increasingly worried that I might miss him. So, I broke in. I've assisted in making up the floorplans in skyscrapers and smaller hotels since graduating College. I was able to pinpoint the weak points in security. I've also dabbled heavily in learning how to crack specific vaults without detection. When I burst through the penthouse, he was stunned. I demanded that he let me join you. Instead of shooting me on the spot, I was tested. I had to break into five specially equipped buildings within a twelve-hour span without alerting a soul."

"Very well." Victor leaned back, lowering his guard towards the youngest member. "You're too nervous when you're around the others. We're like wolves here. We smell fear and become excited when we see it. I need strong men for this, because if I do need to kidnap her, we will have more people to deal with than just three brothers. There are agents looking out for her and searching for us. Keep that in mind whenever you return here. No one is to follow you. Each one of you have their tasks, and I expect them to be done properly. Your task is important, because, if you succeed, capturing this kid will be easy and I will have a better chance of getting her to submit to me. Information, Buddy, is everything. You hold all the cards when you know dirt on your opponent. It weakens them emotionally, which in turn, physically weakens them."

Buddy agreed quickly. The boss stood and strode across the dungy area. On top of the table, a thin folder was produced from a bag and was handed to Buddy.

"Study this. This is Cassandra Waters, our target. You are to become close with her by any means necessary. Keep in mind that our only in is that nobody knows about you, and she requires a counsellor. The brothers will be your first obstacle," Victor stated. "They must be convinced that you are a counsellor. They've had six speak to her with no success. According to school reports, she's completely closed off. I'll show you some manipulation tactics so all four of them will talk. I'm still working on the best course of action for the kidnapping. I may use you to kidnap her directly from her home, though you need to stay alert for this kid." Another, thicker folder dropped to the ground where Victor scowled at it. "His name is Zack Exacil. This will be our biggest hindrance. If she gets too close to him, we will lose every advantage that we carry. She needs to trust you beyond anyone else, otherwise, she will never be persuaded into anything. I want her willing to walk into that tomb and accept either death or the diamonds." His tongue clicked twice in thought. "If you hear his name at all, you drill her about him until she shuts down. The agency he works for is not known by civilians. You will never hear her mention the FUA, but if she's met Zack, she will most likely know something."

Buddy shook his head from the terrifying memory and held his breath after mentioning Zack to his boss. If he couldn't gain as much trust as Zack, his talents may be deemed useless to Victor. Uselessness was not an option.

Victor's nostrils flared. He sprang up and marched around the scratched glass desk. His arms flung forward to throw the neatly stacked papers and books onto the ground. Each second he steamed with more rage and crept slightly closer to the newest member.

"She's becoming friendly with that bastard... the one who sent my best men to prison?" Victor's features twitched, developing an insidious shadow overcasting everything that may have been seemed kind. In a low, incredulous grumble, he stated, "That disruptive runt is going to swoon her and then we'll be in a tighter jam... she'll never leave his side!"

A statue that seemed to be worth millions shattered to the floor. Victor's composure dissipated and he went around smashing his favorite items. Buddy stumbled to the exit. He was finding himself in the crossfire. Fumbling to leave, Buddy burst through the doorway and darted down the steps as Victor hollered loudly.

Sitting onto the springless couch, Victor's head fell into his hands. Becoming close to Cassandra would be near impossible. *Zack's warned her,* he assumed, *about us. She's going to keep her guard up with any stranger that might pass by. Damn! Nothing about this kidnapping feels right. The FUA has already moved in to protect her...*

Pacing about the warehouse overview, Victor tossed more items, growling swears. For half an hour this trend continued with no interruptions from his men. The unoiled doorway opening and a cooling breeze fluttering across Victor's back made his lips flare in preparation to send out whoever invaded his personal bubble that broadened with fiery rage. Mocking laughter fluttered inside. The unexpected voices surprised Victor. His waist twisted as recognition struck like a ton of bricks.

"Now I've seen it all, Jason!" a voice cooed. "I've never seen Victor lose his cool this way."

The mocking man struck his comrade's shoulder with a solid punch.

"It's such a small issue. We can definitely eradicate this with a single bullet." Jason glanced over at their boss, who ripened with excitement to have the original members back in the group. "Eric would definitely enjoy that one shot."

"Hell! You two finally broke out, huh?" Victor crossed the cement flooring, embracing the men's hands in two solid shakes. "How did you find us?"

"First, we had to break out of prison," Jason said. "This buffoon of a guard came at us with his weapon lowered and we were able to pop it right out of his hands to knock him out. We then caught another guard and stole both of their clothes. Out without a single fight!"

"We headed to all of our safe houses in New York. They were completely cleared out," Eric glowered. "We spent a couple of days trying to track down any hint on your new incognito location. We eventually spotted Jonathon in the airport. We assumed he'd still be with you, so we followed. We lost sight of you two when you entered that new, luxury private jet!"

Victor shrugged, grinning at their jealousy.

"Asking around, we learned that it was heading to this unknown, god-forsaken town. This place is so freaking cold, it's ridiculous. We spent some time in a hotel, but five hours ago, we caught sight of Austin. That old asshole is still dealing in that dirty work, Victor. I caught him purchasing some new black-market drugs."

Jason piped up, "I would keep an eye on those. Even he seemed a little anxious with them."

"Anyways," Eric continued once Victor nodded in agreement, "I assume that we are on the hunt for someone again, otherwise, we wouldn't need it. Austin's collected a good arsenal of weapons for us."

Victor narrowed his eyes gently at their brilliant perception. "I would rather have had you two escape than those who did before. I could've used you in our latest hunts."

"That new kid hanging around like a lost puppy is sure going to cause some drama, Victor. The dimwit led us straight to you. He went to some house for almost an hour and a half and then came directly here. No evading or anything. He better learn quickly. I ain't going back to jail," Eric finished.

"Yes, he will be taught swiftly. Whipping him into shape has proven more difficult than Jonathon. He is, however, a valuable part of the group at this time." Victor offered them a glass of whiskey before explaining Buddy's necessity. "A week ago, we found another assumed heir, who lives here." He assembled himself behind the table and tossed the upside-down picture towards them.

"This is him?"

Jason and Eric flipped over the four-by-six photograph and then in unison said, "Holy shit!"

Eric exclaimed, "It's a flipping girl!"

"We're really stretching it a bit, don't you think? Not only is she female, but she also looks young. How sure are we?" Jason logically thought.

Eric fondled the picture, excited to have a female as their potential heir. A smack directed his attention back to Victor's serious face.

"She's fourteen, turning fifteen at the beginning of August. I want to be sure. The evidence just keeps piling up. Her grandfather was the Enlightened One, and when her parents died, we were pinged. Also, when we tried to locate any information on this family, we were blocked within five minutes. The FUA has even gone into high alert."

"Mhmm," Jason hummed deeply, "that's never happened before. Not even with that guy who was directly linked with Obeko."

"Exactly. They wouldn't react this way unless there's more to this kid."

"So, she's the last of the lineage?"

"No, there's three brothers."

Eric swore under his breath. "Why don't we believe its one of the other siblings?"

Victor chuckled aloud, "Jonathon is still caught up with that gurgled comment of one of the group members."

"That whole, 'You'll never find her' bit?"

Victor clicked his tongue and rose an eyebrow in a response.

"I don't mind it being a girl," Eric sneered.

With that comment, malevolent black eyes struck him, pinning his heart in petrified fear. Victor disliked talk like that. To hear it about *his* heir made him grow revolted.

"Forgive me, Victor," Eric inclined his head in shame.

Jason interrupted before any other disgusting comments could arise. "Speaking of the FUA, where is Zack located?"

Victor was dissatisfied to report to his favorite lackeys that Zack resurfaced at a prime position to weasel into the heir's life. Long fingers slammed down as Eric leaned over the glass desk with his bulky arms holding him up. Jason sank onto the moulding couch, aware of something amiss that Victor didn't want to expose.

"He's here in town, huh?" Jason broke the silence and growled.

"Unfortunately, yes. Turns out, this is his hometown. Him and Cassandra met on bad terms, but those terms are becoming increasingly improved, based on Buddy's recon. I have no doubt she'll be made fully aware of our presence. Therefore, we *must* position ourselves perfectly throughout this entire plan. Buddy is our best bet."

Eric used his bulkiness to send a disdain-filled fist into the mildew infested wall. The smaller of the two calculated their options before reacting. Rubbing his chin, Jason strolled towards Victor, admiring the photo clutched in his palm.

"We could get rid of him for you."

Jason viewed Cassandra's photo with awe and surprise that they seemed closer to capturing the heir than ever before.

Victor replied, "No, at this point, we need him alive. He is still useful. Cassandra barely trusts anyone. Buddy tried two techniques with her, and those almost failed. We need someone she trusts around, whether they are our pawn or an actual group member."

"Isn't that what this new kid's for?"

"Buddy has a long way to go. If he screws up at any point, Zack is our last chance."

Eric whined, scouting the hideout with his dark, brown eyes, "What can we do then? I dislike waiting around while the rest get to interact with her or do their duties. I get too restless."

Instantly, Victor found a task for his favorites. "Zack will benefit us in more than one way. Tail him closely for the next few weeks. Not only will that allow us to keep tabs on their relationship status, but I wager that he will lead us to the FUA. Finding those goddamn FUA agents' hidden headquarters will gain us an advantage, especially if we can ambush them. We've never been this close to locating them before. It will slow down their reaction time. Cassandra is as good as ours."

Pleased with this entertaining job, Jason slid the picture across the scratched glass, attentively checking the rusted lockers in the corner along the wall of the entrance door for any spare weapons. Eric whooped at the opportunity to wreak havoc in this godforsaken town and disappeared with Jason to claim any of the few offices left. Victor was suddenly washed over with a brilliant wave of calmness. His best men were in their rightful spots, and soon their plans would set into motion.

• • •

The bright, late afternoon air brought Zack around for a surprise visit. Up the porch, Zack crept cautiously about, anticipating Michael to respond to the creaking boards. Gently, his long fingers pressed the white, glowing doorbell. Still not meeting the infamous brother who disliked him so much, Zack struggled to contain his attitude. There was no answer to the doorbell, so Zack avoided the hazardous meeting. Zack backpedalled several steps to hunt for his assignment. Through the tall, brown fencing, he found Cassy lying on the green grass, watching magnificent figures formed within the clouds. He snuck closer, watching her mumble descriptions of the white, billowing clouds above, laughing at herself.

Captivated by her simplistic pastime, he also looked up into the baby blue skies. He hardly took the time to look at the splendors of the world anymore.

"You decipher the clouds well," he said, finally exposing himself.

Startled, Cassy jumped slightly, rolling onto her stomach. A frown creased her forehead when she realized that his bravado had grown beyond cockiness. Dread welled up.

"What the hell? If Michael catches you here, he'll legit beat you!" she hollered.

Her tiny figure darted up the patio steps to the kitchen's door on the opposite side of the breakfast nook and peered into the window to determine that her brothers were nowhere in sight. Relieved, she sank onto a black, cushioned patio chair, massaging her aching skull. Zack had finally brought on a migraine with his insatiable need to appear at the most inopportune times.

Zack approached with a swagger before sitting in the parallel seat.

"I have something to show you."

"Fine," Cassy groaned. "Hurry up. I don't know when they'll come home."

Zack pulled out several crumpled photos from his jean pockets and handed them to her. "So, a year ago, I arrested two of Victor's men. However, I recently learned that they broke out of jail over the weekend. According to reports, they've been spotted travelling, by plane, to Canada. They're aware of Victor's arrival." He pointed to each individual man as he said their names. "This is Jason and Eric."

"Wait!" she shrilled. The pictures tumbled to her lap, tempting her to witness the criminals about to destroy her life, and then fluttered to the ground. "You said they hadn't found me yet!"

"Technically, I said that we were ninety percent sure that they had. However, during the weekend, we caught sight of Jonathon familiarizing himself with the city. Austin's also been spotted spying on your daily routine by me and another couple of agents." The chair shifted under his weight when he leaned closer to her. "It's no coincidence. If those two are here, so is Victor. They've finally begun their hunt."

"Why don't you arrest whichever members you do see?" Cassy logically complained. "If you have even one of them, couldn't you hold them for questioning?"

"No matter if we catch a couple of them, none of them will squeal on Victor. Especially not while in custody. If they are let loose, and they said anything, Victor would kill them on the spot. He doesn't need anyone to help. He'd just gain new pawns. If it becomes too risky, Victor will escape. That would leave us with little warning on whether he feels confident enough to grab you or leave you be. If we allow them to go about their business, we may be able to determine their plans and catch them all together without a struggle."

Accepting the response, Cassy scooped up the fallen pictures, and studied them, shivering when she realized that men had been following her without her noticing. *Who the hell is this Austin person? If Zack wasn't following me and walking me home lately, would they have grabbed me already?*

The first couple pictures held two men within them, sneering aggressively, half turned towards the camera. Zack's finger prodded at the picture that held the man he introduced as Eric. He was a cocky man that wore expensive clothing and maintained a light tan. In each picture in which he appeared, his hair was meticulously kempt in a subtle faux hawk, and he was prepared to act suave. Eric's square features angled to define his jaw line. No nicks were taken out of his chin from his exceptionally close shave. His large hands always seemed to grip the weapon attached to his hip in paranoia that someone was around them. His dark clothes, a button up, black collared shirt and dark washed jeans, covered most of his muscles, but if he was twisted slightly, she noticed that they protruded and swelled.

The other one, Jason, tucked his longer, dirty blonde hair behind his ears and gelled it back a bit to stay out of his eyes. An air of arrogance surrounded him. His deep, knowing eyes evaluated every situation to find the optimal route before he made a move with a cynical twinkle. This man's arrogant personality worried Cassy. He would be manipulative and able to convince her to do things she normally wouldn't. She fiddled with the pictures, drilling the men's features into her mind. Jason wore loose fitting jeans and expensive shirts. He was not as tall as his counterpart, Eric. However, his angled, lean face, was not someone to underestimate. Both could charm to their hearts' content.

Most of these men are conniving. They aren't about to back down at any point in this fight.

Something froze her hand before she flipped from a picture of a man Zack called Austin.

Pointing at another man in the picture, she asked, "Is this Victor?"

Zack ripped the photo from her grip, startled by the comment. He was there, standing behind a structure, hidden in the shadows. The teen sighed and tapped the photo with an index finger. A couple seconds past before he could do anything. Victor stared off, looking as though he hid while speaking to the others in the open. The other man half faced the camera, unaware of the photo. It was the same for most of the pictures, yet all in different environments.

"Yeah." Zack finally handed back the still shot. "He finds a way into every picture with his men, but whenever we search for *him*, he slips away without a trace. He's good at running, but even better when it's time to fight."

"He doesn't seem like a man I want to ever meet."

"These pictures are from almost three years ago. Meeting him now would mean more trouble for you. He's invested so much in hunting for the heir that he's become deranged and will try anything."

Zack brushed back her brunette hair when it fell in front of her eyes. Her defeated look shook him to show a caring gesture. *If Victor comes for me, he might do a lot of damage,* Cassy thought.

Pulling her head to his chest, Zack whispered, "I don't want to scare you. I just want you to understand what you are in Victor's eyes. If you turn out to be the heir, he *will* keep you as his, to abuse you. If you aren't, well, let's just say we don't want you to ever have to find out."

Cassy closed her eyes, comforted by Zack's softly beating heart thudding next to her ear. "I never want to meet any of those men, especially that one."

Chapter 7

Cassy stretched out her legs along the steps of the front porch after a long day of classes and being barked at for not accomplishing assignments on time. Groaning and complaining, she had strolled home, angry about the double load that she had gained because of the move and the teachers' unreasonable requests about completing all the work. Her detentions with Zack were nearing their end, which brought anxiety to both since they needed to find a new tactic to conceal their newly formed bond with each other. If it became public knowledge, it could worsen his bully friends' actions against her.

The serene environment collapsed into a volcanic eruption when Cassy was met with a shouting friend who was unpleased as she stormed across the grass. Pointing accusingly, Rebecca fumed when she stood in front of Cassy's house.

"What the hell is wrong with you?"

Cassy straightened, unsure how to respond.

"You're dating Zack now? Do you even have any brain cells? Like, are you for real!" Rebecca shrilled. "He's the one who, for almost two weeks, made your life a living hell, and all I heard was you complain about it, but then you go behind my back and start dating that prick!" Her slender arms bent at the elbow and her hands pressed firmly into her lean hips, standing in an unmoveable posture. "I keep seeing you walking with him after your detention, and then yesterday, you were making googly eyes at him with that ridiculous grin you get when you're around him." Rebecca hesitated, annoyed with Cassy's depressed look. "What's going on? Are the rumours going around school for real?"

Cassy shoved her hands out, waving them back and forth as she denied the accusations. "NO! It's complicated!"

"You better tell me, or this is the end of our friendship! I don't need this drama in my life."

Betrayed by this reaction, Cassy felt her walls building higher in preparation to tell Rebecca that she didn't need anyone else. Yet, the trustworthy friend had a right to be outraged by this. Cassy had complained for days that Zack was a horrible person, and then suddenly, she had changed gears once learning the truth about her fate. Rebecca should have been the first to know that they were now developing a friendship. Now, Cassy's dilemma was to explain the truth without explaining the truth.

"My brother hired a counsellor to speak with Zack and me. When we first met, the counsellor demanded that we get to know one another. So, that's what we've been doing. We're just friends."

Cassy fidgeted slightly as she became a guilty liar.

"You swear?" insisted Rebecca.

A pinkie finger shot up from Cassy, and Rebecca locked her own in, intertwining the two into a promise of loyalty.

"Please, don't tell anyone. I'm really trying to work on some things to avoid any more issues."

Rebecca twirled her red hair around her finger, reassured of her friend's want for a better life.

"Want to go to the mall? Mark can drive us."

Cassy leaned back, looking up at the porch's ceiling. "I'm still under punishment, remember? Two more weeks."

Rebecca groaned. "They really locked you down. I thought that once Zack admitted you never stabbed him, everything would sort itself out."

"According to Michael, I still handled everything wrong, so I'm finishing the punishment as if I had stabbed him." Cassy rose, alerted by her disdain towards Michael. "Yeah, let's go to the mall. If I'm being punished for something I didn't do, I might as well do something to deserve the sentence."

After Rebecca led her rebellious friend back over to her house, they dragged Rebecca's lazy brother off the couch where he napped. Sluggishly, Mark dressed in a pair of black sweats and a loose-fitting t-shirt to at least conceal his scrawny torso with the bare minimum of dress. He complained about how Cassy had three brothers to drag her around, but he halted when Cassy gave a sorrowful look towards the jokes. He realized that she couldn't approach her brothers like Rebecca was able to with hers.

Strolling along the mall, they buzzed like bees, trying on clothes and fooling around in different sections of the box store chains. Two hours of fun brought out Cassy's cheery personality that a lot of people missed since the death of her parents. Without even a second to dwell on the changes in her life, she was spirited away from one store to the next.

"Woo, I bought too much! This money was meant to last until summer!" Rebecca said, shaking her head at all the clothes.

They took a break in the food court and drank fruit smoothies in a crowded area. Rebecca sipped her drink without a care in the world, all the while her friend nervously rubbed the nape of her neck to stop the hairs from standing on end. Since the beginning of their shopping spree, a bothersome tickle had crept along her spine, and the joy of rushing around shopping faded progressively. Somewhere in the mall, leering eyes concentrated on the young teenager. *Don't panic,* she mindfully thought. Her heart raced. It pounded hard against her rib cage to produce a hyperventilating breath. The feeling wouldn't disperse, and she feared now that unwanted attention landed on her because of the men hunting her. *I should be at home. It's safer there. Where's Zack?* Repeatedly, she found herself playing with her wrist, wishing that the bracelet had been put on and not left at home.

"So, what's Zack really like?"

Refocusing on the topic shift, Cassy banished away her dazed expression. No one around them was recognized, and so she began to add intellectual conversation.

"He's alright. Zack's actually a decent person when you get over the rotten parts."

"Are you guys officially dating?"

"I don't think that's what we're aiming for," Cassy stuttered. "I think we're better off friends."

Rebecca nudged her brazenly, "Come on, he's a hottie. You two would be a great couple if you both got over each other's differences."

Cassy shrugged, unable to elaborate on anything. "We'll have to see. I'm not expecting anything. If there's no more bullying from him, I'll be happy!"

Their brief moment of laughter halted when Rebecca's purse, which rested on the table, vibrated loudly. Rebecca shuffled inside, searching for the loud device.

"Hello?" she chirped.

Cassy cringed when Rebecca's face paled. Handing over the phone, Cassy clutched it, not bothering to look at the caller ID. She knew exactly who would call Rebecca's cell.

"Hi, Michael..." she thickly mumbled.

"Where the hell are you?"

"I went to the mall with Rebecca."

"Meet me at the First Avenue entrance in five minutes."

The receiver slammed down without another word. The laughter dissipated so quickly; it was as if the world had succumbed to the black plague once more. She handed back the phone before gathering up the few items she purchased on the unforeseen shopping spree.

"Michael's coming to pick us up. He's not happy."

Forcing Rebecca out of the mall was more difficult than Cassy assumed. Whenever a nice top appeared, she wanted to try it on. Cassy was embarrassed for Michael's outburst. He constantly seemed to explode with irrational rage whenever possible. Reaching the entrance, Michael's car was already parked in a loading zone, his fingers tapping meanly on the steering wheel.

"Get. In. Now," he growled through the open window.

Scooting into the backseat, the twosome sat quietly, fidgeting whenever Michael gave a nasty look through the rear-view mirror. He grumbled about Cassy's one small bag that he knew she bought something useless. As they shot forward, his frustrations with city drivers flung him into a flurry to return home as soon as possible. Driving in rush hour annoyed him, especially while driving on Idylwyld. He flew down several streets to avoid being caught by every single light and then parked horribly on their driveway. As Rebecca sulked home, depressed that she caused more tension between the siblings, Michael towed his little sister into the over-bearing house. Flinging her onto the couch, he paced.

"Why didn't you let anyone know where you were going?"

"It's not that big of a deal…"

"Yes, it is, Cassy! You can't just sneak out. Not only are you still grounded, but me not knowing where you are puts us all at risk of you being taken away. Cassy, please, I'm begging you! I need to know!" he pleaded. "At least I knew you weren't out with that boy again." He massaged his quickly aging forehead. "If he hadn't come over, I wouldn't have realized that you were even gone! Luckily, Mark came over and noticed that I was panicked."

Cassy slumped, showing how defeated she was with all the drama. "I didn't think it was such an issue…" she apologized sheepishly. "Rebecca invited me to go."

Michael's hands landed on her shoulder when he squatted in front of her. It had taken years for them to talk to one another so courteously.

"Cassy, I need you to talk to me. I'm only a guardian. At any time, if the government deems me unfit, I'll lose you guys. I refuse to allow that to happen. You deserve a much better life than being trapped at some foster home until you're of age. Please, I'm begging. I get you have some pent-up anger, and I'll have to work on that, but *we*, as a family, need to work together to make this arrangement work. I still love my baby sister and hate that I'm not able to talk to you like Brant, or Vince, or even Buddy is able to."

Cassy redirected her eyes when she realized that she hurt Michael more than necessary with her attitude.

"None of this will happen again, Michael, I swear." Cassy gave him a brief hug before leaving the couch to work on her overload of homework. Reaching the railing, she considered something he had said. "What happened between you and Zack?"

"Nothing," Michael bluntly stated. "I told him to stay away from my house and if I see him again, I will deal with him properly. After everything he's done to you, I can't believe you're so concerned over him."

Cassy nibbled her bottom lip. *Michael, if I told you the truth, do you think you'd understand Zack's position in my life?*

• • •

The discussion between Cassy and Michael caused her to become closed off with Zack. She wanted to stay clear of him so that Michael wouldn't blow a fuse if Zack arrived at his doorstep again. However, Zack quickly devised a plan that had her staying at home, safe and sound, and so Michael wouldn't ever find out. At night, he snuck through her large bay window facing the side of the house, adjacent to the garage. He stealthily scaled a tree every night so they might be able to communicate.

After the first face-to-face with Michael, Zack figured that more work would need to be done to fix the bad blood around his past indiscretions. When Cassy asked why he went to the house, his brown eyes rolled in bothersome frustration when he looked at her still bare wrist.

"If you had been wearing this," he reached over to the nightstand and dangled the FUA bracelet in the air, "you might have prevented the entire event. I can locate you with my watch, so when I noticed that you were at home, I thought, heck, I might as well go say hi and see how you've been doing. You've been quiet lately. I threw a lot of information at you the other day, and I wanted to make sure you weren't freaking out. Michael was not all too pleased to find a strange teenager on his porch asking to see you." Zack chuckled. "It could have all been avoided had you been wearing your bracelet. Try to remember it whenever you leave the house. It's important."

Cassy fumbled to put the jewelry on when he dropped it onto her lap.

"You can pretty much follow me anywhere, huh?"

Not denying it, Zack gave a half shrug.

"Were you at the mall today?" she earnestly queried.

He frowned and shook his head very slowly. "No."

"Oh," she rubbed her goosebumps raising along her arms. *I should've figured. He was being berated here during the time I was at the mall.*

Zack massaged his temples aggressively with both hands. "I suppose we've got to be a lot more careful. Victor's men are starting to get arrogant during their surveillance."

She collapsed to her pillow as soon as he excused himself for the evening. Her world was most definitely falling apart around her. Over the following weeks, though, the nightly visits became a nice routine. When at school, they avoided one another, especially with their detentions finally coming to an end. Zack was watchful throughout the day, but less stalker-like. He became more like a protective entity that sent his beaming eyes to graze her, causing butterflies to flare into the pit of her stomach. He continued to catch her off guard with his flattering side-grin and charm.

During the midnight visits, they sat on her bed, facing one another in cross-legged positions and drilling each other on anything that popped into their minds. Zack typically informed her on the latest Victor news at the beginning, and then Cassy would interrupt him before it stretched further into their time together. She wanted to learn about the agent protecting her, not the malicious man who planned to sever all the good in her life.

Quite a few of his interests matched hers. Their favourite movies, a lot of music and the thrill of outdoor adventures had them dwelling on the simple lives the two led. Zack opened up enough to tell her about his passion for cooking and how he was the main cook at home. They even got into a heated debate on who cooked the best. Zack had laughed hard, saying, 'Well, one day, I will cook for you, and we shall see'. The option of doing a couple's activity enthralled her. She couldn't deny wanting to test it.

Her happy smile returned during their brilliant conversations, though, as the night became late, talk would usually revert to the hell lurking in the shadows. They discussed the outcome if Victor did succeed in his kidnapping. Every day brought more evidence that Cassy was the legitimate heir. At times, Zack noticed her rolling her eyes and an annoyed expression showed how she wanted to be freed from this unending fate.

Cassy chose to keep her mind elsewhere. Curled up inside her quilt, she randomly studied Zack, who, when Cassy would build up her walls again, always shifted to the windowsill nook to relax on the cushions. She wondered when everything had changed so drastically that she hardly trusted anyone. Zack stressed for her to listen to his warnings and the news he was giving her, reminding her that her mindlessness would be their downfall. The bluntness usually ended their nice chats when she clammed up and told him to leave so she could sleep. Without the ability to control the intimidating variables, Cassy decided to face each day with an optimistic view.

Cassy did take Zack's advice on occasion. Even though she rarely remembered the bracelet, she made sure to be aware of her surroundings in case she did have to run somewhere for safety. People around her all became the same: either they scared her or were grey blurs that only got in the way of the scarier people. Sensing Zack's presence had her feeling more secure, since he did follow her everywhere. Dangerous situations would be dealt with by him if need be.

When she needed to release personal and emotional anguishes, Buddy became the friend who listened. Not many listened as keenly to her as he did. She obviously steered away from topics like the diamonds and the FUA, but her security dropped quite low with him whenever something stressful happened.

Eight weeks passed as the counsellor returned on Mondays at four-thirty sharp. Buddy was casual, freely offering the girl stories from his past. She looked forward to her afternoon classes ending and arriving home to find Buddy chatting with a brother and then spending an hour relieving any problems that arose over the previous week.

The eighth meeting became awkward. Buddy was on edge and unprepared for the conversation. His pale face, from lack of sleep, shadowed and sagged, which made him look sickly. His interests, during this odd day, were pushed upon her family. He mentioned her grandfather and mother several times in the session before realizing that she was clammed up again. His movements were twitchy as he scribbled quickly across the notepad. Cassy gave nonchalant, rehearsed answers that Zack had offered if she was ever approached by anyone and interrogated. These responses caused Buddy to lash out at her.

After catching her off guard, he asked, "Cassy, do you have a cell phone?"

"Yeah..." *After a month and a half of being grounded, I finally do again!* "Why?"

Shifting away, Cassy bundled the pillow against her chest, picking at the pillowcase.

"Do you carry it with you all the time?"

Timidly, she said, "Well, uh, most of the time?"

"Can I have the number?" he asked. The man received a startled look. He explained, "In case I ever need to reach you."

Cassy responded, "I don't know if this is allowed..."

Buddy slashed the worries away with a flop of the book in the air. "It's only for emergencies. Here," he dug deep into his pants and handed her a card, "this is my number. If you ever need to talk, at any time, or you feel anxious about something, I want you to contact me."

Obligated, now, to respond with hers, she stuttered through her cell number, filling with a hollow regret swarming her insides. Panic rose, and she hid by crossing her legs and holding her stomach. His erratic behaviour terrified her.

Pleased with the results of the session, Buddy waved a quick goodbye and left to speak with Michael about the following week. The troubled girl began pacing, back and forth, trying to figure out Buddy's intentions behind learning about her family and wanting the phone number. Settling in the desk chair to dive into homework, her focus was lacking in all regards. Nothing she wrote made sense the second read through. Cassy slammed a fist into her forehead, frustrated with the constant distractions.

Michael stormed around downstairs making supper, growling about Brant's math mark that had finally been presented to him. Failing marks never gained university acceptances, nor scholarships. The rants worsened when Vince arrived home tipsy. All Michael could do was slam things down and yell at the two brothers hanging their heads low at the dinner table. None bothered to gather the sister for dinner, since they foresaw her attitude worsening Michael's mood.

My brothers are in such disarray. None of us are handling Mum and Dad's death well... Will they be destroyed if I suddenly just disappear? Should I let them know what's going on before something bad happens?

Sitting in her room, hungry, but unwilling to endure the awkward fights happening downstairs, Cassy scribbled away as she subconsciously half focused on school, half on figuring out her life. As the evening rounded into the later hours, the basement became quiet once Michael surrendered into his study to fume. The others shuffled their feet to their bedrooms to wallow in their disappointment. The silence lessened her ability to study, so she laid her head down on her thick textbook and fell into a content state of sleep.

At twelve-thirty, Cassy jumped up, awoken by the knocking against the windowpane. Standing, Cassy yawned and rubbed her hazel eyes as she went to unlatch the window so Zack could hop inside. Cassy's clean floor became a puddle of water when Zack sprang in, drenched to the bone.

"When did it rain?" she wondered while looking at the glistening streets. She lavished in the sweet smell in the air.

He wagged his head back and forth, drying his brunette hair a bit. "About ten minutes ago."

Cassy went on a hunt for a towel for the boy as he looked around for a good spot to sit while avoiding wrecking her things. Rifling inside the laundry hamper, Cassy kneeled, groaning at the dismay he caused her.

"Zack, it's so late. Don't you think it's more logical to just wait until we're heading to class to chat with me?"

"No, definitely not. Rebecca's with you."

Cassy flung a towel in his direction, prepared to confess something. "Well, she does technically know about us."

Zack's swishing hands halted in mid swipe. His eyes peaked out from beneath the towel, testing Cassy's seriousness with the comment.

"What do you mean?"

"She noticed us hanging out a lot, so I explained that we had seen a counsellor and were told to try to find common grounds. She's been keeping it secret for a while."

"Ugh," he groaned. "That would've been good to know earlier. That's probably why she's been trying to talk with me lately."

Cassy shrugged quickly to dissuade any guilt in the accusing tone. She flung her thick quilt over her head and ducked low. *I should've told him*, she sheepishly thought. Zack's long legs stretched out when he sank into the desk chair. He checked over her homework when he noted how studious she was trying to be.

"Besides, since I've been following you around, coming over like this is a safe way for me to come over and ask you questions."

Cassy popped out from under her blankets. She cocked her head like a curious dog to his words.

"Like today, a man, about Michael's age, was leaving the house around five thirty. For almost an hour he was talking to you."

Suspiciously, he interlocked his hands, leaving the towel on his head.

Cassy giggled at his ridiculous stature, but replied to his unasked question, "He's a counsellor. He was the one who I talked about the fights we had. Once that was all sorted out, he continued to come because he feels that I've been through so much that I might need an ear to talk to."

Zack crossed his arms deep into his pectorals, thinking. "When did he start coming?"

A soft hum showed that she had to think about it. "Around the time we went to the FUA. About eight or nine weeks. Every Monday."

"So, around the time Victor's group appeared?"

Surprised that he made such an assumption, Cassy trembled. *It can't be true... Buddy's not like any of those men Zack's described. Buddy was just off today. That's the only reason why I thought it...*

"Zack, I know what you're thinking, but it's been more than two months and he hasn't tried anything. Even my brothers really trust him."

Zack rose his hands to halt the accusations. "Hey now, I was only thinking aloud. I must check on anyone new in your life. Victor's strategic. Implanting someone into your home would be the easiest route for them to learn about you and, if they decided to kidnap you from here, they could easily because your entire family trusts whoever was implanted."

"I just can't see him doing something like that. He's really a nice man."

"Alright. I'll leave it be."

"You swear? I honestly don't like how the FUA investigates people's lives. It sounds so invasive."

Zack leaned his head back and tapped his hands on the chair's arms. "It protects everyone involved."

Cassy forced a topic change at that point to prevent Zack from becoming irritable. "So, what did your mum say about that last history test we took? You failed, didn't you?"

"She never saw it. I forged her signature."

Cassy gave a short laugh. "No, you didn't!"

"Yup. She hardly ever has to know my final marks. The FUA will alter them so I can continue. Besides, they've made sure that I have the necessary skills and classes to graduate without needing to finish. Most of the classes we take are bullshit. Like, what's the advantage to history?"

"I actually like history. I mean, if you don't know the past, mistakes can easily be repeated. Hell, history is the reason why you have to look after me."

Zack swirled the chair around, embarrassed. "I really don't mind looking out for you, Cassy. I've become quite fond of you. You understand me and accept me for who I am instead of what I pretend to be." Redness flashed across his cheekbones once he halted.

Blushing, Cassy hid the fact that she had longed to hear him say that.

He then stated, "History also destroyed the curse's peace. If historians didn't attempt to learn everything about the past, Victor would never have been able to get as far as he has with the diamond search."

"I guess that's another thing that has a pro and con."

"How's it been going with Michael? Since I've been staying out of his hair, is he less abrasive?"

"Towards you, yes, but towards everyone else, no. Vince got busted drinking again... He snuck out during the night, didn't make it to school, and then came home drunk! It didn't help that Brant came home with a failed test... he's been working so hard, but it hasn't been paying off. Michael isn't handling it well. I'm trying to keep out of his way, otherwise, I'll get into more trouble." Cassy leaned against the headboard before mentioning, "He almost busted us the other night. You just left when he was coming upstairs to make sure Vince was in his room. That would've sucked had we gotten caught!"

"We got really lucky. It sounds like you guys are getting along a bit better."

"Just a bit. He's been making an honest effort to apologize. One day, I'll have to suck it up and do the same."

Zack approved with an appreciated smile. "You'll one day realize how much he actually cares about you." He stood, stretching away the stiffness, and then came over to give her a quick caress of his hand upon her head. "Make sure that you show your love before it's too late. A moment's time can snatch away anything you want to tell him." Yawning, he flashed a goodbye wave before ditching to the window. "Goodnight, Cassy. Sleep well!"

Cassy leaned back, savouring the brief touch from him. Her affection had developed into anticipation of when he might arrive to sweep her off her feet again. Though, that night, while she rested her head and looked up to the stucco ceiling, Cassy found herself contemplating his words. *The pain in his eyes spoke of something much deeper than just my brothers and I getting along. Is he not telling me something?* Nothing reinforced her theories, so she went on to falling into a dream world where nothing dangerous lurked in the darkness.

● ● ●

Sinking into the jeep's driver's side, Zack tapped his fingers in contemplation of what should be done with the new evidence about the "counsellor." The gears shifted and rolled the tires forward as soon as he made a final decision. The agent's nosiness got the better of him. Downtown, he circled several times, turning this way and that, before even heading to the rear end of the FUA building. Pulling into a privately-owned parking lot, he turned the wheel sharply to pull into a stall next to another vehicle down in the basement. The complex made no sound other than echoes from rustling animals. Down into the depths of the parkade, Zack twirled the keys around his fingers as he came upon a thick, reinforced metal entrance. This led into the basement of the FUA, where he would meet with the vehicle registrar.

Pressing his thumb into the ninth brick up and third brick from the doorway, Zack waited for the red beam of light to scan his imprint. A gentle beep permitted him to remove the appendage, and a voice asked for his name and badge number.

"Zackary Exacil, Y-six-P-one-B-four."

This time, the system verified his voice and code connected to the file with the thumb print, unlocking the entrance so he could continue his journey into the FUA.

The cement stairs clanged, entombed inside the building's walls, as he stepped down thirteen steps. Mindlessly, he kept tabs on his footing and speed. He hoped, against all odds, that Cassy's counsellor was who he swore to be. If it turned out otherwise, Cassy's trust would be dashed, and any barriers Zack finally broke through would vanish with the treacherous bastard.

Landing his final step at the basement floor, Zack briskly strode around the left-hand corner to meet with an awaiting agent prepared to relieve any keys from field agents. Zack distractedly gave the man a happy smile.

"Good mornin', Exacil. What brings ya tonight?"

Zack dropped the keys to the desk. "First off, I'm returning my vehicle. I think I've had it for too long."

A clipboard was ruffled under a stack of papers as the man hunted for the agent's name. "Ah, yup, you've had it quite a few days. Ever since last Tuesday. Jeez, you gotta be careful. You get busted with that, you'll be put on probation. Can't do nothin' without your vehicle if you get an out-of-town assignment."

"Yeah, I know, Simon. I thought it was about time." Zack glanced over at the elevator. "Do you know if Mr. Edwards is still around?"

Again, Simon lifted and scrambled his papers. "According to this, he hasn't taken his vehicle from the impound, so he must still be here. That man's been working his tail off lately. Must be a few big assignments happenin'." Handing over a piece of paper, Zack was told to sign. "He doesn't go home much after his wife and kid's deaths. There are too many memories. He's been sleeping in the agent barracks upstairs. I can't imagine what he's going through."

"Hopefully, the team he put on it will finally catch the bastard." Zack knocked on the desk as a farewell. "I'll see you later, Simon. I got to speak with Mr. Edwards."

"Good luck with anythin' you're working on, Exacil."

Zack thanked the man before strolling down a tightly enclosed corridor parallel to the registrar's desk. Offices of specialty agents were all locked and the dim lights showed Zack little of the area around him. Had he been a newbie agent, he may have walked into the inappropriate door, since the stairwell that led up to the FUA was masked by an agent's faux name.

After Zack tapped the door with the name Frederick Aseen, Greg's counterpart for this less popular entrance sidestepped sluggishly. Zack shook his head at the smaller, thin man who longed for his shift to be over to return to a warm comfortable bed. Ushered inside, Zack headed to the less attractive metal elevator to enter the almost empty agency. The elevator lulled him into a calm state as soon as it shifted upwards. Leaning against the metal, he wondered the best route for approaching this touchy topic.

A loud ding ended his ride up, and the metal doors widened to show Mr. Edwards sipping a steaming coffee. He chatted with a veteran agent on the main floor near the glass elevator. Obviously surprised to see the youth, Mr. Edwards briefly acknowledged him before returning to the veteran's topic of failed assignments. Zack pointed towards Mr. Edwards' office and marched over to be shortly joined by the boss. Excusing himself, Mr. Edwards extended a hand of apology and took long strides to reach the teenager patiently waiting on a bench outside. Before Mr. Edwards reached for his office keys, Zack halted him with a shake of his brunette hair. It wouldn't take long.

"Do you have surveillance at Cassy's house?"

Mr. Edwards rose a slightly bushy brow. "Of course not. A legal guardian must sign for that."

"Dammit!"

Mr. Edwards spoke quizzically, noticing the edginess of the agent. "Zack, what have you found?"

Instantly, Zack gave up on the hunt. *I'm just being overbearing.* Mr. Edwards restrained him from rushing off without an explanation.

"Why are you acting irrational?"

"Today I noticed this counsellor leaving Cassy's house. He was so smug and seemed out of place as a counsellor. He was too young. I guess they've been chatting for nine weeks without me knowing. I want to make sure she's not in danger. It's too much of a coincidence that this guy would start to visit more than needed right when Victor is on her tail. Do you think it's possible he's a new member? Technically, since the original sixth member was murdered, they would have room for another one."

Mr. Edwards went into deep consideration of the possibilities with the counsellor's appearance.

"Do you know anything other than him being a counsellor? Whether he's part of the school division or community? What's his name? Anything at all so I can get searching?" Zack shook his head furiously to each question. "Well, once you find that out, come back and we can do some concrete investigations. Honestly, Zack, he could just have despicable timing. She has endured a lot in these last few months. She may just need him to talk about some pent-up issues. The FUA sure has not lessened her worries."

Grumbling angrily, the youth said, "I'm always there for her. She could talk to me…"

"Now, Zack, that's unfair. Have you ever given her a reason to open up to you? She views you as someone who's protecting her, more than likely nothing more. If you want her to open up, you need to open up to her. Give her a reason to entrust you with her problems." Mr. Edwards nudged Zack's lowered chin with a gentle fist. "The conversation we had two weeks ago still holds true. I won't condone it, but I think you have every right to do as you wish, only if she accepts it." He sank onto the wooden bench, rubbing his drooping eyes. "Why don't you check on the counsellor's information and then test the waters with Cassandra? That would be the fairest assessment of her feelings towards you."

"I guess I'll have to; otherwise, we'll be stuck in the same routine."

"In regard to this man, we'll put Mrs. Ember onto it immediately and she should give us something on him as soon as we get, at least, a name. If he turns out to be involved with Victor, we'll stop this man before he hurts Cassandra in any way."

Frustration rattled Zack's bones, and before he knew it, he was strolling from the FUA to make the hour walk home. With his mother asking so many questions, he wanted to avoid her noticing the jeep. His thoughts remained dreary during the walk. *I should've noticed something earlier. She seems so close to him. If he's part of the group, she may have told them something about the diamonds without even noticing it. Damn, I let my guard down. Even Jason and Eric have been lurking about, just waiting to pounce.* The calming walk in the brisk air cleared his head enough to determine what he really wanted to do. *Do I storm into her house and demand for everything that he's told her, or do I coast by until she wants to tell me? She's never mentioned him in any of our talks. Does she not trust me? Am I just her agent like Mr. Edwards said?* This option infuriated him more than the unknown of Victor's plans.

His solid footsteps slammed against the cement as he rounded past the University Bridge and headed towards the university, which he had always dreamed to attend, and yet, as soon as he became an agent of the FUA, those goals were dashed. With a single skip, he began running down Central at top speed, trying to outrun the misery of his heart clenching as it was. Something about Cassy's smile kept him fluttering high into the skies, and the way she spoke with him seemed so casual and light, he comfortably listened without an interruption. Zack breathed out long breaths while the run lengthened down Attridge Drive. The shopping centers continued to expand as the entire neighbourhood grew to have more people. He continued down into Kerr Road, where the houses were all built identically to one another, but the one house he could always locate ended his run.

The quaint house with a garden that soon would be flourishing lifted his spirits. It towered above him with three storeys of white exterior. Rounding to the backyard from the driveway, Zack stretched far, reaching for the fence's lock to wiggle it up. Once in the backyard, with its stone slabs and large, billowing trees, Zack scaled a tree to reach his half-opened window.

Landing in the cluttered bedroom of a working agent and teenage boy, Zack ruffled his hair, unsure about what to do the following day if Cassy was shut down. Leaving the bedroom, he went to the bathroom, soaked his face, and then crept to his mother's bedroom, where he peeked inside to double-check on her sleeping form. As had happened before, eventually he would disappear for a couple days without a trace because of an assignment, and his young mother would become distraught with worry. She slept so soundly in her double bed with no one to hold her anymore. She became adjusted to that fact and really enjoyed whenever Zack spent at least two hours with her watching a movie or eating a gourmet meal that he had made. Their joy together lessened every time Zack received an assignment or she had a court case to prepare for. Slipping the brown, wooden entry closed, Zack sealed her safely inside.

Wrapped up in the soothing nature of his bed, Zack swished about the squeaking mattress. He rolled to his side and a hand struck the wall. His knuckles burned. Deliberations of possible ways to inquire about the man crossed his mind. Making Cassy angry was not an option. All his words would be ignored and then she'd lock her jaw the rest of the day. *Ugh! She's so damn stubborn! Stupid assignment!* The anger flooded away in a flash when he thought that. This assignment had done something for him.

• • •

Cassy swished about in the early morning, relentlessly fighting the enemies of her dreams and the heat that caused a heavy, thick sweat to drip down her entire body. No matter how hard she fought, the enemies clung to her limbs and the chills spread, paralyzing her into submission.

Michael tapped the door, announcing he was entering. An agony filled groan escaped her throat in response to her brother. He tensed, unsure what should be done about her red face that glistened beneath the sweat, attaching her dampened hair to her cheeks. She flipped over with heavy gasps of discomfort. Michael's hand pressed against her forehead to test the height of the fever. It burned his touch. In an instant, he rushed about to search for a washcloth. The damp cloth fell onto her forehead before he excused himself and called her school. Finishing his duty as a mature guardian, Michael headed into Vince's room, forcing the sober brother awake.

Cassy rolled about, struggling to break from the nightmares of fiery beasts chasing her down an unknown path. Soft screams uttered out. The sweat persisted down her arms, and when she jumped up, the hairs behind her head stood on end. The creatures disappeared as the bright daylight blinded her back into reality. Cassy stretched. The now dry washcloth dropped from her forehead. Wondering when it appeared, she decided that she would need to get ready for school. As she shuffled into the clothes she had chosen the night before, the fever made her stumble with dizziness. Holding tightly onto the railing, she rounded to the living room finding Michael flipping through the newspaper. Creaking under her foot declared her arrival.

"Good afternoon, sleepy head." He set the paper down, hurrying to help steady her wavering figure.

"What time is it?"

"Almost two," Michael replied.

Cassy's eyes widened. She wrenched away from Michael's soft grip. "Two! What about class?" she yelled.

"You have a fever. I wasn't about to let you make yourself sicker. Don't worry about school, I asked your teacher to send homework with Rebecca."

"But..." she diverted her eyes to the floor, "I'm so far behind everyone else. It's been hard to catch up..."

"Don't you worry about that. You'll do awesome," Michael encouraged. "Would you like something to eat? Maybe some soup?"

This time, Cassy nodded. Following her big brother into the kitchen, she collapsed at the kitchen nook table.

"What kind? We have..." as he listed off the options, he searched the cupboards.

"Chicken noodle, please."

Michael busied himself with the preparation of heating the soup. Flicking the stove on and reaching for the pot, he dumped the can's contents into it. Cassy's head rested upon her tucked arms on top of the wood. *This is the first time we've sat and talked since Mum and Dad died.*

"What do you normally do when we're away?"

"Well, on days off, I spend them here relaxing or have Mark over to hang out. Usually, I'm at school or work, though. Today was a bit strange with you being sick. I didn't want to leave in case you woke up. You slept forever, though!" Michael's wrist swirled the soup before he leaned against the counter. "I could've finished my errand and still gotten back in time to sit around for hours!" No accusations filled his tone; instead, he tried at teasing her.

Cassy shamefully shifted rather than laugh. She'd ruined his day. Full of racing thoughts, she half-consciously looked at her brother's busy figure. *I really wish my family could be happy again. Michael's been trying so hard to make me comfortable.* Studying him, Cassy held back her tears. *Maybe we could grow closer, like we were before.* Her stomach lurched. *He left us! He could've called more... he could've given me a sincere hug when our parents died! He should've been there, especially after the accident.* She pointed blame at him, exiling him for everything that had occurred. However, she suddenly remembered their conversation when she arrived home from the mall with Rebecca. *He's trying his best… no matter what has happened in the past, he's doing his best now.*

"Michael," she whispered.

The soup fell in front of her, finally finished at a boil. Michael sank across from his baby sister. When her words faltered, he continued a random conversation, things that they once spoke about while he lived in Edmonton. All his wonderful memories of living there stabbed her more as she wished her parents were still able to share in their lives. She picked at a peeling piece of wood near the windowsill. She remained quiet, trying to place a protective bubble around her. Zack's words from the previous night lingered, swooping in and out of her mind.

The bubble popped when Michael spoke abruptly, "Do you remember Grandpa's story about that pharaoh guy?"

Cassy stuttered, "Y-yeah."

"You used to get so excited whenever grandpa was coming because you knew he would tell the story right before you went to bed. You would lay awake talking about it while I was trying to sleep." Michael grinned proudly. "I really miss that smile you used to give whenever you heard it."

"Michael… Do you think anyone could be that heir?"

"Of course not. The heir is just a fantastic story Grandpa used to tell."

Tell him, Cassy! "Michael… if I knew something bad might happen, would you want to know about it?"

Michael's head tilted. "Cassy, what do you mean? Has that kid been bothering you again?"

"No… Zack's actually turned over a new leaf and he's become a really good guy."

"Uh-huh," he growled.

"I've just been anxious about some things."

"Is it because of Buddy? I noticed you were closed off yesterday after your meeting. You didn't even come to eat."

"No." Her hair swished back and forth as she shook her head. "Never mind. I'm not sure how to tell you. I hope I'll find the words someday." Her head dropped and her chin pressed into her collarbones. "I'm sorry for being a brat lately. I probably didn't make your change of lifestyle easy."

Michael lost his smile. "I don't blame you. I should've realized you were suffering too. We just dealt with things differently."

Excusing herself, Cassy hurried upstairs, feeling as though she had lifted a heavy burden that could mend her broken family. She curled into the blankets. *It's going to get better with my brothers.*

Two hours later, the middle siblings noisily returned home after a long day of school. Vince celebrated with the summer coming closer and Brant quietly cheered with him. Michael shushed them. He pointed in the direction of the upstairs, indicating that Cassy still slept.

"How's she doing?" Brant inquired.

"She slept most of the day. I think she's feeling a bit better."

Brant dropped his bag. "Did you even see each other?"

"Actually, we had a good conversation." He brushed his hair back and nervously laughed, "Well, alright, I talked the most. She kinda worried me when she mentioned something, but then she apologized for being such a troublemaker."

Vince, in mid-step, flung around, surprised to hear that. "No, she didn't."

Michael clicked his tongue with a brief tilt of his head. Brant patted the eldest on the shoulder.

"She's definitely maturing. That's a good sign," Brant mumbled.

"I'm hoping when she wakes up that I can get her to help me cook supper. She'll probably appreciate that."

"Weren't you supposed to work tonight?"

"Damn it," he swore, "I almost forgot. I guess I'm not going to be able to spend time with her. We finally had a breakthrough!" he complained.

Michael moped. Their tight budget to upkeep their lives took priority over correcting their family's bond. Even so, he wished to spend time with Cassy. Solemnly, his head bobbed. Brant pulled out his schoolbooks and prepared for a couple of hours of studying.

"Hey, why don't we make it a late supper? When Cassy wakes up, we could make the supper and wait until you get home. You're done at nine thirty?"

"I can do that. I feel like crap leaving her alone when she's sick." *Besides, I need to be closer to her than you do,* he selfishly thought.

Brant took offence to that. He whined, "Come on! She won't be alone! I think I know how to take care of my siblings, even if one is sick. I swear we won't burn down the house," he cracked.

Before Michael could respond with a jibe against his ability to care for the younger siblings, Brant dashed up the steps to check on his little sister's condition. He widened her door slightly from its ajar position. Thick droplets of sweat rolled down Cassy's temples and her skin burned under the quilt. Sinking onto the mattress, Brant sighed. Normally, she slept so soundlessly that her entirety was tranquil. That day, she moved, bidding the nightmarish dreams away. Patting her head, Brant left. Seeing her sick proved difficult. She was still overprotected by all three brothers.

• • •

Vince barged in on the unpleasant dreams to bring a brief message. He shook her vigorously with his lanky limbs. Teasingly, he flicked her nose or poked her forehead to force Cassy to grunt in irritation. Her lean body arched and she swatted away the pestering hands. Vince persisted on, joking about the sweat stinking up his hands.

"Hey, get up! Your *boyfriend's* here," he mocked.

Rubbing the sleep from her eyes, she muttered, "I don't have a boyfriend..."

A startled shadow crossed his foolish grin. "Really? You haven't been dating this whole time?"

"No. Why is he here?"

"He brought your homework." With his efforts to make her laugh unappreciated, Vince huffed out.

Cassy propped up against the headboard and hurriedly fixed her untidy hair. Even if Zack was not her boyfriend, the need to look pleasing always made her feel imperfect. Above everything else, she hoped the handsome boy who protected her would look upon her with awe in his gentle brown eyes and long to hold her. Two soft taps came from the hallway. They shook her out of her daze before Zack strolled in with a mountain of books piled in his muscled arms. Swinging his legs onto the bed, he searched her over.

"How're you feeling?"

The books settled onto the bedspread. He admired the half-asleep girl. Her hazel eyes squinted against the blazing ceiling lights and her hands snaked across her face and neck to rub away the dripping sweat. Zack's jeans were tight over his legs and caused her heart to skip when she noticed how well built he was. His muscles tensed whenever he shifted and his chest pushed forward, showing off his rigid pectorals. Pleased to have the fever to hide her blushing, Cassy redirected her sight to the few duo tangs and three textbooks.

"Fine. How come you brought the books?"

"Rebecca had an early training session, so she asked me to grab the books from all your classes. I also wanted to ask you a question."

Wrinkles forming on Cassy's forehead marked her suspicion.

"That counsellor, where's he from? What's his name?"

"You really want the FUA to look into him?"

Zack rose his shoulders. "I have to, Cassy."

He leaned away from the dirty look.

"He's Buddy Sisk and he's from the school district."

Cassy's shoulders pulled back, unimpressed with his smile. Zack, obviously at a disadvantage against her stubbornness, took hold of her palm.

"Do you think you'll feel better by tomorrow? I want to take you to you-know-where. Mr. Edwards is wanting to talk to you."

As soon as she agreed, Zack hopped up. He released her tiny hands from the pleasant touch of his larger ones. Swiftly kissing her burning cheek, he waved a goodbye. Her stunned expression caused him to stop in mid-step. The hasty behaviour of abandoning the sick girl once he gained the information he wanted obviously stabbed her like a sharp blade. She began fiddling with the quilt, trying to shake the sinking from her chest.

Zack backtracked and kneeled. Taking up her fidgeting hand, he explained that he had chores and homework to work on that nagged annoyingly at him. Cassy exhaled sharply, understanding he'd only come to deliver her continuously piling up homework, and so she permitted him to leave with a curt nod. Standing, he tugged her close.

"I'll come later tonight."

Her head spun, turning the room upside down. Zack's reactions to specific situations unceasingly shifted, worsening from when she first met the boy, and she learned quickly that even beginning to fathom him would be near impossible. Just as she doubted he might ever see her as more than an assignment, a hand lifted her chin to where his soft lips met it. He assisted in moving the books to the ground to allow her to rest her head against the heavenly pillows before her eyes watched his posterior stroll out in a masculine strut. Her heart fluttered, stealing her breath away as soon as he disappeared.

• • •

Zack headed towards Michael's fuming figure at the bottom step. Skipping to the main floor, he tried to reach for his shoes; however, the brother had other plans. He dragged Zack aggressively to the couch and then eyed down the innocent looking boy.

"Is there a problem?" Zack layered his voice with sarcasm.

"What's *your* problem, kid? You harass Cassy at school, frame her for stabbing your pompous ass, and then you ask her out? What are your intentions?" Michael's fist clenched, tempted to strike the boy's sharp jaw, but he controlled the urge.

"I am sorry if I harboured any bad feelings. I carry no intentions towards your sister. We both apologized and our issues have been resolved. It would be nice if you could accept that we are friends now. And don't call me kid; I have a name. If you're finished, I'd like to go. I have things to do." He shoved past Michael and stuffed his socked feet into old running shoes. "See you later, Michael. I *will* be around." He quietly exited through the door.

"That damn son-of-a-" he prevented a swear from welling over. "If he thinks he can just waltz inside my house, he has another thing coming."

Brant, realizing Cassy was awake, flung himself up the stairs to avoid listening to the ravings of Michael's increasing frustrations. From outside the bedroom, he halted his hand from knocking. Voices could be heard. Cassy spoke, and then a boy.

"Zack, you can't be mad at him. He has good reasons not to like you," Cassy reasoned.

Zack's voice echoed in rage, "Well, he's treating me like a felon and acting like an ass!"

Cassy cried back, "I never told him to do it, so don't bitch at me! In his eyes, you're the reason I come home and cry at night. I know you're the one who's protecting me in the long run."

"I'm sorry," Zack mumbled. "I didn't realize that you..." the statement faltered. "Are you going to feel well enough to come to you-know-where?"

"Yeah, I hope so. I'll take it easy tonight."

Brant burst in, searching the neatly kept area. He checked underneath cushions of the bench resting up against the bay window. Nothing. He crossed the laminate floor and opened her closet, waited a second for tension to build, and then pulled all the clothes apart. Again, no one.

"What are you doing?" she giggled. "Oh, you must've heard me talking to Zack. I was on the phone."

Cassy smirked, dissuading him from noticing the cell phone resting on the desk. The FUA bracelet came in handy, except for eavesdroppers, especially with the sound quality that made it seem like he sat right beside her.

Brant bent low. He investigated beneath the bed and then slammed the floor with a fist, frustrated that he found nobody with his sister. Cassy figured he wouldn't finish until he searched every nook and cranny, so, she produced a faux cough that rumbled her throat, distracting him with concern.

Still wary of a lie, Brant ignored his suspicions. "How are you feeling?"

"Better. I'm hoping to make it to class tomorrow. I can't afford to miss anymore. Exams are coming up soon."

"I understand that. Michael's got to go to work tonight, so we were thinking we would make supper for later and we'll be able to eat together as a family."

"That sounds awesome!"

As Brant lightly pressed his lips to Cassy's forehead, a pleasant memory brought butterflies to her stomach. Brant learned a lot from their mother. When they were kids, Brant attempted to diagnose and treat their illnesses under their mother's watchful eye. Kissing their foreheads was a way of testing fevers.

"I'll go gather the ingredients and grab you when it's ready. Michael will be leaving soon."

"Wait! Say nothing to Michael about what Zack said, please!"

Brant gulped. That was his intention, yet he even second guessed it. Lately, since Zack entered her life, the tears and combativeness lessened. Disputes about allowing Zack to come around came up multiple times, and Brant always fought for Michael to at least give the boy a chance. He couldn't make her lose another sane part of her life when everything else crumbled around them. Turning with a large sigh, he accepted her small pleas and received a grateful smile through the pain from the illness. *At least she's happy*, Brant thought.

Brant scurried to the grocery store once Michael announced he was leaving for work. He returned with heavy grocery bags filled to the brim with ingredients. As soon as he arrived home, Cassy hopped down the steps, excited to assist in fixing up a meal long since needed in the household. Vince avoided touching anything but the cutlery as the other two slaved over the hot stove. Cassy laughed aloud when an icing fight broke out between the two brothers and she ended up with a spoonful splattered across her face. Though the fever prevented a lot of the activities, she still spent time with her siblings who, for a time, had never smiled. The clean up of the icing fight took a good half hour, which brought the cooking time for the roast and potatoes closer to the time Michael would arrive home. By ten o'clock, most of the meal was prepared. Cassy looked at their neatly set table, proudly admiring the accomplishment. The aromas wafted throughout the home and their stomachs grumbled in anticipation.

Brant wrapped an arm over her shoulder, touching her forehead with the back of his hand.

"Feel better, Cassy?"

"Yeah. I think it was from stress."

Vince sank to a chair, picking up a slice of meat to nibble on. "What type of stress do you have? You're still a baby!"

Cassy's hands fell onto her hourglass hips, "We're a year apart! Doesn't that mean you're a baby too? Maybe more so!"

A fit of laughter broke from Brant as he listened to the joking argument.

Michael's arrival was first filled with hunting for anything out of place, though he could not find any hint of the sticky icing fight. When he rounded the island, he noticed the magnificent meal set out for them. A roast with lemon potatoes, peas and a chocolate cake for dessert was their first official meal as a cohesive family.

"Damn, Brant!" Vince chomped down before anyone could hardly sit at the table, "You're an amazing cook!"

Michael grinned, appraising the second eldest, "I concur. Maybe you should look into being a chef?"

Brant lifted the full fork to his mouth. After a moment of contemplating, he shook his head. Cooking, unless with the joyous events, was an impossible chore.

"You'll have to choose a career soon, Brant, you graduate this year! Besides," Cassy added, "you're not half bad. Everything tastes delicious!"

All four cleared away the table, washing the grime off pots and talking over the clatter of glassware. By eleven thirty, Cassy was outright exhausted, and the fever imposed on the cheer. Michael noticed it right away. Shooing her off, he demanded that she allow them to finish the dishes so she could recuperate before school started tomorrow.

Snuggling up into the blankets, Cassy faced the beginning of a nightmare not typical in her portfolio of dreads.

Cassy cowered in a dark room. Cold, damp, and scared, she huddled against hard brick of her unknown whereabouts. Frightened whimpers escaped unchecked. Suddenly, a light shone through a crack in the opening door where a brunette head poked around.

Oh god, she thought.

The face was memorable. He strolled in, holding a gun in his hazy left hand, demonstrating his brute force with the weapon, all the while she knew who it was for. Heading ever so closer, he reached out an empty hand to calm her struggle against the heavy, clanging chains that clung to her arms and feet. The man squatted to touch her face sharply with inhumanly long fingers.

The door widened more as another man barrelled in. Her hero arrived in time. The man turned and received a foot in the face. He took the blow without complaint and followed by placing the weapon landing upon her temple. Her racing heart skipped when she watched the safety go off.

The man spoke with a slither. "You can't save her, boy."

Zack stopped in mid-step, reading the predicament clearly. "Let her go, Victor!"

Cassy's eyes watered as Victor began to pull the trigger, forcing Zack to collapse to his knees, begging for mercy and beseeching to be taken instead of her. Victor surprised Cassy. The gun shifted to Zack's head and shot. The loud gunshot echoed in the brick prison along with Cassy's shrilled screams as Zack's figure tumbled to the ground, a pool of blood flowing towards her.

Sweat poured across her face. The screams carried into reality as she awoke to find a protective hand clutching hers, trying to comfort her in her dire time of need. Cassy's widened, fear-struck eyes focused on Zack's disturbed, overshadowed face.

"Cassy, you're okay. I'm here," he whispered.

Cassy exhaled. "It was just a bad dream..." Thanking god for nothing serious happening to Zack, she searched the digital clock. Again, he'd come late. "Why are you here?"

Zack's lips sucked into his mouth as he stuttered, "Well, umm... mainly because... I... I.... couldn't sleep," he chickened out. Covering both her hands, he queried, "What happened? You're shaking."

Cassy gulped. They were not a couple. For her to explain the nightmare, she would be voicing her desire of wanting to date him, and he might believe she was obsessed.

Unable to coerce her to explain the miserable dream, Zack hung his head low. Bursting into speedy words, he spluttered, "Cassy, I know we're heading to the FUA tomorrow, but afterwards..." he paused, "I really want to take you out."

Cassy gaped at him. Her bottom jaw drooped, unable to contain the alarming thudding of her heart. *Was the dream telling me something?*

"Like a date?"

His face buried into his hands. "Lately, I've noticed how I'm really happy when I'm around you. I'm hoping to further our relationship. I want to try officially being together."

"Sure, we can go out." Cassy tightened her grip on Zack's now-trembling fingers. "Is that what you wanted to talk to me about?"

Without a single word, Zack drew her forward, hugging her tightly. The movement caught her off guard. Cassy frowned in confusion once he released and twisted away. His unpredictable reactions to certain things always caused an awkward silence to follow.

"Cassy, I know what your dream was about. I won't, not in a million years, allow it to happen. I swear. I'm not going to be killed by that man."

Briskly, he surrendered into the darkness of the night. She was left, taken aback, in bed.

Chapter 8

Buddy brushed back Cassy's wispy hair. She shifted slightly from the discomfort of his tickling caress. His hand slipped down and tenderly stroked her cheek with a thumb. He struggled with the ultimate decision finally made.

The most recent Monday, Victor demanded to gain as many facts about her grandfather and her knowledge on the diamonds as possible. Drilling into her in such a way made her walls rise so high that when it came time for Buddy to receive her phone number, she was too nervous to even hide that she was uncomfortable with handing it over. It was the only way to directly connect to her.

Then, the evening before, just as all the men settled to lounge with drinks in hand, Victor announced his course of action. Victor had shuffled around the empty warehouse for hours, humming and weighing the possibilities of the kidnapping. He tapped his finger against his forearm, and then singled out Buddy.

"Tomorrow morning, you will drug her and bring her here. It's time to move."

Everyone cheered. It rang in Buddy's ears, but all he gathered from Victor's words was he held the duty of collecting her. The evidence of her being the heir had stacked up to the pinnacle, and she officially became the target of these vicious men. Buddy's job was to get her out of the house without her brothers realizing it, which was surprisingly easy. They trusted him so much. Michael had let him in without a question as he hurried out the door for school, and Brant slumped around the kitchen to make breakfast for his siblings. Vince snored away in the room across from her.

The situation was set and gave Buddy the optimal opportunity to steal her away.

The newest group member hesitated several times. He gulped back a lump. He'd grown attached to Cassy. For weeks, he'd known this would eventually happen, but seeing her asleep, calmly enjoying her blissful dream world, he wavered on destroying her life.

His internal battle ended when he realized that, above all else, he wanted to be praised for capturing the precious teenager. He dropped a blue case onto the bed. He unzipped it, and once inside, he admired the contents with respect for the preparation all the men had done for this one moment. It contained the drug Austin had procured. It would put her to sleep with enough time to smuggle her out of the country. Injecting it while she slept was Buddy's preferred method, but Austin urged him to wake her up.

"We will be able to track when she'll wake up. Besides," he sneered with insidious intent, "don't you want to see her face when she realizes you've betrayed her?"

Victor hit Austin across the head swiftly. "You idiot, if this doesn't work out, we lose our advantage. Buddy, you figure out the best way. We depend on your ability to persuade them that she should leave with you. Be it you lead her out awake or not. Understood? The moment Zack hears about her kidnapping, the FUA will go into high alert and scour the city for us. This must be quick."

Irritated that his joke had received poor reviews, Austin took him through the anesthetic. He pointed out how much to give and warned not to overdose.

"This stuff will knock out a full-grown man. We give her too much, she'll seizure and die. Too little, she'll wake up too early, and that may cause other problems. Understood? You give only this much!" He pointed at the permanent marker line he drew on the syringe.

Buddy pulled out the empty syringe. *Damn it.* He had to do it. There was no other way. The serum bottle shook in his grip as he tried to steady his hands. He pressed the needle point into the top and filled it with his betrayal. He second guessed the quantity. Overdosing her would be the worst possible outcome. Her life was too precious to waste it foolishly. He double-checked the drawn line before accepting the amount. The needle was full to the line. He was resolute.

The syringe pointed to her freckled forearm that he gently uncovered from her blue quilt. It went to plunge into her youthful skin, yet it froze inches from entering. Cassy stirred. He lost his grip on her arm as she raised both above her head in a dramatic stretch, then wiped the solidified sleep out of her eyelids. She yawned thickly from oversleeping the previous day. Her hazel eyes blinked back her hazy vision. She looked directly at him with a frown as though she didn't register what was happening.

Buddy was frozen in place. His nerve was gone, and he was unable to perform the task at hand.

Cassy fell from her bed and struggled to hide her exposed self to him. She couldn't believe he had been peeping on her while she slept.

"What the hell are you doing?" Cassy shouted.

She darted to the windowsill, ready to scale the roof to escape. He instinctually hid the needle and blue case behind his back, concealing his intentions to steal her.

"Wow," he skipped back, pretending to be startled, "sorry!" His false persona bled through, and he became the ever-trusted counsellor once more. He struggled significantly to store away the evidence of his deception. "I was just checking on you because I'll be out of town this Monday. I didn't mean to startle you. I knocked and you responded. I thought you were up. I didn't mean to intrude."

She folded her arms across her chest and attempted to cover herself up from his redirected eyes. Her pajama shorts and small, spaghetti strapped tank top didn't cover much, and he embarrassingly admired her small stature. His cheeks blossomed into a bright pink hue.

"Sorry, Cassy. I'll let you change." He sighed internally, glad for the opportunity to collect himself and to put the needle away.

"What's behind your back?" Her adrenalin had faded enough for her to notice that he hid something.

He had no other option. He had to show her. Victor's careful planning was going to shit! Unless... "It's nothing," he said sheepishly while his fingers twirled the blue case until he found the zipper. He heard the ear-piercing zip as the zipper went up just over the corner. He concealed a wince towards the sound that only he heard. The opened gap was enough to slip the needle inside. He zipped it back up within seconds and flashed her a smile. The case came forward and waved about to show her no harm. "It's just a pencil case. I've been told that I lose my pens too easily, so I've decided to store them in here." He rubbed his forehead to hide his scowl as he flashed a fake smile. "Just watch me lose this entire case now!"

She accepted the response and tightened her arms when he made eye contact again. He knew he wasn't getting close enough for drugging her without a fight now.

His hand went from his forehead to behind his head and he flashed another grin to slough off the awkwardness. "Sorry, Cassy. I guess I should be going. I didn't mean to scare you."

She showed her appreciation with a curt nod. Then, she thought of something important. "Since you're here, I guess I should let you know. Zack asked me out... on a real date. We're going out tonight." She turned her back and headed for her dresser. "You helped a lot with getting me to trust people. Thanks, Buddy."

The whole world aligned itself with optimism. Buddy's smile extended ear to ear and he chirped back, "I'm glad to hear! I hope the date goes exceptionally well, Cassy! I'm excited to hear all about it!"

He shuffled to the hallway and left the house with no mention of a next meeting or even a farewell to Brant, who still busied himself in the kitchen.

• • •

Cassy shot out of the eerily quiet bedroom. Buddy's weird appearance and behaviour put up red flags. Leering out of the living room window, Cassy watched Buddy crawl into his black SUV and then shoot from the street without a second of hesitation. Darkness clouded over her eyes when she sealed her sight away, calming her hyperventilated breath. Brant was at work in the kitchen, already making coffee and breakfast for himself. Still dismayed, Cassy concluded that she would question Zack about Buddy, since he was already apprehensive of Buddy, rather than bringing her brothers into it.

In the clean kitchen, Cassy strolled about, unsure on what her appetite could handle.

"How are you feeling?" Brant blurted out as soon as she rounded the counter separating the dining room and kitchen.

"Better." Figuring cereal was the best option, she fiddled inside a cupboard. "Why are you up so early? You don't have a first period."

"I promised Michael I would wake up Vince. He has a field trip today, which I bet he completely forgot about. I'm excited to see his reaction! Michael tried to wake him up earlier, but with no avail, so we'll see how he likes it when he gets a bucket of cold water landing on him."

"You're so evil!" Cassy chirped. "By chance, do you know why Buddy was here this morning? I just found it odd that he came before anyone woke up."

"Well, according to Michael, he wasn't going to make Monday's appointment."

Brant finished his scrambled eggs, cleaned up, and then went to fetch the sleeping Vince. He wasn't excited to awaken the bear from its den, though he was eager to listen to Vince scream after being drenched. Vince remained the night owl of the family.

Silence crept on as she strained to hear the ruckus upstairs and chewed on her meal. She jumped at the phone's loud ring. Not often did they receive phone calls on the landline.

"Hello?" she murmured in a monotone.

"Hey, is Vince there?"

"He's still asleep."

The moment the words were spoken, a great shrill exploded from upstairs and then Brant darted downstairs. Explosions of laughter showed how brilliantly planned it was.

"Oh, never mind. He *just* woke up."

"Crap. Tell him to hurry his ass. The bus is starting to load up."

"I will."

Cassy hung up just as the dripping wet, shirtless Vince stormed into the kitchen. Brant dodged the brother's attempt to give him a sopping wet hug. She shifted out of the way, denying any involvement in this plot.

"What the hell?"

Brant dug inside the fridge, looking for the brown paper bag already prepared for Vince.

"You have a school trip leaving in ten minutes. It was time to get up!" Brant sneered.

Vince's alertness sharpened instantly. "Dammit!"

He waddled out of the kitchen, trying to keep his wet boxers from touching bare skin, and headed straight for the laundry room, rifling through a hamper in search of half-decently clean clothes. Within a couple minutes, Vince rushed back downstairs and trailed behind Brant with a towel still running through his damp hair.

Left alone in the huge house, Cassy also went in search of clothes in the laundry room. Huffing at the mess, she made a mental note to mention that a schedule would need to be sorted out for laundry. All the clean and dirty clothes were mixed in the small, tiled room, piled high. With the family dynamic improving, a regular chore schedule could be secured. Cassy threw on a pair of clean jeans and found a comfortable black t-shirt. Leaving the house, she made sure she locked the doorway. For once, she was running on time, so when she crossed the green lawn, Rebecca was still eating breakfast in hurried gulps. Unwilling to wait around, Cassy continued the lonesome stroll without her.

Cassy dawdled across the road, heading to the alleyway. The dingy alley led to the paths that curved and twisted to the school. An edgy feeling grazed across her spine, sinking her stomach when two men came into view, whispering in a mutter and leaning against their black sports car. Familiarity struck her, but she was unable to place from where. She hurried her steps; she couldn't get away from these men fast enough. Their eyes penetrated deeply into her, following her every move until she escaped into the weaving paths towards the high school.

The awkward feeling dispersed as she grew closer to school. The sight of Zack, her protector, soothed her. She could sense that he would protect her to the ends of the Earth. All the dread disappeared as he strolled in front of her with his friend Travis. They both made jokes and teased one another.

If we start dating, will I be allowed to be around him during school hours?

In hopefulness, Cassy gave a brief wave when Zack turned around. Her action caught Travis' attention, yet he never noticed the hip height wave from Zack's palm.

"Hey!" Travis called out, "Back off new kid! Quit trying to get Zack! He doesn't want some bitch like you."

Cassy looked up to the sky, sighing and preparing for the harassment to begin. Travis effortlessly hiked up towards her with Zack close behind. Zack's miserable reputation caused them to act as if they still fought. However, he was able to prevent his friends from harming her if he remained on their side. He apologized each time they became belligerent. She understood why it continued and made strides to defend herself.

"I'm not the one with the problem here." She took a few steps forward, trying to stay clear of the friend who could hurt her. "It's really pathetic that you have no life other than crawling out of your hole to torment a defenceless girl while you could be doing so much more with your wasted meat sack."

Cassy coolly walked off from the teenage boys while Travis steamed at how nonchalant Zack was towards her, especially when his best friend was just made a fool of. Zack shrugged it off, concealing his beaming fondness towards the girl. No matter the adversary she went up against, she handled it with such grace. Cassy's strength made him more attracted to her than anyone he'd ever encountered.

Satisfied having dissuaded anything cruel from happening so early in the morning, Cassy leaned against the brick walling. For the past two months, their mornings seemed to start off the same way. Zack and his friends played a rough game of football while she and Rebecca snuck glances over at them. Even if the boys were bullies, they were built athletically. Zack flew passed the others, using quick manoeuvres to receive the ball and then dash to the end zone, leaving behind everyone in the dust. She noticed how the FUA training had increased his abilities above the average person. Cassy glistened when he toppled a friend and hooted loudly at the mock pass that had been attempted.

With five minutes until the beginning of class, Cassy determined Rebecca would be late, so without her friend, she headed into the first class to prepare for whatever she had missed while sick. The teacher already set up the cooking stations, so with a few minutes to spare, he went over the missed lecture with Cassy. Saddled with extra homework on top of her original work, Cassy calculated that her weekend would consist of only studying and sleeping. Her partner greeted her before assisting in getting the proper ingredients for the recipe. He jokingly talked with her until the moment Zack entered the classroom. Whenever her partner was chatty, Cassy felt Zack's presence darken. Looking over at the boy she no longer feared, she gave a reassuring wave towards him and then went on working.

"You know," her partner mentioned, "ever since that incident with him and Victoria, he's less mean to you. There hasn't been a single bad exchange."

Cassy shrugged it off, not knowing how to approach that subject. After their first official date as a couple, they would be able to show their feelings towards one another. Until then, she would need to play dumb.

Her frequent shifts of attention always landed upon Zack. Zack's eyes caught hers, giving Cassy a loving sensation. Secretive smirks were exchanged, blossoming into reddening cheeks as they tittered like school children noticing their first crush. Zack absently mixed his ingredients, making a huge mess as he fell into a dream of leaving the school and taking Cassy out on the date. He was nervous, and Cassy snickered at his foolish behaviour, enjoying it while keeping her guard up so nobody noticed her odd actions.

Cassy wanted to stay in the daydream of what magnificent date ideas Zack may have concluded upon. Putting her back to Zack's tomfoolery, her sight landed upon the entrance to the classroom. The shut metal door had a solitary window. It usually showed the blue from the outer wall across the way; however, this time it held a familiar face, petrifying Cassy, and causing her to inhale sharply. Cocky, sneering features winked when the man noticed her paling face. Her hands gripped the corner of the cupboards to hold her swaying torso from toppling over.

Zack's goofy antics instantly ended, and he scurried to her side to hold her steady. Hyperventilation stole her breath as a solid chest pressed against her head. Zack turned to the window to witness the man's back turn and disappear down the hall.

"Cassy," he whispered, "hold yourself up. I've got to alert the FUA."

Accepting the order, she stabilized her balance. Zack beckoned the teacher and he swiftly asked to go retrieve a book from his locker. Only Cassy's partner realized her panic. She worked on lessening his worry over her by continuing to mix cream cheese and sugar, but at a much slower pace than before.

Without much else to say, Cassy finished class and worried over Zack's sudden disappearance for the rest of the morning. Rebecca greeted her in front of their science room., apologizing profusely for missing their walk in the morning. Cassy was still shaken by the thought of the conceited man strolling around her school halls; every out-of-place sound or movement had her jumping. Rebecca apprehensively sank into a desk. She wondered what had happened, but Cassy had no intention in telling her. So, rather than prying, she flicked her red hair about, unsure how to loosen Cassy's tongue without offending her.

The second and third class were fuzzy as Cassy could only find herself thinking, *Why was he in the school? How can he be so arrogant to stroll around here when he knows agents are nearby?* Each time, she would glance over at Zack's empty seat. *Is Zack alright? Did he catch him?* Without any answers, Cassy hunkered lower, finally realizing how close danger was.

After several offers to walk Cassy home during the lunch break, Rebecca surrendered into the cafeteria as the frazzled girl continued to edgily look around every corner and denied company for a fourth time. Cassy refused only to keep her friend safe from whatever lurked in the shadows. Waving her friend away, Cassy left the school, striding quickly through the paths to reach the streets before anyone jumped out. Vulnerability was unsuited for her.

Rustling bushes caused her to jump. Just as she went to take off, the quick hands of an athletic boy sprang out and caught her wrist. Her scream halted and her full-forced swing stopped at the sight of him.

"Cassy, shhh," Zack murmured.

Flinging her wrist out of his hand, she almost scolded the teenager for scaring her. A rare seriousness had removed the twinkle of light from his striking face. Instead, a nearly mature man stood before her, brushing back his hair and straining from overreacting when he found her still safe.

"What happened to you? You disappeared for almost three hours." Cassy asked.

His right hand disappeared behind his head. "I didn't mean to freak you out. When I noticed what startled you, I rushed outside to double-check my assumption. I was a bit too late, and he had gone already, so I went to send out an alert to all field agents."

"You saw him too? It was Eric!"

Zack dropped his arm, surprised at her recognition. "Yeah."

"Why was he in the school?" she shrilled.

"He's definitely getting brave," growled the agent. "That's why I went to the FUA. According to a few agents, there's been a spike in their movements, and they've been spotted all over town. We've got to be careful. Something got them moving. That's the closest they've ever been to you."

"Aren't you worried, Zack? I mean, they were in our school! They could have hurt our friends to get to me..."

Zack reassured her by touching her hand and hiding it inside his. "I'm always worried when it comes to this. However, I know that Victor will only attempt a kidnapping in semi-privacy, to avoid witnesses. If anything does happen, you know where to go, right?"

"Of course," Cassy groaned, still terrified.

"Good! Now, remove that bothered face. I have to get back to the FUA because I'm needed to figure out what Victor's plan is. I will call you on your bracelet when I plan to pick you up. Mr. Edwards is stressing this visit, so it must be important. Also, we have that date, remember?" He brought her hands to his lips, where a little peck landed upon them. "I am so excited."

Cassy blushed, holding her breath before sighing in excitement. With the earlier appearance of a kidnapper, she had nearly forgotten about the long-awaited date. As Zack began to escort her home, something ripped at her hair, dropping her to the ground. Zack released his grip instantly to avoid tugging her in the opposite direction and causing pain.

"So, it is true!" the gruff voice said. "You two always hanging around and flirting with one another... All this time we've been punishing her for interacting with you, but you're the one who's been following her around, pestering her."

Zack raised his hands. "Listen, Travis, I didn't mean to lie."

"You're dating this bitch, aren't you?" Travis accused. "You broke Victoria's heart for *her*! She's destroyed your reputation. Nobody takes you seriously anymore."

Cassy fumbled to keep up with the forcefully moving boy.

"My reputation sucked anyways. Maybe it's about time I get a new one," Zack grumbled, swearing in a monotone. "Anyways, we aren't dating yet. Tonight will be our first date."

"Then why have you been hanging around her?"

As Travis' foot met her side, Cassy shrieked, "Because of me!"

Both boys directed their attention at the girl, covered in dirt and begging to be released. Travis squatted beside her, tilting her head further back.

"What do you mean?"

"My brothers hired a counsellor. He told us to talk and get to know each other. We've been doing that for my family's sake."

"You stuck-up brat. You honestly thought you'd snatch Zack into your talons by talking with him?"

"Travis, that's enough!" Zack ordered. "Release her. This is my choice. I want to take her out. It's not her fault at all. I made up my mind weeks ago that this is what I wanted." Zack's large hands landed on Travis', demanding the friend to loosen his grip on her hair.

He did so. Travis then hesitated for a moment before he took hold of Cassy's cheeks and forced her into a stolen kiss. She, half-prepared, swung her elbow into his throat and then sprang up. Zack approached her quivering form. Shoving at Zack's hands, Cassy scurried away, wiping the unsatisfying first kiss from her lips. Tears flooded to the brim of her eyelids, though she prevented any leakage at all costs. She refused to spill tears over the abusive nature of boys.

Disgusted with the friend who was sprawled out on the pavement, clutching his wheezing throat, Zack was tempted to chase after the distraught Cassy. Unfortunately, his friend required a bit of assistance, so he extended a helpful hand to lift Travis onto his feet.

"What the hell was that?"

"Zack..." Travis pleaded for mercy. "I just wanted to know. The last few months you wanted us to keep her away from you to the best of our abilities... Lately, I've been noticing you guys smiling and waving at one another when you think nobody is watching. And just now, I heard that you're dating."

"We're not, yet... You might have royally screwed that up!" Zack blew out his cheeks in exasperation. "Why did you frickin' kiss her?"

He shrugged. "I thought it was a good idea at the time." He rubbed his throat, consciously aware of the trouble he caused. "Dammit, I'm sorry, Zack."

Not in the mood for forgiveness, Zack glowered upon him. "You assaulted her, Travis! How could you do that? That behaviour is utterly disgusting! You forced yourself on her and took away her right of consent." He groaned up to the sky. "I've done a lot of terrible things to her. I'm in hot water as it is with her and her family. I've been working on gaining her trust and correcting my poor behaviour. You may have made it ten times worse."

"I never realized you liked her so much..."

"I've fallen hard for her," Zack huffed out.

Travis swung a consoling arm over the taller boy's shoulders and gave him a joking punch. "If you had told me, I would've found some way to stop the others without giving away everything."

"I was hoping to take her out and then see where it led. She might not even want to go out now." *With Victor's men becoming braver, we might not be able to take our date anyways*, Zack added internally.

Travis bowed his head. "I'll find a way to fix it."

"Don't bother. I'll figure something out. Come on, you're a mess."

The two strolled back onto the school grounds with Zack sternly lecturing that his actions could have consequences and he couldn't just slough it off as a boy being a boy.

• • •

Cassy lifted herself from her home's foyer floor. She couldn't skip the last two classes of the day. Rather than sulk, she dragged herself back through the pathway that had resulted in an unexpected attack. No one leered at her during this silent walk. As she arrived at the school, she dreaded sitting in her final class with Travis glaring at her back with no Zack around. He would have headed to the FUA to gather intel on her potential kidnappers. At the edge of the school's property line, what Cassy saw devastated her more than the actual event during the lunch hour. Zack and Travis joked by the fence, speaking with Rebecca, who flung her head back and laughed heartily at the boys' jokes.

Her nerves of steel faded with an instant gasp, and she stormed towards the math classroom. Sitting in her desk, she slumped to hide from whoever already sat in there. A herd of students swarmed the room after the first warning bell rang. Rebecca, Zack, and Travis strolled in together, speaking in a monotone. All three noticed the girl hunkered down. She avoided eye contact.

"Hey, Cassy," Rebecca welcomed.

Zack bolted over to her to check her for any bruises left by Travis' attack. What he saw was the same look he received when they first sat in their cooking class together: complete disgust and mournful outrage. Travis shuffled over, unsure how to speak to the pariah that had corrupted his best friend into liking her.

"Hey, Cassandra," he said softly, "I wanted to apologize for this afternoon. I didn't mean to be such a dick."

Cassy directed her sight upwards.

"I'm sorry. Even though that won't change what I did, I want you to know that I won't do it ever again."

Startled, she watched Zack's approving head bob. *Did Zack force him to apologize?*

The teacher interrupted her response when he commanded the students to sit. Zack surrendered into the far corner and Rebecca sank next to her friend. Travis disappeared from the classroom, rushing to the afternoon class that he would be late for. Tedious note taking was done throughout the class, but Cassy's mind wandered to Zack still being at school, and then to the unpredicted apology from one of his bully friends. Rebecca nudged her to point out how Zack sulked whenever Cassy was upset at him.

In between classes, Rebecca stopped Cassy from storming off.

"Hey, you. Why are you so upset?"

Cassy snarled, "He's a complete asshole! How could Zack hang out with someone like that? He attacked me!"

"You mean Travis?" Rebecca flipped her head around, shooing away Zack's creeping figure. "They told me what happened. Travis admits that he behaved like a jerk. He shouldn't have done that. I'm not defending him, but Travis did apologize." She landed a hand onto her hip. "You should've heard Zack lecturing him. Travis never considered what it was like for you to be grabbed and forced into a kiss. He just thought it was a joke. Zack kept mentioning that it's sexual assault, no matter if it was a kiss or anything more. Travis really freaked out because he didn't think about that. I don't think Travis is a bad guy, he made a stupid decision that hurt you. I doubt he'll ever pull a stunt like that again on any girl."

Cassy admittedly agreed. Her hand smothered her face, unsure how to react.

"Zack and I are supposed to go on our first date tonight," Cassy said. "Do you think I should go?"

"He honestly cares about you, Cassy. He got angry at Travis. Those two never get mad at one another. I have to admit, if you were only a fling, he would've reacted differently when Travis grabbed you." Rebecca met Cassy's eyes and continued. "Even if you don't talk within school hours, he uses his eyes to watch over you. Somebody whose only intentions were to hurt you would never do that." Rebecca's supportive hand slipped in-between Cassy's arm and torso, towing her from the classroom. "I think you should go on this date and enjoy every second of it! You deserve it after all the shit going on around you!"

Grateful for her friend's advice, Cassy simmered down. The two strolled along the hallways and planned a shopping spree for the following day so they could recount the date. Rebecca wanted to know all the details of this first for Cassy. Zack sidestepped towards them as Rebecca waved him down and then disappeared to talk to another classmate. Zack tapped the wooden desk for Cassy to look up at him.

"Thanks for helping me, Zack."

"I will *never* let anyone hurt you," he stressed.

Pleased that she forgave him, Zack leaned closer, touching her cheek.

"I'm going to the FUA. I'll contact you when I'm coming to pick you up."

She watched him stroll from her. She wished that Zack would remain with her and to harbour the fear from boiling over. Knowing he went to protect her, she sat in class, not hearing a single word said.

School ended with a blaring bell that aroused her from her daydream. She slowly strolled home in deep thought of her parents. She usually, during times of troubling anxiety, would crawl onto their bed and sit with her mother to talk about it. She reminded herself that they were long since buried. She wondered how they would react to everything happening in her life now. *Would they have liked Zack? I wonder if they would want to know about me being the supposed heir.* If they learned about the curse and of the FUA, it might have increased their chance of condoning their relationship. *I really wish I asked them more questions. I learned hardly anything about mum and dad.*

She laughed aloud as her legal guardian popped into her train of runaway thoughts. *Michael would put Zack on the definite 'NO' list. When Zack and I start to officially date, Zack will need to prove himself. Michael thinks so lowly of him, I wonder if Zack will ever be able to crawl his way up.*

She laughed harder at the possibility of being the heir. If Michael ever learned about that, she assumed he would blow a fuse. He still teased her about believing in that story. Now, grown men attacking her proved that there was a possibility that the story was real. *Those men are coming for me, and they aren't going to take any chances of me escaping.*

The front porch tripped her while she mounted the creaking wood. Taking in a deep breath, she shoved her thoughts into a locked filing cabinet to be referred to on a later date. She putted around mindlessly, doing random chores throughout the house. Each time she skulked by Michael's study, where he worked on his frustrating schoolwork, she itched to sit beside him and just be with her big brother. However, if she did, something would potentially fly from her unsealed lips about all the craziness happening.

Carrying a load of laundry to her room, she dressed and re-dressed, getting ready for the date. She pondered about what outfit might be appropriate for the date since Zack had given no details to his plans. She rolled her eyes as the floral dress flared at her knees. *We're going to the FUA first. I shouldn't be dolled up. I should just be a little better than normal.* So, she sank in front of the mirror and curled strands of hair, putting half of her hair up. For her wardrobe choice, she decided on a newer pair of jeans, a white t-shirt, and an asymmetrical zippered black sweater. It was simple, but still appealing enough to get gleaming appraisal from Zack.

"Hey, Cassy," her bracelet beeped from the nightstand, "are you ready to go? I'm coming to pick you up in twenty minutes."

Cassy pressed the bracelet close to her glossed lips. "Yup! I'll be ready when you come."

"What are you telling your brother?"

Cassy hummed, confused at the question. "Well, I was going to tell him the truth."

Zack burst into a fit of laughter. "Really? You're going to tell him that you're going on a date with *me*?"

"When you say it like that, I guess it probably won't be the best idea." Cassy scratched her head. "Ugh, I guess I'll call Rebecca."

Clicking off the bracelet, she tossed it onto the bedspread and then she reached for her cell phone on the desk and dialed quickly.

"Hey, Rebecca, I have a small request for you," she said as soon as the phone answered.

"Sure. What's up?"

"I'm going out with Zack. I'm going to use you as my alibi, is that alright?"

"Of course! I hope you have a blast. He seems like he's going to do something fantastic for you. Tell me everything tomorrow!"

Cassy heard the click before searching around for anything forgotten. She slipped her cell phone into the zippered pocket of her jacket before she rushed out. Michael still sat, scribbling on lined paper with a pencil.

"Michael?"

He slightly glanced her way.

"I'm going over to Rebecca's to study, is that alright?"

Stretching back, he searched for the time on his wristwatch. "Holy hell! It's already seven? Why didn't you guys yell at me that you were hungry? You should eat before you study."

"Nah, I'm fine. Rebecca and I will munch on something. Brant and Vince have been fending for themselves. Vince has almost eaten everything in the fridge!"

"Damn, he's going to eat me out of house and home. Do you remember me eating that much at his age?"

Cassy leaned against the frame, mockingly stroking her chin. "Maybe… I think you actually ate more!"

Michael flashed a sneer her way. With a quick wave, he shooed her out. "Be home by ten!"

Accepting her curfew, Cassy darted out to hunt for her runners before Zack barged up to the entrance. It was mere seconds after she shoved her left foot into her runners that a bang rumbled the door. Shouting that she would answer it, she planted her other foot inside her shoe and left through the wooden door. Unlike during their original trip to the FUA, this time the concept of Zack driving hardly startled her as much as what he drove. By the time she reached the edge of the driveway, he was across the street, helmet on and perched on an unsafe-looking orange motorcycle.

Zack chuckled, amused at her sudden unwillingness. "Don't worry, I can drive this too."

Disappointedly, she twirled a curl around. *So much for having nice hair for our date.* "What happened to the jeep?"

"Another agent needed it for an out-of-town assignment."

The amusement in his eyes was lost. Zack grudgingly crossed the street, took hold of her arm, and hauled her to the bike. She resisted the best she could. His grip held strong, and without a voiced complaint, a helmet dropped onto her head and his fingers restrained it to her chin. Zack straddled the front of the bike and revved impatiently. Her helmet clanged against his as she sat behind him and clung to his lean torso.

Gushing winds stole strands of hair partway out of the helmet and whipped them around violently. They cruised to the downtown area, beginning the circles to ensuring that no vehicles were tailing them. She clung snuggly against him, interlocking her hands. The rush of danger she felt relinquished at a red light. There was hardly any space between her and any passing vehicles as the motorcycle came to a steady halt with Zack's legs stretching out.

"Zack, next time we go to the FUA, I vote for an actual vehicle. This is awful."

He twisted, mockingly. Cassy's grip around his waist that had just loosened quickly retightened.

"OOF!" he patted her hand. "Don't kill me. We're almost there. Just three more blocks and then we're off this *dangerous* machine," he joked.

"Don't mock me. I didn't expect this. Besides, you're only fifteen. This is technically *illegal*," she scolded.

"I have a driver's license to prove it's legal."

"Only because of the FUA!"

"Ready?"

He sped off before an answer nagged his ear. Smoothly, his feet lifted to the clutch, and with each shift of gear, Cassy almost relaxed. He obsessively checked his side mirrors in avoidance of leading anyone to the headquarters. Their destination overshadowed them, and he loosened the gas to lose speed. A sudden sharp turn to the left forced her hands firm again. The bike sped up, speeding down the road, weaving in and out of the traffic.

"What are you doing?"

He yelled over the vociferous motor, "Behind us!"

Cassy's head turned just enough to find a closely following car behind them. She couldn't believe that she recognized the black sports car from the early morning.

"Jason and Eric." Another sharp turn almost had them toppling to the pavement. "They've been following me since they arrived in town. They're finally making their move. They've never attempted to get this close while tailing me."

He slowed the motorbike for the men to catch up. In the traffic, the two men were unable to back away fast enough to hit the sharp turn Zack took. For an instant, Cassy and Zack were protected by several buildings separating them from the vicious men.

Zack stopped, cut the engine, and jumped off. Hurrying, he assisted Cassy off, his fingers frantically fumbling with the helmet. Time was limited. His index finger whipped to his mouth to halt any questions. The alley that lay ahead made her wish she hadn't left home. It looked as if it were from an old detective movie: dark, eerie, and forbidding. The dire situation she'd landed in proved that she was the prey now that the real hunt had begun.

Inside the alley, Zack hauled her to an old wooden box. It lined up against the wall, surrounded by metal barrels, crates and pallets. Zack's finger pointed to Cassy and then to the box. Zack's edginess grew as she gave quizzical looks at her surroundings.

"Cassy, get inside," Zack pleaded.

The crate scratched along the pavement as he dragged the wooden, rectangular box. The bulk of the noise was created by the gears of the faux brick wall opening while he shifted the crate. A dark hole inside the wall invited her to conceal herself. Zack's frantic gestures showed the severity of the situation. Cassy's head shook in astonishment. At first, she assumed he was playing a practical joke, but wrinkles creased at his eyebrows that told her otherwise.

She fell to her hands and knees to crawl into the half-a-metre-high hole in the wall. A blanket and pillow patiently waited for the sake of an assignment being hidden. Zack quickly shifted the wall and crate to their rightful places. The "brick" was a type of glass decorated to be the reddish hue of the manufactured clay blocks. The crate had enough openings that when Zack kneeled before it, she saw the terror reflected through his worried facial expression.

"Promise me you won't leave here, no matter what happens," Zack demanded. "As soon as the coast is clear, you call the FUA." He frowned at her hands, which tapped the walling to be released. "Dammit, you forgot your bracelet!" Zack swore. Fists tugged at his thick brunette hair.

Cassy instantly chilled to the bone as she ruffled around hunting for the piece of jewelry. She had grabbed it from the night table when Zack spoke on it and then tossed it onto the bed again.

"Change of plans. Once the men leave, you run. You go nowhere but the FUA. You remember how to get there?"

"I think so," she whispered.

"Once you're there, you stay there! No matter what happens."

"Zack…"

She panicked and attempted to open the wall. Zack firmly gripped it to steady the seal.

"Do you promise?"

"I promise."

Zack took a second to replace a bunch of the barrels into haphazard disorganization. Teeth appeared as he nibbled a lip.

He couldn't look down at Cassy's hiding spot. "Cassy... I love you," admitted Zack.

A solid strike onto the wood caused it to splinter. Showing such emotion at this point of the hunt was a sign of weakness.

"Just stay here. I won't be able to protect you anymore..."

Multiple nearby vehicle doors slammed shut. Zack stared out at the darkening horizon, trying to visualize whoever arrived to snatch their prize. He hastily chanced a glance at the hiding place before he heard it. Cassy listened intently as the soft tap of several pairs of footsteps headed towards them. Zack mentally prepared. Cassy begged for him to stop and prevent him from getting caught up with these dangerous men.

To the rear entrance of the alley, Zack shouted, "Run! Don't look back, just run!"

No longer facing her, his torso rounded in the darkness. He was determined not to give her up without a fight. Four distinct chuckles exposed the men from the shadows along the wall. Zack faced his enemies, slightly stiffer, and settled in a ready stance for whatever they planned. Cassy propped herself onto her elbows to study the men. From her position, she saw four shadowy shapes. Victor's men stood proud in a small group.

Two were recognized straight away. Jason and Eric sneered at the boy, cracking their knuckles. The other men were unfamiliar to her. Their jeering faces glowed brightly at the sight of the lonely agent.

"It's been so long, hasn't it, Zack?" Eric bluntly muttered.

"Nope, not for me. I keep seeing your ugly mugs everywhere I go. You should've stayed in prison."

"I finally saw that pretty girlfriend of yours up close and personal. I just couldn't handle not going to the high school for one more peak." He lavished as he said it. "Oh wait, I stand corrected. You two haven't had a date yet. Tonight was supposed to be your first. So, she's still free game. Maybe, I'll try my hand with her."

Revolted, Zack stepped back, checking behind him to pretend she had scurried down the alleyway. Cassy frowned towards the final comments. *How did they know about our date?*

Jason added, "She's such a slight little thing, she'll be one of the easiest ever taken."

Zack ignored the jibes. Searching the other men, he said, "Austin, you're still a lowlife working for Victor. Don't you ever get bored of taking orders from him? He allowed his favourite goons to be imprisoned without even a flinch."

"Don't act like you didn't know we were in town," an English accented voice said. "The FUA has been keeping tabs on any activities we do."

The man with a closely buzzed scalp growled. "Enough chatter. Where's Cassandra?"

Cassy shivered. *Oh, please, Zack, get us out of here.* The latter of the two who spoke stood between the other three in a perfectly fitted jacket and dark khakis. Sleek blonde hair was cropped short, barely noticeable in the darkness. The enormous size of the man's gorilla muscles overshadowed the others. His neck was thick and his face round since his muscles overtook a lot of him. He wasted no time talking out in the cold, potentially giving Zack a chance to let her escape. A scowl was a permanent facial position for him. Cracking his neck, moving it side to side, he strutted towards Zack, who cautiously stepped back. Cassy prayed that this man was Victor and she wouldn't have to worry about anyone worse than him.

"I told her to run," explained Zack.

"Austin, go find her," the big blonde man commanded. "Keep it quiet."

The accented speaker left in a hurry. As he flew by, Cassy glimpsed at his swift figure. The man's square face twisted in all directions as he scanned the alley with his ocean blue eyes squinting into the crevasses. He was handsome with brunette hair perfectly fixed in place and nicely groomed stubble stretching from his chin to his sideburns. He disappeared into the night seconds before Cassy returned to Zack's predicament.

"Now, I bet Victor would just *love* to see *you* again."

Cassy gaped that the commanding man was not Victor. Unable to pinpoint his name, the teenager leaned in closer, wanting a better visual of the enemies.

Eric and Jason started for Zack. Zack waited for them to be in reaching distance and then kicked Eric in the stomach and punched Jason in the nose. They did not go down, but it did slow them. The boy planted his feet and was ready for their next attack. Both fumed now. Jason spat blood from his mouth. The big blonde man commanded from the sidelines for the fighting men to beat Zack to a pulp. They committed to uncalculated, wild swings; Zack blocked every fist that came in his direction and then hit them in opened areas in their defences.

A resounding thump filled the air as Jason fell to his knees after a swift, hard kick to the head. Eric stumbled, falling against a wall and again received a powerful blow to the chest. He coughed amongst a snarl. Zack had the advantage of training with professional martial arts instructors, and he was at his prime for speed and reaction.

Zack's going to win, and we'll get to the FUA to make sure they're arrested! Cassy praised.

She was naïve to believe this since he didn't have much of a chance. Both men were nearly double his size and they hadn't produced their ace in the hole: their weapons. As Eric pulled out his weapon, winning left Zack's grasp completely.

Shit, Cassy, you're on your own. Get to the FUA, Zack thought, resigned.

Eric drove himself from the wall, whipping a sling shot-shaped weapon from his thin jacket. A small electrical current flooded the center of the weapon. In dread, Cassy realized what it was: a Taser.

Blue zapped into the boy's eyes as Eric's attack narrowly missed his torso. Zack lost his train of thought at the debilitating strike. Jason took advantage of the weapon holding Zack's attention, grabbed a handful of Zack's hair, and flung the agent to the ground. Attempting to be released before Eric came to him, he struck the restraining arm at the wrist. The tugs loosened but did not release. Cassy's whimpers were covered by Zack's profanity and Jason chuckled while Eric reached around to the back of Zack's head, zapping him into submission. Zack collapsed to the ground, wide eyed, and facing Cassy's hideaway. He was full of remorse for losing so easily.

Cassy covered her mouth, preventing any sounds from reaching them.

Chapter 9

The men disappeared to retrieve thick black ropes. They bound Zack's hands tightly, kicking him if he made a noise. Jason flung him over a shoulder to tow him away while Austin returned from his hunt. The big blonde man cheered about finally capturing the troublesome agent, but was unimpressed with the man returning empty handed.

"Where the hell is she?"

"I couldn't find her. The alley meets up with another street. I'm assuming she ran off. That sneaky bastard held us up here so she could escape," Austin complained.

"Or," the commander contemplated, "that's what he wants us to think. She might be here in this wasteland of junk. Don't forget, he is the master hider."

Kicking a crate near Cassy, he groaned at the indecision of where to hunt.

"You weren't able to learn the whereabouts of the FUA?" Austin questioned.

Jason stroked his head as he walked back into the conversation. "Nah. That boy is overly cautious. We weren't able to follow close enough, and then he would lose us."

Cassy curled up. The commanding man sank onto the crate covering the section in the wall. Absolutely absorbed with Zack's predicament, she ignored their whispers. *They took him... What will they do to him? They won't stop until I'm caught. I have to get to the FUA.* Short searches inside crates and the pile of junk metal shook her almost to react, which would bring disaster if they heard her.

"Dammit," one mumbled, "we have no choice. You find her and bring her to Victor." He scowled, aggravated with delaying their departure.

The last approaching shadow that had taken Zack snapped back. "Yeah, whatever, Jonathon. Why don't you stay in this screwy weather?"

Eric folded his arms and shivered in the early evening winds.

The man, Jonathon, walked away, leaving the question unanswered. The remaining two shuffled about to make half an effort in searching. Defeated, Cassy's blanket covered her head. Trapped within the wall, Cassy had few options at comfort.

Listening closely, she heard car doors shut and engines rev. All that was heard next were complaints. The men searched for a long while as she snuggled into the thick, woolen blanket, smothering her face in the pillow. They couldn't see her and yet she felt uncomfortable with their closeness. She saw the whites of their eyes when Eric smashed the largest crate and looked inside. His head turned, glancing at the wall.

Screwing her hazel eyes shut, she broke into a silent prayer. Eric struck the wall and then straightened with an exasperated groan.

"Does that ass really expect us to find her? When Zack hides people, they stay hidden, unless they give themselves away. Remember the guy from Germany?"

Jason chuckled, remembering all too well.

"The FUA could've placed hidden compartments inside the walls or even tunnels leading straight to the FUA. We'd never know."

"Mhmm," Jason hummed.

He moved to the brick wall. Knocking, he listened for hollow parts. His knuckles banged twice at each spot he picked and steadily it lowered only to cause her heart to race. *No! Stay away!* If he found her, she would be stripped from the enclosure, and dragged out to endure a torturous journey. The small hole had limited squeeze room to hide.

Eric distracted Jason from the task. "Why are we always stuck doing the dirty work? If Jonathon thinks he's better than us, then why doesn't he do this?"

"True. I think you should ask him, just to see how he reacts."

They joined in a short snicker and then sat themselves on the partially destroyed box, continuing their complaints about their comrade. Cassy breathed slowly. Luckily, Jonathon had sloughed the chore off to a couple of lazy people.

The comments about their commander finished too soon, and the men fell instead on the topic of catching her. Ideas sprouted in extraordinary detail about what they'd do once they owned her. Every option became more vulgar. She'd never heard such things, but they confirmed how much she preferred avoiding them.

• • •

Zack's head lolled. He withstood the searing that stung his neck and fought the restraints that tightened around his arms. They were bent snuggly at the elbow and horizontally bound. The angle made it almost impossible to loosen the bonds, especially when they started at the wrist and snaked up to the highest point of the forearm. Zack was enclosed within a strange environment of cluttered papers on an old desk and iron walling. The hard, wooden chair creaked beneath him. Sitting across the dusty flooring, on an old couch, was Victor.

The man sat with both arms spread eagle across the top of the decrepit seat. He swirled a drink in one hand while he eyed the agent.

"I never imagined catching you. Even so, I should have suspected it. There was no way you were going to give her up unless we disabled you." Victor swung back a shot. "Now, where did you hide her?"

Zack moaned. The pain became unbearable. A persistent stabbing sucked each breath away; he realized that the men might have damaged his ribs while they assaulted him in the vehicle. Glowering at the man's words, Zack leaned his head back, exposing his bobbing Adam's apple.

"Screw off!"

"You won't tell me?" Victor snapped his fingers. "Let me try to guess! The FUA? No, you never made it in time..." He took another sip. "Your mother's place..." A condescending finger wagged. "No, no, that's not right. She's important to you. You wouldn't land her in danger either. Cassandra's no longer at home. I'm positive about that. Mhmm, where, oh where, could the agent bastard take my heir?"

Zack shook furiously. "She's not yours..."

A half-crooked grin expressed Victor's outright pleasure. "You should learn to trust me. I will not hurt her as long as she's the heir."

"I would never trust you, you sick bastard, especially when Cassy's involved," Zack mumbled.

Victor shrugged with little concern. "You learned who works for me this afternoon, huh? That's why you rushed to take Cassandra to the FUA. You know about Buddy."

"She won't be fooled by him anymore."

Victor clicked his thick tongue twice. "You never warned her, though. I may have a chance to fool her once more before this evening is out. Soon she'll be chained up by my side, accepting the diamonds as hers. How long do you think it'll take until I break her spirit, *Zackarass*? How long will she have to be trapped in the dark before she willingly walks into that tomb?"

"You leave her alone!" the youth screamed.

"Oh, I will. It's my men that won't."

• • •

Cassy listened, half aware of Jason and Eric's conversation. The cold nipped at the tips of her fingers and reddened her nose. The numbing sensations caused wooziness. It took most of her willpower to stay awake; two hours of shivering made the time crawl. Without making a single noise, she struggled to cocoon inside the blanket. Her head rested upon the pillow, trying to forget that if she did not free herself soon, Zack's life might end.

The conversations led from her to previous heirs and memories of torturing the Sacred Chosen for information. Cassy hated it. They abused so many innocent people, and now they laughed at their cries for mercy. Cassy's eyes squeezed shut as they mimicked the pleas for freedom.

The darkness faded from her eyelids as Jason's hands jumped into a ringing pocket. At first, she almost inhaled loudly, thinking it was her cell phone.

"What's up, Victor? We haven't found her yet."

Jason nudged Eric and stood.

"Understood. We'll be there shortly."

Hanging up, Jason stretched, smothering his face between his hands as he wiped sleep from his eyes.

"Victor wants us back at the warehouse to regroup and figure out a plan."

Eric cheered in thanks towards the boss for freeing him from the cold. Both shoved their hands deep into their jeans and strolled to the street.

Cassy ripped from the blankets in readiness to dart from the hole as soon as the men abandoned their post. The car's wheels crunched along the road, zooming down the street. Cassy delayed her escape for two minutes before pushing open the fake brick wall and slithering out. She ran in a frenzy. Huffing and puffing, her feet were an echo as they slammed onto the cement. Cassy was unsure of the true location of the FUA, since during their original trip to it, Zack had done multiple turns. Running along the river, she went straight, always second guessing her choice. A miracle formed right in front of her eyes as she recognized the ominous building. Rushing down the alleyway, she barely searched for any looming shadows nearby before whacking the metal with hard fists.

"Please, let me in! It's Cassandra Waters!" she screeched.

No response permitted her inside. *No… why won't you open it?* Banging harder, Cassy cried out for help. *Zack, you said they would help me. They won't even let me in.* She stepped back, completely defeated by the circumstances. Just as she turned, the metal creaked and banged open as Greg stormed out and grabbed the trembling girl. His huge hands folded over Cassy's forearm. The mountainous man's dreary eyes sulked over the bags under them, obviously too tired to deal with someone not willing to learn her place at the agency.

"Cassandra, did Exacil not explain about the lights?"

Cassy lifted her sight towards the blinding spotlights she'd forgotten from the original visit.

Grunting, Greg tossed her into the building where agents had halted, standing on guard because of her insistent knocking.

"That lazy boy," Greg groaned, sinking onto the swivel chair behind the desk, "doesn't even try to teach you. Ugh! Those lights outside are meant to scan your face so I just double-check the photos to make an accurate facial recognition. Next time, don't even knock. I'll open it once you stand there." Greg leaned back. "Where is Exacil? It's time to give him a scolding."

The surrounding agents finished their gawking, and Cassy now had a chance to clear her mind and search for the FUA's boss.

"Where's Mr. Edwards? It's an emergency!"

Standing on high tiptoes, she hunted throughout the crowd.

"He's in his office. Cassandra, where is Exacil?" Greg asked firmly.

With a skip of her feet, she ignored his queries and dashed to Mr. Edwards' office. Rather than reaching the solitary square room, she met with Mr. Edwards leaving a concealed hallway. She scrambled past conversing agents, shoving them to reach the boss's stiff arm to obtain his full attention. Mr. Edwards apologized to the agent he had previously been speaking with and was dragged off by the distraught teenager. Puzzled, Mr. Edwards directed her to the bench outside of the dimly lit office space.

"Cassandra, I had assumed Zack would take you on that date before coming here," he pondered.

"They attacked us!" she sobbed. "They took him!"

Mr. Edwards dropped his grip. He tried to hide his worry over the disappearance of his agent. "Where were you located? At home?"

"Some back alley. You need to find him! They'll kill him!"

Mr. Edwards ignored her pleas and turned on his communication watch. "I need a Rescue Team to surveil Cassandra Waters' residence. Check on the two agents positioned there and on her brothers. Remain inconspicuous. We are only to ensure their safety and then return."

"My brothers?" Cassy was frozen in spot. "Could they be in danger?"

"It's unlikely. Victor's group normally does not stray from their target. If you don't return home, there will be no need for your brothers to be hurt. This team will only ensure they are safe and that none of Victor's men are scouting for you. They most likely expect you to come here or to return home."

Her trembling fingers scratched at her head. She hadn't considered her brothers might come into danger because of her.

"Cassandra, I need you to calm down." Mr. Edwards patted her shoulders.

"Are they going to kill Zack? Please, we need to find them!"

"*You* are remaining here under the protection of the FUA, and *we* will be sending out a team as soon as possible to locate Agent Exacil." Mr. Edwards sighed heavily. "Dammit…" He checked his watch and clicked his tongue at the crying girl. "Cassandra, you must remember that Zack is your protection. You aren't to protect him."

Her glistening eyes looked at him with sorrow.

"I will find him." Mr. Edwards spun to the busily moving Mrs. Ember as she clumsily fiddled with several folders. "Is it set?"

"Ah," she distractedly said. She seemed not to see Cassy sitting on the bench. "Sir, your meeting will be in board room eleven."

Cassy's chest hurt when she realized that his distracted behaviour was not because of Zack's disappearance. He was more concerned about going to a meeting. Zack's dire state wasn't even considered.

"You're not going to save him?" she said, aghast.

Instantly, she removed herself from Mr. Edwards' reach. *Why would you send me here, Zack? The FUA plans to betray you.*

"I'm not leaving him with those men," Mr. Edwards interrupted, keeping her from storming off. "However, *you* will not be involved. I am placing you in a secure area." He gained Mrs. Ember's attention by taking the load of folders. "Mrs. Ember, you remember Cassandra?" Mr. Edwards interrupted.

"Of course…" she inclined her chin.

"Would you mind watching her? There's an emergency with Agent Exacil that I'll deal with after this meeting."

"He was taken by *them*, wasn't he?"

Darting eyes glanced away.

"Very well, sir. Where should I lock her?"

Cassy sprang into action, enraged with their speech. "You can't lock me up!"

"Enough, girl!" Mrs. Ember snapped. "We are doing what is permitted of the FUA. You are to be protected until further notice."

"Cassandra, you must listen to every order given by Mrs. Ember. If these men abduct you as well, they will leave without a trace. Understand that these men will treat you like a princess until you're put into that tomb.

If it turns out you're not the heir, they will murder you. Do not give them a chance to do so."

"You just want me to abandon Zack?"

Mrs. Ember clung to Cassy's wiggling arms.

"Cassandra, for now, we need you to stay here," Mr. Edwards checked his watch. "I will rush the meeting to be back in half an hour. The Rescue Team will be alerted of this. Do not allow her to leave this building. Zack warned me this afternoon of Eric being too cocky for his own good. He was strolling around the high school, scoping out where the two were. We should've noticed the signs. They've only ever become this brash when they've decided to act."

Mrs. Ember lugged the girl through to the research facility and into the communication room. Cassy whimpered, unable to do anything. *Zack told me to come here because he knew I would be placed under lockdown. He doesn't expect to survive...*

The woman busied herself with filing folders, sorting them in distinct piles and then shoving them into their appropriate cabinet. She winced each time Cassy sniffled back the heartache.

"Will you please at least let me know he's still alive?"

Mrs. Ember rolled her green eyes, impatient with the compulsive behaviour. "Knowing that he's alive will only make you hurt more. Do you realize that he's probably getting beat right now?"

"Please..."

"Very well. It will allow me to get some work done."

Mrs. Ember's statement stung Cassy. She grimaced at the callous woman and dug her chin into her collarbone for comfort.

"I don't mean to be heartless, Cassandra." The woman refolded a file and settled it upon a pile. "This is how agents cope with their job. Do you see these files?"

Cassy nodded.

"These are the ones who won't be coming back. I file them away into a cabinet to collect dust. This is what's left of those agents. Whatever equipment they may have been carrying is recycled and given to the next agent. One day, you'll understand the function of the FUA."

"The way Mr. Edwards is handling Zack's kidnapping, is that how all the rest were handled?"

"Well, that's tough to answer. Agent Exacil is lucky because he is still within our jurisdiction. The moment he leaves, we have no advantage. The FUA is not a 'legal' organization. So, the Board determines specific rules that we must follow. Trust me, he's in a better position than most, but in a worse one based on who has him." Blonde hair flicked back and forth as her curled, loosely pinned locks flipped over her shoulders. "Cassandra, you just need to trust us when we say we will do our very best in rescuing Agent Exacil."

"How many have died because your very best was not enough?"

Mrs. Ember examined the files sorted by if the agent died or had been released based on injury.

"Is your jurisdiction extended for assignments?"

"We are able to travel to a known location as long as a believed sighting has been reported. Though," Mrs. Ember wiped her brow with her wrist, "I bet exceptions would be permitted if you were to be kidnapped." She slammed her hands down, understanding what Cassy hoped to achieve with the questions. "Don't even think whatever you're thinking. It's reckless and tempts those men to abuse you. Let's go." She snatched Cassy's palm. The youth tugged back, startled by the pinching grip. "You wanted to check if he was still alive, didn't you?"

Cassy quickly accepted the chance. Fast feet tapped along the floor toward the doorway on the opposite side of the office. Mrs. Ember shoved her thumb and a thirteen-digit code into a scanner next to the entrance. It was not a system easily fooled even by the most conniving masterminds. As Cassy was ushered within, the first noise she noted was a deafening hum of mainframe computers situated in fifteen rows of three-tiers. Cassy was awed. The rows were tightly situated together in groups of ten. Each computer displayed, at the bottom of the screen, an agent's name, position, and assignment. The rest of the screen portrayed a dot, blinking on a small map of their whereabouts. The dot moved whenever the agent travelled a metre in distance.

Mrs. Ember explained, "This is the Location Room. All four hundred and fifty staff members that work in this agency are monitored and tracked

through their watches or bracelets. That is why it is of the upmost importance that you always carry yours." Her eyes twitched to graze Cassy's bare
wrist. "Unfortunately, you still have not learned the importance of it yet.
Let's go to Agent Exacil's."

Zack's computer was number three hundred and fifty-two. Stopping
at the twelfth row, they gazed upon the topmost system. Mrs. Ember
tapped the screen a few times with a thoughtful finger. The dot blinked
lightly, remaining motionless. Cassy examined others to determine if that
was typical. Some blinked vigorously, indicating a fluctuating heart rate
because the agents ran, or an adrenalin-filled reaction occurred. Zack's
map showed an area of the city nearer the northside highway. Cassy had
only seen the industrial buildings once when Brant took her for a drive
to familiarize himself with the city. She frowned when she remembered
Jason mention a warehouse. Zack's dot remained motionless, gently blinking away in an orange hue.

"Is he still alive?" she trembled as she asked.

"Yes. He's alive. That dot would be a red colour if he were dead. He is
seemingly unconscious or near unconsciousness."

Cassy's hands rose to her chest in relief that he remained partially safe.

A woman with a clipboard rounded the aisle that they stood within.
She was short and lean, bustling about.

A thick German accent welcomed the two females. "Evening, Mrs.
Ember. What brings you here?"

Mrs. Ember gave a short wave and shifted so Cassy was in full view.
The woman lowered the clipboard, unfamiliar with the youth.

"Natasha, this is Cassandra Waters, Agent Exacil's newest assignment."

"Oh, Zackary! Is that troublemaker keeping out of trouble?"

"Not so much."

The woman continued her work of double-checking the systems. Cassy
noticed that the curiosity to learn more had been pushed into the back
of the busy woman's head. *They all have a part and are to keep their business quiet.*

"Cassandra, this is Natasha Fischer, our Location Room's highest
ranked agent. She keeps track of all four hundred and fifty agents to
ensure their safety."

"Umm, Mrs. Ember," Cassy nibbled her bottom lips, "I want to stay here. If something happens to him, I want to know."

Mrs. Ember considered it by looking over at the other woman.

"Would you mind watching her until Mr. Edwards has finished with his meeting?"

"Oh, no worries. If she doesn't touch anything, we should be fine."

"Alright, check on her ever so often." Mrs. Ember strolled passed the woman and said in a monotone, "She's a potential runner."

"I will make sure the doors are locked behind you."

Cassy stared curiously at the system. She wondered how it worked. Miss Fischer shuffled about and rejected any questions before they were asked. She went around into the next aisle, her heels clicking with every step. It became rhythmic; she would take four steps and stop for ten seconds before moving on.

All alone in the twelfth row, Cassy leaned against the iron shelving unit. Zack's little light blinked steadily. It kept perfect pace with his heart-rate, but at times, Cassy noted a slight blip in it, and winced at the scenario he may have been experiencing. Her hazel eyes dropped their gaze to the cool, black cement floor. Her bottom lip fell between her teeth and she restrained a whimper. *He's going to die...* Something caught her eyes when they landed on the computer beneath Zack's. Though the screen showed the agent running quickly across some type of barren wasteland, there was a message saying "Do not contact at this time" scrolling across the width of the bottom of the screen. She bent at the waist to examine it. Zack's did not have that; however, she realized a small, circular speaker rested near a tiny red button. *Is this how they contact agents if they aren't directly connected?* Her nimble fingers struck Zack's button and she cried into it.

"Zack? Where are you? The FUA... they're moving too slow. What should I do?"

• • •

Victor froze his punch at the sound of Zack's wrist speaking with their prey's voice. The watch's face scribbled her words and then the light dimmed. Zack's flinch transformed into panic. Victor had found a secret

157

tool. Quick fingers unlatched the band and the watch dropped into his hands. Austin edged closer, full of obvious intrigue towards the technology that presented itself.

"Now, what do we have here?" Victor slowly wondered. "So, this is your troublesome little secret." Tossing it to the companion, he demanded, "Figure it out so we can track her."

Zack stomped his feet in protest of the men tampering with the device.

Victor massaged his chin in contemplation while Austin sank to a chair and struck the buttons to familiarize himself with the equipment.

"We've never gotten close enough to an agent to notice how you communicate," Victor awed.

Austin grunted for several minutes as he was sent to odd screens or bumped out of what he was working on. Eventually, Zack's watch beeped with a special option of locating the girl's bracelet. It blinked, showing the street name and the address.

"Mhmm, that's weird," Austin muttered. "It's a street that I recognize, but I can't pinpoint it."

"Show me."

Austin tilted it towards him.

Victor burst into a fit of laughter, finding the punch line in the joke. "Dammit! That's her house. I doubt she's there. She wouldn't cause her brothers to get hurt. Shit, we're still going to have to do this the hard way."

Austin turned off the location option, and then slipped the watch into his pocket. It would be fiddled with later. Victor struck Zack again prior to marching from the upstairs room to go on the next hunt for the supposed heir.

●　　●　　●

Cassy slumped her shoulder when she received no response to her urgent question. Depressed and defeated, she sat on the ground to watch the system blink away. *If it keeps blinking, Zack's still alive...*

The agent monitoring the screens strolled nearby, doing random checks on the computers. Cassy scooted to allow her to stroll by. Cassy's eyes resettled upon the screen, but something had changed. The little dot no longer blinked; instead, the map was blank with warnings signalling a severed connection. Alarmed, Cassy sprang up, smacking the computer with all her might.

Miss Fischer heard the alarm bells ringing and asked, "What happened?"

The woman dropped the clipboard, shoved Cassy away and hit the screen to begin typing on a portable keyboard to locate the malfunction.

"What did you touch?" she shrilled.

"That red button near the speaker..."

"We told you not to touch *anything*."

Cassy's only concern was Zack's wellbeing. The woman could yell all she wanted.

"Did they kill him?" she choked.

Calming down at the sight of the quivering girl, the woman huffed out, "No. More than likely, based on the warning we received, they only took off the watch." Hauling Cassy down the hall, she tapped upon Mrs. Ember's doorway. "I have to sort this out and don't have time to babysit."

Mrs. Ember, dishevelled in anxiety, appeared around the door, clearly scrambling to find answers. Miss Fischer shoved Cassy into her arms before storming off.

"Wait, what happened?"

"She contacted the boy. They shut off the location system and have removed his watch completely. I need to figure out whether he has died or not."

"Cassandra," Mrs. Ember scolded, "I told you not to touch anything. Ugh, it's just like having a child around. Come, we'll place you upstairs for a while."

They headed from the research laboratory to the elevators and stepped into the glass and silver machines. Mrs. Ember's nails dug deeply into Cassy's forearm as she struggled against the woman's close body. The elevator effortlessly lifted to the fourth floor, where Cassy was dragged behind the woman past offices upon offices. They eventually landed on an unfamiliar office, into which Cassy was tossed and locked away. Two shadowy figures moved in front of the door, barricading the exit.

Unable to escape her imprisonment, Cassy sank onto the leather couch facing a coffee table and the mahogany desk. The consequences of contacting Zack through his watch now seemed steeper than she ever fathomed. *Did they kill him or just remove the watch?* Curled up tightly into the couch's arm, she dozed off, patiently waiting for Mr. Edwards to save the agent from a catastrophe.

Brring! Brring!

Cassy jumped at her cell phone alerting her of a call.

"I'm lucky that didn't go off earlier," she mumbled.

The phone number was blocked. She determined that the person on the other end would most definitely be an enemy. Clicking the talk button, she put the phone to her ear to hear a menacing voice chuckle.

"Hello?"

"Good evening, Cassandra."

She now knew all the other men's voices, so hearing a new one, she instantly determined who was on the other line.

"Let Zack go, Victor!"

"Mhmm, you're fairly smug, Cassandra. You think you will get what you want by demanding it?"

Cassy took the hint. "I'm sorry. Just let him go. It's me you want."

"That is true. *Zackarass* bleeding on the floor is just an added bonus."

Crying out, she pressed the cell phone so tightly to her ear that it almost cracked under the pressure. "You killed him?"

"Of course not. He wouldn't die from a few good beatings. Oh no, he's too stubborn for that. Otherwise, I would have killed him long ago." Victor shuffled, playing with something metal. "Now, I've gone back to where my men snatched the agent. Interestingly, I found a hole in a wall just the perfect size for hiding a person. You called Zack on that watch, but do not have your device, so I'm assuming you're at the FUA."

Cassy inhaled sharply.

"Excellent! Now, here are the terms of what's expected for tonight. You will tell us where the FUA is, or come to me."

"What if I decide on neither?"

"Then Zack dies. Simple as that. These terms are non-negotiable. So, which will it be?"

I have no choice. I have to go to Victor. Giving away the FUA would cause a worse disaster than me just being kidnapped.

"I have a third option."

Victor snorted, annoyed with her persistence.

"I'll meet you at the high school. It's late enough that there will be no witnesses. I'll come peacefully."

"Fine. You have half an hour to meet us there."

A resounding click ended their connection. Cassy shoved the device back into her jacket pocket before figuring what other plans she could commit to without getting Zack murdered. *I'm not meeting you anywhere, you bastard. You're not bringing Zack... I'm going to find him.* She sprang from the couch and went to tap the door for assistance.

"Excuse me! I need to go to the washroom!"

Whispers and shuffling were heard as the two outside struggled to find a legitimate reason not to accept the request. They were baffled by the circumstances and called Mrs. Embers to permit the latrine break. A frustrated voice was fuzzy as Mrs. Embers agreed with some hesitation. With a warning not to leave their sight, Cassy was freed from the office and headed, with the male agents marching on each side of her, to the bathroom. Every direction that she could take in was calculated as her escape. These agents were uninformed on the predicament and let their guard down frequently when she seemed to be listening to their small talk.

The washroom was just up ahead, but Cassy saw another area that better suited her needs. A sign for a staircase marked a chance to escape this place full of people who disregarded a person's life because of rules. She comprehended little and disliked the resolve of the agency.

As soon as they took two steps past the staircase, where the agents had tensed up, she backpedalled quickly and darted through the metal exit, skipping down the steps as fast as possible. The agents were athletically built and capable of keeping up with her; however, adrenalin drove her speed. They hollered and cooed, begging for her to stop, and then they threatened to call Mrs. Ember to retrieve her. When they couldn't match her pace, they huffed out louder pleas.

She disappeared onto the third floor where agents gathered to eat delicious smelling foods after a hard day's work. She ducked into the kitchen, trying to conceal herself further without the twosome finding her. They already alerted Mrs. Ember of her escape, so all she could do was hide for a moment's time.

This floor carried nothing but a large cafeteria filled to the brim with tables of black metal framed, cushioned chairs, and a huge spread of food in a buffet style. Inside the kitchen, five cooks sweltered over a hot stove, completely ignoring the arrival of a stranger inside their workplace. A large stainless steel expeditor counter stretched all the way to where a cook minced onion and hid their weeping eyes from the scent. Cassy dodged this person and halted just next to a dumbwaiter. It seemed simple in design, but efficient with its duty.

She wondered if going down in the dumbwaiter would be effective, but nixed the option straight away. That would be the first location, especially on this floor, to cause suspicion. It helped little that the twosome sprinted inside, demanding that the cooks point them in the direction of the girl. Unwilling to stick around, she darted from a secondary entrance and hurried along the railing.

Her second choice was the regular elevator. As she peered at the main floor beneath her over the balcony railing, Cassy noticed the higher-up agents conversing, determining her route of action. That's when an idea popped into her head.

Dashing to the elevator, Cassy struck the door, waiting impatiently for it to open. As soon as it dinged, she hit the button for the second floor, sticking close to the farthest section of the window to stop peering eyes from finding her. Once she reached that floor, she allowed it to stop for a second before slamming the button to the fifth floor where, according to the floor map, was the training arena. She wanted them to believe she had escaped on that floor. Up the elevator went. Still tucked snugly with the cool metal to avoid detection, Cassy breathed out, wondering how she was going to get through to the front entrance. Out on the fifth floor, six arenas were soundless, their doors wide open for any willing agents to train. Not a soul disturbed her contemplation, and when she found a new emergency staircase, she wondered if she should travel down it and risk being caught. Without many options, she flew down, hardly holding onto the railing that ran under her left palm. Floor after floor she went, hunting for the main level. Unbeknownst to her, however, she missed it and ended up in the basement.

She stumbled to a sudden halt when an unrecognized agent lounged at a desk similar to Greg's and shuffled papers, seeming busy. Around the corner, she peeked to look for a way out. Two were viewed. The first was to head back into the main building of the FUA to receive a stern lashing; the second was to run into the door directly in front of the desk and hope that it was an escape route. Chancing the unknown, Cassy darted from the concealing corner, feeling her heart race at every obstacle she faced to rescue her beloved agent.

"Yo!" the man shouted.

He sprang from the desk in realization that an escapee was fleeing under his watch. Cassy slipped from his reaching fingers and struck the door with all her might. It sprang open easily, as the entrance was only barricaded from intruders. Out into another hallway of offices, Cassy gasped as she figured out where she could turn. She opened and slammed Frederick Aseen's office door, leaving her in a dreary, decrepit hallway. The agent behind her was nearing, opening the door, so she ran towards a flashing light and found another agent sitting, watching a movie and munching on food. He choked a bit and tried to assist in stopping the girl, but she skidded out of sight before the other agent could alert him of capturing her.

Emerging outside, Cassy's feet deafened her, the streetlights blinded her, and her heavy breaths seared her throat with dryness. She couldn't stop running. She picked up speed, traversing too many streets to count before she no longer heard anything but traffic and the gusting winds between buildings. The agents' voices floated away because of their inability to keep up with the determined girl. Reaching 2nd Avenue, she slammed against the corner of a wall, holding herself up from collapsing to her quivering knees.

"I escaped the FUA..."

Her hands swiped across her face. *Why did I escape the FUA? I don't even know what I'm doing...* Without a second thought, her hands snaked into her zippered pocket and wrenched out her cell phone. Pulling up a map of the city with her numb fingers, she found only a couple of buildings from the map's view that she recalled from Zack's location computer. She checked the time to decide which ones to look through first.

"Which ones are in use?" she mumbled aloud. "They've got to be somewhere that nobody would look. So, either an abandoned one or a rental place..." Suddenly, something dawned on Cassy. *Wait, Jason mentioned a warehouse.*

A single warehouse appeared onscreen, describing all the criteria that she set out. *I'm coming for you, Zack. Hold on just a little longer.*

Cassy began making a call. The phone rang for a short while.

A bored woman's voice replied amidst a yawn, "How may we help you?"

"I need a cab." Cassy squinted at the street signs, "at the corner of 2nd avenue and 25th street."

The operator groaned, "A taxi will arrive within half an hour's time. Thank you for choosing our taxi service, we appreciate your business."

With nothing but fiddling her thumbs and anxiously keeping tabs on vehicles that seemed suspicious to occupy her, she sat on the curb, curling her knees into her chest. Any of the blinding lights could have been Victor's men. Being in trouble with the FUA was comparatively better than being caught by the criminals. She worried, and a slow-developing migraine increased in intensity as the seconds clicked by. *What if I make the wrong choice? If I waste too much time, they'll return and kill Zack...*

A beige car parked near her hunched figure. She gave an obvious shiver before she realized that the taxi had arrived. Rolling down the window, the man rose a bushy eyebrow as he questioned the girl.

"You needed a cab?" he asked.

She mumbled, "Yes, sir." Wiping her rear end from the dirtiness of the curb, Cassy crawled into the backseat. "Umm, so, I have an odd request."

The man tilted his head.

"I don't actually know the address, but I need to get to this warehouse."

She pointed at the map on her cell phone. It seemed the most logical location, since it had been up for rent for quite a few years and now was completely abandoned, the company having gone bankrupt.

"Sorry, kid, you seem sweet and all, but I won't take you to a place like that. Too many kids break into empty warehouses, and I won't support vandalism," he scolded.

"Please, I was called by my friend. He's hurt and I need to get there."

Sympathetically, he twisted his entire torso to face her. "Shouldn't that be an issue for the ambulance?"

"I have fifty dollars. I'll give it all to you. He's in serious trouble."

Her hands dug deep into her jeans, hunting for the cash. It fell out in a single twenty, two tens, and two fives.

Fatigued, and really needing the cash, the man mumbled, "Fine. I ain't sticking around though. Whatever you're into, I'm staying out of."

"Deal!" She pointed at the map again, showing him the directions. "Do you know how to get there?"

"Yeah, it's across from Costco. It's a smaller warehouse which used to be a furniture store. It was a good place until those big box stores came in."

He shifted gears as he spoke and cruised onward to their destination. Not even setting the meter, he hesitantly pocketed the unaccounted fair. The taxi merged into a lane, joining a less hectic street.

Cassy half listened to the rambles of the man. Outside the window, the city lights glistened against the night skies, dazzling her with their brightness. Before she knew it, an unwanted daydream sprang from the reflection of the lights on the black tarmac.

Zack reached out from the shadows, mouthing her name with a muted voice. He twisted, searching the darkness with shock written across his creased brows. Five shadowy figures rounded him, hitting every inch of the young man who failed at defending himself. Blood spilled from his lips. Her slow-moving feet struggled to run towards him as his eyes almost pleaded for a saviour or death. She held his broken torso. He wheezed in her arms; his ribs were snapped, and bruises already shaded his lightly tanned skin with a blue hue. She had provided him with nothing but abuse.

The car jolted to a stop, replacing the daydream with reality. Briskly, she swiped her tears away, and she slowed her heavy breathing.

The outside of the warehouse was unimpressive. A chain link fence would have protected the rectangular, abandoned building from theft had there been merchandise left inside. Most of the windows, which were few, were broken or boarded up. A huge loading dock was sealed with a large, white commercial garage door. In its prime, the building had huge semis loaded to the brim with furniture. At the angle that Cassy faced, only the large garage and a single side entrance appeared. She realized the taxi was parked in the back of the actual building.

"I hope your friend is alright, kid. Make sure to call an ambulance if it's serious."

"Thank you!" Cassy responded.

The vehicle backed out, crunching along the broken cement, and disappeared into the night. Cassy hurried around the chain link fence barrier to find a spot to enter. No recognizable vehicles lay in wait, but that did not mean that a man wasn't standing guard over Zack. The original side door was the least eerie option, so Cassy pushed at the chain link fence, making it creak and bend ever so slightly. Shoving and wiggling the metal, she crafted a hole wide enough to squeeze in. She crept along the brown grass onto black tarmac and reached the door, which had chipped paint peeling away.

"Zack?" She banged on the metal twice before peeking inside. "Are you here?"

•   •   •

Zack's head shot in the direction of the bang. His wrists dripped with blood as he tried to rotate them to break free of his bondage. From the vantage point of the overseeing office, he found himself gulping back a dry lump. The side entrance swung open and slammed shut.

•   •   •

Cassy paced herself inside the echoing building. Each footstep resounded without resolve to keep quiet, alerting whoever was inside that she had arrived. She examined the semi-lit warehouse. Four pillars held up the loading area, all made of iron. At the far end, directly across from the garage door, three entrances were available. A staircase led up to a viewing area, another went into a bathroom, and the last directed her into the rest of the furniture store and offices. She ran straight for the hallway that had five unkempt offices. Inside each one, men's belongings were scattered about the floor. A few were kept meticulously, but most showed the mishaps of a bachelor in hiding. No Zack was to be found inside any of them.

•　•　•

Damn it, Cassy! Go away... get to the FUA.

He struck the floor with both feet to kick away the telecommunication device left underneath the chair by Victor. Austin had informed the group, just as they were about to leave, that he finally perfected the technology and wanted some field testing with it. It hooked up to a receiver which stayed in the hands of Victor. The men heard every word that he might say. Zack couldn't afford to speak to her without letting Victor learn of her whereabouts.

That damn cocky bastard! He knew Cassy would come find me.

•　•　•

Cassy swung open a rusty doorway leading down a long counter and into the front entrance. Only dust, cobwebs, and random mouse droppings remained in the front area. Nobody roamed the front area, let alone held Zack captive. She finally came to terms that she may have gambled away her only advantage while playing Russian roulette with Zack's life. With one area still left to look, she mounted the stairs down the creepy hallway and began plotting how to get to the next place. The metal creaked underfoot, and a rusty door gave her blood poisoning just looking at it. It swung wide, casting a bit of light into the otherwise pitch-black area.

"Zack?"

A grunt responded as a chair scratched against the floor. With a small light tickling his shoes, Cassy saw the shadowed boy bound on a chair. Without a second of restraint, she hastened to him and swung her arms over his shoulders. He sucked in a deep, mournful ouch. Startled by his silence and odd noises, her cell phone flashlight flicked on, illuminating his bruised and swollen face.

"Cassy, get out of here!"

• • •

Leaning on the hood of the car outside of the high school, Victor beck-oned his men towards him when he finally heard more than the grunting of their captive. Their supposed heir spoke first, and then the boy filled with panic.

"What did I tell you?" Victor sneered. "All it took was a little nudge and she came straight to us."

Jason stretched up his arms to the skies, saying, "You're always right, Victor."

"She's quite clever, I must admit. If I were an idiot, I may have suspected her to show up here; however, nothing was going to prevent that girl from trying to save him." Shouting towards his five men, he said, "Let's get back there. She's returning to her rightful place!"

• • •

"Zack, what did they do to you?"

Her hand gently caressed the swollen lump on his right cheek bone.

Zack shifted away. "Jesus, Cassy, I told you to go straight to the FUA!"

"I did. I couldn't stay there. They were moving too slow. I couldn't let you die."

"You being here is definitely going to kill me, Cassy. I'm disposable to them."

Cassy ignored his cynicism. She rounded him to investigate his tightly tied arms. A stunned expression filled her with terror as the knots were complex and unfamiliar. Unless trained, nobody could untie them. She attempted tugging them apart, but it only made the black rope snuggle tighter and pinch the already worn skin. Cassy shrieked as Zack begged her to stop fiddling.

"Jonathon tied those! He used to be in the army. He's the only one capable of undoing them at this point." He shook his head back and forth while he demanded for her to come around in front of him. "You shouldn't have come here. I'm the bait. Victor knows too much for our own good… He knew that the FUA would react slowly and that you wouldn't tolerate it. He learned of how you feel towards me." Zack hunted for the best escape route. "They've been coming through that side entrance. If you escape down that stairwell, and go through the main store, you should be able to escape."

"I'm not leaving you here."

Giving up on untying the rope, she snatched the chair's back, dragging it as far as her muscles could handle. The sound caused their ears to cringe.

"Cassy!" he shouted.

Without warning, the metal side entrance banged open, showing Victor's strutting stance rounding the concealed entrance. Zack snatched a quick glance below him and told her to run. She was hidden in the shadows, so the advancing men had no knowledge as to where she may be in the building.

"Hide over in that locker, and the moment I say go, you go!"

"Please," she pleaded, "don't make me leave you... I love you!"

Zack's heart raced as Victor's looming presence landed on the stairs in front of his men.

"Cassy," Zack said seriously, "I love you, and I won't be the reason you end up being hurt."

Cassy backpedalled to the large locker and sealed herself inside. She was not a moment too late, since the room exploded with men carrying weapons at the ready. Victor swore under his breath as he realized that she already escaped. Enraged, his gun's butt slammed into Zack's temple, toppling the boy.

"All of you, go search the main part of the warehouse and the store!" Victor growled.

Cassy took a good look at the leader through the slits of the locker. His lean cheeks were sunken in frustration and shaggy brunette hair flared when he ruffled it. He was well-dressed in a black collared, button down shirt and business khakis. Everlastingly long legs shortened when he squatted, flicking Zack with an irate finger. His piercing dark eyes sent chills down her spine.

"You smart little bastard, where did you hide her this time?"

Zack directed his sight to the man in avoidance of flicking his glance towards the locker. Victor's head lifted to the roof. He figured that they would have to hunt again. That's when he stiffened, realizing something was amiss. Standing, his back straightened, and he admired the locker which had always remained open throughout his stay. Zack acted the moment recognition struck Victor. Using his free feet, Zack swiped across the ground, caught Victor's ankles, and tripped the man to the ground.

"Go!"

She sprang from the locker without a second of hesitation. Victor scowled at the boy and reached for her feet to trip her. The motion brushed her jeans as she avoided the man's grip. Darting from the overviewing area, Cassy disappeared down the steps to the space from where she had arrived. A man inside the office hallway called for the rest, and stomping feet quickly followed the panicked teenager. Cassy burst across the warehouse. The leader watched from above, holding Zack captive. No matter where she went, he would watch and send the men after her. Heading towards the warehouse's double doors, Cassy's legs lengthened their strides and she only hoped to reach the street before being captured by the shouting men now behind her. She broke free of the dusty building to where nighttime air filled her lungs. Bending the chain link, she shoved her way out and emerged from the private grounds with deep gashes slicing her thin skin. Just as she assumed the coast was clear, a figure rushed next to her with familiar fingers reaching to intercept her.

Her heart fluttered at the sight of a trusted man, but her subconscious screamed that something was off about his appearance. Then, all the puzzle pieces fell together neatly to paint the true picture of Buddy.

"No…" She wrenched back, asking him, "How could you?"

He approached with a satisfied sneer.

"Cassy, don't fight anymore. Everything will be fine if you just come quietly," he said.

"No…" her words stuttered as she back pedalled away from him. "This morning… you were going to take me from my home!"

A hand reached out to snag her wrist.

"It sure took Zack a while to figure it out. He must be lacking the initiative to protect you."

"You used me… you used my brothers!"

She slapped away his extending hands. Her meager might went into calling out for help and keeping distance from Buddy, who calmly strode to snatch and pin her down. Her strides lengthened and she rebounded down the tarmac. Buddy huffed out a curse as he bulldozed forward. She used precious energy to run and wave wildly at any vehicle that might have been occupied in the darkened street.

Yet it soon became too late for Cassy. She'd wasted her chance to escape at Buddy's sudden appearance. Another figure overtook her, a cloth fell upon her lips, and a sweet nectar filled her lungs as she dropped into the arms of the man who stood behind her. The chloroform numbed her before growing into a thrilling high; Cassy's heart raced as she realized it was submitting her into their embrace. Buddy scooped the limp girl up and hid any glimpse of Cassy's kidnapping from the speedy highway traffic. Austin fiddled with the chloroform's bottle while he replaced the used cloth inside his front pocket. Jonathon was at the ready with the chain link gate's main entrance open with a self-praising grin. Buddy struggled with her weight against his scrawny torso.

Inside the warehouse, beneath the watchful eyes of all six men, Cassy had little ability to shift as she became a heap on the cement. She was half-conscious when the needle, filled with a clear fluid, pricked her arm and drained into her skin. Her arms became immobile, and her legs failed in their attempts to kick the men away. Everything lacked feeling. Flickering eyes noticed that they spoke above her. Her attempt to stay aware hurt, and their words melted together. A final image lingered: the first clear visual of Victor, who proudly gleamed at the predicted capture of their heir.

• • •

Eric bent at the knee, brushing back Cassy's delicately curled hair. Jonathon shoved the gentle caress from her. The others cheered at the final capture of the hopefully true heir, while Victor lugged the bound agent down the metal steps. Victor nudged her with a shoe to check her wellbeing. Zack was racked with guilt, as he had led Cassy into hell.

"Excellent work," Victor praised, "especially you, *Zackarass*. How else would we have gotten her here?"

"I won't let you take advantage of her," the agent muttered.

"Too late."

Jonathon barged forward, snatched Cassy's limp form, and tossed her over a shoulder.

Eric grumpily kicked Zack in the gut. "Let's just kill him and leave him for the FUA to find."

"No. Bring him with us."

Jason halted Eric's rebuttal by patting his shoulder. "Zack will keep her calm."

Victor nodded in appreciation of Jason's analytical thinking. "We shall celebrate tonight once we're in the air. I want her tied as soon as we get on the plane." His tight grip scooped Zack up by the hair and shuffled him forward. Leaning in closely so his men could not hear, he muttered, "I have her now, boy, and you failed. You better listen to everything I say, because you are disposable. I am keeping you alive only as a ploy against Cassandra. Do not think of me as simple. Cassandra can be forced into that tomb." He directed his focus to the girl in Jonathon's arms. "She's easy to lug around. If you listen, she will be kept safe. You'll want that, trust me."

Zack broke into a string of swears at the insinuation of torture towards his beloved assignment.

Both teenagers were placed inside the sports car that had followed Zack for nine weeks. Cassy's slumbering form lied against him with her head upon his shoulder. Calmly, he whispered sweet nothings to her to keep her dreams peaceful.

•   •   •

"Where the hell is she? It's eleven!" Michael fretted. The eldest brother's tolerance had grown thin after forty-five minutes of worried pacing.

Brant lounged on the couch, attempting to study for an upcoming exam. "She's at Rebecca's. Just phone and see what's keeping her." He'd heard a week's worth of Michael's heels clicking throughout the last hour.

Calling this late made Michael feel guilty about disturbing anyone who may be sleeping, yet worry promoted picking up the phone.

The neighbour's father answered. "Hello?"

"Hey, this is Michael. I'm sorry to call so late, but I wanted to see if Cassy was coming home soon."

"Is she here? Huh?" he grumbled. "Rebecca, Michael is on the phone. Can you answer it please?"

"Hello?" one line answered while the other hung up.

"Is Cassy there?"

"What!" Rebecca shrieked. "She's not home yet?"

"No..."

Rebecca pleaded, "Don't be mad, but Cassy never came here. She and Zack went out on a date."

Clenched fists made the phone tremble against his ear. "What..." he hissed. "Where are they?"

"I don't know."

Michael slammed down the receiver. Instead of asserting the erupting volcano of rage upon Cassy's friend, he did all he could to calm down before going to hunt for his sister. A second later, he dialled another number. The phone rang and rang, going straight to voice mail. Again, he tried. This time, someone answered.

"Where the hell are you?" Michael growled.

A male voice replied. "Hello, Michael, how are you?"

"Who is this?"

"It's Buddy."

"Where's Cassy?"

"She's here, asleep."

Michael edgily frowned. "Why are you with her?"

"Well, I was out having supper and met up with Zack and Cassy on their date. I came at a fairly bad time. They were arguing and she was crying. I came to console her and then Zack broke into angry rants. I wanted to settle them down before sending them on their way, so I brought them over to my place. She fell asleep on the couch afterwards and Zack is just in the washroom. It's late. I'll take them to school tomorrow, I assure you."

"I'd prefer if she came home for the night."

"They're safe here. You have my word. I've been able to talk to them. Their bond is quite fascinating. This boy has done all this crap to her and she's still fawning over him." Buddy continued, "Are you sure you want me to wake her up? She was really upset. She's content here."

"Maybe you're right. Well, if she wakes up, would you be able to bring her home?"

"Of course. Oh, I'll give you my cell so you can contact me if something comes up." He rattled off a random number, permitting Michael to scribble away on a pad of paper.

"Thanks, Buddy. I'm glad that you took care of her. She obviously needs to get over that prick so he doesn't keep hurting her." Michael sighed. "I'll see you later." Before hanging up, he made a last request. "Buddy, don't let anything happen to her."

"I won't."

• • •

Buddy uncovered Zack's snapping lips. As he was chaining Zack to the wall with short shackles, Victor had stood over the girl resting upon the white bedding. A ringing suddenly made them both aware of her phone. At first, Victor waited until the message machine took the call; however, the person calling was persistent. Angrily, Victor demanded that the 'counsellor' convince Michael to leave it be. Their main concern was the airport security going into high alert because of a kidnapping. As long as they had an evening to travel, they'd be off scot-free.

Buddy replaced Cassy's cell back into her coat. Relief flooded him; he had been convincing while restraining the restless boy. At the sound of the cell phone, Zack began horrific cries out. If they didn't answer it, Michael would continue, but if they did, Zack might have given away the kidnapping. Annoyingly, Victor departed, leaving the youngest man to fight with the agent. Throughout the conversation, Buddy struggled with keeping Zack pinned beneath him and keeping his voice natural. He had succeeded, and hoped for a drink for finally finishing his duty as a counsellor.

"You sick, disgusting bastard," Zack shouted. "She trusted you!"

"Shut up!"

"You just landed her in hell! She deserves to be home with her brothers!"

Buddy straightened his clothes and cleared his throat, trying to ignore how right Zack was. "Instead of being concerned about her, I think you should worry over how long you'd like to live!"

A string of swears followed Buddy out.

Chapter 10

Cassy sickly shifted, coming out of the drug-induced coma. It took a while to focus her eyes. Her hands were sore from being intertwined snuggly at a crisscross with rope, and her lips were dry since duct tape covered her mouth, preventing her from shouting out. Stiffly, she rolled over to find Zack sitting on the floor beside the bed, his head wedged between his arms. She admired the room they were locked in. The bed was large and the room small, but a closet sat open, exposing an empty place to hide, while another area was hidden from her in the corner. *Are we in a hotel room? Do they still have us?*

Panicking, she whimpered as nausea almost overwhelmed her. Zack's head popped up, overjoyed to find her awake. Shackles clanged together as he reached out to remove the tape. She squirmed a bit to allow the longing fingers to reach her. The tape burned as he peeled it off slowly.

"Zack, what's going on? Where are we?"

"On a plane."

Startled, she said, "It doesn't look like a plane."

"Well, this is a perk of travelling with Victor. Only luxury is suitable for him. I'm assuming he rented the most expensive plane available to him. Don't get him wrong, he has tons of money, but he can never have enough. That's why he's so obsessed with that damn curse. He'll become a wealthier and more powerful man."

• • •

Victor toasted Zack's compliments, sipping back whiskey as he listened to their conversation. He had slipped Austin's small listening device between the mattresses before excusing himself to lounge.

• • •

Zack unwrapped her sore wrists with trained hands when she came closer to him. She rubbed them, unsure of their predicament now. Zack almost seemed relieved that Cassy had awoken. He knew that she had awoken in hell. He tugged her into a sympathetic hug before curling back into his spot of self-mourning.

"How long has it been?"

"Two days," he chuckled, the sound muffled inside his knees. "Austin got a decent beating for purchasing unsafe drugs. They usually get stuff from a more reliable source, but Saskatoon didn't offer much of what they specifically look for. You should've only been out for a couple hours. The wooziness and nausea should pass after a while."

"I guess I have no tolerance to drugs, huh?"

Zack gave a ghostly smile. "You said it, not me... but I think they over-dosed you. Even Victor freaked a little when you weren't waking up. A sick supposed heir is an unable-to-walk-into-the-tomb-heir."

"So, I guess we're almost there..."

"Not necessarily. They must take their time because the FUA will be powerless until they get a sighting in Egypt. The longer it takes, the fewer options the FUA has to rescue us."

"Then they could literally take months!"

Zack burst out in laughter. "If any of them were patient enough for that, then yes. I doubt it'll take too long, but who knows."

• • •

Austin and Buddy lingered inside Victor's chosen lounging area. They both had to prove their worth because of stupid mistakes. Each one nervously waited while the teenagers conversed in a separate room.

Attentively, Victor turned to them. "Go get Cassandra. I'm dying to meet her."

• • •

Cassy drunkenly stood to explore the solitary room. Zack followed suit, though the chains gripping his ankles permitted only a two-metre distance from the wall.

"Why did they chain you?"

Zack pointed at a spider web crack stretching its length across a small circular window.

"I tried to break out while we were still in Saskatoon. They heard the first strike and reacted fast for buffoons. They decided to rig up the shackles by using a bit of chain Jonathon was lugging around and these stupid braces screwed into the wall." Zack struck the wall with his head when he leaned against it. "Well, I figure we'll need to do more to get out of here."

While he explained, Cassy continued searching around the prison. She found herself facing a washroom, which was small and keeping with the luxurious theme of the plane so far. Blacks and browns accented a countertop that was barely a metre in length. A black toilet with three buttons on top of it sat at the ready, and a shower, made of crystal-like glass, showed how rich Victor was. She returned to Zack's company, unsure how to react about the whole flying thing. Now aware of being in the air, she felt the turbulence and the shifting of the plane.

"How could a pilot fly kidnappers and hostages around?" she asked.

"The pilot doesn't know. Victor is keeping him out of the loop so they don't ever have to worry about betrayal. They told him that they were businessmen flying around to several parts of the world." Zack cupped her hand. "It may be another reason we'll be taking longer than necessary. They have to stop at least a couple times to make it seem legit."

Two men barged into the prison, startling Cassy and causing her to jump into Zack's arms. Zack brought her behind his shielding body, going as far toward the men as the chains allowed. Austin stomped toward them, raising an eyebrow at this weak attempt at security.

"Come on, Zack, really? Victor just wants to talk to her. She is *his* now."

Zack flicked his wrist, bringing Cassy close; she breathed in his scent and grabbed the fabric of his shirt. No matter what the men did, Zack refused to release her. Austin, tired of Zack's overbearing nature, used a single hand to dig into his jugular, almost breaking his windpipe from the force. The agent's grip loosened.

Under his breath, he muttered, "Cas-sy… Run…"

The man's fingers tightened every time Zack mumbled this. Zack dropped to his knees with an agonized groan and completely released Cassy's wrist. Austin steadied his grip around Zack's neck. Zack's back arched, trying to take in as much air as possible with every wheezy breath. His mouth pleaded for Cassy to move.

Only one place caught her sight. She raced to the small closet, slamming its door behind her, and sank to the floor. Unfortunately, without anything to lock it, the murderous criminals could enter. She sobbed loudly. Escape on a plane was impossible.

The darkness vaporized when Buddy widened the slit door and blocked all routes out.

"Cassy, it's alright," he encouraged, reaching out a gentle hand. "We're not going to hurt you."

"Screw you, you traitor! You betrayed me! You lied about everything! You should paint yourself as you really are, a lying scumbag who would rather gain wealth over somebody's life!"

Cassy shoved away Buddy's fake-concern-filled palm and curled deeper into the corner, protecting herself in the fetal position.

A rage, never before displayed by Buddy, erupted. He took a knot of hair, tugging her out from the depths of the hiding space. He slammed her into the floor and towered above her. Austin stopped him before he kicked her stomach. She was their priceless artifact until proven otherwise, and harming such a trophy was unthinkable. Shoving the youngest member of their group out of the way, Austin ripped her from the ground by the upper arm and forced Cassy from the prison, leaving Zack wheezing on the floor. Cassy deafened the plane's inhabitants as Zack's name echoed off the walls. Buddy remained with her agent to vent his fury on the already-bruised male.

Cassy screamed, "Let go!"

She wiggled out of Austin's grip as she kicked him in the back of his thigh. He landed on his knee, half-supported by the walling. She ran straight down a short corridor, witnessing lounging plane seats as it widened. Barricades, similar to walls, separated specific areas so the men could gain an ounce of privacy. A few of the men slept in a living room setting. A large couch and television relaxed them as they watched a sports game and worried little about the girl escaping, hooting that they were pleased to see her awake. Cassy trembled, petrified at the entire predicament. As she reached an open doorway near the front of the plane, a blurred hand snatched a handful of her shirt. Jonathon stepped out of what looked like a kitchen, shaking his head and twisting the shirt slightly to choke her.

"Princess," his lips fell near her ear, "where do you think you're going? Victor wants to meet you. It's not polite to ignore someone's wishes, now is it?"

His choking hand dropped, and his burly arms held her around the waist. Backtracking, he drove her inside a dimly lit room, causing her fumbling feet to trip. Once the door locked behind her, Cassy unwillingly gazed about to determine her whereabouts. A small dining area surrounded her.

At a table, a man held a glass in one hand while another played with a silenced pistol. His head turned, sprouting a kind grin to dazzle her into submission before she made a condescending comment. The man situated the glass and gun upon the table, and then a hand tapped against the seat next to him with an inviting gesture.

Cassy was rooted to her spot. She admired the man in front of her. He seemed so delicately kind with his soft brown eyes and chiseled face. Bits and pieces of this man had been viewed in the past, and yet she was still in awe of him. His white collared shirt shifted as he moved, allowing a peek at his meticulously kept abdomen. Long legs stretched out in a relaxed position, and his dress pants rose to show off his black socks and ankles. Everything about him was enthralling, and he seemed out of place as the bad guy. He belonged as the hero. Cassy gave her head a shake. He was no hero.

"Come sit, *my dear*," his bass voice boomed.

The man gave an air of safety, and without another option, Cassy shuffled towards him with her head down. She sank next to her abductor. Her shoulders were tense as he flicked strands of hair off her shoulders.

The man introduced himself. "I'm Victor."

"I know who you are," Cassy snapped with venom. She added, "You're twisted to even believe I'm the heir to some non-existent diamonds."

Victor's smile became crooked. "You must have no idea what I have seen to even make that statement. They're real, just as you and I are. You're the reason I have become addicted to the diamonds. If I'm twisted, you're despicable for staying hidden all this time and allowing me to hurt so many people. It could've been over three years ago."

"Don't blame me!" she shouted. "This is all your fault. How many people have you killed to find this supposed heir?"

"I must admit, I've lost count. That group was quite large and led me on too many futile paths."

"You know about the Sacred Chosen?"

Victor tapped a finger, considering how to explain. "Why, yes, I do. They are the main reason my men were able to locate the heir."

Cassy rolled her eyes, "Don't be so confident. I haven't been proven to be anything yet."

The gun twirled around on the table as Victor showed his frustration towards that truth.

"Do you know the truth about your grandfather as well? The 'Enlightened One' is what they used to call him."

"Yes, parts of it."

He stroked his chin and then twisted completely, bending a leg at the knee and leaning against the wall. "So, the FUA has informed you of some privileged information."

"How did you learn about them and me?"

Lifting his glass, the man swirled auburn liquid around, and the ice cube clanged against the glass. "I would have to explain from the very beginning." Victor slung his arm over the table, preparing for his story telling. "It was more than three years ago that I met Jason and Eric. They had just recently found Obeko's tomb in Egypt, which gave them control over its excavation, and yet a complication ensued on their first day. They knew of the curse, and many civilians warned them that if they entered, they would die. Not believing their superstitions, Jason and Eric moved forward by getting a team of archeologists together for the excavation. On their first day, a friend of theirs entered ahead of them, too excited for his own good, and once inside, a seizure dropped him to the ground. Jason and Eric helplessly watched while their assistants stopped them from entering the tomb to rescue their friend. Several minutes past before the convulsions ended. According to Jason, it was silent as they waited for a sign of life from him. Eventually, he flipped over and stumbled out of the tomb, wrenching at their arms, begging them to never set foot inside it unless they had a death wish. Jason and Eric rushed him to the ER to check his mental state. As they drove, their friend explained he had a vision. Obeko had stood before him, speaking Ancient Egyptian, which he barely recognized. Out from the darkness, Haeibba, filled to the brim with rage, grabbed a sword and ran at Obeko. The Pharaoh moved from the strike and the sword struck their friend in the chest. That is when he woke.

"The doctors diagnosed him as physically healthy and just experiencing a traumatic episode. Once released, they noticed nervous movements from him, like he saw horrifying creatures. At the hotel, they were packing him up to return home, since he refused to enter the cursed tomb. He continued to ramble on about there being no point in packing or worrying over him because he had been denied as the heir and would be dead soon. Both chuckled, thinking it was a joke. The peculiar body movements worsened and three hours after leaving the tomb, their friend died, clutching at his chest. No one could find the cause of death, except for the slightest scar where a sharpened blade had struck him."

Cassy remained like stone as she listened. The story only worsened her fears; if she were not the heir, she now knew what would become of her.

"Do you know what he saw?" she interrupted.

A scolding click of his tongue answered the question. Victor continued. "I overheard them in the bar while visiting the desert. Their mournful gossip piqued my interest. Before approaching them, I researched Obeko. I found that over the past several centuries, anyone who has set foot inside the tomb has been found mysteriously dead afterwards. Parts of the information were missing, torn from the archives or completely deleted from mainframe systems. Suspicious, I dug harder. That is when I came upon the mention of a group that held all the secrets of the curse and the heir's whereabouts. The mention was brief, but was a lead that I could not pass up. I then went to Jason and Eric, offering my findings. I required their assistance because their additional knowledge would help greatly. Jason has been addicted to Obeko's tomb for years and Eric was intrigued by the money, so when I offered my help in finding the heir, our hunt began within Egypt.

"We assumed that the heir would still be amongst the Pharaoh's line. Through countless hours of research, we found a small family tree, the members of which we sought out and questioned. They suspiciously had the same story, which rose many red flags. It was all too neatly presented. I resorted to torturing them. They turned out to be members of the Sacred Chosen. Each one broke after a certain amount of time, giving out tidbits of information on the heir, and yet they never once produced a true name or mentioned a female. It was always a male. As we became increasingly frustrated, the group members disappeared to other regions of the world.

"At the beginning, I hardly fathomed it to be this troublesome to break a damn curse. Jason and Eric always asked why I assumed the heir was alive in our era, and I always said, 'I just sense it.' That's when a Sacred Chosen member came to find us. He had information and wanted in on the hunt. He proclaimed that the heir was living based on whispers from the other group members. Even he could not tell us who it was, but he gave us other opportunities. He could give the names of several higher-up group members so we could question them. The puzzle slowly formed into a picture, which we took advantage of. Any group members we caught, we murdered after long interrogations, and anyone we found that was an assumed heir was taken, unless they willingly joined us, and then we sent them into the tomb.

"Now, the curse acts differently depending on the person. Some were killed instantly; others went through horrifying events beforehand. Our last attempt was fascinating. He lasted twelve hours. He told me," Victor rose an eyebrow, finally answering Cassy's question, "that shadows will chase after you, whispering that death is coming. They reach out their hands to snatch your throat just to torture you before you die. There's no escape."

Cassy clenched her fists.

"This went on for about half a year before Garrett, our traitor from the Sacred Chosen, made the stupid decision to leave us. He disagreed with how we handled the Sacred Chosen members or supposed heirs. The men, which is the group you see now, except for Buddy, had grown frustrated and were less kind to liars. The instant we figured that the group would tell us nothing but lies, we started *being rid* of them after mere hours of torture. I suppose they were lucky, since at the beginning, the torture would be long. Around this time, the FUA stepped in. Garrett worried more and more about being caught, so as a parting gift to him for alerting the group of us arriving, as well as assisting in contacting the FUA, I demanded that he walk into the tomb to double-check that the heir wasn't always with us." Victor laughed. "Jesus, he pissed himself as he walked in!" The laughter died out as Victor returned to the FUA entering the picture. "Zack's brother— "

"Zack doesn't have a brother," Cassy stated with a frown creasing her forehead.

"He really told you nothing about him, huh? That stupid boy doesn't trust you at all. Yes, he *did* have a brother, but I got rid of him."

Cassy's heart sank, finally understanding why Zack pushed for her to forgive Michael. He had lost a brother without having a chance to say goodbye. "You killed him…"

"Tomas was a pain in my ass, though I was actually aiming for Zack. But," he slashed the air, "we have digressed. I will explain things properly. Tomas was sent out to hunt for us once I killed Garrett." Victor sipped his liquor, growing in anger as he explained the past events. "Tomas offered to train Zack on the field since Zack had recently joined the FUA. They assumed that we would be a safe bust for his first one. Quite a few times we met up with them as our search continued, but it wasn't until a year ago that they set up a trap. We had received an anonymous letter stating that the heir was found and captured, and we were told to meet the sender inside an old graveyard, safely away from prying eyes, for an exchange of money for the man. I was unsure about this, so I set up a backup plan, just in case. When we arrived, there was, as we suspected there would be, a young man seemingly bound and gagged in the center, while nobody else was there.

"We approached, suspicious of this perfect predicament. Just as we predicted, the man's hands ripped forward, wrenched off the gag, and raised his gun towards us. Tomas played the bait while Zack hid in the bushes, anticipating when to alert the awaiting agents. I refused to give them a chance for that. Instead, my men fired their guns instantly. Tomas ducked beneath the bushes and showed us his athletic prowess as he shifted from bush to bush, striking down any one of us that got too close. Zack followed suit, swiping our feet to knock us down. A swarm of agents flooded into the cemetery, and that's when it seemed like all hope had been lost for us." Victor groaned and straightened to lean closer to the supposed heir.

"Those boys really pissed me off. I worried about nothing but taking out the two who set us up." His gun landed inside his hands as he spoke, demonstrating the events with a visual. "Zack was caught off guard. He had his back turned on me and was warning Jonathon to back down. I aimed straight between his shoulders and pulled the trigger. Tomas had seen me aiming at his kid brother and flung himself in harm's way." He slammed the gun down. "It was an amazing shot!" A deep sigh boomed in his throat. "However, a distraught Zack is fairly devastating. He took all his sorrows out on Jason and Eric, who were caught a moment later by him and another agent. The rest of us escaped with our pride trashed. Ever since that fateful evening, we've been in hiding, keeping our business less noticeable. Fewer people have entered that tomb because we've been stricter with the selections of the heir. Your grandfather remained a prime resource, so whenever any mention of him appeared, we quickly moved. When your parents died, your grandfather's name resurfaced, and with it, we learned of you... the only female in his family line. It turns out you were the only one he ever told about the diamonds!"

Cassy shrank from his touch when he reached out to her. *They know so much about me.*

"And now, we're here!" Victor finished in conceited triumph. "It's been a long time since I captured a supposed heir, let alone capturing *Zackarass*. He's a stealthy little bastard. He's always been this close," he pinched his index finger and thumb almost together, "to catching us whenever they send him out!"

Cassy gazed into the features of the leader, finding so much hatred in his eyes. They were like Zack's whenever Victor's name was mentioned. The man who slaughtered his brother and the man who kidnapped innocent people just to shove them into a tomb and watch them become too scared to run deserved all the anger that festered inside Zack.

"I finally understand why Zack hates you," Cassy mumbled.

Her abductor snapped back, "He should really hate you."

A snake of icicles slithered down her spine.

"Tomas died because of you. Had you been easier to locate, those people would still be alive. Tomas risked his life for your assignment. Look at all the good it did." Victor tapped his left index finger against the wooden table. "You came right to me." Changing up his tactics, the man patted her shoulder. "You're so naïve. You sacrificed your own freedom for a boy who has used you from the beginning."

Cassy's upset rose to its limit as he continued to bring doubt between her and Zack. All she managed to do was bury her head into her palms and control her weeping so it wouldn't be observed by him.

Victor's speech progressed. "He has never shown you any care, and yet you fawn over him like a lost puppy. What you don't realize is Zack's job is to protect. He feels nothing towards you, especially since you're the cause of his brother's death."

The spiral of misery halted in an instant with that last statement. Springing from the seat, she backpedalled to the furthest corner from him.

She hollered, "You manipulative prick! How dare you think that I would listen to your poisonous words! Do you really think I'll trust you over Zack? I love him, Victor. I'll always have a reason to fight with Zack around! I will fight for my freedom every day until I'm free and away from *you!*"

An eyebrow arched, irked by her defiance. "Then maybe, I should remove this *thing* that makes you fight..."

Her bravado tumbled to a bottomless pit of dread. Victor slinked out of the booth-style seat and towered above her. His knuckles cracked in preparation for the fight between the agent and himself. Cassy squatted, holding her head as he came closer. Instead of reaching for Cassy, Victor bulldozed through the entranceway, slammed it behind him, and then disappeared down the hallway as he hooted of Zack's soon-to-be execution.

The excitement from the men overwhelmed the plane. Cheers burned her ears as she realized that she had been insubordinate against a man who only lusted for power. The moment he lost it, he violently acted.

Clanging of chains stumbled behind Victor as he led Zack to the dining room where Cassy still hunkered over in the corner. Zack grunted as he was thrown brutally to the floor. A herd of men clambered within, glancing at the twosome on the floor and their boss, who fumed from the ears.

To distract her from their jeers, Zack hugged her while she sobbed.

"Cassy, it's going to be alright," he promised.

Victor commanded, "Now, Cassandra," a thick arm wrenched her to his chest and wrapped around her neck, "I suggest you think of the appropriate answer to this next statement, or you will see Zack bleeding on the floor." Victor spun about, showing off his pistol to the teenagers, but also gaining support to murder the boy. "All I want is for you to listen to my orders, no matter what I ask. This talk of fighting me will end today, *or* I shall end the very thing that gives you the strength to fight."

Blurred visuals of the men hanging off one another and booing the option of letting Zack survive made Cassy's tears leak uncontrollably. A shove dropped her to shaky knees beside Zack to give her a chance to say goodbye. Zack's chained wrists flung around her and clung to her trembling shoulders for however long humanly possible. Soon they would be torn apart. Victor approached. A trained hand loaded the weapon with a single click and then directed it to the back of Zack's head.

"I own you, Cassandra. Defiance will only cause death. It's your choice to make this trip pleasant or miserable. Once we have determined your place in this curse, I swear to release you."

Cassy viewed Zack's face as Victor proposed his deal. He frowned, obviously confused about something Victor had said. She waited for him to give her a response on what she should do and when he gave it, she could only grasp him tighter. A shake of the head told her not to trust a word spoken.

"One." Victor squatted down.

"Two." The weapon pressed tightly into the base of Zack's skull, drilling as deep as possible.

"Three." He began to squeeze the trigger.

Cassy interrupted the trigger motion. "Stop! Don't do this! I'll listen to you... I'll try... Don't. I can't..." The words faltered. Biting on her lip until blood spilled, Cassy said, "Don't hurt him. I'll willingly walk into the tomb..."

Her breaking point was thin, and Victor was pleased it took so little to make her submissive. Lugging her to Egypt would be a simple task while she remained complacent.

"Good girl." He bent two fingers twice, signalling for the two teenagers to be gathered up.

Jason and Eric jumped forward, all too happy to return them to their cage. Cassy was dragged up. Jason towed her back through the plane's hallway. Zack evaded any more violence by rising and shuffling to Eric's outstretched arms. He was permitted to walk on independently and keep tabs on the whimpering girl in front of him. The closer they grew to the solitary bedroom, the more the men mocked Zack.

"He should've killed you," Eric grunted.

Jason added, "He should've put that bullet straight through your head to teach her about the hierarchy."

Cassy sucked back her bloodied lip, tasting the coppery flavor. *All they do is viciously attack us. How are we going to survive this, Zack?*

Jason was full of disappointment at not witnessing the triumphant day of Zack's death. He flung Cassy onto the bed in disdain. Corralling both prisoners was becoming tedious. He huffed out a swear and bent to gather Zack's ankle chains. Withered ankles were fastened to the wall once more. Eric took in a hungry gaze of the supposed heir. Cassy shamefully lowered her head at her apparent lack of courage and fidgeted with the pillow.

Eric's face appeared next to hers, as he grumpily disliked that she refused to admire him as well. "Little one," he said, "why won't you look at me?"

Jason finished with Zack's leash and called for Eric to finish with the girl, but he was still hatching plans against her. He grasped her cheeks and forced her gaze upon him.

"Don't be scared to bring down those walls, sweetie. I can see through everything you're trying to hide. Those lovely hazel eyes expose everything."

He surveyed her long brunette hair and diamond-shaped jawline. He wiped away streaming tears, streaking her freckled nose with wetness before touching her rosy, cut lips. She shifted back to remove herself from his sensual caresses. His mannerisms made her skin crawl.

"If we were alone, I'd torture you with all your fears to prove I own you..." He said, just loud enough for Zack to hear.

Eric continued to push the limit of Zack's tolerance by touching her shoulder seductively. Zack's body stiffened. He couldn't prevent it, and so he silently set a shadowed glare upon the man's back.

"Come on, I think that's enough fun and games for you today." Jason ushered him out. "Don't worry, Cassandra, he only jokes. You're safe as long as Victor's around."

Her face plastered into the pillow. Chains scooted near her, but inhibited Zack's ability to comfort her. The new terror placed on the beloved girl made Zack erupt with murderous wishes. He breathed in before speaking.

"Cassy... you've got to stop crying. It'll be alright. None of those men will harm you."

"What will stop them?"

"I'm still working on a sure-fire plan." Zack reached out a palm for her to grasp. When she made no such move, he said, "Eric talks big, but he'd never hurt you. Victor won't allow it."

A long, withdrawn silence filled the room as she sniffled back her last tears and then turned to face the agent. "Why..." she twirled her fingers along the pillowcase. "Why didn't you tell me about your brother?"

Resentment entered his tone. "He told you?"

"He told me the truth, then... Why did you keep it a secret from me?"

"Because it's my business. I didn't want you thinking lowly of me once you learned that I was the reason my brother died."

"If Victor told the truth about that, then maybe he told the truth about other things," Cassy mumbled. She fiddled with the bedspread. It finally all made sense. "When you first found out about me being the heir... you were overly cruel."

Zack flinched at the mention of his mistreatment of her.

189

"Was it because—"

He couldn't hide it any longer. He had to come clean. "Yes... I hated you. I blamed you for his death. When I found out that you were the heir, all I could feel was anger. I resented having to protect you when Tomas should've survived. All I could think was, 'If this stupid girl had just come out earlier, he would've lived.'" His knees supported his weight as he kneeled and inclined his torso low. "But I got to know you! I figured out that you wouldn't have wanted anyone to die because of the diamonds. It wasn't your fault at all. I was able to lower my guard around you, and I was able to fall in—"

"I'm the reason all those people died... The FUA or the Sacred Chosen should've approached me earlier and told me the truth, then Tomas would still be alive..." Utterly defeated by Victor's brutal honesty, she toppled again onto the pillow. "You should hate me, Zack! I killed all of them!"

He scolded, "Don't you dare believe that bullshit! None of it is anyone's fault but Victor's. If he didn't obsessively hunt for the heir, none of it would've happened." His fists clenched and struck the plane wall. "Tomas died because Victor pulled that trigger. I'll kill him for making you believe his bullshit."

Cassy sprang from the bed, kneeled in front of him and cupped his hand in between both of hers. "Zack, you can't kill him. It's not right. Death will only lead to more death."

"Do you know what that man did to his victims? What he'd do to you if he ever got the chance? Mercy and forgiveness are completely lost to that man. I can't forgive a monster!"

Yanking her hands away, she snarled, "I never asked you to forgive him! All I'm asking is for you to not look for revenge and just move on. Once this whole trip is finished, we may be able to walk away unscathed... if I can deliver the diamonds to them."

"You're acting like an idiot if you really think he'll just let us go..." Zack commented, filled to the brim with anger.

"Why can't I hope for a bit of humanity amongst these beasts?"

An awkward stillness raised the tension to its limits. Zack punched the wall again, enraged that he had broken her spirit even without the help of

Victor's silver tongue. Cassy stayed in her kneeled position and refocused on the clouds outside the cracked window.

After long contemplations, Zack relinquished his stubbornness. His heart ached whenever she suffered, and when he caused it, he had learned that apologizing was the best course of action.

"I'm sorry, Cassy. I don't want you to lose your optimism. It will help you fight against them."

Cassy hiccupped, shaking her head, "I'm not allowed to fight, or they'll kill you..."

"Fighting will be your sanity. The moment you lose that, Victor will rake his talons into you and take advantage of you however he wishes. Promise me that you'll always fight!"

With a nod, Cassy leaned into his chest, breathing in the attractive scent she always enjoyed during her time near him. His hands ran up, gliding across her arms. She shivered as adrenalin gripped her. The hands now lied above her shoulders. She straightened herself and a yearning grew while his intentions with the gentle caresses were obvious. Zack's fingers felt the nape of her neck and rested beneath Cassy's loose hair. A small tug drew her closer to his body, and before she knew it, the sweet taste of his lips met hers and they forgot the rest of the world.

Their relationship had progressed slowly. Victor's ever-growing goal to hurt them through their emotions had made it so. It hadn't helped that their strained relationship kept reappearing at the most inopportune times. She longed for the day that he would hold her softly and provide her with the love she required. Zack's lips pressed harder, and his hands squeezed her forearms before loosening in a passionate cycle. Cassy realized since her parents' tragic death, she'd never been so happy. Cassy pressed his back against the wall, controlling his movements a little, while she almost lost complete control of her tingling body.

Zack broke it off, retracting from wanting anything further. Not while they were in hell. Cassy rested her head onto Zack's chest and listened to his healthy heart.

A pause in their joy caused Cassy to ask, "What are they going to do with us?"

Zack tenderly hugged her to avoid responding.

• • •

Michael bustled in from a late morning of rushing around. He'd taken to frustrated shopping to rethink what should be done once Cassy arrived home from school. He planned a serious punishment the moment she entered the front door. As he juggled an armful of groceries and school texts in his arms, the phone rang loudly, and he was forced to shuffle around the items. The receiver was held to his chest to allow him a second to calm his breath, and then set onto his ear.

"Hello?"

"Good morning, Mr. Waters. This is Mr. Blake. I'm the principal at Dolesia High School. I've been concerned lately with Cassandra. She's been distracted, and now, today, she's not in class. I realize she may still be sick, however, I'm just worried about how she's been handling the bullying lately. Has she been mourning alright? The tragedy your family has faced can't be easy."

Michael frowned. "I believe she is, and I don't think there's been any new incidents with the bullies..." *Except for going out with one of them.* "Though, I'm confused. She should be there. Mr. Sisk was going to drop both her and Zack off for class this morning."

"Who?"

"Mr. Sisk... the counsellor from the school. He's been talking with Cassy for the past couple months."

"I'm sorry, but I have no staff by that name."

The brother defended against the nagging reality. "No, there has to be! He was over yesterday!"

The principle grew concerned, "I will double-check, but I'm a hundred percent positive that I have no staff by that name. Mr. Waters, I recommend you call the police."

"Can't you ask Zack about where she is? Zack... umm, dammit, I forget his last name. He's in four of her classes. They were out together and met up with Mr. Sisk."

"Umm... one second..." he rustled through some papers. "Ah, Zackary Exacil. He's also absent today."

Michael gagged. The phone dropped to the tiled flooring. His sister had disappeared into the night. Scooping the receiver up, he dialled Brant and Vince's school. He waited painful minutes before Brant took the call from the secretary.

"Brant, have you heard from Cassy today?"

"No..." Brant questioned Vince before continuing. "We both haven't. Shouldn't she be at school? Buddy said he'd take her."

"The principle... he just phoned. She's not there." He gulped a lump forcefully down his throat. "Buddy doesn't work at the school..."

"What!" Brant explained to Vince in a monotone before he returned to talking to Michael. "We're coming home."

"I'll phone the police."

Michael slammed down the receiver and screamed. *What has Buddy done to you, Cassy?* Beyond the point of figuring out what could be done, Michael collapsed to the kitchen table. He refrained from crying. On the day of his parents' funeral, he had sworn to keep each sibling safe while under his guardianship. Now, it seemed that the people he should've been able to trust had betrayed him with swift ease. *Buddy, you sick-minded piece of shit! How could you do this to our family? Kidnap our baby sister... we invited you into our home! We've already lost everything!* A cold went deeper than his spine. "Oh god! He's taken Zack too!" The brother lost all ambition to consider what Buddy had planned for them. Michael buried his face into the palm of his trembling hands as his reddened eyes gleamed.

Brant and Vince hunted for Michael once they returned home. Vince was sickly, his narrow face paling at every word spoken by the eldest, and he couldn't support his own weight. Brant's jaw tightened, choking on tears. The brothers sat around the kitchen nook in utter shock, baffled by this malicious thing done to their sister.

●　　●　　●

Cassy and Zack laid on the floor, side by side. The clouds flashed by, and the lights splashed away with the sunset. Zack hummed a nameless tune while Cassy contemplated how fast everything had changed. Eventually, she concentrated on Zack's music. She stroked his chest, enjoying the tranquility that they could have while in such a horrible predicament.

Eric and Jason burst inside the prison, shattering their serenity. Trays, held in their captors' hands, brought food for the evening. A small bowl of soup and water were their only sustenance. Hunger grumbled Cassy's stomach as she realized she hadn't eaten for at least three days. Jason dropped the tray on the bed and took Cassy from her spot, tossing her onto the bedspread. Zack's food dropped, splashing most of it onto the floor.

"Eat up. We'll be back in ten minutes," Jason stormed out after speaking and commanding his comrade out.

"Zack…" she eyed the meal suspiciously, "want to switch?"

Zack bit a lip. Poisoning him would be the easiest route, and if they had been so ruthless, Cassy potentially could become sick. She stubbornly jumped from the bed and took several sips of his soup and handed over her fuller bowl. He gave her an uncomfortable glance before accepting it.

• • •

Jason leaned against the doorframe, folding his arms over his chest as Victor chuckled at an inside joke.

"You didn't need for this morning to escalate so far. She wouldn't be able to fight against us anyways. Why not just let her have her tantrum?"

"That is true. However, I needed to assert myself as the one in control. If she continued to rebel, she could potentially add complications during this trip. Besides, I gave her some hope for survival, so with that, I should find them less willing to place themselves in an annoying battle against me. I prefer not killing them until we reach the tomb. The way she was behaving, I may not have lasted another twelve hours."

"Makes sense. So, why drug them? Aren't you worried about her not waking up?"

"As long as we don't mix drugs, she should be alright." Victor stretched his arms out. "I want a peaceful night. She's not as I suspected, even after Buddy's intel. She's a goddamn volcano of attitude."

Angrily, Eric flipped a knife around, trying to contain his irritation.

"We should've poisoned him," he hissed.

"Cassandra is too smart for that. I wouldn't risk it. Besides, we don't want Zack dead until the diamonds are in hand. He'll know that he failed, and then we can kill both, maybe Cassandra first," Victor chuckled.

Their leader sipped his whiskey. His rage from hours ago had worn away into a numb happiness. Victor relished in the small battle finally won against the FUA and the group that once protected the heir so futilely. Raising a glass for a toast, Victor sighed gratefully.

•   •   •

Cassy finished her meal. It warmed her belly and increased her mood for dealing with Victor and his men. As soon as she finished, she admired Zack's cautious slurps. Even when he was starving as well, he only thought of the food as dangerous. His assumptions were validated when wooziness and nausea erupted with vindictive rage in Cassy's head. She rubbed it.

"Zack, I feel sick…" Cassy yawned.

Zack's eyes drooped. "Shit! Cassy…" he fell to the solid floor mid-warning.

Cassy jumped, alarmed that she made a grave mistake in exchanging their food. She nearly reached the edge of the bed before she lost the strength to combat the numbness.

Eric returned, depressed that no teasing could occur before the teenagers fell into their slumbers. He kicked Zack's tailbone to check the likelihood of him faking it. Not even a moan escaped. Pleased, Eric ensured the shackles were done properly. As for Cassy, Eric covered her in the quilt and sat at the foot of the bed, guarding in anticipation of some fun later.

•   •   •

Zack blinked back the darkness from his deep sleep. Unsure whether the men had tossed him somewhere rather than returning him to the plane, Zack struggled against the ropes that now bound him. It was fruitless, especially as a blinding light brightened his horizons, revealing the malicious, startled face of Victor. Fascinated as to why a prisoner was secured in his lounging space, Victor closed both eyes, massaging a single side of his temple.

"What's going on here?"

The agent growled, "I'd like to know the same thing!"

"Ugh," Victor groaned.

Victor marched towards a locked cabinet, unlocked it with a key from inside his pants' pocket, and lifted out a remote control. A screen flicked on to reveal Eric hovering over Cassy's slumbering form in her prison cell.

"That damn bastard couldn't control himself."

Zack strained to see around Victor's bulk. "You said that as long as Cassy listened, this trip would be peaceful. Why the hell is that asshole creeping around?"

"Unfortunately, Eric's leash is not as short as I would like." Victor sank into the booth. "You didn't actually believe that I'd let her go, did you?"

"Of course not. I knew instantly that you lied through your teeth. Whether or not she's the actual heir, she's not going to be free ever again."

"Exactly! I get to kill her either way."

The agent stopped in fighting the tethers restraining his wrists and broke into a fit of uncontainable laughs. Zack dripped with a mocking sneer towards Victor, who was questioning Zack's sanity.

"Shit, so it's true!" Zack scoffed. "You know nothing about the actual heir? I thought your comment yesterday was odd. If you truly knew, you would've never promised for Cassy to just walk away."

Victor faced him. "What do you mean?"

"I *mean*, the heir is the only one capable of controlling the diamonds. The curse states that the heir can use the diamonds as *they* wish. You can't harm Cassy. She's safe from you as long as she's the heir."

Victor's response was interrupted when the agent's name was shouted. Cassy shifted and rubbed her drooping eyelids, half aware of the man standing above her. She shoved by him and slinked to where Zack should've been chained. A loud, hysterical scream proceeded. Slamming the doorway with a fist, she called out to whoever might listen. Even when the banging persisted, the confinement held steady.

A swear demonstrated Victor's awareness of the impending abuse. His neck tensed and Zack noted his stiff posture. Cassy's place in Eric's eyes was only for one thing, which Victor detested more than Zack.

Eric scooped Cassy off her feet and pinned her to the ground under his bulk. The man mentally attacked her. He dripped with ridicule at her naïve belief that she believed she could save Zack without the assistance of the FUA. She had landed in Victor's lap, and now she was going to be his puppet.

Cassy maintained a cool head for a few of the jibes.

"You'll never see your family again." He rubbed her trembling shoulders. "You fell for a boy who doesn't give a crap about you. If he doesn't ditch you, we will ensure that you're covered in his warm blood as he chokes to take his last breath. He's landed in a den filled to the brim with starving lions that crave his blood." His lips landed beneath hers and his hands were exploring down her waist. "Then, you won't be so protected... I'm going to enjoy every minute I get alone with you until we kill you..."

"No!" she snivelled. "Victor promised to let us go!"

Zack listened to the half-audible conversation as he watched Victor's rage fume like never before.

A single laugh was all Eric needed to do for her to comprehend that Victor lied. She fought, twisting and thrashing to escape from underneath his weight. A survival instinct took over and she dug her teeth into the nearest piece of flesh, puncturing his wrist as deep as possible. He wrenched back and snarled at her cheap tactics. He swiped the blood with the other hand and lathered it thickly across her face to punish her for her actions. Her head then slammed into the plane floor as he gripped her hair and crashed it down. Disoriented, Cassy felt his body shift, so he could straddle her waist and restrain her arms roughly.

His mouth slipped close to an ear, "Oh, I enjoy your spunk, Cassandra. Fighting still proves to be one of the best ways to relax... among a few others. This has begun a good morning!" A burning sensation fell on her cheek. His hand struck again before he leaned forward.

Zack turned away from this assault of his would-be-girlfriend. Cassy was ensnared underneath Eric's bulk with no escape in sight, not five metres from him, and he could do nothing. Neither voices nor shifting were heard. Nervously, he glanced over at Victor's unimpressed features. From the corner of his eye, he witnessed Eric lean forward and kiss her cheek. His lips nibbled at her earlobe as the trauma of the extensive assault caused her to tremble. A silent comment left the men watching in the lurch and caused a distressed expression to grow across Cassy's face.

Victor remained semi-cool. He stiffly strolled towards the screen and flicked off the camera. He disliked Eric's sneaky behaviour and he plotted a punishment to soon meet the man.

Caring about nothing but the girl who had recently been thrust into such a dire state, Zack begged for Victor to release Cassy. The pleas halted when Eric stealthily entered the dining room, unaware of what Victor had seen. When he noticed both men conversing, he swore under his breath. "Shit!"

"Shit?" Victor rebuked, "That's all you have to say for yourself?"

Eric raised his hands, submitting for an ounce of forgiveness.

"I should make you grovel for your life!" Victor struck the man down to size with a single punch across the face.

Eric rubbed his jaw and remained pathetically on his ass. He babied his arm as it hit the table's corner and now bled from an open wound. He breathed once before another strike doubled him over. It made the hits on Cassandra almost even. Polished shoes met with his ribs twice, and then Victor commanded Jonathon into the dining space to wrangle Zack and return him to his room. Halting Jonathon's intent to lift their prisoner, his leader leaned in close to whisper something.

"Make sure she gets cleaned up, check for a concussion, and then come back. We have some things to discuss."

Jonathon accepted the role of transporting a prisoner. Victor then bent to mend Eric's gushing arm that rightfully deserved the wound.

• • •

Eric withdrew from Cassy with a little laugh playing at his lips. He took a real liking to the memory of kissing her even while she was messily smeared in blood. Surrendering Cassy to a solitary couple of minutes, it left her time to crawl into the washroom, lock the door and cringe at the sight of her red face. Heated water poured into the sink. She quickly scrubbed the blood away and watched the crimson swirl down the drain. Once all she saw was her light skin tone that had slowly become pale as the trials with the men worsened, she pressed her hands over her lips to hide the quivering cry creeping up her chin.

She jumped back when Jonathon broke down the doorway, impatiently looking to finish his orders. Checking that she cleaned off all the blood, he ripped her from the bathroom and back onto the bed. Zack instantly accompanied her. Curling her into his recently untied hands, he encouraged her to cry out the innocent tears. Jonathon growled that he needed to check for a concussion but was berated with shrieks and any objects she was able to find.

"Then you look after her, dammit!" Jonathon huffed.

Protective arms brought her into a security blanket of kindness as soon as the man stormed out.

• • •

Dammit... Victor considered Zack's statement about the heir and the diamonds while he waited for all five of his men to enter the dining room. If it proved true, the men needed to figure out a different exit plan than separating into other regions of the world and never having contact with one another.

Jonathon froze at the entryway as Victor tossed a glass. It shattered into a million pieces and crunched underfoot. The ex-soldier tilted his head like a dog in curiosity.

"Damn," Victor said barely audibly.

"What's wrong?"

"Though I don't agree with his methods, Eric did exceptionally well at exposing an awful truth."

"And what is that?"

The others quietly whispered, scattered in haphazard organisation, wondering what could have irked their boss so severely.

Victor lounged on a chair. Several gulps of alcohol ran their course as Victor searched for words to explain the change in plan. Jonathon sat on the table's ledge and repeated the question. Victor brushed back his thick hair.

How didn't we know this? We've looked at the curse so often and learned so much about it. How did we miss that simple fact? Obeko made the curse unisex so we couldn't tell the gender of the heir, not because the diamonds will listen to anyone.

"According to the agent, Cassandra is the only one capable of using the diamonds."

Jonathon's brows furrowed heavily, and his chin dropped into his collarbones. "You actually believe the twerp?"

"He has nothing to gain by telling me this…"

"Except for ensuring Cassandra's life," Jason muttered as he caught onto the insinuations made. "However, I have considered the prospect as well."

Victor sharply twisted his neck at Jason's matter-of-fact tone.

"Well, while we were in prison, Eric and I spitballed that since Obeko was the only one capable of controlling the diamonds, then why would he let whoever use them? Nah, he would permit only a chosen person to inherit them." Jason chuckled for a split second before he glanced over at Victor. "There being only one person gifted in controlling the diamonds doesn't seem too bad. Imagine if she had been a full-grown man. Do you realize how hard it would've been to control him when he found out about that? Cassandra is easier to manipulate. She won't have the ability to defend herself. Once the agent's dead, she'll be nothing."

Jonathon howled aloud with the concept of being trapped with the five other men for the rest of his life just to maintain wealth.

"So," Austin intruded in, "I guess we are stuck with one another, unless someone wants to take her from the rest of us."

Victor nipped that in the bud by stating, "We shall retrieve the diamonds and move on to another country. Once we all have collected our wealth, we will decide on one man to own her. The others will be able to contact him for money, but until she is submissive, all six will stay together. We won't be killing her, but she will be a captive from now on. If it turns out Zack is lying, then we will remove her from our sight and return to the original plan. Agreed?"

Anxiously, each one agreed to Victor's terms to avoid becoming a target to "be rid of."

• • •

"Zack... Eric attacked me..."

Zack rubbed her back. To admit he watched the entire ordeal would devastate her further.

"I'm not strong enough. I can't live like this! These men are monsters!"

Into the fetal position, Cassy strained to not let Zack feel her shiver under his touch. Eric had terrorized her into cowering even with her loved one's embrace wrapped tenderly around her.

"He got on top of me and kissed me... and whispered in my ear. He said that I'm going to retrieve the diamonds so he can become rich... if I don't do as they say, he'll torture me. He'll take pleasure in slicing me and removing everything I hold dear." She mumbled, "They only seek to cause pain." Rolling over, she faced Zack's concerned features, curling deeper into his hold. "I always told myself that there would be threats and that they would be cruel, but I never expected this. How can they hurt us like we're nothing?"

Anger flooded Zack as she described Eric's aggression. If they lengthened their stay any longer, there would be more frequent physical violence The previous evening showed a glimpse of how much Victor detested Cassy. If she kept testing his limits with her unpredictable behaviour, Victor would react much worse. Zack squeezed her waist. His chin rested on her shoulder and his smooth lips played at her ear.

"We're getting out of here, Cassy, before any of them hurt you anymore. This plane needs to land for gas, and if we can, we could fit beneath the flooring and wait there until security comes to check on the men. We will be in a new country, and they will have to deal with customs. More than likely, Victor will hide us somewhere in the plane to avoid us being on record. Before they get a chance to do that, we will hide ourselves." He sprang up from the bed and rounded it to fiddle with the floor inside the closet. "This will lead to the landing gear, Cassy. We won't be able to leave until they lower it, but I bet we will be able to slip through the space. It's a fairly large plane."

"Zack, it won't work."

"Shhh," he warned about her volume. "Yes, it will. Once we land, customs will come immediately. They aren't allowed off the plane until they come, and the men will be too distracted to focus on us. While they're wasting time with the security, we'll be outside, running."

Cassy said in an undertone, showing how hopeful she was, "Let's do this, Zack."

The iffy plan made them edgy, but if they fit through the landing gear, they would for sure escape. For hours they anticipated the descent. They started holding one another on the floor. They touched openly on topics that they previously had been avoiding. To keep his mind from building barriers, and to ensure they were unheard while they spoke, Zack searched through the room for the hidden camera's location. It was mere minutes before he found the tiny camera attached to a glass light shade. Zack was disappointed at how easily it was found and assumed a rushed job had been performed.

From the vantage point at the bed, they were able to keep tabs on it. It seemed to only be on when Victor watched them, so they attentively checked for the red light. Zack wanted to make sure they weren't caught crawling into the space. Zack paced around, throwing out ideas for how they would commit to their course of action. Upon descent, the pilot would force the men to buckle up, making Victor leave the privacy of the dining room. They would gamble on their safety to escape without detection. Comfortable and in agreeance with the plan, Zack curled onto the bed with Cassy.

"I love you, Zack," Cassy said, ensuring him that her love had not faded.

"Cassy," Zack shamelessly said, "I want, even if we haven't been on a date yet, to be in a relationship with you. I want you to depend on me like a girlfriend would depend on her boyfriend. Are we able to have that?"

The girl stiffened when he mentioned this. A blossoming, real relationship had been her goal ever since Zack seriously asked her out.

"I would like that a lot, Zack."

Kissing her luscious lips, he wrapped an arm around her shoulder. "Even through this crap, we can love each other openly. I'm ready to stay with you, even if I have to travel across the world to be with you."

Butterflies fluttered in her stomach. It thrilled her that finally something fantastic came from a bad situation. Straddling over his lap, she took advantage of the pure emotions and kissed him passionately. Zack gripped her hips, pulling her close. His touch was too real for her and she burned with the excitement of finally being bonded to him emotionally.

The moment ended instantly when Jonathon disrupted their kissing session with a disgusted grunt and parted them. He retreated satisfied back into the plane's depths once they remained separated. Random intervals had the criminals storming in, trying to stop their lovey-dovey conversations. At that point, they gave up on speaking and settled to cuddling on the floor. None of them, luckily, had chained Zack back up. The men found it soothing to have them less uptight, so in turn, everyone remained happy.

Jonathon entered the most frequently, obviously suspicious of their compliance to being quiet. He never spoke, but his eyes questioned the high stakes of kidnapping a female as the heir, even against all the protests of the other men. If he were wrong, he'd never hear the end of it, or be "rid of" because of wasting Victor's time. When Eric sauntered in, *almost* as often as Jonathon, he showed his God complex by proudly heading for the bed and sitting next to the recently proclaimed girlfriend as she sank further into the nook of Zack's elbow. He would attempt to touch her, sneering at her every flinch. Jason eventually rescued the two and reprimanded Eric, forcing him to exit. Buddy would randomly appear in the prison's entranceway. Cassy realized from his short visits that he was a young man who had played a game out of his skill set and now had become a pawn in it all. The others shouted for him to be their lackey and his bravado quickly dissipated.

Laughter followed for half an hour without interruption as they argued over a reality show they found that they both enjoyed. Their smiles slipped when a shadow cast impending doom over them. The leader had left the dining area. His broad shoulders and his gun, attached to his lean hip, created a nefarious aura.

Zack hopped from the bed, holding out his arms to shove Victor out.

"Boy, sit down. I am here to speak with Cassandra," he calmly stated.

Cassy now hid behind Zack's back. "What would you like?"

"Come here," he pointed beside him, "and I'll tell you."

"I can hear you from here."

Annoyance flared his nose and the man reached behind Zack briskly, seizing her hand. Cassy, scared of Zack charging forward, placed a tranquil hand on his chest. Fighting with the leader only brought death.

"There, that's better." He bitterly stated, "We'll work on your listening skills… Now, we are landing soon. One of us, after landing, will come in here to grab you. I want absolutely no fighting or resisting. If any rebelling happens, this bastard," Victor jabbed a finger at Zack, "will be dead."

Cassy resisted making a snarky comment back. She finally gained a devoted boyfriend who filled her with joy. Risking his life, just to provoke Victor, was not worth it.

"We will be dealing with some government protocol and will therefore need to hide you. Make even a single noise, and I assure you, you will be unhappy with the consequences."

Cassy forced a nod.

Victor glanced upon the supposed heir, deep in thought. He brushed her cheek softly with a smooth backhand. This action surprised even him. His brown eyes widened with shock and flicked from Cassy's startled face to his hand. Zack's glare penetrated a stronghold of barriers and Victor was shunned away, reflecting on the many thoughts that had crossed his mind. The deadbolt quietly locked the prisoners within.

Zack was petrified in place by Victor's emotion shown to his girlfriend. Cassy tilted her head, confused by the sudden action. A brush of her hand on Zack's broke the spell and he quickly dashed around, double-checking that he hadn't forgotten anything. From underneath the bed, he reached inside the mattress, feeling around for a specific object. The item that he groped was not what he expected. The listening device blinked at the tip.

"Shit…" Zack looked around. Taking it into the bathroom, he set it near running water, while he rushed over to Cassy. "Cassy, bang on the door. Make sure no one is outside there. Victor planted a listening device. He may know our plans already. If nobody is out there, then they may be unaware of this." He then turned off the water and stuck the device back into the bedding. "Alright, Cassy, do it."

Banging loudly, she asked, "Umm, I'm hungry, can you please bring us some food?"

No response. Zack's concern was lifted with a grateful sigh. A shifting of the plane's altitude prepared them for its descent. He immediately returned to hunting for the hidden object. It settled into his hand. Cassy became excited when the wristwatch was strapped onto his wrist.

"You still have it? Can we get home with it?"

Zack shook his head. "Nah, Austin fiddled with it and wrecked part of the system. It'll take some time to fix and send out a signal."

He strolled by her, preparing the crawl space for them to enter.

"When I contacted you from the FUA, your signal went out… Victor took the watch off, right?" He nodded. "How'd you get it back?"

Lifting the cover, Zack grunted, "Austin isn't the cleverest of the bunch. He was carrying it in his pocket. While they were chaining me on the first day, he got too close, and I swiped it. It's been hidden here until we could escape. With you being unconscious for two days, I worried that we might never have the chance."

Further questions were cut short when the plane jostled them about. Motioning for her to enter the crawl space, he assisted her as she ducked inside. One final check ensured Zack that he had grabbed the most important items, and then he squeezed in beside the girl. Laying on a bunch of entangling wires and close-nit frame beams, they waited until the plane officially landed. Cassy pinned Zack's torso to the beam as he rolled onto his back and replaced the cover to the crawl space. His manoeuvring only worsened her anxiety. Once he properly lied on his stomach and tucked Cassy underneath him, he held onto the beam with both hands and then gazed about the surrounding area. Not much was seen, and until they finished the roughest patch of landing, they were stuck in place, hoping to escape safely and without injury.

The turbulence was unpleasant, and the landing gear deafened them along with the whistling wind when the folded wheels shifted from inside, far off to the front, to straighten out for the ground. A lasting glimmer of hope twinkled through the now-awakened opening. Cassy awed at the sunlight; just the sight of it produced a song of freedom in her mind.

Landing jumbled them around as the wheels touched the hard cement in whatever country the men had deceptively chosen for their worldwide tour. Cassy pinched her eyes closed until they leaked with scared tears.

Her hands clung to any vantage point to avoid bouncing around. With the use of all his muscle strength around the metal brace, Zack secured her beneath him and stopped himself from sliding forward. Relief settled around them when the plane officially halted, unmoving for a long while.

Above them, Cassy cowered, hearing the plane shake from heavy footsteps of the rummaging of Victor's men. The steps approached their prison cell.

• • •

Austin and Jonathon wasted little time before heading to collect the hostages to hide them in the arranged compartment in the front of the plane. Austin rubbed his drooping eyes; he had slept through most of the landing. Jonathon stretched, too stiff to complain about the cramped living conditions with so many other men. Austin absently looked around as he was trying to figure out the type of questions the custom officers were going to ask. Their attentiveness instantly became conscious panic as the twosome realized something was amiss.

Austin remained as calm as possible as he searched in every possible hiding spot. He looked inside the closet, underneath the bed, inside all the cupboards of the washroom, and he even removed the venting system above the bed to peek inside. Nobody appeared.

Jonathon growled, "Where the hell are they?"

Intolerance shot back at him when Austin snapped, "Don't bitch at me! I don't have a damn clue!"

Austin wasted no time in fetching Victor. Jonathon scurried around, desperately searching for the teenagers before his boss ripped him a new one. The same results turned up.

Victor stormed in, saying, "If this is a joke, I won't be impressed."

He bent low, doing a solid examination for himself and became unsatisfied with what he found. Dumbfounded at the vanishing act, Victor scowled at the two, calculating what could have happened.

"Was the door locked?"

They half nodded, half shrugged, unsure of the true answer. Victor slammed the closet door shut and then swung his index finger towards the entrance.

"Was this room unlocked at any time in the past half hour since I left and locked it myself?" he roared.

Jonathon gulped in response. "I don't believe so."

"You find them while the plane fuels up or I'll personally kill you all!"

Glancing through the cracked windowpane, he swore under his breath as the gas jockeys drove up their vehicle, closely followed by the security.

"Damn it. Hurry up. Customs is coming. Do a quick look throughout the plane and then join us in the main area. We all need to be there."

He stormed off, infuriated with the incompetency of the people around him.

• • •

"Go, Cassy," Zack told her.

The men just entered the bedroom and began their frantic search. Underneath them, the couple moved quickly, slithering through wires. They avoided bumping anything only to ensure the men weren't alerted of them because of a power outage or an alarm going off. As they reached the topmost joints of the landing gear, Zack army crawled by Cassy to check if this plan could work. Manoeuvring his legs around, Zack wedged himself inside the square shaped opening. He barely fit. Just as Cassy went to follow suit, he halted her. He needed to check that nobody stood near them. Hiding to the best of his ability, Zack ducked his head from side to side, locating any potential witnesses to their escape.

A gas jockey wore ear plugs and busied himself at finishing the job quickly. Four other men in uniforms marched up the motorized stairs to question the group for their reasons of a visit. All the men would soon be distracted by customs to prevent them from hunting extensively.

Zack jumped from the rubber wheel and whistled at Cassy. She slipped through much more easily than the developing boy and landed into his arms when she misstepped. Luckily, Zack was ready to assist whenever she required. Sitting, pinned against the wheel, they looked out into the horizon while basking in the sun, and then hunted for a good place to run.

Cassy's hand slipped into Zack's. They had made it so far because of him.

"Did you hear Victor?" she whispered. "Do you really think he'd follow through with killing them?"

"Yup!" Zack's acceptance of that had been long overdue, unlike Cassy's. "He murdered two of his comrades already because they withheld information. There was a man from the group helping them, and when he wanted out, Victor gave him only one way. He's also, since I've been involved in this assignment, killed a girlfriend of his. She was pregnant and demanded that he stay with her, or else... well, suffice to say, the 'or else' happened to her. Stay on his good side for however long he'll allow it because he'll treat you like scum once he turns sour towards you."

The wrath of Victor had already befallen her. Cassy wrinkled her shirt. *Victor can be much worse. I've got to be careful.*

"Alright, Cassy. We're going to be out in the open, so we have to act fast."

Zack pointed to their destination. A building of shining metal stretched as far as the eye could see at their angle, but where Zack pointed was in the direction of a fence that was a blind spot for any peering eyes. The section of the fence he saw was tucked behind a part of the airport with only a few visible windows. It was their best shot. If they went to security, Victor's smooth tongue would dissuade any arrests. They already had planned for issues with customs and for security hold ups.

"We're running there." He pointed determinedly. "You run as fast as possible. At the corner of the airport building, we don't stop. We're going to break through that chain link fence and then run again until we find a cop. Are you ready?"

Cassy gulped back dread and said, "I have to be, otherwise, we're back to being trapped with those men."

Zack hopped up, snatched her thin arm and sprinted from the plane wheel. Cassy trailed behind, trying to keep up with his long strides.

• • •

Jason was finished being questioned as the customs officer checked over his passport and frowned. Jason stood near the window, boredom overwhelming him greatly as he responded with rehearsed answers. The officer handed back the passport, said his good days, and then moved on to the next awaiting man. Two other officers spoke in monotones to their chosen man.

While lollygagging, Jason peered out the window and caught onto something interesting. The two kidnapped teenagers were outside, sprinting from the plane. He slammed a fist into a padded chair. *How the hell did they get off the plane?* Politely interrupting Jonathon's conversation, he asked if he were permitted to use the bathroom. The custom officers agreed, since the search for contraband was finished.

Jason strolled towards the teenagers' imprisonment and re-searched the space. With a confused hum, he sank onto the bed. Nothing seemed out of place. Rechecking the closet, he stepped inside, feeling around the walls for hidden compartments. As he stepped towards the farthest right corner, a creak underfoot caught his attention. The cover to the crawl space popped open and he dipped his head inside.

"Hell, that bastard outsmarted us again..." he groaned.

He poked his head through the bedroom entrance and watched as the customs security prepared to leave. As soon as Jonathon finished, Jason flagged him down and ushered him towards the rear of the plane. Victor was heard growling swears about the airport security before heading to the pilot to discuss their travel arrangements.

"I found them," Jason whispered, bending closer to Jonathon's ear.

Jonathon gaped, searching around in astonishment. "Where?"

"Outside..."

Jonathon darted from the room to gather Victor for this disturbing news. Clearing his throat, he beckoned Victor closer, straightening his shirt to avoid the obvious shaking. Victor excused himself, apologizing for the interruption. Once he was close enough, Jonathon sealed shut his eyes to not witness the face Victor was about to make.

"We have a slight problem."

Victor half twisted. His face creased as he raised his eyebrows and pressed his piercing, thin lips together. "It had better be a slight problem we can fix right away."

"The twerps aren't in the plane anymore. Jason saw them running away."

"YOU DAMN IDIOTS!"

Victor's feet rumbled the floors as they stomped and made tread lines as he paced around, his cheeks puffed out in exasperation. The other five men stayed clear, though they stuck near enough to be commanded if necessary. Buddy lingered back, clearly at a disadvantage by not knowing how Victor dealt with situations of this sort. The others scattered the length of the plane, most of them sitting perplexed while Victor's breaths cut into harsh little growls, determining a logical strategy.

A contemplative tick began when he folded his arms and tapped a single thumb as he considered every option. He could forget about the two now free of captivity or call someone in the local area. His head fell back in frustration with his own curiosity spiking with the want to learn the heir's identity. To leave the girl behind without guaranteeing she was not heir was unthinkable. Victor racked his brain for contacts, which brought more stressful swears. *Damn it!* He very much disliked the nearest contact to their location. He tossed a coffee mug from a table, narrowly missing Austin's unperturbed head. The men were used to Victor's methods for finding a way out of a mess. Buddy gulped, feeling his Adam's apple bob as Victor stormed further into the plane. Victor was furious at what he had to do. *She's the only one available... Shit!*

"Jonathon," he barked, "phone Susan and describe them to her." When Jonathon moved leisurely, Victor spun around, and restrained from swinging at the ex-military man. "NOW!" He then turned to Austin. "You find a way to stall for as long as possible. Literally do anything to stop this plane from taking off until we find them. They won't allow more than a few hours here if there's nothing wrong with the actual plane."

Austin stroked back his gelled hair, groaning at being forced to break such a gorgeous machine. The course of action to which he committed had him disappearing into the cock pit, hidden from any of the others.

Victor removed his trusty pistol from a concealed compartment, preparing it for use.

"Those goddamn kids are going to get a beating for this bullshit."

Chapter 11

Zack's legs stretched as far as possible when he darted from underneath the plane. Cassy huffed beside him. Adrenalin filled her entirety during this last-ditch effort. As they rounded the airport, they found the chain link fence was unguarded, with fewer windows than expected looking down upon it. Zack sighed in relief when he stopped. Rattling the fence, he found the durability of the metal was strong.

"Zack," Cassy whispered, "how are we going to cut this?"

The reinforced metal hardly worried the agent as he glanced around once more for pursuing security or criminals.

"No matter how much Austin tried to tamper with my watch, he couldn't remove my *toys*."

A grimace showed her confusion. He explained silently by fiddling with the buttons on his watch. He mindlessly scrolled through the items and accepted one he required. The watch beeped and a hologram of wire cutters formed into a three-dimensional blue light. Zack reached inside it and they fell into his palm as though they had always been there. Stunned, Cassy touched the tool, mystified that it was a physical object.

"Mrs. Embers is a genius and figured out a way to make a holographic three-dimensional object into a physical one. We can store up to a hundred and fifty items on this watch. I don't think Austin, even with all of his tech knowhow, realized it had so many capabilities other than just communication."

He snipped the chain link enough to bend it forward and then replaced the wire cutters into the watch. Once both were out of the airport area, he manipulated some metal cord from his watch to reseal the opened escape route. He then snatched Cassy's hand and took off running again.

The run lengthened from fifteen minutes to half an hour with Zack pulling her forward as she whined, wanting to stop. They slowed their pace as a section of the city became vaguely familiar to Zack, though Zack's firm grip tightened, and he neared Cassy's puffing chest to his. The only reason he would remember an area was because of an assignment, and with that being the case, he could have dragged Cassy into an area not safe for her. Cassy poked his shoulder, distracting him.

"Zack, where are we?"

"We'll find somewhere safe for the night..." He declined to admit that he was not sure where they landed. "I have to figure out my watch, or if that's unlikely to be fixed, we'll go hunt for cops."

He heaved Cassy a couple more blocks. He peeked into windows, wracking his brain for any hints on why he felt a distant pang of recognition. Finally, it dawned on him that they strolled through a rough part of the city. Towering brick buildings were covered in graffiti that clearly showed a gang's territory and the dangers around them. Zack securely tucked Cassy behind him. They edgily passed suspicious people on the streets. The brisk stroll brought them around a corner and facing the first true sign of where they had landed. Even if Zack couldn't remember exactly where they were, at least he had the neighbourhood's name.

"Hackney," he muttered.

Cassy caught the name and smiled. "Do you know where we are?"

Upset that he still failed in remembering, he lifted his head to the sky. Something had to spike his memory eventually; all he had to do was keep looking. That's when he noticed the small, horribly aged inn. It awoke something inside him. Whether it was good or bad would not be seen until Zack chanced venturing inside. He gave his precious girlfriend a sorrowful look. He hadn't been able to please her with a romantic date, and now, he wanted to force her inside a shoddy inn to familiarize himself with their location and to escape the jeering men that were tempted to hoot at the scared teenager.

Cassy shrugged, moving closer to him when a drunk man sauntered by and asked if she would come home with him.

"It's alright, Zack. We should stay here, at least for the night. It's getting dark. Besides, I think you're right with wanting to fix the watch. It's our best shot at getting home. Local police won't be able to deal with us."

Zack kissed her pale cheek and hauled her inside before the drunk rounded back to pester them. Inside, the lobby of the inn was no better than the outside. Outside, the siding was decaying from lack of upkeep and spider webs gathered so thickly they could ensnare even the largest of people. The interior helped even less to make it seem inviting. The glass door banged shut without even a warning to slow down. In front of the two escapees, a ratty wooden desk sat low with a woman, uninterestedly, painting her nails. It was a makeshift desk made of patch jobs. The desk faced the entrance, and around the right-hand corner, an escape route for the clerk was available only if she opened the sliding lock gate that was about waist height. A disgusting brown carpet, which at one point might have been beige, was littered with garbage and shards of glass. Zack instantly regretted bringing Cassy inside this place. In the left-hand corner of the desk, a hurricane of dust pans and brooms rested, not used for months.

The agent went to peer down the hallway a bit to see the extent of the horrors that might await them inside a room. Just as he peeked down a little bit, the woman popped her head up and startled Cassy, causing her to jump and grasp Zack's upper arm in fear.

"Good evening!" an English accent spoke.

That was the moment Zack realized where they were. Excitement brought him high as he finally gained an ounce of an advantage. *I can call the London branch!*

Snatching Cassy's wrist, Zack reassured her that they needn't stay in this place. They reached the exit just as the woman welcomed them.

"Do you need a room?"

"No, we're fine. I was only trying to get my bearings. We're alright."

The woman shrugged, unfazed by the rejection. Cassy clung tightly to Zack's hand when vehicles drove by. They weren't out of deep water yet. At any moment, Victor's men could round the corner. That's when the woman placed her nail polish down and attentively watched the twosome.

"Are you alright, deary?" her accent rose three decibels in fake concern.

Zack hugged Cassy closer, noticing how scared she was to venture out there again.

The woman rose and rounded the desk. "We have an option of paying by the hour. Why not collect yourselves before leaving again?"

Cassy's spirits jumped at being able to hide out in a room without being found to fix the watch. Her boyfriend wearily shifted. Something seemed off by the woman. A snuggling arm tugged at him, and he grasped the necessity to hide for a few hours.

"I guess we could," he whispered in a slightly bothered tone. "I'm exhausted. Besides, it may give me time to fix the watch."

Cassy kissed his lips, pleased to hear it. The woman rounded the desk again and began typing on the old desk top computer. She hummed away before asking them anything.

"We need a room for two, please."

A snide giggle asked, "Would you like a single bed? You two may have a chance for real coziness."

Disgusted by the comment, Zack slammed down his hand. "No, that's alright. We want two separate beds."

Zack turned his back on the woman as she tapped away, fiddling with his reclaimed watch. Scrolling through currencies, he found he had limited funds. *Damn, I forgot to transfer money into my other accounts. I probably don't have enough to pay with pounds… maybe she'll take Canadian.* He pressed the option for an amount of Canadian dollar and then snatched the money from the blue glow. Returning to face the silky-haired and green-eyed woman, he guiltily admired her attractive figure. The skirt she wore embraced lean, long legs and a flashy halter top flattered the woman's shoulders. She caught his gazing eyes and winked at him while Cassy jumped at another vehicle driving by.

He scolded his mind for his lustful thoughts. Zack shook his head and looked over at Cassy. She was a charming, beautiful girl with her short frame. Her mahogany hair was standing because of knots and static, but the curls had all dropped to become an enchantment of waviness. Stroking the strands caressing her back just below the shoulder blade, he felt her jump at the touch. Zack gazed into her hazel eyes, connecting to the soul that provided him with the love needed to survive this hell. All the interest he previously had in the woman faded when it dawned that Cassy's simple beauty and care was all he desired to feel complete.

He pulled Cassy into him and kissed her cheek. Then, he slid the money across the counter.

The woman almost laughed aloud when she saw the monopoly money. "Don't pay now." She reached behind to the wall where fourteen keys hung with only one missing. She snatched a brass one and plopped it into his hands. "I always wait until the end. You never know how *long* it might take and I love when I get a 'room service' call," she flirted thickly.

Cassy caught onto the devious words from the gorgeous woman. Zack encouraged Cassy by sliding his hand up to her freckled face and stroking it with his thumb.

"You're in room twelve. Call if you need *anything*."

Slipping the money into a pocket, Zack led Cassy down the hall. The brass key slipped into the rusty keyhole, and the door swung open to expose that the mouldy carpet worsened inside. It was a tight squeeze and despicable. All the windows were mended together with duct tape, layered in an inch of dust. Springless beds sunk deeply, and the shadows of rodents scurried about. From inside a small foyer, a bathroom filled to the brim with leaky, rusted taps and an old lime green tub only enticed them to run away faster, as the dripping would become a nuisance if they stayed any longer than an hour. Further in, a round, seventies-style table sat in a corner beneath a window. No chairs were available to sit at the table, but a couch was placed unsystematically in the center of the room, facing the beds. It was yellow, and the cushions sank deeply since the springs lost their life from abusive patrons. A ratty old television collected dust, unable to be plugged in because the cord was ripped from the socket.

Zack smoothed out his hair. Outright, he hollered, "This is horrible! I honestly had no idea. I'm sorry. We can still leave and find the FUA located here."

Cassy swung away from the disgusting environment and gaped at the comment. "You know where we are?"

"Somewhere in London. This is the neighbourhood of Hackney."

"Wow, the men sure aren't messing around in trying to dissuade the FUA."

Zack tested the sagging bed, grimacing at the sound it made and the feel of it.

"Since you managed to warn the FUA, they'll be on high alert. When an assignment is taken, the FUA is given a specific range of time to react. One FUA cannot invade another's territory unless given permission from the Board or if they have proof of the assignment's whereabouts. Victor's instincts are good to slowly make their way to Egypt. Mr. Edwards would have sent a report to the Cairo FUA to forewarn them of the kidnapping, and all he can do is sit and wait until there's a sighting. None of the FUAs, except for Saskatoon, the Egyptian Branch, the New York City Branch, and the highest members of the Board know the truth about your assignment. New York only knows because when the assignment was first offered, they made a bid for it. Thankfully, they lost." Zack stiffened when he started to notice a smell and plugged his nose. "Victor's exceptionally good at wasting time and detouring the FUA. If enough time elapses, then the Saskatoon FUA can't do diddly squat."

"Is it possible to contact them?"

"I'll need to sit down for a couple hours and attempt to fix the signal in my watch. It's been awhile since I took one apart and fixed equipment failure."

"Doesn't the FUA have a phone number we could call?"

"Nope," he grunted. "They're completely off the grid. The only way to communicate to them is through the watch or your bracelet." He eyed her bare wrist.

She blushed, ashamed for forgetting it. Zack stepped forward and slipped Cassy's shoulders beneath an arm.

"I'll fix the watch and we'll be heading home soon."

Cassy huffed in exasperation at the unknown.

"I'm going to start working on the watch. I could probably find something for you to do."

"Nah," she said, "I'm going to check on the shower. If it works, I'm going to have a nice hot one. I feel gross."

She headed to the bathroom, leaving the door open an inch so steam would pour out, and stripped. Zack began by shifting the couch closer to the table to sit on the back and then took off his watch. With a sigh, he contemplated the best route to delve in. It was difficult when rodents ran across his feet. Closing his eyes, he pretended not to notice and popped open the watch's face.

• • •

The front desk's phone rang loudly, which led to ruined nail art. Snatching it in a huff, the woman answered, "Thanks for calling Dream Inn, where all your fantasies can become reality. This is Susan," she chimed.

"Good evening, Susan. I hope you remember me, it's Jonathon. Victor's in town and requests your help. We're looking for two teenagers who escaped from the airport about forty-five minutes ago. The girl is a small fourteen-year-old with brunette hair. She's wearing a white shirt with a black, oddly positioned zippered sweater. The male is quite tall, fifteen years old, with messy brunette hair. He's got a black t-shirt on with some logo written in blue across it. Both are wearing dark washed jeans. They're Canadian kids, may look overly cautious. The girl will be outright nervous, while the boy is confident and reassuring. If you could keep an eye out for them, and contact us if you do see them, Victor would appreciate it."

Susan snapped at Jonathon, "Then why doesn't he contact me himself?"

Stutters broke up Jonathon's ill-conceived words and the woman rolled her eyes. She leaned back in the old, creaking chair in a huff.

"I won't need to watch out for them. They just checked into a room."

Jonathon almost dropped the phone as he rushed to the other men to alert them of the abducted teenagers' location.

"Make sure they stay there!"

Susan raised her eyebrows, intrigued by their need for two kids, but also surprised to gain an order from Jonathon when he provided nothing in return.

"Really, Jonathon? I will only keep them here for a price. Call me when you've decided upon something that I might want."

Jonathon's feet slowed down. Having previously worked with this con-niving woman, he already knew what she wanted. His voice deepened, sourly admitting that it was a fair trade. Before he could even agree, Victor interrupted him by asking for news.

Jonathon quickly said, "I'll call later after I negotiate with Victor." He then hung up the line to announce the price for the two kids.

• • •

Cassy finished her shower after twenty-five minutes of harsh water spraying down her skin. The bruises already caused by the men stung under the pelting stream. The maintenance on the shower was neglected to the brink of it being ready to explode; regardless, she basked in its delightful steam and cleansing properties. Drying off with an itchy towel, Cassy ran her hands through her soft hair and admired her sunken eyelids in the mirror. Outside in the smelly, despicable excuse for a room, she found Zack hunched over the table using exceptionally small tools to fiddle with the watch. Trying to locate how Austin had tampered with it frustrated him. With no signal transmitting a general beacon of hope, Zack tossed a screwdriver and slammed his elbows on the table.

Cassy bent to pick it up. Their only saving grace was Zack's ability to fix the watch.

"Zack?" she whispered, handing over the screwdriver and wrapping her arms around his tense neck. "Why don't you take a quick shower? Clear your head a bit."

"We don't have time for that. I need to be able to contact Mr. Edwards or we'll have to go hunt for the London Branch. It could literally be any building. If I had my watch, I'd be able to detect them in a flash," he complained.

Cassy looked at the scattered pieces of the watch. "Zack, go have a shower, please, I'm begging you."

He finally focused upon her when he accepted the small gesture to relax him. Her hair had been thrown up into a messy ponytail which curled as it dried. Zack appreciated her diamond face that was enhanced without hair to hide it. Her hazel eyes glistened with tears; he knew she couldn't conceal the fear of Victor coming for them. He cocked his head as if seeing a girl was something new. Cassy straightened, tilting her head awkwardly, and tried to understand his reaction. She glanced behind her, curious if he saw something strange.

"What?"

His hands snaked up her arms and pressed her into his chest as he breathed out a passionate gasp of air.

"I just realized how beautiful you are!"

"Zack..."

Zack defended his words. "I've never met someone so unselfish that they would stay by my side even when I've failed them."

"Zack, you haven't failed me. If anything, you've done your job better than any other agent. You're still here, fighting for us, and you've been keeping my faith that we will be saved."

Zack released his grip, suddenly awestruck. He'd realized something. "Holy shit!" He swiveled back to focus on the watch and fiddled with multiple pieces. "Cassy, you're a genius!"

"Huh?"

Using tweezers, Zack pulled a small, disk-shaped item from three wires.

"Austin is the best at manipulating technology; he's the *best* at his *job*. If he can't figure something out, he'll add a piece of his own equipment... just like he did here to make sure this wouldn't send out a signal!" He flashed the silvery disk in front of her, unable to contain his joy. "I was stressing over finding something out of place, but never thought that he would replace something with his own. I think we're going to be able to get home, Cassy!"

It took ten minutes for him to piece the watch back together and Cassy hung near his shoulder, anticipating success. Clicking the watch on, Zack held his breath for the moment of truth. It blinked with a green light and then only showed the time from Saskatoon. As he pressed two buttons in a specific sequence, an option screen popped up, allowing him to search through and turn on the location signal. It never blinked like it should have, but it did give them a small map of London.

"Damn," he mumbled. "It's not transferring a signal to the FUA... there must be something else wrong with it."

"But isn't that map able to help us?"

Zack breathed in through his teeth and made a sucking noise. "I think we should be able to get a fairly good idea of where the London Branch is. We've got to be careful. This isn't a place we want to be at night."

Cassy massaged his shoulders. "We'll be careful."

A knock halted their celebratory planning. Three more taps hit, and they both called in unison, 'Come in!' without even thinking about who might be outside. Luckily for them, it was only the woman from the front desk. She brought a tray of food with an expression of hospitality towards the youngsters. Zack sprang into action to deny the food and tried to escort the woman back out. He had hardly any patience with a nosey, lewd woman. Cassy exhaled anxiously, wanting to ask how much she overheard.

"Oh, that looks delicious, ummm..." Cassy muttered, "We never got your name."

"It's Susan." She shoved the tray into Zack's hands, pouting at his dissuasion to her advances. "I wanted to ask if you two plan on staying the entire night. It's getting late. There's a curfew for teenagers under the age of eighteen. If you're willing, have this food, on the house, and stay as long as you like tonight. Your, girlfriend?" she twittered at Zack, slipping in a seductive voice unlike he ever heard before. "She's looking worn down... Why don't you rest up and continue whatever you two were doing later?"

Her tickling fingers slid up Zack's arm, tempting him to join her in some alone time. Enraged at the woman, he shoved the tray of food back into her hands, gathered his things, and snatched Cassy's unprepared hand. With determined feet, he marched down the mildew-infested hallway and left the inn completely.

Cassy struggled against his paranoid fingers as she slowed down his pace with her resistance. A block swept by before she finally broke free.

"What's your deal?" she exclaimed. "She was being nice."

"Yeah, she was being nice alright..." he murmured, fiddling with the malfunctioning watch, which, in certain areas, struggled to maintain the map. "Ugh, Austin really did a number on this."

He attempted to move on and forget about the girlfriend who fumed in his grip, directing the watch to the skies to get some form of satellite signal. Cassy stomped her feet, determined to learn the truth.

"Zack! Tell me what's going on!"

"I just got uneasy about that place." He took hold of her hand. "Come on, once we find the London branch, she will be the least of your concern. She's sleazy anyways."

"Wow, you're a warm and fuzzy guy, aren't you? She didn't seem bad to me," Cassy pouted. "We at least had a place to stay until we do get home."

Zack carried little endurance for an emotion-driven argument. His sleek hands slid back onto the watch's buttons and pressed it distractedly several times. Arms folded over her chest, Cassy stayed put as Zack moved onward to a better destination.

Unwanted people studied the couple from the sidelines with their crooked, greedy grins lapping up the foreigner in dark washed jeans. They needed to move away from this neighbourhood, and travelling down the street in the direction of the FUA would promote that.

"Cassy, come on! You really wanted to stay in that dump for an entire night?"

"If it meant we stayed out of harm's way, then yes!"

Exasperated, Zack flung his arms into the air and wrenched her forward, submitting a great need to shake her.

"Want to make a deal?" Cassy leaned her head over to the side. "If you give me two hours to find the FUA, then I promise to apologize to her."

"How are you going to do that? Send a post card?" she snapped.

"No! If we don't find the FUA tonight, we'll go back to the inn and sleep there until we can get the watch working properly. In the morning, whether it's fixed or not, we will continue the search. I'll also keep an eye out for cops. They won't do much, but at least they will be a bit of protection."

Cassy dropped her head in disallowance of the raging anger within. "I'm sorry, Zack. I'd rather get home safe than have you apologize to some lady."

Snatching her clammy hand, Zack steered her down the street and followed the watch, which flickered frequently.

• • •

Victor climbed from the taxi, unimpressed with the dumpy inn Susan ran. His long strides towards the aged brick building halted just outside its broken glass entrance. Inside the hazy, dully lit lobby, he frowned at the conditions his supposed heir stayed in. Behind him, the others dug their hands deep into their pockets, fiddling with their loaded guns in case this exchange went sour. Victor gained the stamina to greet Susan after an extended stretch of time. Opening the door, the woman sprang into action, plopping down on the desk and crossing her exposed, sleek legs. A couple of the men, who were unable to contain their lust, whistled at the sexy woman. Jealousy greened their eyes, as Victor would soon be enjoying the willing woman.

Victor pretended to give a captivated smile towards her, but within his mind, he reverted to only wanting another girl. He approached confidently and placed a seductive touch onto Susan's bare shoulders to heat his skin. He was impressed that she hadn't changed since their last meeting. *She's still got the body I remember. Tonight may not be a waste.*

"Hello, Susan. Where are the brats?"

Susan hopped from the desk to plant a wet kiss on his shaven chin. Her sultry body pressed tightly against his solid torso. She stroked his chest with a seductive hum as she realized he was built more than before, and wanted to take him then. During the negotiations, all Victor could do was growl, disliking how he became a prize to be exchanged for the teenagers. She demanded that he spend one night with her, and then he would receive the two on a silver platter. As Victor's hands explored her voluptuous hips, he realized that one night of relaxing with her might prove to be a pleasant change from the testosterone surrounding him and the challenge of dealing with two teenagers.

"I don't get why you're after those brats, Victor. Weren't you the one who said you wanted to be *free*?" She giggled in a fake tone as she winked at a few of the adrenalin filled men.

He tugged her away to study her. Something about the comment had awoken a huge concern.

"Susan, where are they?"

"They left when I went to the loo," she whined.

His hands, dissatisfied by Susan's inability to control two scared and lost teenagers, dropped. Raising his sight to the rotten and sagging ceiling, Victor considered the next measure they may have to take. A grunt showed his unpleasant nature as he rounded the desk and hunted through the keys.

Jonathon demanded for answers, "Did they even come here?" He gripped Susan's shoulders and shook them with his beefy hands.

"Of course, they did. The boy tried to pay with Canadian dollars and the girl, as you said, was petrified. She jumped every time a vehicle drove by and hid behind that boy like he was a bulletproof vest."

"Where did they go?" Jonathon asked.

Victor listened intently, fiddling with the keys in front of him.

Aware that these men were not playing games, she rebutted, "Somewhere... I don't know! They spent the hour hardly talking to one another. When I came in, she had freshly showered, and he was near the table with some tools. They didn't even take the food I offered. He grabbed her and took off."

Jason loudly chuckled, amused. "So, they didn't leave when you went to the washroom? They took off right in front of your eyes and you never stopped them."

Susan bared her teeth at his sharp comment. "I, ummm, I tried my best! I needed to keep them calm, or they would have scattered. The girl seemed disappointed that he was forcing her from here, so they might return tonight..."

Victor despised the unknown, but something piqued his interest. "Does Zack know your name?"

"Yes, the girl asked."

The leader scoffed and shook his head at the ludicrous situation they landed in. "You're an idiot. I can't believe you don't recognize that boy."

"Who is he?"

"We had you try to seduce his brother about two years ago."

Susan squeaked with excitement. "You mean Tomas!" Her heart fluttered at the thought of the young man who had stolen it with his mysterious ways and his handsome looks that flattered him at every angle. "They truly are brothers! Both never succumbed to me."

Eric groaned, "I'm actually surprised Zack doesn't remember you." He rubbed his chin. "Unfortunately for you, Susan, you ain't nothing compared to Cassandra."

"She isn't anything special..." Susan jealously snarled.

Victor banished any retorts from continuing the conversation. "Did they say anything about where they were headed?"

Her hands slipped underneath her breasts, popping them higher for all the men to drool over.

"I overheard them talking about some London Branch... and then something about some form of tech being screwed up."

Five distinct groans and a yelp broke into the lobby; the men knew what the London Branch meant. Victor then pointed out Austin, who clambered to hide in a corner while hunting for the small device supposedly in his pants' pocket.

"Austin," Victor clicked, "did you, by chance, lose that watch of his?"

He stammered, oblivious to the reason behind the missing watch.

"Were you able to shut off the location signal completely?"

Scratching at his head, Austin stated, "I did. I placed a decoy chip that was obvious, but as long as he hasn't found the actual signal disrupter, then he should still be dealing with a piece of shit."

"Ugh, I work with a bunch of buffoons! Now, we will see if they even return here. They may happen upon a police officer, or better yet, Zack may remember your connection with me, and never return."

Susan weakly stuttered out inaudible words before she faced Jonathon's snarling features.

Eric leaned onto the desk in contemplation. "What are the odds that either of these situations play out?"

Jason replied, interested in the nightlife outside the dusty windows, "Actually, both are fairly high. We underestimate Zack, but he's still a smart kid with resources up his sleeve. I could see him figuring out Susan before finding cops, though. This part of town isn't frequented by them. If anything, he may find the London Branch, and then we're screwed."

Victor spun to face his men and the petrified woman in Jonathon's grip. "Susan," he threatened, "come here."

Susan huffed and marched behind the counter.

"How many guests have rented a room for the night?"

"There's one couple that will be here for a couple hours and the brats were only going to stay for a few hours. When I tried to get them to eat, it seemed like they were thinking about staying."

"Very well. That's a good sign. They may return if their quest turns out futile. Besides, they won't have money for anywhere else. We shall stay the night and wait until they arrive. If they don't return after six a.m., we will separate and search every alley and store until we find her."

His men all nodded.

"Good. Now, Susan, which room were they in?"

"Room twelve," she whimpered.

"Can I have a key please?"

Rolling her green eyes, the woman hunkered over to shuffle through the desk's drawer. She had hidden the key in anticipation of the men backing out of the deal before she received her prize. The key was chucked at him, and she was told to sit at the front. Following the orders, Susan grumbled, irritated that they planned to break the deal.

Before leaving her to stew, Victor leaned in close and whispered, "If they don't show up, expect to be punished for this ridiculous excuse for capturing them. However, I do promise to show you a good night. You have riled me up, just like the old days."

Victor marched his snickering group to the worn-down room. Susan shivered and prayed that the two returned soon. If they didn't, every passing hour would only make the punishment more severe.

Moving through the door, the six clambered into the tiny space and gawked.

"No wonder they left... This room is worse than the front entrance," Jonathon jeered.

Victor ordered them to gather around. Tools were scattered about the table, neglected by Zack's speedy exit with their supposed heir. Pointing it out, Austin bent low to examine the pieces Zack had removed. They needed to know the probability of Zack having contacted the FUA.

"It's only the decoy. I don't see the actual disruptor. It shouldn't get them anywhere important. Besides, Zack won't force Cassandra to stay out there all night. There's a good chance she'll convince him to return here."

Victor sank to the bed and folded his arms over his chest.

"Here's what we're going to do..."

●　●　●

Cassy followed closely behind an anxious Zack, who swore whenever the system went fuzzy for a few minutes. As their hunt for the London Branch increased the distance from the inn, the watch became less cooperative, making the map out of sequence and unable to lead them anywhere. Cassy wrapped her arms around her waist, trying to hide the chill caused by the wispy breeze sweeping through her light sweater. Zack's rage fell onto the watch and he began jamming the buttons, trying to fix the damn thing.

They strode through a small park filled with rolling hills and soon-to-be-flower-filled gardens. As Zack gazed at the night sky, trying to figure out what he could do with a malfunctioning piece of equipment, he turned to find Cassy admiring the stars that seemed abnormal in this new country. Zack took in an everlasting picture of her contemplating gaze.

"Cassy, let's stop for tonight. If Victor doesn't find us, we have tomorrow as well."

Breathing in, Cassy asked, "Where should we go?"

"Well, I promised to apologize to Susan, so why don't we go back to that inn? I'll work on the watch a bit more."

She sank into his outreached arms as he neared her shivering torso. His hands stroked her upper arm, relieving the cold from her raised skin.

"I thought you didn't trust her?"

Zack poked her cheek, teasing her. "I don't. We just don't have the funds to go anywhere else; besides, my tools are still there." Kissing her forehead, he added, "You're comfortable there. I want you feeling safe, rather than tossing and turning all night."

Accepting his excuses, Cassy followed his lead. Yet as they strolled through London's narrow streets, they found themselves caught up in hunger. A delicious aroma aroused growling in their stomachs, and before they knew it, they sat inside a small café, wanting a small bowl of soup each to relieve themselves from the spring air. The café was quaint, and it felt like they were on an official date, even if they were still on the run from monsters.

Zack clutched her hand, intertwining his fingers between hers, and embraced the sensation of her smooth palm against his. Cassy sipped the steaming soup, suddenly aware of how frightened she was.

"Zack, how sure is the FUA that I'm this heir?"

Zack scolded, "Stop worrying about it. We're going to find the London Branch, contact Mr. Edwards, and then we're going home." Amidst a thought, he undid his watch and handed it over. "I want you to keep this. This is my promise to you that we will get home. You look at this whenever you feel lost." He tapped the flickering screen. "We will get out of here, Cassy. They're all going to jail. No matter how long it takes, I won't stop hunting for them until I know you're safe."

The screen elevated her emotional turmoil; however, it reflected Zack's solemn features. "But, Zack, if we're caught again, what if I'm not the heir? I'll die… and you'll die! What if Eric told the truth, and they don't plan on letting us walk away?"

"You knowing won't stop your worrying, Cassy." His hand landed on his chest. "I won't let anything bad happen to you, I swear it!"

Zack forbade the sadness welling up from the pit of her chest. He leaned forward and kissed her trembling lips before continuing his soup.

Cassy recognized his unwillingness to lie to her as he hid his knowledge behind her questions. So, instead, she pondered aloud, "How did you get involved in all of this?"

"How do you mean?"

"With the FUA?"

"Well, Tomas was recruited at fourteen because of his martial arts background. The FUA started a recruitment program for underaged agents the previous year, and he was invited to be a guinea pig. Kids make it easier for the FUA to infiltrate certain areas without any questions being asked…"

"Like when an assignment is a teenager going to school."

"Yeah, exactly. Obviously, we report to higher up agents, but the same training is given to any agent, whether they are of age or underaged."

"Tomas must've been pretty amazing to be selected for that."

"He was. He became a Team Lead by sixteen, and was allowed to take on assignments in other countries because of his expertise. His old partner, Mitchell, always says that he'd be in the running for Mr. Edwards' replacement if he were still alive."

"You joined because of Tomas, right?"

"Yeah. I looked up to him so much, and took all the same martial arts programs he did. I wasn't as awarded as him, but I was still on top, and he thought that I'd be great for the FUA. He approached me when I was eleven, and of course I wanted to do the same thing as my brother. I trained hard and eventually became an agent. Tomas even requested me for his field team because he wanted to keep tabs on how I was doing."

"How could you hide it from your mum? Obviously, you're away for long periods of times for assignments, and get called out of school."

"Well, the FUA assists in that. They'll make up excuses for the school and to my mom. They'll fabricate school trips and events so that I can be gone for long periods of time. It's convenient. Mom has never found out, even with both Tomas and I being agents."

Cassy twirled her water glass around. "It must suck having to hide such a big part of your life from her."

Zack shrugged. "The downfalls of the job. I enjoy it and I can't really see myself doing anything else. My life has never been boring."

He hastily finished his soup to avoid any further questions and escorted her from the restaurant. She slipped the watch into her jeans' pocket as they slowly migrated back to the inn. Zack dreaded the night of worried pacing he'd soon commit to. Standing outside the dreary place, Zack sighed, hating that he took his girlfriend back into the disgusting location. The door chimes sang as it shut behind the two.

The woman behind the desk welcomed them back, grinning from ear to ear. Cassy elbowed him directly in the ribs, hurrying his apology. Hesitantly, he approached Susan, who still gleamed whenever she admired him.

"Look," he mumbled, "I'm sorry I was rude earlier."

Zack shot Cassy a look meant to say, *See, happy?*

"It's fine. I was pushy. Don't worry 'bout it."

Appreciating the woman's unperturbed nature, Zack handed over the key he had forgotten to give back and asked if they were able to stay again.

"Sure. Keep the key. You can stay in that room. I noticed you forgot some things when you left."

Tossing the key into his hands, she waved a goodnight to the twosome. Hand in hand, pleased her boyfriend broke down his walls and apologized, Cassy pecked his cheek. In time, she'd make up for causing him to do so. Zack inserted the key and swung the door open wide.

Cassy breathed in sharply at the shadows and stumbled backwards, fumbling to find the parallel doorway to lock herself away. Instead, a soft wall grazed her back. Zack's hand stayed on the door handle, frozen from the shock of finding Victor cockily sitting on the couch's arm facing the two escapees.

Victor bobbed his head once and Zack spun around to assist Cassy at the sound of her shrilled, "Let go!". Jason, Austin, and Buddy enclosed the circle around them. Austin blocked the main entrance, behind which he had been hiding in the first room. Buddy barricaded the exit in the rear of the building, and Jason towered behind Cassy, gripping her waist with both arms. The others prevented Zack's escape.

Zack never fathomed them finding their hideout with such ease. His first instinct was to attack Jason, but Cassy's thrashing torso was in harm's way. Instead, he went up against Austin; if Zack could get rid of him, he would open the main entrance back onto the street. Austin swung back his fist and tried to strike down the agent. It missed. Zack ducked low and tripped the man. Austin slammed his head into the wall, yelping at the pain. Zack hardly had time to regain his balance after his sweeping motion before he took off down the hallway. If he could at least make it out to a public area, the men would be less likely to follow.

Glass crunched beneath his feet. He searched for any of the others who could be nearby. Susan was standing in front of the desk. He calculated her threat level. It was low, as she admired her fingernails with nonchalant care.

Zack hit the main entrance with force, but rebounded off. It was locked with a chain and padlock. Frustrated, he kicked the glass once. It would take too long to try to break through. A jolt of pain smoked him across the temple as something that felt like a wooden baseball bat made contact. Zack heard Cassy's screams in his ringing ears, and then suddenly felt the mildewed ground against his bare skin. His mind was fogged and willing him to drop into unconsciousness. He tried to crawl onto all fours, but a heavy heel landed between his shoulder blades.

"Poor little boy," Susan sang, "you try so hard for that bitch."

Finally, recognition struck Zack. Two years earlier, as he was training, Tomas had informed him of a woman who had helped in a few violent murders with Victor, showing the then thirteen-year-old a picture of her, Tomas warned Zack not to be tricked by a seductive smile. Victor and Susan had planned for her to seduce Tomas, lure him to the inn and murder him in the suite. Tomas was much stricter about relationships than they had anticipated. After that failed attempt, Susan became involved again as she helped murder and conceal the evidence of a supposed heir, as well as assist in Victor's escape.

Zack punched the floor. He should've known better than to stay in an unknown environment, especially when it came to the safety of his assignment. The nagging voice in his head had screamed so loudly, it deafened him. If only he'd listened. He'd apologized to a murderer and Victor's most recent girlfriend. *Dammit! I should've just gone with the plan and let Cassy fume!*

His rage fueled his ability to flip onto his back, grip Susan's thin legs, and toss her to the ground. Zack landed a single punch on her face as punishment for betraying them to a psychopath. He struggled to stand and gripped the wooden broom used to hurt his head.

Buddy and Austin stood nearby. They watched the scene go on as they tried to calculate the most effective route to capture the agent. Zack held his ground. He wouldn't return to that plane without telling someone, anyone. Even if he was dazed, Zack held a weapon now. Keeping a close eye on Buddy and Austin, he turned sideways and used the handle of the broom against the glass door to break it.

Susan swore under her breath about her bloody lip.

"You arse!" she kicked Zack in the hip with a heeled foot. "How dare you hit a woman!"

Zack dropped the broom and slammed against the door when the men standing by acted. Austin jumped over Susan and wrapped his arm around Zack's neck. He choked the boy into submission. Buddy assisted Susan up. She screamed and hollered at the impertinence of the boy. She took off down the hallway angrily going to scrub her face clean before she showed Victor the disgusting swollen lip. In Austin's grip, Zack was towed backwards with no resistance to room number twelve.

The six men cluttered the room with bulk. Cassy remained in Jason's hold while Zack was released and struggled up onto all fours, searching for a solution to this predicament.

"Well, good evening, you two," Victor sneered. "I'm quite glad that you could rejoin us." He then ordered, "Tie them."

Jason clung to Cassy's waist while Jonathon strung a rope around her, and then pinned her wrists together. Jonathon forced her around the wall and toppled her onto one of the beds. Zack hopped up, glowering at Victor, wanting to slice the grin off his lips. Eric rammed into the boy, shoving him forward. Somewhat ready, Zack stuck out a foot and stumbled a few times before regaining his balance. He pinpointed where all the others were and calculated his readiness for the next attack. The circle surrounded him tightly. Jonathon, after demanding Cassy stay on the bed, placed himself behind Zack and swiftly landed him onto his back, then following with landing a knee squarely in Zack's chest. Zack twisted and squirmed to get from underneath Jonathon's mass. Another man snagged his legs to prevent them from kicking wildly and striking any of them.

Victor wearily held him down to control the boy and let two others tie him. Once Zack's thrashing was restrained, the leader landed beside his supposed heir, reclining to brush back her messy hair. Nothing was said, but she briskly leaned away.

Zack's head cracked into a decaying wall after being thrown across the room. Noticing the panic in his girlfriend when Victor caressed her, Zack wrenched at the ropes. Victor's hands snaked up to pop her chin to force her to maintain eye contact with him.

"Stop it," he growled, "don't you dare touch her!"

Victor beamed at Zack's reaction, replying, "But she's mine. I get to do as I wish." His attention shifted to the bloodied agent, who had a cut dribbling down his right temple. "You're a clever boy, *Zackarass*. I never even thought about that crawl space! Make no mistake, I won't underestimate you again. No matter how smart you may be, you are still stupid." Again, his outreached hand touched Cassy's youthful jawline. "You brought the heir to the wrong place. This is a past lover's inn." He widened his arm in welcome and yelled out, "Susan, are you out there? They're tied!"

Cassy squirmed away, trying to stay far from the treacherous woman. A moan demonstrated her misery as Jonathon scooped her up and tied her waist to the headboard.

"You shouldn't run from Victor anymore. He's already pissed at you. You don't want him more so, do ya?"

"As long as he holds me here, he should get used to being pissed off."

Jonathon rolled his eyes in irritation of her attitude. Cassy's bravado was lost when Victor eyed her down without a single word.

As Susan strolled in, her provocative personality engulfed the attention of all the inhabitants. Victor's previous rage had evaporated, allowing Susan to relax around them. Whenever a man randomly came too close, she cringed, showing that her position between them all was a toy, nothing more. If Victor found her necessary, he would keep her for himself. Susan sat across Victor's inviting lap and crossed her sleek legs that were barely covered by the skirt.

Victor clicked his tongue in disappointment at her damaged face. "Oh, Zack, you ruined such a beautiful specimen." He kissed Susan as she shied away from showing her bruising face. He ran his hands down her legs to show that he still found her attractive. "Cassandra, Zack, this is Susan."

Cassy muttered, "We've already met."

"Which I'm quite happy about. We called, and, luckily, we didn't have to look far because you had just walked in," Victor commented.

Jonathon butted in. The murderous woman slipped her succulent lips to her lover's mouth and passionately kissed him. Even with the teenagers found, Victor was unhappy that it had been such a trial. She had to prove herself.

"Since you good-for-nothings ran off, we had to *break* a few things on the plane to have airport security let us stay until we found you. It should be fixed in the morning, so we'll stay for the night." He then turned to his mute companions, who averted their eyes from watching Victor enjoying himself with the British woman. "We'll take an hour shift each, but I think for safety, we should have someone on duty for the entire time."

Eric instantly volunteered. Cassy's eyelids shut as the most detested of them so far went to make himself comfortable on the couch. The matter resolved, Victor lifted Susan off his lap and turned to Cassy. He shifted closer, kissing her forehead.

"Have a good evening, Cassandra. Don't you dare attempt anything else." A hand slid behind her head and he pinched her neck viciously.

Cassy filled with loathing towards the man. The pit of her stomach sank, and her waist twisted to rebel against the men.

Victor planted his feet, escorted Susan with him for their private time, and led the group from the inn's room. Jonathon and Eric lingered behind, double-checking the bonds strapping the teenagers in place. With a displeased grunt, Jonathon noticed the already withering strands that Zack vigorously worked on breaking apart. So, rather than bothering with periodically checking on them, he ruffled through a duffel bag and brought out two sets of handcuffs. Releasing the ropes, his manipulative hands pinned Zack's down until the handcuffs looped around the headboard's center wooden column and clicked into place. Both of Zack's wrists were tightly latched on.

Cassy did not make it easy for Eric to shift her to another position. Her defiant foot clipped him in his privates, dropping him straight to the ground. Wild legs thrashed about as she screamed to be let go during his curses and grimaces towards the untouchable girl. Jonathon took over before Eric could strike the weeping girl on the bed. Instead of untying anything, he snatched her flailing legs and restrained them onto the squeaking bed, making the ropes pinch the skin beneath them. He retightened the cinched waist and left her to wheeze in the upright position.

Shuffling about, Eric rifled through a camping backpack in search of a book to breeze through before he sprawled onto the decaying couch. Admiring the struggling girl, the man presented her with a pompous shake of his head.

"You're lucky that Victor is being nice to you; otherwise, you'd be a bloody mess on the ground. If you were anything other than a teenage girl, he would've punished you for today's events."

She denied him the thrill of a combative response and drifted her thoughts to the small glimmer of a smile on Zack's face, which kept her spirits soaring while stuck in the silence of the smelly inn. The ropes cut into her wrists and waist during her shifts to find a suitable position to sleep in. Eric began a furious race of reading against himself, flipping through multiple pages in record speed. Each crackle of the pages, every mouthed "I love you" from Zack, and the cooling temperature drooped her eyes further after such a daring day. Her final memory before lolling off to an awkward deep sleep was Zack's pensive face. It fluttered her heart with his love.

Eric licked his fingers every five pages. They slammed each page down before the energetic sweeping of his eyes sprang into action. It took quite some time before he lifted his gaze and noticed that Cassy slept soundly. Her head hung against jutting collarbones. She looked so peaceful. After determining the threat level of a sleeping teenager to be low, the kidnapper unknotted the complex knots that he had recently learned to undo and settled her on her back. Eric settled her arms along her sides, impressed with her uncanny ability to entice him. He stroked gently up and down her shoulder. He couldn't wait to have her all to himself.

Zack only needed to scold him for being too forward before the man fell back to the couch as if nothing had occurred. Once Eric surrendered back into his hovel, Zack studied Cassy's delicate features. The way her mouth parted just slightly to allow the air to pass by without much force drove his heart into overdrive. Her tiny hands that could be folded between his fingers clenched often, prohibiting a nightmare from breaking into reality. A temptation to feel her fair skin and the texture of her hair-covered forehead made him tighten his fists with a passive breath. This stupendous sensation relieved all his worries, but the following days would turn traumatic as the men grew closer to Egypt. Soon, the torture would continue until he became a bloodied corpse.

The agent's look shifted as Buddy strolled in, his hands dug deeply into his pockets and his head hung low as he was forced to take on the first watch with Eric. Buddy sank onto the arm of the couch, since Eric stretched right out across it, and admired the sleeping female.

"She's so sweet when she sleeps, huh?" Eric said, gleaming.

Buddy gave a simple nod, redirecting from his stare. "If only my attempt on Thursday hadn't gone so awry. All of this trouble with the damn boy wouldn't have happened."

Eric *tsk*ed at his hastiness. "Yes, well, I think it turned out to be more entertaining. Besides, Victor preferred taking her how we did since we had an easier time escaping the city. The moment one of the brothers realized what happened, an amber alert would've cancelled all flights until a thorough check was complete. This ain't all bad. We get to beat the boy whenever one of them rebels, and once we get to Egypt, Zack will die by our own hands."

"You must really hate him, huh," Buddy commented, "to wish him dead."

"He's been a thorn in our asses ever since he became a primary agent. Jason and I were sent to prison for a year because of him. Getting in Victor's way is a sure-fire way to get yourself killed, but Zack keeps on doing it. He's a good-for-nothing twerp that won't derail us this time." Eric announced, "It's finally time for payback!"

"Yeah, sure, but…"

"Quit defending him. You joined us, now live with the consequences. Zack deserves all the bullshit we throw at him. It's more fun this way. Watching him fight to keep us under control and defend her, it's outright hilarious!"

The book pages crumpled in his fist as he became ecstatic for this round of kidnapping. Buddy raised an eyebrow, bringing Eric to groan. He swung his legs from the low-dwelling couch and massaged his forehead, baffled by the younger man.

"Come on! You really find no thrill in this? No matter how hard he tries, he'll fail. We have her, and obviously, she's the heir. The FUA never protected an assignment to this extent before. No one has witnessed the inside of the FUA unless they are an agent, yet she's allowed to walk right in?"

"You really believe she's the heir?" Buddy asked, intrigued by the notion. "After how many?"

Eric cleared his throat. "Twelve…" He defended, "I'm sick of looking for the heir, though once you're in, you're in. She'd better be it, or no one will be kind when they kill her."

Buddy, full of depression for the girl thrown into this world, sighed. The ending result had someone dying, whether it was two or one.

"Zack is gone this time, mark my words. No one is allowing him to escape again."

• • •

Zack listened to the conversation. He understood the significance of their words. Whichever way it played, Zack would die. If Cassy proved not to be the heir, they would slaughter her and then torture him until his last breath. The savage men wanted her unrelenting rebelliousness to fizzle out, and watching his life drift away would accomplish that. She made a promise to fight, but after his death, would she keep it? Taking an eyeful of his girlfriend, Zack dreaded the curse ensnaring her.

If I attempt to negotiate with Victor, would he rethink being rid of me? Zack chuckled silently, realizing his stupidity. *Cassy, I can't beg for my life. I can't just let a monster kill me while I'm on my hands and knees.* All she hoped for was to view the men as more than soulless humans. Zack saw them as nothing more than evil. At least he could give her a bit of a civil world if he were willing to be peaceful. *Cassy, I won't forgive that man for killing Tomas, and I won't become a snivelling idiot when the time comes, but I can give you the goodness of the world before they rip me from you...*

• • •

Rubbing sleepy eyes and stretching her stiff torso, Cassy awoke in the early morning after a recuperating sleep. She frowned when she noticed that the ropes were scattered on the nightstand, releasing her from their grip. Zack's handcuffed hands were tucked underneath his head while he quietly lied awake.

"Zack..." she froze in mid-sentence as Zack shook his head in urgency to shush her.

Eric was cramped on the couch and wheezily snored; his hands covered his face from the rising sun that slightly brightened the room through the grimy windows. Jason's head leaned back against the couch's armrest near Eric's feet as he slept on the floor in a seated position. His legs crossed over each other and stretched straight out. Neither of them shifted as the teenagers conversed.

"Cassy, you've got to escape while you can. I haven't heard anything for a few hours, so no one should be awake," he whispered.

"What about you?"

He twisted his wrists around, demonstrating how shackled he was. "I can't."

She refused. "They'll kill you if I'm gone."

A crooked smile showed his appreciation towards the girl's determination to rescue the both of them.

"Once I get out, I'll come find you," he promised.

"Don't lie! You won't get out of here!"

Zack tilted back his head. There was no argument about that. Victor would kill him the second his usefulness ended. Cassy kept Zack alive.

"Cassy, I'm begging you! This may be our last chance," he reasoned. "You're our only chance to contact the police, the FUA, somebody... anybody! Once we're back on that plane, we're stuck!" He pointed where she hid the FUA technology. "You use that watch to save us, Cassy. Go... please!"

His eyes glistened with desperation. Even if she reached the police quickly, Zack would disappear, along with the men. The hard decision solidified her in place longer than Zack could handle. Urgently, he pointed towards the doorway.

"Do you remember the neighbourhood we were in yesterday? Go back there and just start banging on any warehouses. I think that should be the area. Ask anyone near you about the FUA."

She choked back a whimper. She had to go. With a small kiss, she dodged between the beds, sidestepped over Jason's guarding limbs, and headed into the hallway. Her feet tiptoed on the moaning ground, cautious between the quiet rooms in which the men slumbered. Many were cracked open and pitch black from the curtains that shielded the sun's rays. Nearer the front desk, Cassy slithered along the wall, unsure of whether Susan sat at the ready to sound the alarm.

A gasp lodged deep in her chest as a person cleared their rasping throat. It seemed too deep for the high-pitched woman. She peered around the corner. She exhaled in misery.

Victor reclined on the wooden chair, swaying it back and forth on its back two legs. His shoed feet were planted on the desk. A song sprang from him, the beat hummed as he tapped the table in absolute boredom.

Cassy sank down the wall and curled her trembling legs into her chest to reduce the quick thumps of her racing heart. Somehow her path would have to lead by Victor and out the door without him catching her. *Well,* she thought, searching for options. The back entrance was chained up and sealed with an industrial lock. Without the key, exiting there was unmanageable. *I could crawl. I'll get to the door and dash as fast as possible.* Determined to attempt this plan, she moved onto her hands and knees, crawled by the short door which separated the desk space from the lobby, and then took a moment to check how fast she needed to move from the front of the desk.

As she set her hands down on the carpet, a yelp almost exposed her. A stinging shot up both arms. In awe, she investigated the rotten luck she had. She'd left a trail of bloody handprints along the floor. It stained the brown, once beige, carpet with crimson red. Overlooked shards of glass clung snugly beneath her skin as small trickles of her blood smeared her palms.

"That must hurt," a suave voice boomed from above.

Cassy shivered as black shoes rounded the desk to tower over her. Before she even fled the building, her ill-conceived plan failed. Victor joyfully squatted between her and the entrance, took both of Cassy's hands, and yanked a clean handkerchief from a pant pocket. Picking at a few exposed pieces of glass, Victor could only chuckle at her feeble attempts while ripping the white cloth apart.

As he tied one half of the cloth to her stained left hand, he kindly stated, "You just won't learn, will you?" Cassy groaned. The leader tightened it beyond measure and painfully patted the uncovered right hand. "I'm glad I stayed up once I finished with Susan. So far, it's been an eventful morning. The pilot just called ten minutes ago and said that by seven the plane issues will be fixed. Austin sure is a master of destruction. I was just about to awaken the bears so we could prepare to leave, and I noticed these small, fresh handprints exposing an escapee."

The man's voice was layered with a soothing tone. It lulled Cassy into a state of utter misperception. He was gently stroking her palms with the tip of two fingers and held her hand steady from beneath with his other hand. She shook her head before she became too caught up in the daze and removed her hands from him. He could act tender, but she saw that it was all just that... an act.

Defiantly, Cassy muttered, "Don't touch me. No matter how you treat me, we both know you're a greedy man who only wants me compliant."

He shifted, landing his elbows on his knees in the squatted position, and then rubbed his chin. His patronising nature made a faux shocked expression. His head tilting as though curious, Victor mystically said, "On the plane I was thinking..." he chuckled.

Confused about this odd statement, Cassy thought back to when he touched her cheek.

"I thought about how close we were to getting those diamonds, but my main thought was that it's nice to have a girl around. I'm always around men. You help break up the testosterone, and your uncanny ability to rock the boat has definitely piqued our interest."

Piercing her lips, Cassy was disgusted in how he stated this without even a wince of repulsion. "Why can't you take Susan with you instead of me, and enjoy her *company?*" Cassy snarled within, *All the men doted and fawned over Susan, and she would have been willing to enjoy all of them had she gotten the chance last night.*

"Oh, we had to 'be rid' of her. After I was finished with her last night, she overheard Eric and Jason talking about the diamonds. Guess what she did? She demanded that she get one of *our* diamonds since she had helped more than once in the process. I couldn't have that. You're too much as it is. Having another bitch around would give me an aneurism. Jonathon is disposing of the body as we speak."

Cassy's back pressed tightly against the hard, wooden desk. He lavished in ridiculing his murdered girlfriend.

"You bastard! You killed her!" Her hands flung out and shoved his shoulders. "Stay away from me!"

Regaining his balance after almost toppling over, Victor slammed both of her hands above her head as punishment. A squeal produced an odd fondness to her in Victor, and he exhaled the anger before leaning forward.

"Acting ruthlessly will cause you to be injured, Cassandra. Be careful, because when Zack's not around, punishments will land upon you." Victor snaked a hand up to her face and pulled strands of hair that had fallen from the ponytail behind her ear. "I watched you sleep last night. You're like an angel when you dream. You don't talk back!" he snapped. His thumb landed beneath her eye. "Finally, I get to see those hazel eyes up close. They are so dazzling. I see why Eric kept that picture Buddy took; he was admiring them."

Cassy turned away to face the far wall.

"Come. Let's get back to Zack." He stood and extended a hand to hers. "You'll be safer with Zackary and *us*." His hand landed on top of her head and patted her messy hair; her aching heart only felt her father's hand land atop of her. "It will be over soon, Cassandra."

Cassy's naivety saw him as trying to be good willed, but her subconscious screamed out that he used her innocent, child-like mind to play malicious games with her. Cassy became hypnotized by Victor's ever-growing considerate gestures. Did she really want to leave the inn without knowing what type of world she might step into? Staying with this man who proved difficult to fathom meant staying with Zack as well. Victor's gesture had set her mind to genuinely believing the man's intentions were to free her in the end. Everything would turn out.

Chapter 12

Victor re-extended his hand to Cassy, and she took hold of it, lifting herself from the stinky ground. His other hand fell on the small of her back as she headed down the hallway. He escorted her calmly by applying a bit of pressure on her spine. Cassy liked the feeling of his palm's soft touch; it caused a flutter of safety while with him.

They arrived at room twelve. Cassy slammed on her brakes before it swung wide. Her head spun with indecision as she considered, *Why am I following him? Why do I trust him as though he were Zack, or my brothers? He took me away from my home... There's no way he's going to let Zack walk. I blew it! I needed to escape so I could save Zack!*

Common sense appeared swiftly. This horrendous man, full of greed and anger, was trying to befriend her after committing threats and years of murder. She wouldn't tolerate his manipulative ways when he wanted to kill the only sane part of her life.

She hollered, "You lying asshole!"

Her feet planted into action, sending her in the opposite way of the man, but a quick response snatched her shirt. He swung her to face him. The faux smile dripped away to leave behind a cold and furious man that held her captive.

"Let me go!" She swung ineffective fists towards his chest. "I'm not at all safe with you!"

Victor choked her with his arm and pinned her into his swelled chest. "You should learn quickly that I am not someone to test."

"You are nothing but a monster!"

"If you wish to stay unlocked from a dark room, you will learn to respect me. You will be learning all about me for the rest of your life, so you'd better become pleasant quickly, for your sake, or you will see the real monster."

Cassy shrieked, denying the implications of his words. "You said I would be free once I walked into the tomb!"

His hand snuck beneath her chin. It forced her to view the sneer that replaced his frustration.

"Your boyfriend has informed me of something that I never even considered. He has condemned you to a life of prison."

Her chin wobbled. "What do you mean?"

His lips pressed tightly onto her forehead before he said, "If you are proven to be the heir, you are the only one gifted to control the diamonds."

"No... you're lying..."

"Oh no, I would not lie about this. You are no longer going to be free, Cassandra, until the day you die. I own your life!"

Jason burst through a room offset to the one Victor and Cassy fought near. Subtle panic filled him when he realized that his boss caught the girl who had been gone when he rose. Apologizing for falling asleep, Jason brushed back his hair, unsure of what Victor's temperament was like this early in the morning. Sending Jason to the front to watch for anyone who tried to enter, Victor propelled the crying girl into the aged room.

Eric had awoken. He straddled Zack's torso, and throttled a gun in his throat. Eric jerked the agent's hair back as he screamed commands to uncover Cassy's whereabouts. The gun butt met with Zack's jaw and left a gaping wound.

"Put that *filthy* thing away!" Victor blared. "I have her! The brat tried to escape *again*!"

Victor propelled Cassy at the other man, who rebounded quickly off the bed to ramble apologies before catching her in a death grip. Instead of punishing the men who had neglected their duties by falling asleep, Victor stormed up to Zack and solidly punched him across the jaw as penance for promoting another escape.

"Tie them. I'll send Jason to help you. We are leaving straight away."

Zack sucked back the pain. His lower jaw shifted back and forth only to hide how distraught he was with seeing Cassy being towed around by

Eric. Eric struck her across the face, and when she landed on the ground, stunned by the smack, a foot contacted her stomach, causing her to curl into a ball. All she could think of, over the pain, was the revelation Victor had exposed.

"Zack," she choked, "is it true?"

Zack's cries for Eric to stop hurting her ended. "What?"

"Is the heir really the only one capable of using the diamonds? Am I going to be stuck with these men forever?"

Eric raised her from the ground and stroked her neck, his excitement subtly rising. "You truly thought we'd release you once we got you to the tomb, didn't you?"

She applied a harsh tone. "Zack, is it true?"

"Yes… If you make it to Egypt, then one way or the other, Victor won't let either of us walk away."

Adrenalin shot from her toes up to her chest, pouring into an unbreakable abyss in the pit of her stomach. Cassy's head swung back and clipped Eric's nose. She broke free of him. Eric's red blood dripped all over while she shoved him down and then rushed over to Zack's handcuffed arms.

"I just want to go home!" she shrilled.

Zack struggled to maintain his grip on the girl sprawled across his chest. Her quivering shoulders heaved up and down throughout each laboured breath she made.

"Calm down, Cassy. It's going to be alright."

"I failed, Zack!" she bawled. "I should've escaped sooner… I shouldn't have left the FUA… I should've never trusted any of these bastards! They only lie and cheat their way to what they want. Please," she crumpled his shirt, "tell me what I should do. I'm so scared."

Crimson fingers ripped her from the agent's consoling figure and tossed her to the rotting carpet. Eric's silver gun pressed snuggly against her throat as his profusely bleeding nose made his eyes weep. A yelp broke free as Cassy realized her mistake in hurting this man.

Zack grappled with the handcuffs, now fighting for the life of his dear assignment before an irreversible doom befell her. His arms tugged at the cuffs, rubbing the skin raw. With a last-ditch effort, he yanked once more so that the wooden column attached to the headboard splintered and he broke free from his imprisonment. Jumping from the bed, Zack tackled Eric's threatening torso and removed him from Cassy's sight.

Eric and Zack skirmished for the weapon, rolling around on the floor in a raging battle to defeat the other. If Eric permitted the gun to leave his palm, the agent received an advantage against all but Victor. As they swapped positions from top to bottom, Cassy cowered in a corner to avoid getting caught in the crossfire.

Jason lost his strut at the sight of the grappling twosome and the screaming girl. Blood and limbs flung everywhere as the gun was gripped by a hand of each and their other hands punched wildly. With no end in sight, Jason decided to create one. He dashed to the girl, grabbed her, and held a knife to her throat, hollering at the two males to stop this ridiculous behaviour and to release the gun completely. Cassy exposed her neck and inched from the blade held steady beneath her chin.

"Yo! Both of you, enough!" Jason demanded. "Exacil, if you don't want her bleeding on the floor, you'll let go of that gun now."

Beneath Eric's weight, Zack grimaced at the position he landed Cassy in. Both of his hands rose, admitting defeat, and then his head met the ground as he received a punch across the temple. Cassy told them to stop hurting him in shrilled shouts.

"Cassy," he mumbled, "it's alright. I'm fine."

Cassy's struggle against Jason lessened, and then ceased altogether once she determined no amount of fighting would protect them. Eric stood straight and wiped the drying blood from his nose before he checked that his eyelid wasn't going to swell from Zack's vicious punches. Zack sat up and rubbed his head to diffuse the throbbing, but any motions to pick himself completely off the floor were ended. Eric retaliated again by swinging back the gun's butt and striking him behind the head. Zack collapsed. His movements ceased as he slipped into an unconscious state.

Eric retorted towards Cassy, "Now, it's your turn, you bitch."

Jason swore beneath his breath. Instantly, he advanced in front of the supposed heir.

"Calm the hell down, Eric!" He leaned into his partner, snatched the gun, and wrenched the man's sight onto his serious face. "You're threatening to kill the kid who's going to make you rich!" he coaxed.

"Look at my nose! She deserves the same punishment."

"Shit! She did that!" Jason flicked Eric's nose.

The wounded man winced and whined before being smacked by his partner.

"Tie up the boy." He nudged Zack's torso. "Jeez, Victor's not going to be impressed with the boy being knocked out..." The ropes from the previous evening were snatched and brought close to Cassy. "I guess we'll have to tie you as well."

Jason mocked Eric's simplistic aggression just because he was hit once. He tugged the black ropes tight. His comrade took out all his rage on the defenceless agent and tied the ropes snug enough to leave behind red and purple skin.

Jason, the calmer of the two men groaned, "You stupid brat... It's too early for this shit."

"He started it!" Cassy defended. "He threatened me with the gun."

Jason picked up Cassy by her arms, bound in the front, and raised them above her head. She dangled in midair while he used his strength to shake her about. Her shoulders rolled in an awkward direction as she protested in agony.

"No, that's the wrong answer. You started it by trying to run away again. If only you'd learned from the first time."

Her legs toppled beneath her as he dropped her from the air. Jason grumbled and went to check on his partner. Cassy heaved air out of her sore lungs. Her ribs were severely bruised, if not broken. She directed a swift glance to Zack's unconscious body. He didn't move at all, and his breath was shallow. She wormed toward him and nudged him gently. *Zack, wake up...* Her bound hands shuffled his head towards her knees. She softly sniffled while Eric and Jason disappeared into the bathroom to clean their blood.

Victor rounded the room's doorframe, seeming much less abrasive, and announced that the men should gather their things to leave as early as possible. Both his manicured brows rose as he rounded to find the teenagers on the floor, one unresponsive.

"Which one of you did this?"

Jason popped his head out of the washroom, rolling his eyes to condemn Eric. The boss crossed his arms. This was hardly an issue, so instead of picking a fight, he shifted away, demanding that they hurry in gathering their equipment. Buddy dashed around in the hallway, double-checking his jobs before he heard the barked order to enter the teenagers' room.

"You stay here," Victor commanded Buddy. "You two, follow me."

The three left Buddy alone to listen to Cassy's weeping. He clambered in and sat on the springless couch. Cassy, edgy about a traitor being near her, stroked Zack's hair back. She pleaded for him to wake up. It seemed hard to fathom that this would always be her reality: trapped with kidnappers and abused by them.

Buddy invested interest in her grumbles.

"You're such a troublesome kid."

"Screw off," she snapped.

Relentlessly, he bulldozed on. He forced small talk while he awaited new orders. "When I first met your brothers, they told me about your previous suspensions while living in Edmonton..."

Cassy recognized the shift in Buddy's behaviour instantly. He was not the sadistic man who kidnapped her, but her counsellor who helped break through her bubble.

"Yeah... when Michael moved, I was devastated to the point of rebelling. I put cherry bombs into desks, broke into the school after hours to steal things, and pulled the fire alarm once or twice."

"Did you get caught?"

"Of course I did. I turned myself in," replied Cassy.

Buddy played with the springs and mocked, "Why turn yourself in?"

She shrugged. "I felt guilty..." Staring at the young man, she asked, "Buddy, I've always wondered, how old are you?"

"Twenty-two."

Cassy laughed at herself. "That should've given us a hint about your lies."

Buddy stroked back his sporadic blonde hair, unsure how to comment about that accusation. "When I told Michael, he was really shocked..."

"I always assumed you were older, turns out you're the same age as Michael." Cassy brushed Zack's hair less frequently while she talked with the man. "What's your real name?"

A chuckle escaped. "Actually, Buddy is my real name. I was honest with you the entire time we saw one another. I told you about my own personal life whenever you asked because that was the easiest way to sound sincere. Well, okay, that's not a hundred percent true. Mostly everything was true except anything revolving around Victor." He leaned forward, touching her slumped shoulders. "How do you think Michael reacted when he found out about your disappearance?"

"He's probably doing all that he can to find me. The FUA *will* rescue us, and I'll see my big brothers again." The darkness of her rolling glare beset upon Buddy's dripping sneer. "I won't let you bastards get the best of me again."

• • •

Mr. Edwards slammed a wrinkled fist against the sturdy conference table. A female agent, dressed in a police uniform, clenched a notebook near the doorway to announce another foiled attempt to find the abducted teenagers.

"Those abductors have found a way to prevent us from finding them." Sinking into a chair, Mr. Edwards admired the strict blonde woman who kept herself prim and proper. "How has the Waters family been?"

"They are dealing as every family has during these types of circumstances. Michael has taken a leave from work and submitted forms to be excused from classes. He's heading his own amber alert. I must admit, he's impressive. He's gone beyond any family I've ever encountered. He approached all the news stations in the city to send out an alert across the country and has been scouring the internet to see if she's escaped and alerted any police. That family is holding strong, but..." she slicked back the sleek hair curled into a bun, "I believe that's all a front. The youngest brother, Vince, has started to drink heavily, and Brant has engrossed himself in solitude. He won't leave for anything, unless Michael asks for his help. Michael has admitted that he's walked into her room every day, hoping that she'll be smiling at them again, and yet, even before he rounds the entrance, the walls crumble, and he finds himself staring at the empty bedroom."

Mr. Edwards clicked his tongue to hold back a mournful sigh. The family displayed enough sorrow to last them a lifetime. This worsened their predicament.

"Sir, can I please have your blessing to tell them of us? We could prove how we are contributing and... They are desperate for answers... they don't get why they were the targeted family."

"No. I don't want to bring them in when all that will do is bring pressure on us. We will find them."

"You better hold to that, Mr. Edwards. I wish not to be the barer of bad news."

He inclined his head. "I will not make you. What of Arlene Exacil?"

The agent halted in mid step, intending to leave before having to explain the mother's predicament.

"She's lost her entire family. How do you think she's handling it?" she snapped. "When I called to inform her of their kidnapping, she could hardly control the hysterical crying. After Tomas and her husband, she can't handle the loss of her beloved son. She doesn't even know that Tomas died because of these men. You know how I know that?" she bristled. "I'm the one who had to file the report of him dying in a car accident!" The agent gritted her teeth to hold back the wounds left by the FUA's inability to rescue innocent lives. "She couldn't even have an open casket on her firstborn's funeral. Zack was the only reason she fought so hard as a lawyer to put criminals into jail! He's vanished and now she's all alone."

Mr. Edwards strode across the room and embraced the middle-aged agent who sourly disheartened his attempts to fix the mistakes done long ago. She accepted the hug before scurrying away to wipe her reddened eyes and to head out to speak with the families again to announce that still no news had come.

The FUA boss sank back down, looking through all the records gathered inside the warehouse. They had found plans about their travels, but without sightings of the men anywhere, he was trapped in his jurisdiction. Their saving grace was that the Egyptian FUA Branch was tracking the tomb in anticipation of the group's arrival.

A knock jolted his attention towards the door where a scrawny communications agent nervously held a piece of paper. It shook as it was handed over to the gently aged man.

"Sir, I just spoke to Mr. Ebni from the Egyptian Branch. We may have a bit of an issue."

"How so?"

"He's taking his agents off of the recon."

Mr. Edwards frowned, startled to hear that. "We have another forty-eight hours before they can make that call."

"According to him, the Board commanded him to do it, saying that protocol has been neglected and that you weren't supposed to involve another agency until sightings had provided evidence of such action."

"Get me a phone... I wish to speak to Tiy."

The agent said, "He assumed you might want to, so he sent this." He pointed to the folded piece of paper.

In accordance with the FUA Board's procedures, I have removed my undercover agents from the assignment of gaining intel on the kidnapping of the potential Egyptian Heir and Agent Zackary Exacil. My condolences to the families involved and my deepest regrets for this course of action.

Agent Tiy Ebni
Egypt Federal Undercover Agency Head

"Dammit!" he swore. "So, the Board is really corrupting this entire assignment to figure out her position as the heir..."

"Sir?" the agent wondered while Mr. Edwards muttered to himself.

"Never mind. I want my most trusted agents on this and searching for any sightings by any means possible."

"We only have a few. Would you like to lead this investigation, or should I appoint one from the Rescue team?"

"I want Agent Rognas on the lead. Choose three others for this that are trained in dealing with hostage situations."

The agent acknowledged his orders and hurried off in search of the four chosen agents being offered an opportunity to rescue a comrade. Mr. Edwards leaned back, frustrated with the miserable circumstances.

•   •   •

Back on the dreaded plane, Zack paced about. The chains were unnecessary now, since Victor and Jonathon had spent the early morning barring the crawl space and the windows. Once they returned to the inn, Susan had outright demanded for a diamond, or she would expose them. Victor took the threat as an assault and silenced her once and for all. The opportunity to escape was lost when Cassy was caught without an effort.

Cassy leaned against the wall on the floor, studying Zack. He awoke hours after returning to the plane. She spent the time cleaning the dried blood from his forehead once she was unbound. Buddy's conversation with her had raised some hope that a couple of the men might hold a bit of empathy, but it was dashed when halfway through her cleaning of Zack's neck, Jonathon stormed into the plane's backroom to beat the unconscious boy with his foot. She attempted to stop the aggression, but was locked away inside the washroom for the five minutes the beating happened. It was punishment for trying to run, and the muscled man was delighted to exact the sentence. Afterwards, with her hair falling in front of her blurred vision, she rose Zack to the bed and cleaned him to the best of her ability. Reminding herself that she had caused the beating by trying to run, she tried to remain as good as possible while he was knocked out.

When he first regained consciousness, Zack shifted his stiff, bruised arms about, causing a groan to escape his bobbing throat. Then, he rose his head as high as possible, to only slam it down again when he realized where they were. Cassy petted his thick hair, kissed his cheek, and fussed about. Quickly, he nipped it in the bud, sat up, and hugged her close before beginning his pacing to loosen up his sore limbs.

"Where's your dad?" she finally queried.

Zack stopped pacing, a pained expression sketched all over his wounded face.

"He died six years ago. He was in the military as a sniper. A mission went haywire, and he was shot as a result."

"Oh, Zack, I'm sorry. I didn't mean to bring that up."

"No worries. Sooner or later, it had to come up."

Cassy nibbled on a red lip. She began to tear up as it became clear Zack's fragile life was quickly growing shorter and shorter with every minute they travelled. Surveying him carefully, she engrained every thing she loved about him in her mind.

"Zack, it's all true, isn't it? They're going to kill you..."

Zack sighed. Over the course of the trip, he'd heard them talking about the ways they planned to kill him. The worst idea was strangulation. They would pin Cassy nearby and make her watch the life be sucked from him. Stroking back his crusted hair covered in dried blood, Zack sank next to her. Cassy's dazzling eyes settled on his to beg for him to lie just to calm her down.

"Yes, they are."

He turned away with shame for having to answer truthfully.

Cassy curled her short, lean legs, clothed in now-dirty jeans, tighter against her chest. Feeling that all that she worried about may come true, she thought, *I'll be all alone... beat and used.* Unable to accept the fate, she honestly prayed not to be the heir.

"Zack, this isn't fair! Why can't they keep you alive?" she whispered. "I wish I could die with you! I hate being this supposed heir! Why can't I just be a normal teenager? I'd rather die than spend the rest of my life trapped with these monsters!"

Zack shook her. His fingers burrowed deep into her shoulders, enraged with her words. He asserted, "Don't you dare think that garbage! You should be proud of who you are! Your grandfather was goddamn proud of you! One day, you'll see that the diamonds can be used for decent things, not just corrupt ideas that these men might have."

Her head was tugged snuggly into his shoulder. He placed his chin on top of her mahogany hair.

"The moment I walk into that tomb, my life will be determined, Zack. Either way it happens, they're going to murder you in front of me and then abuse me whenever they feel like it until I die."

"Yes... unfortunately," he muttered in an undertone.

A resolve fixated Cassy towards the dark pit in his chest. "Zack... I'm going to find a way to rescue you. We're going to get out of here. I won't let them take advantage of me. I'll fight them until we get home... All those lies Victor told me... he has no right to those diamonds. Whether I'm the heir or not, I'll fight those bastards!"

"That'll be a tough promise, Cassy, but never forget that you promised me that." He played with her hair. "Mr. Edwards will find you. You're definitely going to return to your family."

Cassy ripped from his grip, snarling, "They're going to make it in time to save you too... I'm going to find a..."

"Cassy," he bluntly interrupted, "this is no fairy tale where everything goes well for everyone good, and evil is defeated. More than likely, I'm not going to be around much longer. You will have to fight to survive against them."

"Don't say things like that! You told me to have faith in Mr. Edwards and the FUA. They're going to rescue *us!*"

The door unlocked to intrude on their heated argument and expose the leader and Jason stomping inside. Victor fixed his steely gaze upon Cassy, but Zack dissuaded any brash actions when he protectively stood up. Victor shoved him away and knelt beside Cassy, pulling out his trusted pistol. The metal caught rays of the sun and as Victor put it up to her eyes, demonstrating its threat was real. Cassy squirmed to resist listening to any manipulative words about to slither out. Instead of settling upon Cassy's temple or neck, Victor pointed the barrel towards Zack, who stood erect with Jason sticking a knife towards his stomach. Cassy settled underneath Victor's shadow and shivered in expectation of his threat.

"You can fight all you want but, understand that will surely lessen Zack's days." Double-checking that Jason kept Zack under control, Victor took hold of Cassy's neck and pinned her to the ground. "Let's clear some things up because I'm sick of your bellyaching. We own you now. You will do as we wish." He smacked her with half strength using the gun butt. She wheezed beneath his clutch. "You understand? Stop talking about going home or being rescued because you'll never leave us. Forget about your old life. It's time that you accept this and move on."

Zack stayed where he was pinned behind Jason's barricade, but he rebutted, "Victor! That's enough! You'll kill her."

Victor quickly released when he realized he potentially could do just that as her skin had started to turn blue. Cassy choked back a cough. Crawling from his reach, she rubbed her sore throat.

"You're full of bullshit! You come in here just to threaten me and Zack while, just as you said, *you* have the power over *us* for the time being. However," she straightened herself and tried to become courageous, "I won't do anything to help you and your bastard lapdogs! I have every right to talk about going home and I always will. My brothers are searching for me, I know that! You just hate that my family would do anything to find me because that will always give me hope, even when trapped with you. I can hold onto something to keep me strong, no matter what you do to me." A fist balled up when she boldly stated, "If I am the heir, I'm the only one who can control the diamonds, so if I want to, all I'd have to do is refuse whatever you want, and I'll win. You don't own a goddamn thing!"

Victor ripped back her hair when she struck that nerve. Slipping away the gun, he extracted a knife. Her head yanked back to expose her bare throat. The silver blade brushed against smooth skin.

Zack reacted swiftly to remove the blade threatening himself and rescue his girlfriend. His hand popped the weapon out from Jason's grip and then held it at the ready to slice open the man's neck after he got the upper hand and pinned Jason into a corner. Victor showed no dismay at his comrade being threatened and pressed his knife tighter onto Cassy's neck.

"Lower it, boy."

No more words were expressed; Victor obviously cared little for an idiot of a man. Zack carried nothing more than a toothpick in the eyes of the leader. Victor went on speaking with Cassy as though nothing happened.

"Are you prepared to make us angry enough to kill you? You're leading to this possibility."

Zack lowered his guard. Cassy's life, other than the fact that she may be the heir, was useless in Victor's eyes. Annoying him would bring about her death whether she was the heir or not. With his guard dropped, Jason struck Zack directly in the throat with an open-handed jab, dropping him straight to his knees to wheeze. Three kicks hit Zack in the stomach, and he ended up on his side, clutching his stomach and unable to help Cassy.

"KILL ME!" she hollered. "I'd rather die than be trapped with you! If I'm dead, nobody will ever get their greedy fingers on those diamonds!"

The knife slipped lightly across her skin steadily, to not cut her. Wearily feeling Victor's temptation to teach her a lesson about defying him, Cassy gulped down a solemn lump.

"I *could* slit your throat right now, but you're no good to me dead." He sneered, "This way, I can torture you for as long as I'd like. I could slice open your skin to make sure that the heir actually does bleed, or, my favorite, lock you up, gag you, strap you up, and leave you until your cries drift into the winds of nobody-gives-a-shit." The blade slipped away. "Now, no more talk of heading home or refusing us the diamonds. I already told you, to make this trip pleasant and have Zack survive, I'm going to expect you to remain obedient. Just a few more days and then we will know if we wasted our time on you."

Cassy's head bobbed from fear, and she found no response to lessen her welling tears.

"Now, enjoy your lunch."

He hopped up and beckoned Austin inside to set two bowls of salad and water on the floor. Victor checked over the boy and grabbed the second bowl of salad.

"I don't think the boy deserves to eat today." Nudging Zack with a foot, he rolled his hands to move everyone out. "Cassandra needs to eat in peace."

Cassy scrambled up, swearing and stomping around in the prison. Falling into complete helplessness, she slammed her knuckles against the floor, hurting them.

Just let us out of this hell!

The girl disregarded the bastards who interrupted their solitude and put all her efforts on Zack. Crawling over to him, she helped to flip him over and opened his wheezing airway. His head lay on her knee, and she began to stroke his hair and caress his cheeks with her thumbs. Zack closed his eyes, enthralled by her touch.

She flashed the food a dirty glare. If she wished to die, she had to do it herself because they weren't going to murder her. Zack moved sourly, distracting her from her thoughts.

"Zack, are you alright?"

"Yeah," he choked, "I think so. Nothing's broken yet."

"Are you hungry?"

"What about you?" He eyed the singular bowl of salad. "You should keep up your strength, otherwise, you might..." He said "Oh" as she averted her eyes to the ceiling.

"I'm not hungry. Go ahead."

He boosted himself and ate the salad but handed Cassy the water.

"You can't last long without water."

Awhile after lunch, they shifted into refreshing past times. Cassy even smiled for the first time in three days after Zack told a joke. The rest of the afternoon went by smoothly. Zack clutched her waist as she rested on his shoulder, and he played with her hair until she slept from watching the pink hue of the setting sun. He sadly grimaced. Cassy starved herself to avoid an eternity of confinement. He brought her closer, resting his chin on her head.

Chapter 13

Cassy rose early the next morning to find herself lying with her eyes closed, but not on the hard floor. Instead, a soft plush bed supported her aching torso. The quilt uncovered her head as she popped out to look around. Zack churned and twisted with nightmares creasing his brow in a parallel bed. The room was different from the plane's dark décor. Around them, a large balcony window glistened in the overcast skies' moon. Cassy snuck from bed and shook Zack's built upper arm until he opened his red eyes from a disturbed slumber.

"We're not on the plane anymore!"

"Didn't you know?" he questioned in surprise. "They decided that the pilot should rest up, so they've been carrying us to a hotel and back again. I thought you would've woken up with all their grunts this time."

"How many times have they done this?"

"Um, four. Twice before you woke up those first two nights, and two since then." He suddenly looked around. "Wait a sec. Is Jonathon asleep?" He stared over at the snoring man. "Shit, you're lucky! Last time I got up, he tied me to the bed until they carried us out in the morning."

Cassy scurried over to the man who was crammed on a small hideaway bed. Waving her hands in front of him, Jonathon didn't flinch. Relieved that this savage man wouldn't harm her while she strode about, Cassy headed back to kiss Zack's blackened face.

"How much longer will they travel?"

"Well, we've been flying for six days, give or take. So, depending on how long they want to take and how many more destinations they have on their itinerary, it could take upwards from three days to another week.

Don't become anxious about getting there. It's better for us to take as long as they'd like." He rolled over to permit her to lie beside him. "Come and sleep before you get into trouble."

Denying his offer of a nice cuddle, Cassy instead ripped the blankets off the bed and sat on the floor near the balcony entrance. She wasn't tired enough for sleep, and the rolling in storm charmed her. Lightening streaked the black skies with dazzling zigzags of unpredictable excitement and static while heavy drops of rain splattered the tarmac beneath them and the window with its wetness.

Zack lied awake as long as possible, trying to enjoy Cassy admiring the skies. He soon soundly slept. Finally, she gave him the comfort to lessen his guard over her and think of himself for a while.

Cassy pressed her forehead on the cool windowpane. The rain droplets reverberated the glass and sent chills down her spine. All she could do was imagine when her family once sat around a fire in their cabin in the mountains of British Columbia. It had rained heavily, and the thunder rolled, scaring Cassy and Vince, and driving them to huddle into their parents. Michael told scary stories. He held a flashlight to his face causing a gloomy aura to surround him. Their parents laughed aloud when the youngest three shrieked at the ending punch line as their wild imaginations formed the beastly monsters from the stories. It was a peaceful time. A simple time. Nothing harmed their small family.

Cassy bashed her head against the glass. Jonathon's snoring reminded her of her reality. His bulk tensed whenever he gave a slight shift. At any point he would rise, and the man's threatening persona would return. *This is my life now...*

• • •

Cassy jumped on the hard ground when a grunt signalled that Jonathon found her. His burly fingers wrenched her up. Zack was nowhere to be seen, which petrified her. She turned in Jonathon's grip to find Victor already in the doorway and Jason sitting on her bed. Victor strolled towards her, wishing her a half-hearted good morning. The ex-military man traded her off before storming out. He was annoyed for the early awakening. The panic of losing the innocently sleeping girl, who had slept every evening during the first nights without movement, had Jonathon in a frenzy. Now, Cassy seemed to find herself in a predicament of waking up early each morning.

She released Victor's death grip from her shoulder. With a sweep of the hotel room, she found no logical reason for her stoic hero to be missing.

"What have you done to Zack?"

"Nothing. He has been sent to the plane with Eric to prepare for our flight. Jonathon is damn lucky you never fled. I'm assuming you and the boy spoke while that lousy oaf slept. I wanted the two of you separated to shut you up."

"Then what are you doing here? Shouldn't you also be preparing the plane so you can continue this shit?"

"Don't get smart." He growled, "The jackass pilot doesn't think it's safe to fly in the middle of a storm, but it's just a small thing, nothing worrisome."

Glancing towards her sleeping spot from moments before, she found beautiful bolts of lightening through the grey sky with sad clouds and thunder rumbling. The storm pleasantly gave them some leniency. Overjoyed, she hugged her arms across her stomach.

"It's still raining! I guess we can't go anywhere."

"Keep dreaming, kid. I will make that damn pilot fly, or he'll have a price to pay." Then, he broke off to think. "Does Zack know how to fly a plane?" Victor struck his own head at the humorous joke. "That won't work at all... he'll just take us back to Canada."

"You know," Cassy inserted, "if you just let us go, this wouldn't be such a hassle."

"Shut up. We're going to the plane now, my sweet treasure. Jason," he barked, "go help Austin and Buddy convince that pilot to take off. The rest will wait on the plane."

Cassy disliked what he called her. "Now I'm treasure?"

"Of course, you're a rare artifact. You were once hidden, but now that I found you, I get to harbor you all to myself."

Her hazel eyes rolled. The hatred towards him grew every day they spent together.

Victor snuck his fingers around her increasingly bruised arm, the same spot where all the men kept snatching her, and hauled her from the hotel room. They paraded down the carpeted hallway and burst through the elevator doors as they landed on the ground floor. People discretely stared at the youth struggling to be free. In the eyes of the teenager, every person encountered was a potential rescuer; however, as she became riled up, Victor rumbled a simple threat next to her ear: "Don't, or I kill him." The fighting lessened, and the welling scream died in her throat. Cassy dug her heels to put the brakes on him, yet his mass overpowered her.

Outside, cold winds and freezing rain splattered against her face. The storm raged in an act of the heavens being outraged by the treatment of the abducted girl. Cassy hoped it was a sign that Egypt would never be reached. The hope faded quickly whenever she glanced towards Victor's face. Far too long had passed since the mission began. He would never cease unless he was caught, found the true heir, or he died.

A chill planted itself deep within her bones. Cassy hugged herself as Victor waited for a sleek black rental car to pull forward. Black leather met her when she fell behind Austin in the driver's seat. Victor planted one foot inside the vehicle just as he was waved down by Buddy, who spoke to a man in a pilot's uniform. Groaning, Victor commanded that Austin go on ahead and waved goodbye before he slammed the car door. Austin revved and accelerated, moving through the atrocious weather.

The windshield wipers squeaked, back and forth, as they were pelted with raindrops. Cassy reverted to remembering her family as she had the evening before. Austin's silence lengthened the five-minute trip back to the private plane. It took all her might to avoid tearing up again. Weary and exhausted, Cassy slumped her shoulders and placed her head between her legs to hide that she was nauseous.

Airport security grilled Austin at the gate, and as the security checked the car, Cassy answered any questions directed at her to the best of her ability. Otherwise, she was silent and looked ahead. Struggling to silence her clicking tongue, Cassy snuck looks at the four guards dressed in black while they shuffled through the fake suitcases planted the previous day. Once they finished, they permitted them through with a cheery smile, and the car moved along towards the huge private plane.

Austin hurriedly dashed to the passenger's side rear door. Cassy instinctively listened to him when he unlocked the child-locked door and ushered her out. Her arms rose to cover herself with her thin sweater against the cold rain. It poured heavy drops and soaked the fabric in an instant. They scurried up the plane's staircase and found themselves inside the heated living space. Austin shook his head to dry it a bit while towing her past the cockpit and further into the plane.

In her haste on the first day after she regained consciousness, she had hardly viewed the entire plane. The private Boeing jet spread out into a long aisle, broken up with liveable conveniences. Along one side of the plane, ten modern, black-leathered plane seats were lined up in pairs, facing the cockpit. On the opposite side, a kitchenette and dining room had the option to be walled off rather than open concept, which the men preferred for the sake of privacy. Victor's favourite sitting area, the dining room, was the smallest space, and the one in which he confined himself to avoid anything bothersome.

Behind the ten seats, a decently sized storage space was cluttered with alcohol bottles and used as a small pantry for snacks. It was just large enough to fit a few people inside, and had the back bedroom not been available, Cassy and Zack might have found themselves locked up inside the otherwise bare room. A bathroom with nothing more than a sink and toilet was littered with male grooming products and had been well used during their trip.

They marched underneath an archway-like entrance, directly centralized for the convenient flow of traffic, into a recreation room. One round glass coffee table was nailed down at the legs, closely situated near a black leather sectional. Beneath the flat screen TV, a small dinner table with an ongoing chess game atop it was sandwiched between two swivel chairs, which were also bolted down, but able to rotate completely around.

A small bar where flight attendants would've had the duty of preparing beverages was located just inside the recreation room's main entrance, around the corner of the wall. This gave easy access to their alcohol while Victor's cronies lounged on the couches. Unfortunately for these men, Victor cheaply refused flight attendants and forced them to get their own drinks. They could hardly complain when they travelled in luxury.

Though Cassy disliked flying more than ever before, she understood the rarity of flying on such an expensive jet. Had it not been for Victor, commoner travelling might have been their only way of transportation. Cassy liked the dark colours that accented the walls and carpet. The black of a starless night darkened the baseboards that spread throughout the entire plane, but the mahogany finish enhanced it to a primal elegance.

Lastly, her gaze landed on the rear part as they left another archway into a tiny hallway. To her right, an exit was securely locked up. If the teens ever found another chance at escaping, they had a shot just outside their sleeping quarters. Their prison took up the rest of the tail end, with its single door tucked on the far left-hand side.

Austin unlatched the makeshift locking system made with two dead bolts. The first was a simple lock and key, with three keys for one deadbolt. The other was a keypad glowing near the door handle. It obviously had been put in by the men when they first rented the plane, because it contrasted with the modern look of the jet. Breaking down the door would be impossible.

An unforgiving thrust lunged her forward unexpectedly, and Cassy fell to the floor. Cassy growled at Austin as he chuckled at her scraped palms. He finally gained some enjoyment from abusing the girl. Soft hands halted her swelling shout and lifted her back onto her feet. A soothing hug followed, alleviating her worries over her missing companion.

"Victor thought you'd be able to fly the plane!" Cassy giggled to Zack. "But he doesn't trust you."

Zack stuck his hand to his head in the shape of a gun and pretended to shoot.

"He knows I wouldn't assist him in taking you anywhere near that tomb."

Cassy kissed his lips in appreciation of the sincere words. "He's an idiot if he believes that the pilot will fly in this weather."

A familiar voice snuck up from behind her. "Now I'm an idiot?" Victor asked. "That's a bit harsh, isn't it, Cassandra? Especially considering that the pilot is getting ready to take off."

Cassy lost her sneer and paled as a fear of entering the rumbling storm clouds claimed her cockiness.

"But," Victor continued, rounding the twosome in a strut, "if there are any problems, I've agreed to let him land at the nearest airport until it ends."

Instead of losing face, Cassy plastered on a confident grin and hid the fact that she shook inside. "I still think you're an idiot. Is it really worth risking your life to rush to Egypt?"

"I'm sorry you feel that way, my dear. However, I've been itching to get to Egypt the last few days, and slowing me down causes that itch to become irritable. Since it is a risk, we're all going to spend a bit of time together in another section of the plane."

Victor pitched her out of the prison towards the recreation area. Wedged between the two teenagers, Victor fiddled with her hair and ushered her towards the five rows of seats. A couple of the men had already drank their fill in advance of the turbulent flight. Prior to sitting, Victor flung Zack to one of them, and then plopped Cassy into the nearest seat to the window. Victor strapped the seatbelt snuggly around her waist. He then disappeared to speak with the pilot about the finalization of the flight plans. The rest of the men scattered about, preparing for takeoff, which the pilot announced would be within five minutes.

Cassy edged closer to the wall when Austin planted himself next to her, flopping a leanly muscled arm around her shoulders. In front of her, Zack took a strike to the head from Eric and grumbled inaudible words.

Victor reappeared from the cockpit and slumped to the front of the group, secluded from the others. The engines whirred and squealed in the rain as the jets rumbled. Cassy pinched her skin. Her chest throbbed. Every inhale stung. All her previous bravado dissipated when the wheels outside shifted and they rolled forward. She hated takeoffs the most.

Zack, unable to console the girl making small, scared noises, stared out the nearest window to distract himself. She needed to learn independence because they would have her alone and at their mercy soon enough.

The plane leveled off; however, no one left their seats. The rollercoaster plane bounced up and down, feeling every gust of wind imaginable. It made a couple of Victor's men swear harshly. The storm was persistent, and for two hours this trend of miserable flying continued.

Austin's arm remained over Cassy's shoulder, shrinking her. No words were spoken. Eric leaned in close to whisper into Zack's reddening ear. Cassy noticed her boyfriend's fists clench and body stiffen while Eric jeered. Shaking his perturbed head, the agent tightly locked his jaw.

Zack, keep calm, Cassy begged internally. *They'll punish you.*

Zack couldn't hear her pleading thoughts. After a good amount of time elapsed, the torment became unbearable. Zack snapped, yelling at the man to end the ongoing taunts.

Cassy defended Zack against the mockery that followed. "Leave him alone…"

Leaning uncomfortably close, the only one capable of hearing the soft words leaned in.

"Nobody can hear you and nobody cares what you say. Haven't you learned that we are in control?"

"And yet you're taking orders from Victor, when you alone could probably take him," she snapped.

Austin hummed condescendingly. "The boy never told you who you're really dealing with, did he?"

"What do you mean?"

"Don't underestimate Victor. He became the leader for a reason."

Cassy gaped at Victor's inclined head, his brunette hair situated in the meticulousness ordinary of this man. *Who are you really, Victor?*

Austin raised his eyebrows in secret.

The weather worsened as the day progressed, and along with it, Victor's mood became outrageous. He swore under his breath every time the plane made involuntary groans and jumps. Accepting defeat against nature, Victor stomped out to tell the pilot to land. He could no longer handle Cassandra's whimpering or the complaints of the flushed men.

The landing shook them when the strained pilot struck the ground more roughly than intended. The six men shuffled about to unload and enter the packed airport. Cassy smacked Austin's hands away from unlatching her seat belt. She screamed at him to leave her be, flinging open handed slaps to dissuade his reach. Austin grunted and smacked her against her cheek. Cassy sucked back the pain. Her knees came up and she huddled into the leather seats to hide from him.

Eric was shoved from hanging off the seat to watch the action unfold by Zack, who removed Austin and clutched Cassy into his chest. He whispered for her to follow without a fight before unbuckling her and snaking his arms around her shoulders to lead her towards Victor's impatient form.

The boss resented the teenagers who relished in the delay. They huddled close, and Cassy's head rested protectively in Zack's chest. The rain pelted down upon them as they strolled towards the terminal gates. Inside the cluttered space, people assembled themselves with children and luggage, cursing the bad weather. Victor growled at the mass of people before he snatched Cassy's wrist to drag her into the corner with the fewest people and planted her onto a silver seat.

Buddy disappeared to purchase water for himself and the teenagers to occupy the time. Jonathon paced, babbling a string of swears. The rest lounged or stood, stretching after such long flights. All of them grumbled about the unforeseen length of this storm.

Cassy sipped the water, grateful that the progression towards Egypt finally took a step back. Zack confidently held her hand. She was petrified of how long the men's calm act would last for. Nausea stirred her stomach.

"Cassy, are you alright?"

"Zack... they're going to beat us because of this."

Zack rubbed her knee and pecked her chin. "Look around us, Cassy."

She did. She found children squealing, adults chatting in several languages with coffee cups steaming in their hands, and security guards nonchalantly sauntering along.

"We are surrounded by security. They are our ticket to safety."

"Until we get back onto the plane..." she mumbled.

Suddenly, anxiety snatched her, and she hopped up to rush towards the exit. The men inconspicuously darted glances towards their boss who sprang from his conversation with Jason and hurried behind the girl. His suspicion ended when she disappeared into a washroom.

She entered the stall and finished with her business hurriedly, comprehending that Victor seethed with embarrassment from her rash action. Nausea rose from the pit of her stomach to her throat, which caused her to kneel over the toilet and gag. A couple minutes of dry heaving passed, and she wiped her wet lips. She dreaded exiting the washroom to find Victor looming over her once more. She massaged her forehead. She concealed her trembles as she stumbled her way out of the stall to hastily wash her hands. She couldn't dawdle for long.

The appearance that faced her in the mirror abruptly halted any intention to return to Zack's side. A mess of hair matted her head, and a dirty, ripped sweater covered her upper torso. Attention then fell to her eyes, bloodshot from stress. She despised the look of it all. Running warm water, she soaked her face and dampened her hair.

Depressingly, she stripped off her sweater and bunched it into a ball. Nothing could be done with her unclean clothes. A large lump prevented her from dropping it into the garbage. The black, sleek cellphone dropped into her palm. It was long since dead, and she could only smack the screen with desperation. Once it was finalized that the cell phone would make no calls, she slipped it into her front jean pocket along with Zack's hidden watch and covered the lump with her blouse. *It might come in handy.* The sweater then landed into the garbage, poking out from the top. It stung to have to toss something that her mother purchased for her less than a month before she died. She hadn't appreciated the small things in life when they were the things that meant the most.

She ran her fingers through the tugging knots of her shoulder-length hair. Her scalp stung as she pulled out strands. Smoothing out the unruly hair, she re-examined herself. Physically, she felt disgusting. With nothing left to do but mourn over the loss of her family again, she swung open the bathroom's metal door and departed.

Victor noticed the slight appearance changes instantly. Leading her to the most secluded area of the airport, he shoved her into the wall.

"Ouch!" she rubbed her shoulder. "Leave me alone!"

"Where's your sweater?"

"I threw it away. One of you ripped it…it won't keep me warm anymore."

"We will be kept warm in Egypt." He softly touched her cheek. "You washed your face." The hand slithered up her neck to her hair, where he appreciated the fixed strands. "You are gorgeous, my sweet treasure."

"Quit touching me! You're a kidnapper. You can't hit me and then touch me as if I'm yours," her voice rose louder with each word she hissed.

"Stop making a damn scene," he sharply whispered. "You are mine, so stop fighting."

She snapped, "I wouldn't be making a scene if you weren't holding my arm so tightly." She wiggled in despise of his grip. "Just let me go and I'll stop."

He did as she commanded and casually wrapped his hand inside his coat. A security guard strolled by them without even a questioning look. The youth rolled her eyes. Victor deceived those around him with ease.

Cassy stormed off to head back to Zack, but quickly rethought it. Jonathon hung around him and she had little nerve to deal with him. Instead, with the eyes of all six men upon her, she headed over to Eric, who ordered food. He welcomed her with a curt nod. Cassy leaned against the counter next to him. Victor was close behind, weary of her being left alone with this specific man. Eric smirked when she stared at the menu postings. Her eyes widened at unreadable words. Her blank face made Eric chuckle.

"Intimidating, isn't it?"

"Where are we?" she queried.

"It's Italian." He placed his order with the server, and she began preparing his food. "Can you guess where we are?"

"Well, I suppose, somewhere in Italy."

He made mock praise, "Very good. A little generic, but accurate."

Cassy squinted in curiosity as she asked, "How can you speak Italian?"

"I'm a multilingual, which means..."

"I know what it means. Why did you learn it when you based most of your work in Egypt?"

"I have travelled the world since I finished college, Cassandra. When I was an archaeologist, you got more jobs when you could read more than a couple of transcripts. I can almost speak six languages fluently."

Cassy tilted her head, thinking about that. "What about Jason? He was also part of your archaeological dig of Obeko's tomb, right? So, he's also an archaeologist? Does he speak lots of languages too?"

"We have been partners since we met in our first year of college." Eric eyed Victor, cautiously wording the next statement properly, "Egypt was the start of everything." A warning cleared Victor's throat when too much information could be exposed. "Jason only speaks three. He focused on Ancient Egyptian texts, so he's learned a few ancient languages, but not many. He thinks I've wasted my time learning all these languages, but it's really quite fun."

Cassy plucked his fork from his lips when he plunked a mouthful of noodles into his mouth. Startled at this action, he hummed, lusting over her young features. He carried the tray of food towards the group to avoid Victor's darkening eyes. Cassy wanted to take advantage of his chattiness for as long as possible.

"What did all the others do before joining?"

Eric reached out and patted her head while shaking his. "Don't ask me. Ask them."

They returned to witness Jonathon finish his pestering of Zack, who swore and snarled at the man's persistent presence. The others sprawled out their legs to try to find comfortable seats during this horrible waiting game. She pouted that they refused to enlighten her about where they all came from.

Her head cuddled against Zack.

"Zack, how come I can't learn anything about these men? I know nothing about them. What did Victor do before he became the leader of this group? What about the others? Why are they so scared of him?"

Victor sent a daring motion towards Zack, who flinched at the questions.

"Cassy," he stated as diplomatically as possible, "no matter what, learning about these men isn't going to benefit you. All it will do is make you someone to be rid of. I'm sorry, but I'm trying everything to keep you safe. Just drop it."

Cassy folded her arms underneath her small chest and accepted his warning. He beckoned her to lean in so he could place his chin on her shoulder and whisper ways they could escape in the crowd. Victor complained to the pilot while the rest left and grabbed food randomly. Cassy offered that while the men were busy with their food, they could sneak away. Zack reclined back, unable to pretend it was a possibility. Victor may have been speaking with the pilot, but his attention was fixated on Cassy, observing her carefully.

Their plans became fewer when nightfall dropped and the storm hadn't calmed. The men clambered closer, restricting them even more. Zack lied on Cassy's knee and stretched across a few seats to rest.

Cassy stroked her boyfriend's hair soothingly as Jonathon seated himself beside her. Grumpy, sunken eyes were heavy beneath his eyelids. The smell of alcohol wafted towards her, making her squirm.

"What you staring at?"

Startled that he noticed her gaze, she looked away quickly.

"Nothing…" she muttered. "Jonathon," she asked, "what did you do before joining Victor?"

Her curiosity was overwhelming. She couldn't help herself. If she would be stuck with these men, she wanted to understand them.

"Huh?" he densely responded. Eventually, the question was comprehended. "I was in the army. When I came back from a tour in the East, I met up with Victor in New York City. I'm glad he took me from that bullshit! That job was a waste of goddamn life!"

Any more questions were silenced.

His drunken stupor swayed him about. She disliked when people drank, especially since Vince had come home every day plastered out of his mind, unable to focus on anything except for his mournful sadness.

"Why do you care where we came from, you stupid bitch? Victor is going to toss you into a prison cell when we find out that you're the heir."

"You really think I'm the heir?"

"I should, because I'm the one who found you. You were *my* gamble. If you aren't, I'm going to really enjoy slicing open your neck and watch that attitude ooze away."

She scooted from him when his hand swung widely to stroke her hair.

"Don't touch me," she scolded.

"Whatever you say, *princess*," he mumbled. "You're Victor's precious trophy…" he struck his head with a bulky fist. "I shouldn't be drunk around you…" Concern made him glance about the airport. He seemed disturbed that he might be busted by Victor.

"I'm not anybody's trophy."

"Sure y-your aren't." His words, as he stressed, were slurred. "Wh-why don't y-yo-you sleep? These men enjoy watching you sleep… did you know that? They hover over you like you're an exotic animal. Y-you should sleep. If you do-n't, Victor punishes," he sang. "Oh! Yo-you'll be punished more often. Victor wants it his way and you're his now! *All* of you!"

His lips slurred the vulgar comments thickly. Cassy was completely emotionally drained from hearing that she was owned by these men. She truly landed in hell and Victor was the devil.

"Is there a problem here?"

The voice startled Cassy. She wrenched her neck around after the jump caused her heart to skip a beat. The "devil" stood behind her. He studied Jonathon, contempt filling his tight jaw. Victor dragged the ex-military man off. Outside, behind two glass doors, they swore at each other. Jonathon retorted against the boss's words and Victor's arms flew up, relinquished of all hopes to prevent the man from drinking. Red faced, Victor returned and hurried over to a solitary corner to calm down. He dug his hands into a pocket, contemplating his next move. Austin carefully assisted Jonathon back into the airport. Cassy, astonished about this happening, gaped. *Aren't they supposed to be organized?* They worked so hard to conceal any dysfunction that when she saw it, Victor swiftly reacted.

Victor examined her from a distance; he finally began making a move towards her when he realized how stunned she was. Taking hold of her hand, he studied the bare skin, like he expected cuts on her body. She shuffled closer to Zack's sleeping form.

Victor's fingers rose to rub her face. "He didn't touch you, did he?"

She banished his hand. "What does it matter? You're always touching me."

"I'm not drunk," he hissed.

"Shouldn't that mean you touch me less?" Cassy argued. "At least drunk people don't know the difference between right or wrong. You're fully aware, which is disgusting."

A clenched fist froze in mid swing. Victor couldn't risk striking her in the open. Instead, he checked the time on an expensive Rolex watch, and clicked his tongue at the lateness.

"Get to sleep. We have a long day tomorrow. We need to make up for lost time." He petted her head and marched away to deal with Jonathon's misbehaving.

JANELLE FILTEAU

Her new life proved difficult to adapt to. For that evening only, Cassy chose to accept his orders. Zack's head slipped to the chair softly and she laid hers next to his. Lifting her legs onto the grey, metal chairs, Cassy listened to the commotion around her.

Throughout the night, the men restlessly shifted on the benches. A few slept for five minutes, but any more was deemed improbable because of the lousy makeshift beds. Around five that morning, they were given a reprieve when the pilot announced that the storm was dispersing, and it was safe to leave. Victor, already shaking the grumpy men, awoke the teenage girl.

She shouted at him to leave her alone. Sore and stiff from the uncomfortable arrangement, she snapped, "What?"

"We're leaving."

Springing up, she investigated the windows where the dusk light was clearing, and a shimmering rain caressed the ground. The other men hauled Zack, now awake, to the terminal exit. Victor fought with her. She heard people talking and security guards strolling about, but everything just flashed by as she tugged her arm. Her concentration flooded from the people to Victor to Zack's waves for her to come with them. Shock persisted. The battle against them was infinite.

Victor's fingers slipped. Escaping, she dashed to the woman's washroom. Tears steadily fell. Sitting in a grimy stall, Cassy breathed in her fears. Her fist quaked the metal stall as it slammed against it. It didn't matter if she exposed the men, or even if she escaped; her whereabouts could place her in a worse danger than she was already in. She had to go with Victor. Zack remained in their captivity, and she couldn't leave him behind. The uncertainty of surviving crossed her mind several times before she vowed that crying was unacceptable until they were tears of joy. Gaining courage from the thought, she abandoned the stall and approached the sink. As she rinsed her streaked face, a woman entered.

With concern in her tone, the woman began rambling in another language. Cassy's resigned face made her stop and speak in broken English. "Your father ask to check on you."

"He's not my father!" Cassy spat. "Please, I need your help!" Cassy tugged the woman's sleeve. "Phone the..." This woman could be her final chance of alerting the FUA of their whereabouts.

Victor's head poked in, "Coming, *darling?*"

"No."

"Come... we are *all* ready to go."

The woman interrupted. "Phone who?"

Victor's face flashed violently into a malevolent shadow. Cassy noticed movement behind the door and instantly regretted involving an innocent woman. He reached for a concealed weapon.

"Never mind, ma'am."

She hurried to follow the aggressive leader. He twisted her wrist behind her back to punish her.

"You pull that bullshit again, I'll kill him."

Cassy whimpered in pain as her bones protested. "I understand."

Roughly escorted into the plane, Zack was now pummelled by the men to settle him down. Their assaults were nothing compared to Victor's. After being thrown into Zack, she hunkered into the corner, protected by her boyfriend's guarding form. The man's face reddened, and Victor punched Zack in the gut. He then tripped him to the ground to beat him bloody. Zack's face bruised, and his skin opened with deep gashes stretching along the bridge of his nose. Cassy begged Victor to stop. Once Zack took a sufficient beating, Victor stood and wiped his hands clean of the red blood. He left without a word to threaten the panicking girl. Her punishment was to tend to her half-conscious boyfriend.

●　●　●

It took another day and a half of straight travelling to arrive in the blazing hot sun of Cairo, Egypt. During that time, no troubles occurred. Victor avoided the captives and none of the men bothered them. The physical threat of Victor brought such terror to Cassy that she influenced Zack to stop being so abrasive against them.

At touchdown, Cassy carried a deal of frustration inside. Its explosion from her made it hard for Jonathon to tie her hands. Whenever he grasped one, the other shoved him farther away.

"Come on, princess, we're going to the tomb now," he cooed.

"NO!"

Her small wrists slipped from his bulky, rough fingers. Jonathon, his wide nostrils flared, was ready to tackle the youth and knock her out. Victor commanded that she remain unharmed, so he endured the one-sided game.

Jonathon dropped his arms. "Buddy! A little *help*, please!"

"Jonathon, you're doing it all wrong. For a military guy, you sure don't know how to make a hostage move."

Buddy leaned against the door, pleased with the struggle between the man and teenager.

"Shut it and help!"

"Okay, okay, don't get your bloomers in a bunch."

He straightened and glared at Zack.

Jonathon registered Buddy's words and halted his reach for her. "Hey, that's women's clothing!"

"You're not one? Oops, my mistake."

Buddy fixed his shirt and then stepped towards the agent, who remained near the washroom, waiting to intervene if they became vicious. Jonathon swore at both Buddy's small joke and Cassy's fist hitting him in the shoulder. Buddy pulled out a revolver, newly entrusted to him, and aimed it at Zack's head. His hands were steady; all the time spent with the others had him prepared to finish off the agent whom he still hadn't grown to despise.

"Hey, *Cassy*," he sang, "stop hitting Jonathon and face me or I'll shoot Zack."

She stopped amid a swooping kick that was intended for Jonathon's calf and glanced over, mockingly. The ridicule dripped away when the weapon pressed hard against Zack's temple. She unwillingly listened and turned to Buddy. Her hands were ripped back and her torso bent over the bed as Jonathon tied her hands securely. Jonathon had his revenge as the rope dug into her wrists.

"Good girl," Buddy complimented. "Now, you're probably going to fight, huh?"

"Of course. I don't get taken easily," Zack snapped back.

Zack bent his knees, swinging away from the gun's aim.

Buddy, who cheated whenever he fought, took advantage of the close combat to slip into his pocket and grab a Taser. Zack charged, a fist raised to strike down onto Buddy's head. He second-guessed it when the man seemed willing to take the hit to conceal a weapon. Zack sidestepped and missed the first swipe of the electricity as Buddy produced the taser. Buddy tilted it back and forth, showing off his new skill in using this less lethal attack.

The Taser bounced securely from hand to hand. A ravenous howl from Buddy escaped his lips as Buddy charged Zack. They both dodged each other's attacks and blocked any flailing limbs. They attacked each other several times, their movements not even coming close to connecting. Jonathon became bored of watching their dance. Outreaching his foot when Zack agilely avoided the Taser, Jonathon tripped him. The agent fell directly into Buddy's welcoming arms, and the Taser contacted Zack's shoulder, jolting every inch of his body. Dropped to the ground like garbage, Zack was unable to resist when his hands were tied back, and he was dragged from the plane's prison for the final time.

Jonathon gathered up Cassy. She kicked at him, slung over his shoulder like a sack, and was moved to the outside. Victor did a double take of the three vehicles waiting for them. At the sound of Cassy's voice, he smacked a hand down onto the hood of the car, infuriated with her insistent obsession with maddening him.

"Put them in that one." He pointed towards a black SUV. "I need to speak with them." Then he disappeared around another vehicle.

Unable to read the circumstances for Victor's eagerness, Cassy kicked Jonathon in the stomach. The well-built man took the kicks without even a flinch.

"Let us go!"

"Here you are, princess: your freedom."

She fell onto a carpeted floor. The exit slammed shut and she crawled onto the leather seats to concentrate on the outside action through tinted windows. Egypt baked her with its intense heat, but it was unexpectedly a breathtaking sight. No pyramids were visible. Instead, it looked like any flourishing city might with its large buildings, though the dense dunes of sand swirled in the gentle winds in a grand mysticism. Tentatively, she almost felt at home in Egypt, and it awed her with its wonder. She prayed that sensation meant something different than being bonded with mystical gems.

Buddy caught her dreary eyes as he dragged Zack along the black tarmac. Scrapes kissed the agent's skin as he moved. Cassy realized that they now stood on Egyptian land; Zack not lasting another day crept to the front of her mind.

Shifting the pain to his core, Zack took advantage of the lessened guard of the men and tripped Buddy, making him land on his face. Buddy managed to regain his balance after the unexpected action, but, still unsteady, he landed on his butt. Zack was disoriented from Buddy's previous attack. He noticed his loss of mobility as he swung his shoulders around in helpless flails to keep the men away and fumbled to stand. He had come to the same realization as Cassy. As soon as they reached that tomb, he would die.

Jason and Buddy tackled the boy, using their weight to pile atop Zack's already weak torso. He was punched once more for the pure satisfaction of feeling the flesh beneath their fingers. Once the beating ended, they scooped him effortlessly into Victor's SUV.

Cassy scooted to Zack to comfort the gasping boy, who tried to hide his pain and readiness to die. The men conversed outside, leaving the two time to speak.

"Zack, what should I do? Just tell me!" She rested her cheek gently across his wounded cheekbone and felt the warm blood smear her skin. "Oh God! You're bleeding, Zack. You can't keep this up."

Zack pecked her luscious, pale lips before consoling her horribly, "In awhile, Cassy, it won't matter how much I bleed…"

"Please… don't… I don't want to hear it."

"I'm sorry, Cassy," he nuzzled into her collarbone while he spoke. "I love you more than anything, and if I could, I'd stay right by your side when you walk into that tomb."

"Isn't there any way to stop them now?"

His words were cut short. Following Jonathon, who sank into the driver's seat, Victor mounted the SUV's tall entrance, strode in, and snuck between the two to separate them. Dissatisfied that blood stained Cassy's face, he swiped it off with a handkerchief which he then tossed to Zack, telling him to clean himself off despite his arms being tethered behind his back.

"Now, no matter how much I'd love to take you directly to the tomb, the others have convinced me that trying to get through the miserable side roads to the tomb is nearly impossible in the day, let alone during the night. The sun will be setting in less than an hour, so we are heading to the safehouse for the night. This provides us with ample time to prepare and for you time to say goodbye to your damn boyfriend." He rethought that. "I guess it would be wiser for us to separate the two of you, seeing as you've tried to escape, what, four times now? Cassandra, you'll stay with Austin and Buddy. And *Zackarass*... I suppose you have some catching up to do with Eric and Jason. I bet they'd enjoy it."

Cassy attempted to haggle, "I'd prefer staying with Eric and Jason. Can't I stay with them?"

"I wouldn't put you anywhere near them with a ten-foot pole. The last time, Eric nearly killed you. Besides, they are both riled up and they might get a little antsy if I'm not precautious."

Victor was not about to change his mind. Cassy glanced at her boyfriend's bloodied face. His jawline protruded awkwardly from all the swelling. Bruises nearly sealed his right eye shut and his skin was cut and scraped to almost being unrecognizable. His sulking eyes met hers; however, he still promoted encouragement when he smiled and accepted his fate. Appreciating his full-hearted bravery, she chose to enjoy whatever time she had left with him.

Dust flew out from under the window, fueled by a whirlwind of memories and appalling images. She reverted to the night her parents were killed in the car accident. They had waved their goodbyes, hugging their kids, who joked that they were being saps and should go ahead and enjoy the housewarming party at a friend's. Cassy sulked on the stairs, wanting to go with them. She couldn't even work up the nerve to say goodbye. She pouted angrily that they left her with the brothers who already planned to go out to a movie to which she wasn't invited. She had sat alone on the couch watching television until she was intruded on by the return of her rambunctious brothers. Snarling at them, she went to bed in a huff. Hours later, she had awoken to Brant towering over her, his sullen features showing something happened. When she was led up the stairs to the living room, she found Vince with bloodshot eyes and police officers mournfully apologetic for the news they were about to speak. All she heard was one word. Dead. It echoed in her ears and seared her skull. The word was final. Her parents were gone forever, just as her grandfather.

Cassy pinched her palms with her nails to awaken herself from the daydream. The "devil" still sat next to her, humming a tune, and Zack was still physically battered. *Zack, I'm not letting you die here… If you die, I will die too. I'll find a way to make it out of this.*

The heavy shackles were clamping down. Soon, they would chain her in the grasps of Victor's wrath. Freedom, the only sensation she desired, would be lost forever the moment the following morning rose.

Zack absently gazed through the window and saw nothing. *This will be my last night.* He miserably sighed. At the beginning of this assignment, he'd come to terms with the inevitable. Up in the skies, the blue horizon and a few puffy clouds permitted the setting sun to beat down on his brow. He may not have been religious, but at a time like this, Zack found himself praying to a spiritual being. *Tomas, help protect us from the men that murdered you. I'm desperate. I can't lose her like this. Seeing her cry and suffer hurts so bad. I love her.*

The quiet trip to the barren wasteland of sand dunes and heat was full of tension. The silence lasted the forty-five minutes out of Cairo. Victor was disinterested in continuing his patronizing. He flared in annoyance while Cassy sniffled back her building fear, and Zack was overly interested in where they were traveling. The FUA had never known where Victor's group hid during their time in Egypt. He was finally learning the inner workings of the group.

The lead car drove smoothly along the suspicious, sand-covered side road. It was infrequently used. Twists and turns sent the sand spiralling. Mountainous sand dunes towered above them as they turned and began to drive down a steep hill. Small wooden, cookie-cutter buildings were perfectly situated in a straight line. They were uninhabited for an extended period, as dust had collected on the windows and doors. They were all dark inside.

The cars squealed to a halt in front of the center building's entrance. Jonathon shifted gears and shuffled in front of them. The men stretched and approached the hostage's vehicle. Austin disappeared behind one of the buildings, and soon the lights flicked on in all of the buildings as a noisy generator started up. Buddy stepped into the SUV. Cassy squirmed, compressed between both men's girth.

Victor removed his contempt towards the loud noise and the living conditions to focus on Cassy. "Now, I trust we won't have any issues tonight. I'm untying you. You attempt another escape, I'll beat both of you." Victor brushed her hair out of her sullen face. "I hate the idea of hurting you." He tugged her arms to untie them.

Cassy and Zack stepped out to be grabbed by Jonathon and Buddy. The group moved as one towards the first building. The buildings were deteriorating wood that creaked underfoot on the small porch. The unclean windows were barred from the outside and three deadbolts maintained the hideout's security. They'd be well secured for the night.

Victor's heavy presence remained nearby. It suffocated her in the cooling heat as he breathed down her neck nearby Jonathon's bulk. Jason flicked through a huge keychain to locate the appropriate key for the cabin they approached.

Cassy clung to Zack's nearby palm. She noticed his anxious looks while the men secured them there. He was stupefied at their well-hidden location. The FUA had never fathomed they would set up such a well-developed system for their hostages and their own safety. It was truly unlikely that they'd have a swarm of agents hunting for them in this barren wasteland.

A jerk brought Cassy into the kempt place. A closet ran along a wall that led into an open concept living-and-dining room and kitchenette. A small fridge hummed after several months, if not close to a year, of disuse. Two doors were laid out along the righthand side. The first led to a washroom, and the second a bedroom. Someone would most definitely be sleeping on the couch in the living room.

Victor did a quick sweep of the setup, and then pointed at Cassy to sit on the couch. She did so and crossed her palms tightly together.

"Damn," Victor clicked his tongue, "we should've grabbed food while in Cairo. Jonathon, you're in charge of grabbing something. Austin, when he gets back, make sure she eats! If she doesn't, you force it down her throat. Understood?"

Jonathon disappeared in a flash once he received his evening orders and the vehicle revved loudly. An acknowledging nod showed Austin's understanding.

"We'll be heading out at seven sharp. I expect everyone to be ready to go."

Zack bulldozed through the men as Victor attempted to exit. He hugged Cassy's stiffening torso. His lips pressed against hers and he swept a palm through her hair several times to settle them both.

She fumbled to take a good grip on his waist. "Zack, don't leave me... Please!"

"I'll see you tomorrow. I swear. Sleep well, and remove that worried look."

She spluttered inaudible words as she gulped dense air. Clasping her palm, he kissed her forehead and slipped something into her hand before following behind Victor. Cassy clutched the folded piece of paper safely into her palm. She was unable to read the words written across it. Two of the remaining six men slammed the door shut, and the outdoor deadbolts sealed them inside.

Austin sank onto the couch next to her. Unable to contain her thudding chest, she sprang from the couch and hurried to the bathroom to hide. She locked herself in and hunkered into a corner to rock herself. The note crinkled in her hands. It was a looming doom of Zack's final words. It could've said anything. Instead, she searched around the bathroom for a towel and turned the rusting faucet in the tub-shower. Washing away the grime with chilly water would soothe her heartache.

• • •

Zack's predicament had drastically shifted. His feet scarcely met the hearth of the entrance before his body was against the wall with Jason clutching his throat. The man tightened his grip with clenched teeth in a proud grimace. He cared little about choking Zack; he only hoped that the agent die in his own hands.

"So, how does it feel to be trapped like a dog?" Jason mocked.

"You... deserve to be trapped!" Zack gasped.

"If it weren't for your dear brother, you'd be dead right now. That would have made her capture much easier! Who would the FUA have sent to get friendly with her? I doubt even the great Tomas Exacil would've been able to convince Cassandra to trust him. Once we caught her, she wouldn't be causing so many issues. She would be nothing." Jason pushed his thumbs into Zack's throat. "You'll finally die and leave her all alone, Zack. We can—and will—do anything to make her listen."

"Go ahead and kill me! Cassy will never let you control her."

A crooked grin tilted with his head as Jason tightened the grip. "No... I'm going to rip out her heart when we waste you right in front of her. She'll scream your name, but you won't respond. That is going to be the most poetic death we could ever provide you."

Zack toppled to his knees, coughing for breath with exasperated lungs. Eric kicked him. Zack curled up and held his stomach. He prepared for the long night of torture. His likelihood of leaving this suite unscathed was zero. He supported himself up, ready for whatever the men would do.

● ● ●

Cassy wrapped a towel over her before she leaned against the sink's cabinetry and sank to the creaking floor. The letter patronized her in her tight, unsure fingers. It was unravelled. Zack's neat scroll was scribbled across the torn paper. With one deep inhale, Cassy began to read what most likely were Zack's final words.

Cassy

I've thought about how to write my final words, always erasing because I want to express them properly. I love you with all my heart, and I wish I was stronger. I wanted to protect you from these men, but they just wouldn't stop. I did all I could. I will never be like my brother. He would have succeeded in stopping them, but I failed you.

Never forget that you come from a loving family who would die trying to make you happy. If I never see your beautiful face again, remember that I am watching over you. You will eventually return home and be free of these beasts.

I love you and please don't hate me for letting go.

Cassy wept. Zack could no longer survive the abuse. His scarred body was testament to that, even if he tried to fake a grin and encourage bravery. These were Zack's final words, with the unknown coming the following day. She hunkered over, swaying about. She had lost her entire life in six days. *I never said goodbye to Brant or Vince. I'm going to die here. Eventually, Victor will control my very being...*

Logic broke the barriers of melancholy thoughts and reminded her that she was stronger than to believe that shit. Even during the worst moments during Zack's bullying, she held strong and endured. This became a resolve of determination.

I'm getting out of here. Whether it be through suicide or because I'm found, I'm going to escape. If I'm not the heir, at least I'll die alongside Zack and I'll be able to find peace from this horrendous life.

Determined to defeat the oppressive men, she rose to dress in her dirty clothes and glanced at her dirty reflection of the cracked mirror. Cassy convinced herself that none of the men would take advantage of her through their conniving tactics. *I'm keeping my promise, Zack. I won't be degraded to nothing by any of these bastards.*

Leaving the bathroom, she clenched Zack's note, holding it to her chest. She found one man fiddling with the beds to determine which one would be suitable for the girl. Buddy sat on the couch in the following room. He flipped through an outdated magazine and nibbled on a newly arrived meal. A small bowl of soup was cooling down atop the rundown table. She supposed it was for her. Ignoring the meal, she went to stand next to the window to look out at Egypt's land.

Austin barrelled into the living room when he realized she had snuck from the bathroom and now sulked in a corner. A spoon landed on the table next to the soup. He snapped at his partner for not instantly coercing her to eat, and then growled at her to sit. Cassy listened to the fuming man. She settled at the table. She slurped her meal; after three days of not eating, it burned her throat and made her stomach grumble in upset. Austin pushed Buddy's feet off the couch then flopped down himself, eyeing the girl who ate the smallest of morsels. She took a couple of spoonsful before replacing the spoon into the brown broth. Cassy noticed how uptight the two were. They spoke little and hardly acknowledged each other. They had been forced into a companionship without consent.

"Where is everyone from?"

Austin lowered the weapon that rose when her soft voice startled him. She bowed her head, swirling the spoon around as he shifted to put it away.

"Jeez, kid…"

She apologized and lost the nerve to ask another question. Austin landed his elbows on his knees as he hunched over, nibbling on a chicken wing.

"Victor and Jonathon are from New York. Jason and Eric, they've spent most of their time here in Egypt since they graduated college, but they haven't told us much about their past. Buddy said he came from California," he said as Buddy shrugged. "Me, I lived in Vancouver, but am originally from London, England."

Buddy edgily shifted during the explanation.

Cassy trudged on. She took advantage of them being talkative. Knowing who she was up against helped her deal with them. Her head bowed, nervously pushing their leniency.

"What did you use to do for work?"

Austin sneered, "Why the sudden interest?"

"You know all about me, why shouldn't I know anything about you?"

"Touché." Austin rose and rounded her. "Our little chat piqued your interest, huh?" His hands fiddled with the damp hair clinging to her shoulders. A deep hum exposed his thoughts. "Let's make a deal. I'll answer only one more question, and then you'll go to bed with nothing else said, understood? Victor wants you bright eyed tomorrow when we arrive at the tomb."

Cassy made an obvious shudder but accepted his terms.

"So, I worked as a gunsmith in Vancouver. Didn't pay well until I moved to the US, but it paid the bills. I also did a bit of work as a computer technician. Do you really think those buffoons, especially Jonathon, could work their way around the computer systems of organizations like the FBI without my encryption program?" Austin boasted. "Nope, Jonathon may have nudged us to hunt, but it was my system that actually located you."

With surprise etched across her face, Cassy realized that they were men who each held secret talents that should not be trusted.

"What about you, Buddy?"

Austin became outright frustrated with her blatant disregard to his set rules. Rather than politely ushering her off, a hand smacked her to the ground and then tossed her into the bedroom to commit her to her end of the bargain. Buddy hurried along behind him, unzipping a small package that had been stowed away in a duffel bag. Cassy screamed out apologies to stop them from their abusive reaction. Buddy's hand was sweaty while it covered her lips to smother the noise. He handed the needle over to Austin, who sharply jabbed it into the fleshy part of her upper arm, draining it completely before both men calmed down.

"You should never go back on your word, Cassandra," Austin growled.

Her eyelids drooped more heavily than she ever experienced. She curled into herself as the nausea curdled her stomach. Paralyzed into a hunched ball, Cassy barely noticed that they were arguing about who would stay with her. Neither wanted to sleep in the same room as the girl. The moment Victor walked in the next morning, whoever slept in that spot would be accused of attempting something. Once it was decided on, and Buddy had lost, Austin leaned in to pat her cheek.

"Ignorant girl, you should learn to leave things be. However, I'll be nice, and as a goodnight, I'll let you know what Buddy used to do. He was an architect in New York City with a good mind for unlocking safes."

•   •   •

"What the hell is your damn problem?" Buddy nagged. "Victor told us not to toy with telling her anything and you go off—"

"I told her nothing. She's been bugging all of us, so if we just tell her bits and pieces, then she's more likely to drop it."

"Then why did you have to hit her?"

Austin hoped that he hadn't hit her cheek too hard. "She needs to learn that you follow through with deals, otherwise there's consequences. I taught her a well-deserved lesson that she should not soon forget."

Buddy flicked his hand back and forth, shoving away the lame excuse. "Yeah, how about you tell Victor that when he comes in to find Cassandra not only knowing something about us, but also carrying a bruised cheek."

Austin grumbled from the bedroom, rubbing his chin in thought as he considered the rash decision to strike her.

Buddy double-checked the girl after the drugs settled in her system and then went to the bathroom to take a shower. Austin settled into reading an old magazine after setting up his less-than-preferred bed.

Chapter 14

The previous night was hazy, and a nauseous sensation twisted her insides, making her mouth grimy. Saliva layered Cassy's lips as her thick tongue licked them to remove the feeling. The lump rising from the pit of her gut to her throat assisted little. She sprang from bed and rushed into the bathroom in the eerily quiet morning. As she sat over the toilet, her lips quivering in preparation to throw up, she found herself thinking of the day's events. Trembling fingers brushed back her hair as she heaved out air. This feeling would not dissipate.

Stumbling from the bathroom, she wondered if it were worth trying to escape. She was a couple hours away from viewing the tomb that had overflowed her nightmares for months. She shook her head as if she made a sarcastic joke. To leave would condemn Zack. She couldn't even pretend to consider such an option. If he didn't survive, it was not by lack of trying. Instead, she went and settled next to the window. She lavished in the sunrise's pink hue before the men stirred to destroy it.

It took two hours, until exactly seven, before any movement was seen. Shadows shifted outside. It reinforced her decision to stay around. Zack and Victor burst inside at the lead. Snarling that Austin and Buddy should've been up already, their boss hollered at them. It took a few scared sweeps before anyone found the quiet girl sitting upon the floor. Zack went straight to her, welcoming her into his recently injured arms.

"Zack..." she shrilled, "what are those on your arm? They look like burn marks!"

All over his arms, his neck, and some on his face were sections of seared skin which darkened his usually lightly tanned features. The wounds festered, potentially infected. Swiping back his delicate hair, he winced when she brushed a couple.

Victor was pleased to see that placing Zack with Jason and Eric had been successful; however, he also noted how the girl's fondness for Zack had her jumping up to run cold water onto a cloth in the kitchen sink and then hurrying to clean the burns to the best of her ability. She found many more underneath his shirt that he edgily tried to stop her from fussing over.

"Leave them. Don't worry about them," Zack said.

As she dabbed one that seemed a few days older, she recognized his neck injury.

"This is from a Taser... they tortured you all night, didn't they?"

Zack's lips cracked when they tensed. "I assure you, it could've been much worse. Please, Cassy, stop worrying about me. I'm just glad I get to see you again."

She curled into his arms to watch the action around them. The men groggily scurried about, searching for packed items, and setting them either by the front door or on the table where Victor inspected that they had done their job. Guns, drugs, and a map scattered across the glass as they double-checked their chosen route to get to the tomb.

They then gathered in the living room. Victor stood in the middle to look at his men, and then landed his malicious gaze upon the kneeling two teenagers.

"Who wants them?"

Jason instantly grabbed hold of their hair and towed them through the front entrance. A parked black jeep was their destination as they fumbled across the deep sand. They toppled upon one another in the rear seat and then Jason sank into the driver's. He patiently waited for the rest to load into two other vehicles. One drove ahead of them and one followed behind, keeping close tabs on the middle jeep.

Cassy and Zack settled in a seated position, remaining unbuckled. Cassy burst into sobs half an hour into the trip. Her chest rose and sank between every breath that stung her throat. Zack pinned her closer to kiss her forehead.

"Stop crying, Honey. It's going to be alright," he awkwardly swooned.

Cassy leaned closer to whisper, "This is it. We can't stop them anymore. I'll have to go into that tomb."

Jason jeered at the desperate cries and watched from the rear-view mirror. Zack endeavoured to console her by sympathetically patting her back.

The men turned off the seldomly used road and drove onto an even worse road filled with drifting sand. Unable to thwart her emotions, Cassy's clenched fists struck the rear window, struggling to shatter the glass in a last-ditch effort to escape.

Zack took hold of her arms and relentlessly restrained her. She struggled against him and shouted for him to leave her be.

"I need to get out!" Her shrills increased in volume.

Zack lost his grip. She had landed a solid strike on a fresh wound. It caused him to curl into a defenceless ball. He begged her to stop, but she heard none of it while she bled from her hands from her constant strikes against the glass.

Jason sighed and moved to the side of the road, stalling the group without warning. Facing the mirror, he warned her to stop. As the glass began to give way, he hurriedly unbuckled and stepped out into the morning heat. He counted down to two, preparing for her to jump out once the back unlocked. The girl sprang forward. She scratched at his face and scrambled to get over his shoulder. Cassy weakly punched his shoulder blades, yet nothing ended the torment. Another warning was given before, on a low setting, he touched her neck with a Taser. Her squirming stopped as she was struck by a jolt of electricity. An unbelievable cold slithered straight down her back. Just thinking of moving stung too much.

Jason plopped her back onto the seat where Zack winced from his wounds and carefully assisted in lying her across as Jason roughly swung her legs inside. Her body was tense. She found Victor's grumpy grimace, which wondered why their process had slowed. Cassy's agonized moans caught a questioned look.

"She broke down and almost broke through the window," Jason replied bluntly.

"We finally resorted to stunning her, huh? Damn. Buddy mentioned that he had to drug her last night to stop Austin from beating her. We've got to be careful. We don't want to risk killing her."

"Would you rather her cut herself?"

Victor flicked his fingers up and down in irritation of Jason's smart mouth. Noticing the gesture, Jason stepped back and apologized.

"It was on a low setting..."

Encouraged by the man's loyalty, and his understanding of his place, Victor accepted the excuse. His pawns yielded when they needed to. Rolling his hand in a three-hundred-and-sixty-degree motion, the group started up once more.

Zack admired his girlfriend. She had tried to be strong for a long time, even before the men, and now, her bravery seemed futile. Everything they did to prevent this outcome was inevitably useless and within five kilometres, they would witness the dreaded tomb that dictated either life or death for Cassy. It would be Zack's gravesite no matter the results. Not even an empathetic tear would drop from the men's eyes when they slaughtered him. There hadn't been a chance of defeating these men from the start.

Cassy tensed repeatedly. Each movement was calculated to avoid flaring up the burning hot jabs that sucked the breath from her lips. She kept thinking that if she could move, Zack and she could escape before reaching the tomb. Zack snatched her hand and demanded for her to stop.

"Relax. There's no point in hurting yourself. Just rest. It's almost over..."

Haggardly, she curled into a ball and twisted to her side to see the black interior of the vehicle rather than the outdoors.

The access roads went straight to the tomb, yet they were infrequently used and in the wide open, which permitted gusts of wind to pile sand drifts over them. Jason cursed under his breath as another vehicle sank and then became unstuck. The first documented discovery of the tomb, almost two hundred years ago, had swarms of archeologists visiting it, but they required faster routes. So, the first path was built. When it was rediscovered by Jason and Eric four years ago, the left behind road had been untraceable. When they proclaimed the whereabouts of this tomb, the Cairo government funded maintenance of the old road. This remained

Jason's favourite drive, even when he got stuck and swore. The history behind it enthralled him.

Cassy saw her first sight of the tomb from the backseat, leaned up against Zack's shoulder. The enormous architecture of the half-buried tomb was mystifying. Yellow stone, tanned from centuries of sun, glistened in the rays of morning light. On an odd, tilted square, clay bricks had begun their degradation and collapsed in certain points. Directly in front of the semi-excavated wonder, ten uneven steps led up to the clearing to which the only entrance was ajar. A large, solid, rectangular stone had been pried open multiple times before being replaced by the people who learned their lesson early enough to not promote anymore death. It now stood open, inviting anyone inside, though it would only accept one. Hieroglyphics introduced the curse of Obeko, forewarning the disaster of entering if arrogant people believed themselves to be invincible.

The men parked nearby the steps of the partially buried tomb, and Jason unbuckled to join a few of his comrades outside. Cassy silently hoped against all the odds for a beneficial outcome, whatever that may be, to release her from this torment. A pulling sensation, not caused by Eric's tugging arms, drew her into wanting the tomb's ancient heritage to finally grow into a new light. It sucked the heated air from her weary lungs and caused her to close her eyes to lavish in its pleasure. She dreaded that this feeling gave a hint of her truth.

Cassy was dropped back into reality and onto the sandy dunes once Zack was separated from her grip by Jonathon and they marched up the steps only metres away from the entrance. A devastating event would soon transpire, and she accepted the fate to the best of her ability.

Victor bounced on his heels, brushing Cassy's hair back as he embraced her from behind. He scanned the tomb and then looked over to her trembling chin. His arms extended and draped over her shoulders to relieve Eric of her.

"Isn't it beautiful? I'm quite envious of you. You get to enjoy the wonders of the tomb's secrets."

Cassy glowered, "Lucky me..."

Before she could restrain herself from being tossed within, Victor dragged her nearer and then shoved her forward. She stumbled to regain her balance. Taking a deep breath to steady herself, she thought, *This is it.* A final look at Zack's struggling form caused her to seal away her sight and take her first step into the darkness. Cool air tickled her bare skin. Her breaths rapidly choked her. The heat dispersed completely, and the air became stale. Yet the tomb maintained a potent aura; the sensation of its presence enthralled her.

Six steps into the mouth, a sharp pressure struck her shoulder, and an invisible wall obstructed her path. She felt around for what might prevent her from moving forward. As she hunted, an uncontrollable twitch shot up her arm, dropping Cassy against the wall before she slumped down it. The violent seizure spread throughout her torso, sprawling her across the ground.

Outside, Zack broke free from Jonathon's hold. He had made a promise. This one he intended to keep. His long strides headed straight for his girl-friend and none of the men hurried to stop him. They assumed the curse would kill him for them. All he saw was Cassy's panic filled eyes rolling to the back of her head when he entered the darkness. He began to seize even before he met Cassy's form. Stretching out his hand, he found Cassy's palm, clinging to it.

Cassy's mind vibrantly showed the ancient tomb's narrow passages as it had been centuries ago. Her steps echoed in the corridors full of flickering torches that led her down several unfamiliar tunnel systems. Cassy franti-cally searched through each turn to a new hall that might contain what she searched for. The lost and precious items called out to her, but they gave no direction as to where she should look. As she shrieked in frustra-tion, nothing in the square, dank and empty room gave her the relief she desired. She approached the final doorway at the far end. With a plea, she shoved at the stone. Amazement flooded through as the great, embellished stone widened. She became blinded in a light that enveloped everything. Her arms rose to protect herself, and all she could do was allow it to pull her in. Soothed by the light, Cassy's screams halted in her throat before she found herself inside a great hall.

Golden encrusted columns supported the stable ceiling. Silken drapery concealed a figure that moved gracefully about. They strolled back and forth to determine the intruder. They disappeared completely behind a raised throne of gold. Cassy called out to the figure. In curiosity, she asked who they were and where she stood. The figure's hands appeared, crumpling the drapery in a fist, and then spread apart.

A man, dressed in a knee length, pleated skirt that was white with golden accents on the belt, tightly cinched to his lean, bare, tall torso. Sandals wrapped up his ankles. His feet stepped nearer her. He towered above Cassy. His features seemed young, and his head was glistening bald, covered by a head dress of blue with gold threads and buckles placed in specific locations to show off his status. A statuesque jawline inclined down. In all the stories she heard, Cassy always imagined him to be a middle-aged man, but the pharaoh who stood before her was no more than in his late twenties. The man strode, his bare calves tightening with each step, to the throne. His royal strut had been perfected during life.

Many had dared to tempt fate, and during the centuries, the man obviously lost hope to ever witness his heir's arrival. He lifted a kind grin towards the young girl as he sank to the throne and beckoned her forward. He had killed several hundred people who preyed on the diamonds, and now his centuries of waiting ended. She appeased the fates with her acceptance of her duty. His tight fingers gripped the throne's blocky arm rests.

Cassy shuffled ahead, unsure what he might do if she displeased him. Obeko's beautiful garments swirled around his body, but the spirit cared little about the girl's appearance. Her ragged clothes and unwashed skin with blood and dirt was at the back of his mind.

An accented dialect spoke to her. Unlike with Victor's other victims, he spoke English, giving her the ability to understand his words, which were filled with delight.

"Cassandra Waters, you arrive to take claim over the diamonds which have entrusted you as the inheritor. They are sacred, and their intent is to be used for the good of this modern world." He braced himself and rose. "You are now the diamonds' host. I have given you a truly potent, unimaginable gift, and yet," he bent, almost apologetically, "I fear I may have burdened your life. I truly pray that you have a kind and peaceful one. Be weary of using them inappropriately. War should never become your ending, as it was mine."

"Obeko," she wept, "please... I don't want the diamonds."

"It is already done. You have broken the curse and now I will permit one other to join you to retrieve them."

Her courage was slightly masked by dread when she sank to the floor and asked, "How do the diamonds work?" She no longer could deny this fate.

"To use the diamonds, you shall speak your true will and they shall grant any wish."

Cassy, bewildered and dazed, bobbed her head.

"You are such a strong girl, Cassandra. I applaud the choice in you being my heir." He spoke appraisal while looking up to the skies. The gods of Egypt had assisted in the destiny. "You shall do wonders with the diamonds."

He mystically waved his right hand and brought all his fingers gently to a close, starting with the pinkie. A twinkling light appeared as he fetched another figure.

"Zackary Exacil."

Cassy lifted her gaze from the bright flooring to face her right side and found Zack behind her, listening carefully.

"I have always permitted Haeibba to kill all who is not heir..."

Cassy instantly sprang in front of Zack, protesting the course of action. Obeko silenced her with a single look. His hand waved back and forth, moving her aside to approach the young man. His finger pressed onto the center of Zack's forehead, causing an agonizing groan that worried Cassy.

"I see you carry no foul intent towards my heir. Cassandra loves you dearly. You will be her protection, Zackary. Whence your last breath has been taken, your duty to this girl will be broken. Guide her in using the diamonds properly."

A simple flick of the wrist ended Zack's conversation with Obeko, and his form disappeared into the blinding light that swallowed him into an abyss. Cassy remained in the vision with Obeko. She was now aware that she must learn all she could about the curse to survive with the vicious men preying upon her.

"What are the diamonds capable of?"

"Capable of?" he hummed. "They are magnificent energy. Their potential is still leashed within their forms. They have rules, such as anything in this world. You are to learn about the diamonds. Travel to my Sacred Chosen and they shall assist in the diamonds' understanding."

"But… they're all dead…" she mourned.

"They are in hiding. Search for them and they will emerge." He touched his heir's weary head with appraisal. "You will develop your bond with the diamonds as you move through life. This bond will be unlike anything you have ever experienced. They will attach themselves to you, expressing each emotion that you feel. Each diamond is unique, and based on the way you use them, they will form a different connection towards you."

"They aren't going to hurt me, are they?"

"No, it is their duty to protect their chosen heir. I, however, forewarn you that death and revival is strictly monitored by the Gods. It is not something to be tampered with lightly, nor is the yet to come. The future is meant to be mismatched pathways of choices that may lead to one future or another, if one path is altered prematurely, it will cause a disjoint in that path and produce something much worse. Never change a future. What is meant to occur, will occur. Do you understand these warnings, sweet heir?"

Cassy accepted her role in determining the diamonds' powers.

"The diamonds are now yours. When you claim them, they will accept none other than you." Obeko proudly patted her head in a fatherly gesture. "My heir, you will forever be a brilliant light."

The heir's body jerked backwards. She found herself back in front of the entrance, and then, suddenly, at the end of the long, everlasting hallway. The feeling of being rewound swept Cassy from Obeko's sight and back into the reality of the ancient tomb's cool stone. Stiffly, she raised her sore torso once the twitching finished. She scanned outside the tomb from the vantage point of the mouth, and saw Victor and the others intently hovered nearby, lying in wait for her to exit. She delayed leaving the homey tomb. It was Cassy's heritage and forever hers.

Zack stood between two of the bulky men and demonstrated concern with his eyes; he knew the curse had befallen Cassy. He frowned at the men, and then looked back at the despised tomb, angrily wishing that he could've done more to prevent this outcome.

Cassy appreciated the sacrifices he made for her own wellbeing. She wouldn't allow it to be in vain, and she committed to the promise she'd made days back. Stepping from the stale dark air, mentally she prepared. Her feet shook underneath her, and her head was held high. It was ending soon. Cautiously, she approached Victor.

"Obeko," she began once Victor inquired about it. She shook her voice, pretending to be fearful. "He said... I'm not the heir..."

Victor's entire demeanor became malevolent. This was his true self. His men became stone around him. They genuinely thought they'd found the heir. He undid his holster and brought out a pistol to aim it squarely at her forehead.

"What-did-you-just-say?" he hissed through gritted teeth.

Zack, forgive me. "I'm not the heir, I'll die in three hours."

Throttling her, he growled at the never-ending nuisance of teenagers. "Tell the truth!" he blared at Zack's stunned figure. "If she's not, I'll kill her and then you can join her quickly!"

Eric encroached on his enraged boss, and interrupted, "Where's the mark?"

All the men snapped their heads to the girl.

"Where's the mark of Haeibba's sword? If she will die, where is it?"

Taking her chin up to force direct eye contact, Victor snapped, "Where did Haeibba strike you?"

Cassy remained silent. Of course, she wouldn't have a mark, even Zack wouldn't have one. Her mind reeled to find a plausible excuse.

"Not all of the assumed heirs had marks after death," Zack interjected.

Eric rolled his eyes, "True... But where did Haeibba strike the two of you? Both should have been attacked, so at least one of you should have a mark."

Jason tugged Zack from his silent captors and then towed him to the entrance again. "If the curse is still active, then he will enter another vision, and maybe die straight away."

Zack grunted as he was slammed into the stone entrance and collapsed to the ground. He tried his best to fake a seizure. Jason followed close behind and kicked him. It was true. The curse had been broken.

"Let's try this again," Eric barked at Cassy.

She squirmed in Victor's tightened and perturbed grip.

Word vomit spewed from her lips. "The curse... it is broken, but I'm not the heir!"

Victor frowned at the lunacy she spoke.

"I'm like my grandfather. I am part of the enlightened ones. I can take one of you with me to retrieve the diamonds for the rightful heir, Zackary Exacil!"

Jason snatched Zack's slinking form that itched to dash away as she shouted out the nonsense. Zack knew she wanted to die, yet she went about it in the most torturous way if they believed her.

Victor's head tilted, even when he understood the words. "Excuse me?"

"Zack is Obeko's heir!"

The men were mortified at the words. Zack lessened in his struggling when everyone stiffly turned to him.

"Bring him here!" their leader spat.

Zack was towed to the center of the group and Victor dropped him to the ground.

"What the hell is going on? If this is true, I won't waste time and I'll kill her now!" Tugging at her hair, the pistol pressed against her neck.

Cassy's determined face shot Zack a look of daring, but even when Zack guiltily looked at her, he continued to sentence her. She told such a horrific lie. To watch another loved one die in the hands of these beasts would utterly destroy him.

"No, she's..."

Cassy screamed out, "He knew from the beginning! He planned to enter the tomb with me ever since we were kidnapped. He would pretend not to know if I were the heir and then he would get you to kill him! With him gone, nobody would be able to get near those diamonds."

"You're lying," Jonathon uttered.

Victor struck both teenagers to the sandy ground, howling to the skies. Without any indication of what to believe, he was at a loss for words. Jason, methodically thinking, hauled her up.

"We can sort this out, Victor. Trust me. Once we retrieve the diamonds, we can just get the real heir to use them."

Agreeing, Victor towed Cassy forward and tossed her into the tomb. Jason pursued her. He would escort her through the cavernous chambers.

Chapter 15

The entrance stretched along a straight corridor of brick. Jason nervously fiddled with a flashlight removed from his hip and shone it against the interior of the tomb. Cassy pushed forward, determined to play this through. She half-expected them to kill her the moment they found out whether she was the heir, and yet they were calculating, especially the man who strode behind her. They wanted to be sure. She kept her head down, not turning to say anything. She feared Jason's logical mind. If he determined that she was lying, he would dish out the repercussions.

Cassy, however, second-guessed whether Jason would take dealing with her into his own hands. As had been observed throughout the trip, Jason feared someone too. When Victor's demeanor darkened, the men all cringed and walked on eggshells. If they were not able to figure out her lie, he would lash out. *What's his past like?* Cassy wondered. *What's allowed him to gain control over these men?*

Cassy dropped back into reality when she almost fell. She extended her arm to take hold of the wall and heard Jason sigh. It was too dangerous for her to fall in the uncharted tomb. Traps may have been set from ancient times. He settled her back upon her startled feet and marched on.

She was pleased that Jason held the flashlight in haphazard directions to read the hieroglyphs along the walls because once it landed upon her, he would probably notice the welling tears trying to escape. She used the sleeve of her shirt to avoid sniffling and wiped the salty wetness away.

Everything had fallen apart so fast. The day her parents died changed everything. *I've got to convince them that Zack's the heir. If I don't, he'll die, and I'll be left alone with these bastards.* With her newly obtained diamonds being spectacular in theory, she worried what the men had in store for their abilities. The diamonds sentenced her to a life of entrapment, unless she found another way out of it. The girl followed the shadowy, swallowing corridor, dreading to lose the upper hand against the men.

Jason, bored of just hearing the footsteps stomping on the clay bricks, queried, "What was the vision like?"

Squeamish about being questioned, she hesitantly replied, "It's hard to describe. It's almost like the whole world is brighter and more vibrant. It's magnificent!"

Jason chuckled at the explanation, "You were high then?"

With a short shrug, she honestly could not reply. Cassy had never dabbled with drugs.

"What about Obeko?"

A sheepish smile exposed her fondness of the Pharaoh. "He's a kind man. I can tell that he believes he's doing the heir a great favor by giving them the diamonds. He didn't mean for savages to kidnap us and stick us inside this tomb. He truly wanted to help fix the problems in the world."

Jason twisted, catching up to her in an instant, and scowled at her comment as though he clued into something. "So, you were able to understand him?"

"Zack did too." Cassy reverted the conversation back to Obeko to avoid misspeaking. "Obeko's a really strong man. He was actually quite young. He looked barely thirty."

The man scratched his chin, surprised to hear that. "That's interesting. The scholars make him sound much older."

Cassy wavered in her closeness to the man who only asked questions imperative to self-gain. Her tiny form shivered in the cool air of the tomb; the air burned with staleness against her throat. It was tiring to keep up with these men.

"Jason," she inquired, "is Obeko described as a good pharaoh?"

"Not a lot is known about him. The diamonds are considered a myth by a lot of scholars, and when he passed away, his children and the Sacred Chosen did all they could to hide information about him. Even hieroglyphics have been intentionally damaged. That damn group hasn't assisted at all. They destroyed a lot of Obeko's artifacts. I'm the first archeologist to view the hieroglyphs in this tomb since its fruition."

"How did he find the diamonds?"

"Nobody really knows. The Sacred Chosen seemed unsure on that topic as well." He chuckled at the past. "Victor and I once spit balled about finding the source of the diamonds and recreating them rather than hunting for the heir." Jason tilted back his head as he laughed harder. "That proved even harder than finding the heir!"

Thoughtfully, she followed Jason's flashlight. Jason had pursued knowledge, and he hardly boasted unless he was correct. A civil conversation finally happened without a vulgar comment being spouted. She commended him for the peace.

A stretch of silence caused the eeriness of their environment to claim their calm breathing. Jason examined the walls randomly, stealing the light to read the hieroglyphics as quickly as possible. He fawned over Obeko's story. He was overly excited to find the lost information. Cassy froze whenever the light swept to the walls. She worried about tripping again.

Jason finally refocused on strolling forward. "What do you see in that damn agent?"

Cassy span, raising her eyebrows. "He's kind. Even if we started our relationship by fighting, he turned around and looked out for me. Turns out, I should be the one looking after him..."

Amidst viewing a section of the wall, Jason snapped back a reply. "We shall see about that, Cassandra."

They rounded a bend and froze. A long plank bridged across a pit. The width of it was mere centimetres, making whoever wished to cross unable to balance properly and potentially causing them to fall into the two-metre-deep hole. The hole, however, was not the issue. It was the sharp jagged spikes jutting from the pit of darkness and the creatures slithering between the crevices of the spikes. Brown, crowned snakes slithered in the pit, low enough not to be able to escape, but shallow enough to strike them with their fangs. Cassy inhaled sharply while Jason tossed a pebble inside. Harsh, venomous teeth plunged toward the echo, expecting to catch prey. Jason made an obvious gulp.

"Damn," he muttered, "they're cobras..."

"Cobras?" Cassy uttered.

"Shit! They must have fallen down there and have been feeding on one another for sustenance."

Cassy hardly cared on how they got down there. Either way, being bit would kill them, and make them fall. They had limited choices.

Close to the plank, but still far enough away from the snakes, Jason measured the distance from the plank to the side walls. They were too far apart to hold onto. This was a serious trap. Cassy slid down, hugging her knees. *This is good. Getting the diamonds is harder now.*

Jason picked her up and dragged her towards the plank.

"You're joking!" She squirmed within his grip. "We can't do this!"

Jason shoved her onto it. She balanced herself, one foot in front of the other on the thin beam. It barely supported half of her tiny feet, let alone Jason's mammoth ones.

"I want those diamonds. I'm not missing my chance to witness Obeko's sarcophagus or figure out who the real heir is." He ushered her forward as he stepped behind her. "I'll be right here. I will catch you if you fall. You won't get bit, I swear."

"Yeah, that's reassuring."

Cassy shuffled to cross the plank made of clay chipping away from ancient degradation. Jason edged directly behind her. His feet slid across it, unwilling to remove themselves from the semi-secured land source. A few snakes attacked their feet. The younger ones showed their annoyance by flattening their heads and showing off their crowns. They penetrated the humans' loose pant legs, unable to reach the skin. Cassy shrieked each time. Jason held his gun for security. He shot a few rounds, which increased the frequency of strikes, even when some fled. Cassy moaned with anxiety as the silenced bullets ricocheted on the dusty ground and hit a snake.

As soon as she reached the end of the three-metre plank, Cassy collapsed against a wall. *Thank you!* she praised to no one in particular. The gun clipped back into the holster as Jason continued his determined stroll. When he realized he went on alone, he marched back, hands falling on lean hips.

Cassy begged, "Please, give me a minute. I hate this so much."

Jason refused and propelled her onwards. She restrained from combatting him. If she infuriated him enough, he could potentially threaten something that she held dearer than her own life.

Up and over slopes of shifting ground, down uneven sandy areas and rounding corners, they came up to a caved in portion of the tomb. The roof had collapsed, which halted all process. Jason swore and drove the flashlight into the ground. They should have suspected an unclear path to the diamonds. He drove his bare hands into the rubble and removed chunks of bricks in the dust. He hoped it was a small section that caved in, rather than the rest of the tomb. Cassy hunkered against a nearby wall, satisfied with watching him labour away to greedily retrieve the diamonds. His dirty hands slammed into the wall when he noticed her grin.

"You know," he cooed behind him, "if we take too long, Victor may just kill the boy, no matter if he's the heir, and leave us in here to die. His commitment to this can be severed like that," he snapped two dirty fingers together, "if he believes he won't gain anything."

Her shoulders sank. It was true and more probable than not. She sulked over to him, kneeled, and dug her fingers into the sandy clay to make a dent in the cave in. The hole deepened into a human-sized one that Jason could squirm inside. They crawled into the tunnel, Jason in front, raking his fingers along the way. Cassy lazily dragged herself through, and held the flashlight as claustrophobia took over. Her mind raced with worry that at any point they might shift a support and have the tomb crumble down onto them. When they met the end of the tunnel's ten-metre length, Jason broke through. A short laugh celebrated his hour-long struggle of digging. He slithered his way out, using his arms in army-style form. Cassy crawled behind him, finding him grunting about the mess covering his once cleanly manicured person. Trying to make it seem like she expected this, she hardly brushed anything off and strolled onwards.

Jason hurried along, wiping his hands clean, to keep up with the speedily moving girl. He worried that she might know of a hidden entrance and disappear within to leave him in the darkness. His concern was accurate, since the following turns reminded Cassy of the vision. Hard stone chambers were haphazardly placed in no particular order. Jason itched to open some, but Cassy led him straight. The farthest entrance would be the one they needed. It was closed, guarded by a large statue of an ancient Egyptian soldier. The man briskly went to shove at the stone. Cassy paused for a second. It seemed so familiar. *We're almost there. I might expose myself.* Using the few muscles that she had, she helped shift the door open.

It was unlike the vision behind it. Down another empty corridor with jutting turns in all directions, the labyrinth of the tomb continued. This was supposed to lead to the grand hall. Her mind went into overdrive. *How could this not be right?* That's when she realized that the blinding light had swallowed her. *I was not taken to his resting place, but to a throne room. His spirit is not anywhere near the diamonds.* She stepped into the vast darkness, leaving Jason to look at the hieroglyphics behind her. She shrilled and landed on her butt. Tricked by the illusion of an assumed great hall, Cassy was surprised by an uneven stairwell. The girl froze in place. Her bum was numb, and Jason sucked back a breath, worried she had fallen into a booby trap. Pointing the beam of light down, he saw the stairwell of sixty-five steps.

Jason forcefully tugged Cassy from her seat and towed her down the steps. He held her up. It was coming. Any moment, they would witness the gems she disdained, and she would somehow have to convince them that Zack was the heir to save his life.

Jason prodded his fingers between her shoulder blades, distracting her from worrying. Things would happen as already predestined.

"How come you wanted to come down here?" Cassy asked, hoping to distract his focused mind.

"Ever since Eric and I found Obeko's tomb, I've wanted to be the first one to set my eyes on its secrets and treasures. Obeko has been my main goal ever since I was a child, and now, I have a chance to see his actual sarcophagus and try to learn about the man who captivated me since I was a little boy. The diamonds will make this all worth it."

"You're disgusting. You're inside this magnificent tomb and all you can think about is how much money you'll be counting."

"Well, of course! It's been a long time coming. We've hunted for the heir for three years, and no matter which one of you is the actual heir, we'll keep them hostage and be taking our worth from those diamonds. Taking both of you was the easiest thing in the world!" Jason sighed. "I honestly hope you are the heir, though. We need a female among us. If you aren't, Victor's going to rip you apart for the hassle you've caused."

Cassy cringed; unfortunately, that was her plan. She hoped they would remove her, take Zack with them, and give him a chance to survive long enough for the FUA to find him. It wasn't worth her living when all she would cause was misery for everyone else.

Jason snatched her shoulder and turned her to face him. Ready for him to strike her, she recoiled.

"Quit being so stuck up. Why don't you just tell the truth? Then you wouldn't have to hear the truth that we will kill you the moment you're useless to us."

"I have told the truth."

"Uh-huh, we'll see."

He flung her from his arms in disgust as they reached the bottom step. Another stone wall, unlike the one above them, stood in their way. It was heavily encrypted with hieroglyphs and did not show a seam to shift the section. In the middle of the stone, two handprints rested.

"What does it say?"

Cassy knocked on the door while Jason rubbed his hand along the symbols as he read.

"These are some complex hieroglyphs. They're all jumbled together, almost like they need to be reworded." His head tilted. "Huh? What I can get, is that the 'chosen' one is supposed to place their hands on the prints and the doors should open." He attempted a bit more. "That's it. I guess, you are the 'chosen' one."

Cassy instantly considered his words. *The chosen one would mean the heir... but what if because Obeko allowed one more person in here, that it means the one that I chose to bring? I may get away with this if those doors don't open. But how would I convince Jason to put his hands on there?*

First, Cassy slipped her palms onto the imprints nervously. She prayed for the gentle touch not to cause a reaction. Luckily, nothing happened while she stood there awkwardly shoving the clay. She removed her palms, and turned to watch Jason frown when she disappointedly glanced behind her and raised a questioning eyebrow. Recalculating, Jason stroked his chin. He shuffled towards the steps and sat down.

"Maybe…" she said, "because Obeko allowed one more in here, you're supposed to help, to prove your worth?"

"I read nothing of the sort…"

Frustrated, Jason swore gruffly and then sauntered back over to the barricade in hopes of finding another hint.

"Well, right here, it says the chosen one will be led by the all-seeing to reach their destination."

He prodded at a few worn hieroglyphs in hopes of making them readable.

Cassy tilted her head sideways when he spoke. *The all-seeing? Is that Grandpa? Was he supposed to lead my way to the diamonds? He was the Enlightened One and he was the first person to know the true identity of the heir.*

"Can you humour me," Jason begged, "and try once more? It should've opened if you are who you say you are."

"Alright…"

Cassy pressed harder, wanting to dissuade him from coming upon any conclusions. Still nothing happened. Confused, she wondered internally, *Ugh! Why would Obeko make this when his heir can't open it?* As though the door listened to her thoughts, a burning instantly stung her palms. The hieroglyphs suddenly glowed a bright red that followed a seamless line between the glowing handprints and formed two visible doors, which buckled and moaned wide. Jason gave her a condescending pat on her head as he hurried over to witness the unveiling of the mystical diamonds.

A golden sarcophagus was placed on a rectangular platform, risen above the square flooring inside the chamber. Three diamonds sat on each side of the sarcophagus, and a singular one rested near Obeko's head's location, floating three inches above their embellished pedestals. The diamonds were smooth, orb shaped objects. Colours swirled within them; navy was the primary constant, but all imaginable colours jumbled around like lightning bolts, swirling throughout the orbs. Casually, they spun, waiting for inspiration to awaken.

Jason shoved by the youth and strolled to the first, right-hand side diamond. As he brushed his hand against it, the diamond blackened in anger and flung the man backwards. He struck the wall with his spine and slid down it to land on his knees. Coughing, the tall man spat out sand. He struggled to regain his composure while Cassy asked him what she should do. The diamonds weren't allowing him to touch them. Would they allow her?

"Well," Jason growled, "that was unexpected." He leaned against the wall, massaging his chest from the force. "You're supposed to bring the diamonds to the heir..." he snapped. "Check if you can touch it."

Cassy edgily approached the same diamond. It had swirled wildly, almost enraged at the intruder that touched them. She reached out and touched the smooth surface of the diamond. A light, more blinding than the sun, caused a chain reaction from all seven diamonds as Cassy took claim over them. Their warmth trickled along her blood stream, proving their loyalty to only her. Their colours exploded and she indulged in their seduction of power. The high was too much to handle. Cassy moaned before releasing the gem.

The man shifted to stand next to her, making her cringe at the reaction of the diamonds. He nibbled his inner cheek, unsure if he should attempt grabbing it again. He risked being shot across the room once more and snatched the diamond to toss it into the air. She had removed the untouchable curse over them. The men could handle them without concern. He pulled a purse-sized burlap sack from his pant pocket.

As he piled them on top of one another, Cassy approached the sarcophagus and patted the surface. *I'm sorry I took so long. Your spirit stuck around just for me. I'm going to do what's right. I won't let your diamonds get caught up in evil.*

"Hey!" Jason barked, "Take this one. My bag wasn't big enough."

He pointed at the central one near Obeko's head and then began shuffling to the exit. Cassy plucked the diamond from its pedestal. The mass of a two-pound weight landed in her palm. The diamond fit perfectly in her hand. Tingles shot up her arms as her grip tightened around it. The diamond recognized its owner. *If only you knew how much trouble you've caused.* She stuffed it into her front jean pocket. It made a slight bump, but it comforted her with its magical warmth.

Jason took the steps two at a time to leave the tanned stone. Cassy lagged behind. She was exhausted with the lies and dreaded who would be slaughtered once they left the tomb. They both crawled through the tunnel stealthily, only faltering a bit at the pit. As they reached the snakes, the hissing was more vicious. Even with fewer among them, they snapped angrily. Snake corpses were being devoured by their community while others searched for live prey. The man ushered her up front so he could watch over her. The cobras' tails vibrated when they crouched and sprung. A few got further up the fabric on their pants and shoes, but none punctured the skin. Cassy kicked one off her the instant it latched on, shrieking in panic. Jason clung to her wrist, holding her balance. He waited until the end of the thin plank to kick and stomp the cobras. The man was uncontrollably excited to leave the tomb and wasted as little time as possible to show off their reward of three years of hard work.

Hurriedly, he went down the last stretch of the tomb. Jason exited into the sun; Cassy soon followed after a slight hesitation inside. Against all odds, she would have to convince them wholeheartedly that Zack was the rightful heir. She covered her eyes to adjust to the change of bright light. The heat beat down on her now, penetrating her skin. Jason instantly headed to Victor. A diamond dropped from the sack and showed off its beauty to the men. Victor's hand softly rubbed the diamond. His eyes sparkled in wonder. They had won.

His next problem, now that he clutched onto the ever-sought-after diamonds, was to figure out which prisoner was the heir. That problem seemed to weigh heavily on all the men's minds. Jason leaned into Victor's ear to whisper something that brightened his boss's eyes. Curtly nodding, Victor told Jason to grab the girl. Cassy accepted his grasp. She was ready to die.

The sight of Zack stung her. Austin entered the circle of eight with Zack struggling, his arms pinned back. Austin flung the agent to the ground. Blocking his face from the sand, he landed beneath Victor's gaze. Fresh bruises and cuts wept across his face. The five men had taken advantage of Cassy's absence to abuse her boyfriend, despite the possibility that he was the heir. Victor's hand reached around his hip and hoisted his trusted pistol to Zack's head.

"See, I've won! We have the diamonds, and you have death!"

Cassy wrestled hard! She thrashed about, yelling, "NO! He's the heir! If you kill him, you'll have nothing!"

"Cassandra," Jason mocked, "you really thought we would fall for such a half-conceived lie? When the FUA became involved, we investigated the Exacils to make sure they hadn't put the heir further away by putting them closer. Zack's heritage is no where close to being the heir. You, on the other hand, were able to walk straight into the tomb and touch the diamonds." He dropped her to the ground. "You are most definitely the heir."

Victor kicked her torso. "You tried to save your wretched boyfriend with such a disgraceful lie, you stupid little bitch."

"I... I..."

"I caught on straight away," Jason continued. He announced his reasoning for all to hear, since quite a few of the others had been fooled by the girl. "First off, you took much longer to speak with Obeko in the vision. Had Zack been the heir, you would've been the first out. Secondly, when you mentioned that you were able to understand Obeko, it most definitely meant you were the heir."

"But Zack could—"

"Yes, I have a working theory about that. When you entered, you broke the curse; since Zack entered the vision with you, he was able to hear what you heard and was fully connected with you, rather than being connected to Obeko. Lastly, inside the tomb, with those handprints on the stone, it didn't say the 'chosen' one. It said, 'Only the heir may open it'. Which I sensed you caught onto. That's why you tried to convince me that we both needed to open it. That bullshit about the all-seeing one was false. I bet you assumed instantly that the Enlightened One was supposed to lead you here. You are a naïve little girl who fell for every trap I set for you."

"NO! Please! I'll do whatever you say! I need Zack."

"Cassandra," Victor snapped, "his life is worthless now. He's survived far longer than we intended, but now, it is time for him to accept his death."

Zack kneeled. His hands folded into each other on his lap as he looked at his beloved girlfriend. "Cassy, stop. It's alright. I'm just glad you weren't killed because of me."

One of the men straddled Cassy's back and wrenched her neck to witness Victor nearing Zack. Zack reverted his eyes to the man. He was unable to watch Cassy cry while he accepted his death.

"Zack," said Victor, "you are before us for your execution. We find you guilty of interfering in matters you have no ties to, and in turn, we sentence you to death by our own hand." Victor lavished in the heir's pleas to stop. "Our witness for this amazing event will be Cassandra, our newly imprisoned trophy. Now," he grinned maliciously at the boy who did not satisfy his need to watch him beg, "do you have anything to say before you join your brother?"

Zack ignored his budding anger. Their mock sentencing pissed him off. It was only meant to torture his girlfriend. And yet, relief washed over him. It would soon be over.

"Cassy, forgive me... I'm sorry for leaving you like this." His brown eyes grazed her form, sobbing and fighting the restrainer's grip. Tears reddened her cheeks. "Keep fighting them. Never stop!"

He was ready, and Victor took aim.

Chapter 16

The shot penetrated her ringing ears. Slow motion brought every gesture to a frame-by-frame standstill. Zack dropped to the sandy ground with a soft thud leaving the wound to blossom in his chest. Victor holstered his weapon and cheered along with his men when he nudged a foot into the lifeless agent.

Cassy kicked and screamed. She wanted to assist in stopping the blood before she lost him forever. Eric rose off the sobbing girl and swung a congratulatory arm over his closest comrade's shoulder. Cassy fumbled across the sandy land, tasting sand in her dry mouth. Upon reaching Zack, she struggled to stop the blood by pressing on the wound. She turned him over onto his back to find a pool leaking into the draining sand. Subconsciously, she accepted that he was gone, but her mind could not break through to her heart.

She knelt, scanning Zack. His eyes were dull like a grey, cloudy day. The cheerful, overconfident glow had dimmed. His perfect smile disappeared, and his straight posture now lay on the ground, bloody and awkwardly bent. Already the sand blew over his body to remove the lost teenager from existence. He was going to be buried, and she would be unable to expose his murderer. Her head dropped to his chest, and she cried into his stiffening pectorals. Nothing of Zack's personality or brilliance was left, just a limp, empty figure.

She comforted his body, brushing off any sand trying to cover up the homicide. *Zack, don't leave me here alone. I love you. I've lost everything...* A pinch from within her jeans' pocket prompted her to pat it. Everything held dear rested there. From Zack's note in the back pocket to the warm diamond that snuggly clung to her hip concealed by her shirt, all of her most prized possessions were nearby. Beside her hidden cellphone was the watch Zack gave her for safe keeping. The men had searched Zack inside Susan's motel, but never patted her down. It had been a symbol of hope, yet, with Zack gone, it became a lasting memento to a lost soul. Digging it out, she attached it to his wrist and crossed both arms over his still chest.

"Zack, I won't need this anymore. I suppose..." she gulped. "I won't be free..."

Cassy pressed her shocked lips onto his and caressed his flowing hair. *I'm theirs.*

Behind her, she listened to the men shuffling around, preparing to leave for the plane. They spoke in undertones. None bothered her while they moved about. It was like they hadn't done anything. The heartless monsters each grasped hold of the diamond Victor carried. They awed at it. She couldn't help but feel the overwhelming magic the diamond produced penetrating into her leg while she sobbed.

Zack's murderer squatted down to embrace her shoulders. "Come, Cassandra. We're leaving," he layered his voice in fake sweetness.

"I'm not going anywhere with you! You slaughtered him!"

He took a fistful of hair. She used her legs to move with him when he propelled her onward. Cassy yelped in pain as she was hauled down the stone steps away from the tomb. She elbowed Victor in the stomach. It winded him, but grew his resentment. He tossed her into the back seat of an SUV with a savage shove of her back. His companions waited for orders behind the man.

Eric, about to retrieve the body, straightened when his leader barked out, "Leave the body! Cassandra is developing a temper that will soon be eradicated."

Eric followed suit with the rest, and they separated into their designated vehicles. Victor piled in with the heir. The SUV's backseats faced one another, so he sat across from her, flopped his arms across the backrest, and crossed one leg over the other. Streaks of dirt and tears were smeared on her pale cheeks as she swiped lingering ones away. She could ignore the man's giddy grin, but unfortunately for her heart, the pain of the loss was hard to ignore. Cassy welled up with furious rage against Victor. All blame landed on the man who made her suffer so relentlessly.

She examined her hands where red blood tarnished them. Zack's blood had been spilled. *He's gone...* She scrubbed her hands along her jeans, trying to remove the stain from them. Her chin wobbled again, and shivers pierced her spine. It took all her efforts to stop the tears from overflowing.

Victor leaned forward to cup her cheek with fake empathy.

"Cassandra, enough tears. I'm sorry, but I needed to be rid of him. Would you have preferred me killing him in another way?"

He asked as though she would sadistically want to watch him die.

"You made it an execution! You made me watch!" she hiccuped. "You act like a kind person because you think it will manipulate me. You're a greedy," her voice rose, "selfish man and I'm not going to give you anything, you asshole! They're my diamonds! They will never be yours!"

She spat on his polished shoes. This irked him. His leg uncrossed, his murderous hand grabbed above her elbow and wrestled her to the floor. She was bent on her hands and knees with an ear next to his mouth.

"Listen carefully, my dear. I'll only say this once. You will never swear at me again. You will cooperate and submit to me, or we'll kill you. You will be tortured, left to bleed in the dark until you take your final breath."

"I'd rather die slowly than stay submissive for even a minute!"

Victor slipped a pocketknife out. It glistened in the sun as it drifted next to her eyes. It passed her lips and landed on her neck.

"Shall I give you a taste?" he wondered.

The knife grazed gently along her jugular, which bobbed as she swallowed in anticipation of the upcoming sting. The blade was unnoticeable when it shifted from her throat and slipped elsewhere along her body. It struck her upper arm quickly and deep. A scream boomed. The pain was unexpected, and seared with white hot heat. A steady flow of her own blood wept down the stabbed arm with thick, copper-smelling intent to stain her innocent self. She doubled over in paralyzing agony. Victor released, leaned back to sit in his comfortable seat, and watched the action unfold. Sagging to the ground, she clutched the wound. Zack's blood was soon blended with Cassy's, and she lost the last proof that Zack had once lived. She willed herself not to show the ache. That would satisfy his merciless need to watch. He drank from a whiskey container before he took a piece of scrap cloth from a cubbyhole to wipe her hands and then tied it tightly to stop the blood flow.

"It hurts, doesn't it?"

Cassy refused to answer. Without someone to defend her, she needed to situate herself as a strong individual, otherwise, they would eat her alive and do more heinous crimes than they already had.

Their drive through Cairo increased Cassy's anxiety. They had all they needed to take her anywhere in the world. Victor was outright perky about it. The drive uncomfortably lengthened as they drove to the airport to leave Egypt as soon as possible.

Victor tapped his hand against his bristled face, making movements like something bothered him greatly. He lifted his lean hips so he could grab his phone.

"Buddy, turn around," Victor growled. "I'm telling you, turn around now, and get Zack's body. Something is bothering me about the FUA. Meet us back at the plane and we'll dispose of it over the ocean."

Cassy dropped her mouth into a gape while Victor hung up.

"What?" he snarled.

"Why do you suddenly want to get his body?" she wondered softly.

He covered his lips while he admitted, "I was careless. The last few times we took someone to the tomb, we had to linger around, moving to different regions of Cairo as often as three hours because there was a Cairo FUA branch hanging around the tomb. However, suspiciously, they weren't around this time. If they find Zack's body too early, it will lessen our chances of escape, so collecting the body will remove that risk."

What happened to the Egyptian branch? Didn't Mr. Edwards warn them that they kidnapped me and Zack?

Victor's short comment left Cassy worrying over whether the FUA would be capable of finding them. They couldn't move to another jurisdiction unless evidence appeared. Without Zack's body, she could be lost in an unforgiving world.

Cassy curled into the seat's base. She reverted to remembering that first day of school when Zack attacked her. She giggled internally. Those were much happier times, even though they seemed miserable. Surviving the bullies' abuse was a million times easier than dealing with these brutes.

The car crunched to a stop at the airport security. They opened the door to check for passports and asked Victor's men questions on where they planned to head next. Victor spoke in an undertone with them. Once they were cleared, the car shifted on, moving towards the grounded plane. It screeched to a halt.

Jonathon slid from the driver's seat and opened the child-locked door on Cassy's side. Victor paved the way to leave the cool jeep. No one followed him out. Egypt's entire atmosphere eased her. Her ancestors came from there and protected her. The lingering thoughts of Zack had her covering her face with both hands before she slumped forward. Wanting to remain where her boyfriend rested, Cassy fought her demons. *He won't even have a proper funeral... I'm leaving with these monsters that will kill me in the end.* What had she done to deserve such a life sentence?

Victor poked his head back in and bestowed a smile on Cassy. It faded into a glower. Cassy's middle finger rose and without even glancing at him, she said, "Get lost, you asshole!"

Snapping hands grabbed her nearest foot and pulled her from the vehicle. The black cement scraped her skin, causing a stinging sensation to run its course throughout her wounded limbs. He cast a heavy shadow above her and denied her from seeing beyond him. Tugging her to unstable feet, the man gripped beneath her lean jaw to gain her attention. She whipped her head around wildly to dissuade him from the upcoming threats.

"I told you not to use that language with me! You will never use that gesture again or I'll cut off that finger," he snarled. "Now, let's go to the plane quietly."

"SCREW YOU!"

Cassy kicked his kneecap with a strong swipe of her runners. It dropped him instantly to the other one. Releasing herself, she tried to run and search briskly for an escape. Any chance of momentum was unsuccessful as Victor clipped her shin with his arm. She slammed into the ground; her head bounced with a grunt. His weight crushed her. Her flailing arms were restrained, and Cassy's anguish spread through her adrenalin filled body.

"You're stupider than I thought!" He silenced her cries for aid. "Just for this *useless* act, you'll be locked away with no food for a few days."

"Good, I'd rather starve to death!"

She fought harder as soon as his weight lifted. She kicked her feet upwards, producing a couple injuries at his side. He strived to gain possession of strands of her hair or an improved grip on her. Her shirt became caught up in his fumbling hands, giving him the advantage he required. Holding her close, breathlessly, to his masculine torso, he called out for the men gathering around to move inside the plane.

Refusing defeat, she spun, her shirt choking her slightly, and stomped on his feet. Victor lost his grip. She gathered herself from the unexpected force of freedom and spun to glare at him with squinted hazel eyes. She struck her closed fists against him. *This*, she savagely thought as she took revenge, *is for Zack!* Her fist met his face and formed a small cut along his eye line.

Victor's muscles rippled in their tense state of holding her back. The other men used their bulk to hide the fight and forced Cassy closer to Victor. His tight grasp outdid her, ensnaring by the neck and making her inoperative. The ground cooled her back as she rested on the tarmac, getting struck by Victor's fists. She shouted between each strike. Victor instinctively covered her lips and beat her until she bled. As Victor resigned from her thrashing body, Eric grabbed his Taser and moved it to her neck.

Cassy jerked while the numbness burned. She was elevated into Jonathon's arms as he manhandled her onto the plane. Victor, in the background, shook off the won battle, straightening his expensive clothes, and then followed his trophy to the plane's ramp. Jonathon excused himself from the group, who prepared to celebrate their kidnapping of the heir, to return her to the back bedroom. He dropped her onto the bed, moaning and stinging. Jonathon's bulk briskly scurried from the room to revel with heavy drinking.

Slowly, Cassy regained mobility. Her sore, beaten body laid still, with only her toes wiggling first. Zack's advise on not forcing movement until the pain subsided was taken. The diamond jammed into her hip whenever she shifted. It held nothing to help her. She wanted to destroy it, to toss it at the window and watch it shatter. The inanimate object was just there; not even the power that coursed her veins could soothe her ache.

Cassy slid off the bed, searching for the embrace that Zack continuously gifted her. The pain throbbed against her electrocuted neck.

"Thanks, Zack, for your love. I wish you were alive. I want to see you again... to be with you like we should have been," she pleaded.

The denim around her waist suddenly glowed brightly. The orb-like diamond listened to her words and reacted. Cassy realized it when she whipped her hand to her pounding forehead and faced down. It burned worse than the electric shock. She rolled across the floor. *What's happening?* The strange event sent Cassy on the hunt. She slipped the diamond out to admire the colours spinning wildly. The lively glow dimmed, and then settled to a lessened brightness. Multiple colours swirled lazily at their original pace. Her eyes drooped tiredly, since the diamond seemed to suck her entire reservoir of energy. She examined it, flipping it from hand to hand.

She drunkenly perched on the edge of the bed. She hadn't expected this type of reaction by using the diamonds. *I'm their host... I need to be strong for them to work.* In an instant, her lips gaped open, realizing what she had said. *Could he be alive?* In awe of the diamond, a short giggle burst out. *Did I save him?*

The small moment of rejoicing ended abruptly with a short knock, and Victor entered. Before he could find the diamond, she tucked it between the mattresses. Her painful cringe became a distasteful glare towards Victor as he sank next to her. He most likely assumed the pain was formed from the assault only twenty minutes ago. He rubbed below her eye to check the sensitivity of the swelling lump, and sighed back anger when she winced.

"I'm sorry for hurting you, Cassandra."

His legs kicked up and he strode to the bathroom. Gushing water was heard before he returned with a wet cloth. It landed on her face. He wiped away the dirt, blood, and grime so he might see the damage from a better vantage point.

"If you keep a cold cloth on it, the swelling should go down."

Victor's soft tone was used just how Brant spoke whenever he tended his siblings. His soft hands gently nurtured the open gashes just as the middle brother had done the day she was beaten by Victoria. Her inner eye flashed to images of her brothers' loving care from which she was ripped prematurely away.

Michael was most likely on a rampage hunting for his missing sister. He loved her dearly. Having finally reached a point in mending their relationship, to only have Cassy disappear without a trace, he probably lost all willpower to do anything other than search for a needle in a haystack. The kidnapping, she assumed, was viewed as a random act by a sick pervert. *He probably only thinks that Buddy took us for some twisted fantasy. If I ever get home, what am I supposed to tell them?*

Brant, being the most empathetic and parental figure in their shambles of a life, probably hid his emotional breakdowns behind school. She assumed he maintained a tedious study habit to avoid losing his sanity. That was how it was after their parents' deaths. He had worked on ensuring that he had all the proper paperwork sent to Michael or signed by himself, and he settled on packing whatever they found necessary without missing a beat. His younger siblings were his priority.

The night the police offered the ghastly news, and Brant became their temporary caregiver, the three siblings stayed up just hugging one another. The youngest two cried like children while he held his head strong, stroking their backs and giving them a shoulder to cry on. The officers gave their condolences, and then excused themselves from the threesome who endured an unfathomable ache.

Brant offered to call Michael. He marched to the phone, and pretended that he was calling Michael for a pleasant conversation. What Cassy saw was a defeated brother that slipped around the corner to hide while the phone rang. Cassy had entered a state of shock, but heard each of Brant's shaken words.

"Michael," he controlled the weeping tone, "I know it's late, but something happened to Mum and Dad." He listened a bit before answering Michael's questions. "They were in a car accident. A drunk driver... he hit their car. It rolled..."

Unable to handle Brant's rasping voice, Cassy rose and clutched his trembling hands upon the receiver.

Brant wrapped an arm around Cassy's shoulders as he mumbled, "Michael, Mum and Dad passed away tonight."

They heard Michael's line clatter to the floor; he had not anticipated such a harsh comment.

Beside Victor's prodding form, she then understood Michael's behaviour at the funeral. *The entire funeral, he was too upset to approach us. He wasn't being cold. He was mourning the only way he knew how. He had to be solitary to move on from our loss. He felt guilty for leaving so abruptly like he did… Each of them reacted differently… They all took it in stride. How are they going to handle me not coming home?*

At the beginning of the dawn light, the following morning after the accident, Vince had disappeared into his room to think. After a few days, Brant and Cassy noticed the signs of alcohol abuse. He would arrive home drunk, skip classes, or not even return until late into the night. Vince acted so cool, yet, in truth, he drowned the inner pain with the buzz he gained from drinking. Not long after the funeral, he was expelled from school. This gave him more time to drink, but also help Brant with whatever was necessary.

They tried to keep Cassy out of the loop. Many tough decisions had to be made. Being doted on enraged her. The entire three weeks of her brothers' overprotectiveness after their parents' death increased her dislike for it. It was not directed at anyone specific until the day they headed to Saskatoon. All the blame for all the misfortune landed on Michael. *If only I had realized why they were keeping me out of these struggles, I would've had more pleasant memories with them. Instead, I lashed out. I'm such a horrible sister. I even got mad at Mum and Dad for going to that party. I'm so ungrateful. All their sacrifices, and look at it now… I only produced more suffering.*

Cassy inclined her head when the cloth brushed a fresh cut caused by Victor's knuckles.

"Please, leave me alone," she pleaded to Victor, self-conscious of all her short comings. She banished the cloth from touching her and curled into a ball against the wall.

Speaking as though she hadn't spoken, Victor chirped pleasantly, "We're going to travel the world. How does that sound? Where would you like to go?"

Cassy fiddled with the corner of Zack's note hidden in her jeans with a finger and requested, "Can't you take me home? I'll let you come and use the diamonds whenever."

A chilling sneer came from the kidnapper. *He'll never let me go.*

Victor scratched his chin. "You know... I'd really love to meet your brothers. Buddy says they are some interesting individuals. Maybe we'll visit some time. Pop in and say hi."

Fury flashed into her eyes. "Would you let me stay there?"

"Of course not! If I were to ever take you back home, your brothers would not have such a good reunion. I would eliminate them from your thoughts."

He mocked her by dangling her brothers out of reach. The moment she found peace with keeping them as her iron defence, Victor would destroy the last people in the world who loved her. *Does he carry even an ounce of compassion?*

"You're so cruel..." she whispered.

Victor patted her head, reassuringly saying, "In the near future, I will build you a new home that you will not resent me for."

Cassy scooted from him, disgusted by his words.

"My family will be the only place where my home truly is. I despise you. No matter the effort you put into making my life decent, it will never be enough to remove my anger towards you."

The man rose to leave her to wallow in self-pity. Her chest hurt against her ribs with each deep inhale she took. She cautiously stood and edged towards the window. People waited in the terminals to be called for flights. Families and businesspeople chatted. Cassy missed her brothers. She ached to just sit with her family and listen to their simplistic words that always cheered her up. *If Mum and Dad hadn't died, we would've still been in Edmonton. I wouldn't have met Zack. Victor would've kidnapped me more easily... though, if they hadn't died, would any of this have happened?*

"Mr. Edwards and Victor mentioned that they were pinged because of their death. They caused this all to happen..." Cassy shook her head, stopping herself from blaming her loving parents. They wouldn't have wanted this. "Great... now I'm talking to myself."

Her attention settled back on the window. A sleek, black jeep drove up, screeching to a halt before Buddy sprinted up the ramp. No corpse was lugged from the vehicle. His footsteps slammed across the floor as he searched for the boss with shocking news. Cassy slid down the wall. When news reached Victor of what she assumed was about Zack, she would be in trouble. Pressing her hands against her face, the heir moaned, infuriated.

"I wish I had someone to talk to other than these men."

Cassy's head seared again as the diamond under the mattress glowed. It took advantage of Cassy's willingness to use it. It had waited far too long for the heir. Her unused cell phone rang. Loud! Before it chimed again, she ripped it out and pressed the talk button. Her smile glowed at the blissful sound. The device died days previously.

"Hello?"

"Hey, Cassy," a cheery, friendly voice spoke. "It's Tanya. It's been like a month since we last talked! How's it been going?"

"Tanya, listen!" she said frantically.

• • •

Victor turned to Buddy as he rushed inside. Jonathon leaned against the wall underneath the round windowsill. Buddy silently closed the door, his lips pursed together, twitching nervously.

"Well," Victor glanced around him, "where's the body?"

Buddy edged back. "There wasn't a body."

Jonathon tilted his head, perplexed by this statement. Victor swung wildly, hitting Buddy.

"What do you mean," Jonathon queried, "there wasn't a body?"

Buddy slumped against the doorframe as his face swelled from the assault. At first, he muttered, "Jackass." Then, "When I arrived at the tomb, there was no body. It was..."

Victor raised his hand to silence him. A voice spoke through Victor's hidden speaker and camera. The girl speedily explained how to find them. Jonathon clenched his fist.

"Is anyone with her?"

"No," Jonathon answered.

"Does she still have her cell phone?"

Buddy gulped because of another mistake he had committed. "You told me not to get rid of it..."

Victor swung around, swiping his hand through his hair. "You were supposed to get rid of it once we left Canada." Something bothered him about the usage of the phone. Ripping open the burlap sack of diamonds, he spilled them onto a soft surface. After counting hastily, he dodged to the door. "Get to her now or we'll *all* go to jail!"

●   ●   ●

Cassy hung up and tossed the phone beneath the bed. Buddy, Jonathon, and Victor stormed in seconds later.

Buddy took up her wrists and rose her to unsteady feet. Jonathon and Victor commenced in searching her recently, and cleverly, emptied pocket. They found only the note, which was instantly torn up, and then they began to rip apart her prison. Jonathon disappeared inside the washroom. Buddy maintained his grip on Cassy; she sulked in his arms about losing the last of Zack's words. If he was not revived, she lost her last chance of keeping sane. Victor rummaged in the closet. Finding nothing, they reassembled in the main section and wracked their brains for where she may have hidden the diamond or cell phone. Victor's search landed upon the bed. Groaning, he reached in between the mattresses and snagged the smooth diamond. Jonathon dropped to his stomach when Victor shook his head about not finding the cellphone. The man reached with a grunt to grab the abandoned device and broke the screen from the keypad.

Transfixed on the diamond's magnificent beauty, Victor awed at it for a moment. It then dropped into his pocket for safe keeping. His gaze maliciously observed the shivering girl who lost her only advantages against the men in a gamble that her message would reach someone. Victor's eyes glinted with greed and flared fiercely.

"When Buddy arrived, he told me that Zack's body was gone. No matter how quickly the FUA might mobilize, it is too early for it to be found by anyone. Mhmm, I thought," he scratched his head to ridicule her, "how could a teenager, who I personally killed, disappear from the middle of a barren wasteland? In my bag of diamonds, I counted six, which is odd, since in all the research I've ever done, there was supposed to be seven." Victor edged her onto the bed and pinned her beneath him, strangling her with his forearm.

"What does this have to do with me?" Cassy asked, digging her fingers beneath his forearm to pry it off.

"Because here's the seventh." His weight increased its pressure. "What did you ask for?"

A deep resentment furrowed her brow as she realized what he asked. *Did I ask for something? How did I activate the diamonds?* Her memory was sent spiralling. *I wanted Zack alive so badly... I was scared of being alone, and then the phone rang. I asked... no, it's stronger than that. I wished for those things. I wish to use the diamonds.*

Her words were short, but full of sass. "Absolutely nothing."

Her throat closed, collapsing under his sudden rage.

"You obviously used them. He may be alive." The revelation of his spoken words had Victor aghast that Cassy was powerful enough to bring back the dead. Victor dropped her to the floor, choking for air. Turning to his companions, he began the march out while saying, "If he's alive, he'll come back for her. Make sure nobody enters this room!"

Cassy laid her head onto the cool floor. She really did bring back her boyfriend. Her parched, cut lips separated into a glorious smile of victory. She sprang up, spinning about the prison. The FUA would soon travel to rescue her and, somewhere nearby, Zack searched to protect her from the tyrants. She slammed to the ground as a terrible rumble and shifting came from the plane. She hardly felt it with the excitement that she carried.

•   •   •

Inside the dining area, Victor snapped, "Get me Austin and Jason."

Buddy ducked out, escaping whatever Victor planned by reacting quickly. Austin appeared along with Jason before Victor drained his large glass of whiskey, feeling an unusual sensation. Anxiety. He leaned over the table while Austin and Jason worried over what may have caused such a reaction. Buddy hunkered down, tensing his straggly arms over his chest in preparation for Victor's wrath.

"Does the boy still have his watch?"

"Huh?"

Victor repeated with a hiss, "Does he still have the watch?"

"I don't... know. When I searched for it in London, there was no sign of it anywhere," Austin stated.

"Is that the last time you looked?"

"Yes. I didn't think anything of it. I assumed he tucked it somewhere safe."

"Like on the girl? Did you ever look on her?"

"No... I didn't... It would be inappropriate."

"So, there's a loose agent somewhere with the means to fix the equipment that will contact the agency which will *most definitely* catch us if they have even an inkling of where we are?"

Jason gulped back a lump when he remembered the half-witted decision to hand over a diamond. "She brought him back?"

Victor faced them with a condescending grin, "Of course she did. She even used it to contact someone with her phone. Once this plane is in the air, we do a sweep. I want that damn agent found! Keep the pilot vigilant about what he says to towers. Anything could alert the FUA. His butt planted on the bench, and he pointed directly at the three most in trouble. "I'm not impressed, and a punishment will be coming as soon as this mess is cleaned up."

They accepted it before rushing off to tell the rest of their group of the return of the agent's life.

• • •

Michael sank on the couch, swears swarming his mind. He should've prevented her from leaving the house that night. He should've noticed the signs and paid more attention to what she told him. His wavering hand swept through his hair. There were so many "should haves," he lost track of them.

He bolted upright as the phone rang. The rushing to the phone had occurred on more than one occasion through the week. He hoped to just receive a ransom and be given an opportunity to pay whatever sum for his sister. The second option was that the police finally located her, and she would safely return home. No other possibilities were even considered.

"Cassy?"

"Michael?" the voice belonged to Cassy's friend.

"Tanya, ummm, listen… Cassy is…"

She cut him off with a heavy exhale. "I know. I just spoke with her. She sounded really freaked out and rambled off a message for you. What's going on?"

Michael briskly explained it all, anticipating what type of news the friend may have.

Tanya shrilled, "She was kidnapped! Why did that man take her?" She rethought the need for a response. She was overwhelmed already, and she only wanted to help with Cassy's rescue. "Why doesn't she call the police with her cell?"

"I've called her every day, every four hours. Her cell phone has somehow disconnected since I spoke with the kidnapper that night."

"You talked to the bastard?"

"Yes." He stroked his head, "I regret that night more than you know."

He urged for the message to ease the impatient worrying.

"She says she's okay," she paused, thinking. "Go upstairs to her bedroom…"

As she spoke, Michael took the steps two at a time. Hastily, he burst into her untouched room.

"There should be a charm bracelet somewhere, possibly on her bed. Did you find it?"

The slightly imperfectly made bed was ruffled as he hastily looked for it. In an instant, he remembered that he had placed it securely in the nightstand to avoid losing it. Shuffling books and papers out of his way, it rested, shoved far in the back. He snatched it.

"Yes, what else?"

"You're supposed to press the charm twice, speak into it, and say, 'Cassandra's safe. She's in Egypt about to fly off somewhere in a private plane.'"

"Egypt? Why did he take her there?"

"I don't know!" Tanya yelled in distress.

"Sorry, sorry. What do I do after?"

"Press the charm once more. That's when she hung up. I think she was in trouble."

She got herself into trouble just to contact me...

He hit the end button after saying thank you. Unease built up, and then he grew the nerve to press the metal charm. Once his finger hit it the second time, another world erupted from the small device. A man barked orders at another person, not noticing the brother who listened to the words.

"Hello?" Michael awkwardly placed it too close to his mouth. Trembling, he feared what this man would do or who he was.

Rather than be angry, he seemed startled. "What the hell!" He figured out the source and replied, "Ah... who is this?"

Michael hid his identity and gave the first part of the message before the other man interrupted.

Surprise filled his gruff voice, "How do you know this?"

Perplexingly, the mystery man seemed calm even with this unpredicted interaction. *Is this another kidnapper or someone that is going to help?* Cassy might have given him the chance to contact the person responsible for asking for the ransom.

"Where the hell is my sister? Tell me, you bastards! I'll pay anything!"

"I wish I knew for sure. I need you to tell me how you learned about the bracelet."

"One of Cassy's friends somehow got a hold of her."

"What else did Cassandra tell this friend?"

Michael relayed the message. "Who are you? What is Buddy doing to Cassy? Do you think he's forced her and Zack to do something..?"

The man halted the very idea, "No, nothing of that sort. Listen, I'm going to help find her. That's all you know?"

"Tanya said Cassy hung up right away because someone was coming."

"Thank you, this helps a lot."

Michael's tone weakened, "Is he hurting her?"

The man softened from the excitement caused by a lead. "Let's hope not. She will come home. If that's the last thing I do, she'll return to her family." The man's voice disappeared as he hung up on Michael.

Michael pressed the charm and crumpled to the hardwood flooring. He spread out, sticking his face against it. *What's going on, Cassy?* He prayed for the assistance of a kind stranger.

• • •

Mr. Edwards escaped the dingy office and burst through into the conference room. Six agents scanned maps and used computers to track sightings of any lost teenagers. He excitedly took his position in front of them.

"Cassandra has entered the tomb and they've retrieved the diamonds. We know they're in Egypt. We have confirmation that they are travelling in a private plane."

A young agent raised a hand. "How do we know this?"

Mr. Edwards explained Cassandra's brother's unexpected message. "Another issue is Cassandra never mentioned Zack in her conversation. He might be critically injured, or worse. For right now, assume he's alive and that we're saving both. If it turns out it is just one, then at least we'll be sure to give a proper burial. We've got to hurry. Those diamonds are an unknown element and might be more potent than expected. We may be endangering agents by going after them in the air."

The agents bowed in acceptance of the plan. Gruesome thoughts were shaken from their heads to focus on getting a plane prepared. Every minute wasted was a minute Victor got away.

• • •

As Victor promised, Cassy sat in the back room for two days. No food was given, and the flight was full of loneliness, as none of the men wanted to step on Victor's toes while he was paranoid of an FUA raid. Zack stayed concealed wherever he hid. She spent her time curled up on the floor daydreaming of the day she would escape and arrive home to welcome her brothers' loving hugs. With their tight arms around her, she would apologize sincerely for all the tension caused throughout the previous months. Apologies were then required for Mr. Edwards for disobeying his orders. She heartedly admitted that it had been stupid to run away. This may have all been avoided if she stayed at the FUA and not fallen for the trap. While cuddled up near Zack's chains, she had a schoolgirl fantasy of a true date. Zack would treat her to a wonderful date of dinner and a movie, something that had been neglected in their relationship. This prompted a giddy grin to overwhelm her features.

During the second evening, Victor intruded with a sneer tracing his lips. He brought forth a diamond. She was lifted onto the bed from her position on the floor; and Victor arranged himself beside her, fiddling with her messy hair.

"I want a thousand dollars."

Cassy almost commented on how useless he must've felt. The previous evening had been a loud party with many of the men drinking and celebrating. All six attempted to demand something from the gems. If even one could control them, their need of the girl would end. None of the men were capable of it, and she, regrettably, was still necessary. Now Victor wanted to witness the mysterious diamonds in action.

Thrusting the diamond into her palms, he caressed her shoulder, which made Cassy's rejection swift. Moving the hand to her throat, he tightened his grip. She yelped. It hurt so much. Victor towered above her when she fell back, gasping and scratching his face. Without another victim to threaten, Victor resorted to torturing the heir, since physical pain convinced almost everyone to submit. There were few choices for Cassy to take. If she hoped to survive to see her family once more, then listening to his orders was necessary.

Cassy agreed, restraining depressed tears. The man released leisurely, grinning in self-praise. Victor retrieved the dropped diamond from near the edge of the bed and plopped it back into her lap. His hand lied open with anticipation while Cassy coughed a couple times before straightening her torso.

She eyed down the diamond. It swirled in her palm, calming its master's nervous heart. *Please, let me be right.*

"Give Victor a thousand dollars."

The diamond remained calm. A soft release of tense air exposed her relief. She played dense for as long as she could. If she couldn't use them properly, the men remained unfulfilled.

"What's wrong with this damn thing?" Victor snapped.

"I don't know. I'm not really sure how it works."

"Liar!"

A shrug showed her inability to assist. "I've only used them twice. Each time, I used different words."

Victor stroked his shaven chin and paced tread marks into the floor. "Mhmm," he hummed and raised an eyebrow after a long, silent twenty minutes. "When the heir is revealed, they will be able to control the diamonds as they wish…"

Cassy shivered at the words. What had he clued into?

Snapping his fingers, he bent at the waist to meet her. "You don't just simply ask for something, you must *wish* for it."

The diamond clenched in her palms. The reaction was all he required.

"Excellent! Now, let's wish on those diamonds."

Without any options, the susceptible girl spoke the accursed words, "I wish for Victor to have a thousand dollars."

The diamond glowed. The swirling colours spun faster as the light grew. Cassy watched for the first time with fascination. This was her power, for her own use. Her attention shifted as a mixture of numerous bill denominations floated like rain all over the bedroom. As the money formed, Cassy's head spun. It killed her thoughts of pleasantness. Her faltering strength was unnoticed while Victor rushed about, collecting and counting the multi-coloured money repeatedly.

"We'll have to learn how the diamonds work. You may need to be specific in your wording." Handing over a solitary bill to Cassy, he brushed the top of her head. "Maybe Zack isn't alive…"

Biting down on a lip, Cassy whimpered. The mixture of several countries' bills blended into a rainbow of colour. Cassy clamped the diamond down in her tight fingers. The wished money was useless to Victor in this form, yet he still awed at the magnificence of the gems. To be able to appropriately incorporate numerous monetary notes to make a solitary coherent dollar bill showed their all-knowing power.

He took the diamond and left her with a chilling peck on the cheek. Icicles viciously slid down the length of her back. He now carried more power with her as a personal bank.

She scowled at the shut entrance for a while. Her headache attacked more vigorously. And as it did, she cradled her head while all the happiness from beforehand vanished, bringing negativity to sprout. *He must be alive. They couldn't find a body! How come he hasn't come to rescue me? Why hasn't the FUA found me? Victor has it all in his clutches now. Anything he wants, I'll have to give it!* For hours, tears leaked down her sickly face. After all the fighting, nothing mattered. She was trapped.

The unbearable following night worsened her mood. Cassy was taken to the dining area, where abductee was forced to eat with abductor. They sat at the same table, with Victor across from Cassy, and quietly they ate with utensils clanging the glass plates. Picking at her food, she progressively received butterflies from the way he studied every move she made. A few bites were forced down before Cassy requested to leave. Victor declined swiftly. He chewed unhurriedly and then mockingly sawed at the steak. After he wiped his mouth with a napkin, his elbows rested atop the table and his long fingers intertwined. A priceless, living artifact sat across from him, one that he fawned over with lust in his brown eyes.

"Cassandra," he paused.

Cassy sunk down her seat in anticipation of his slithering tongue corrupting her hopes of a rescue.

"What is your opinion on Zack's survival?"

Her chin tucked into her collarbones as she glanced away.

"You truly think he's alive?"

No response enticed more jibes.

"If he is, do you believe he's coming back for you?"

Cowering at the very thought, Cassy's small form squirmed.

"I don't believe he will. He's already caught a plane home, relieved you're out of his life. All you brought was misery."

Victor's sadistic lips, filled to the brim with lies, sipped alcohol before he sombrely chuckled.

"You don't know Zack at all," Cassy defended tiredly.

"You think you do? Listen closely, *my dear*. Zack's kept more secrets than you'll ever learn. Why care about someone who keeps secrets?"

"Because everyone keeps secrets. He's a loving person and would never abandon me. I brought him back because I love him!" stated Cassy. "You talk highly of trust, and yet you've lied more than Zack ever has, and I've known you for less time. How can I ever trust you?"

Victor acted baffled, "When have I ever lied to you?"

"When you said you'd let me walk out of here after going into the tomb... You also lied about letting Zack live. You've been vicious and sadistic ever since I met you. You even said you'd kill my brothers. You're a monster. Why would I ever trust you?" She rose from the seat and positioned her back towards him. "You won't even tell me who you are!"

Victor burst into laughter. "You should not wish to learn about my past, Cassandra." He stroked a finger around the rim of his glass. "Don't you think, if he was alive, he would've saved you already?"

"He'll come."

"Hope is a toxic thing, Cassandra. It keeps you stuck in the past. We should look into the future, our future... together, and find common ground."

"Zack's coming for me!" Cassy rounded on a pivot and landed her fist against the table. "Hope is the only way I'll survive! Don't you dare think that you can manipulate me again!"

"Cassandra, think back," Victor stated calmly, "to when he kneeled in front of me without a fight. He'd given up. He even asked for forgiveness because he was weak. Someone like that, when their duty is ended, will leave because they can't face the enemy any longer. Face it, Cassandra, he's not coming. That so-called boyfriend *never* loved you."

Without the patience to deny his words any longer, she stormed off to the entrance and hurried out, hiding tears when Eric closely followed her to her prison. The heir slammed herself away from the men's leering eyes and squatted in front of the wooden doorway. Her nose squished into her knees, which concealed the sniffling made after every sob.

"Zack, where are you? Didn't I bring you back when I had the chance? Or... did you really abandon me?"

She fell asleep, infuriated with the world.

Chapter 17

An uneasy feeling of somebody stalking around the room aroused Cassy. She rose from her lying position and casually hunted around in the small light within the darkness. Tiptoeing into the bathroom, she swung the wooden door wide to holler at whoever skulked in her prison. However, the bathroom held no one within. She listened for the sound again. A scratching noise beneath her grew louder. With a frown, Cassy bent low to pinpoint it. Something rested underneath the flooring. Remembering the first escape route, she slid the closet open and sank to her stomach. She flipped her hair out of her face to press her ear against the crawl space cover. The tapping noise became repetitive. The girl lifted the cover and cautiously examined all the electrical wires for the rodent that might've caused the noise. As far as the bars permitted, she bowed her head to look inside. There was limited viewing from where she sat. With nothing apparent in there, she rolled onto her back beside the crawl space. Being brave and hopeful proved to be a lost cause.

The scratching continued for a long while. She found a vague familiarity to it, so she stayed on the floor, just listening. As an hour ended, Cassy frowned. It seemed too repetitive, like a code. Sticking her hand through the bars, she twiddled her fingers to show that she listened. The scratching abruptly stopped, and another sound occurred. It shifted closer to reach for the girl's dry, cut hands. Cassy rolled onto her stomach and called out to the advancing creature. A tiny gasp emitted. Disbelief formed in Cassy as kind and soft human features came from the shadows.

Zack reached through the barred area to wipe away a tear. A smudge smeared on her face from his dirty hands. They were rough, yet Cassy noted that he had no scratches or bruises on them. Cassy rubbed his smooth cheeks, enjoying the sensitive touch.

"You are alive!" she giggled cheerfully. "Zack, thank god, you came back for me!" His cheeks were gaunt, deprived of food and water. "How long have you been down there?"

"Since the plane took off. When I woke up, I had a bit of amnesia. I looked around for about twenty minutes, confused about my surroundings. As I entered the tomb, a bright light struck me, and I heard Obeko's voice telling me to get to you, to protect you. I remembered everything until the moment it went black. All I could think of was to get back to you, to save you from them." He shuffled, pulling his shirt up to his collarbones. "Look! There's not even a bullet wound! Their torture has completely healed. I feel better than I've ever felt before! I assumed you used the diamonds to save me, but while I was figuring my next move, I saw a vehicle speed towards me. One of the men was coming back for my body. I buried myself underneath as much sand as possible just in time for Buddy to scramble around in search of me. He even went into the tomb. While he was in there, I snuck into the trunk of the SUV. He had no idea he transported me here. When he ran inside, I snuck into the crawl space and have been here ever since."

"I needed you so much," she cried.

"I realize that, but I needed time to fix my watch." He patted it on his wrist. "Thank you for returning it, Cassy… I know it was probably hard, but it helped."

Cassy whimpered, pinning his hand to her lips. "I wish I'd known you were down there sooner. I would've at least been able to endure this bullshit a lot better."

"I couldn't. If Victor pushed you hard enough, you might've given me away. Cassy, all the crap he said to you was sickening, and I wish I hadn't left you behind, but I swear on my life, we're getting you out." Zack shot forth a bright sparkling grin. "I reached Mr. Edwards. He told me that he and the Rescue Team were already heading our way. He received a message from Michael," he explained, giving her a surprised raised eyebrow. "I suppose you forgetting your bracelet gave us an advantage."

Cassy blushed, pleased to have finally done something useful.

"The team will be close enough to us in about twelve hours. You mustn't talk to me for any reason. Act like I'm not here. Remember, he's probably listening to you."

"I know... this is going to be hard."

"We've gotta try."

"I'll try..."

Cassy lost his palm, closed the crawl space, and slumped to the bed. With his newly refreshed life, Zack seemed rejuvenated, ready to combat the oppressive men one last time.

As though on cue, Victor sauntered in. She tucked her legs into her chest and cocked her head, snarling towards the man. No words were said, but none were needed when his knife was whipped from his hip holster and flung in her direction. She jerked instinctively away from the blade that whizzed by her shoulder and hit the wall. Unable to ignore the murderous threat, she spun, and within seconds, she was hugged to Victor's burly chest while withstanding another knife's touch on her throat. Cassy stayed quiet when he shushed any words.

"Come out, *Zack*, or I'll slit her throat," Victor emptily threatened. "Where is he?" he hissed at Cassy.

"What are you talking about?" Cassy stammered.

"Don't lie, you bitch!" Shaking her, Victor grunted, "If he doesn't come out, you'll end up hurt."

Holding strong, she played dense while he thrashed her around. It took all of his self-control to not strike her with his clenched fists. Instead of using her as a ploy, Victor cold-bloodedly tossed her against the wall hard enough to cause her to stumble down the hall. Automatically, her adrenalin moved her body to crawl into the living room's archway. Her racing mind had no plan. Cassy scrambled to run as far away from the man as she could and hold out until her saviours arrived. In the living space, the men reacted slowly. Reaching the dining room, she heard Victor swearing under his breath, displeased with her uncooperative behaviour. She dipped inside and slammed the entrance. Unfortunately, an unexpected man choked on his food as she pressed her back on the cool doorway.

Jason shovelled a sandwich with lettuce and piled on meat into his mouth, sitting at the table. Victor's usual spot still had a half glass of alcohol near it. Based on his prompt intrusion, he obviously still listened to her even while she was secluded.

Jason set his delicious sandwich down before approaching the teenager with an awkward shuffle. Her bottom lip disappeared inside her mouth to be nibbled on. Her choice of hiding place proved unforgiving. Jason's youthful hands seized a knot of her messy hair and bulldozed her out of the dining space.

Victor approached with his nostrils flared. Her captor pinched the knot of hair and then jostled her from side to side to demonstrate she was restrained.

"What happened?"

She attempted to hide behind Jason but was tugged forward.

"The damn agent got onto the plane. I'm going to move her into another area," Victor replied shortly before gripping her wrist. "Watch for signs of him. I want that entire room torn apart."

Jason released Cassy and hurried along to grab another man for assistance. It was strange that none of the men seemed overly concerned with the appearance of the supposedly dead agent. Being tugged by Victor's biting fingers, Cassy realized, *They've been waiting for him. They always suspected that he would rescue me! Victor's manipulation was not against me, but on Zack, to make him expose himself because he could hear that I was losing grip.*

"Now," Victor grunted, "you are increasingly getting on my nerves."

"You're getting on mine!" she hollered back.

Next to the main washroom, a new imprisonment was opened. He smiled and urged her inwards, leaving her in a cramped space of shelves and empty alcohol bottles.

"Maybe if you were more effective with your threats this wouldn't be an issue," Cassy said.

Victor *tsked* her, giving her a short response, "Why would I kill you when I could torture you instead?"

He locked the door behind him, trapping the heir in the petrifying darkness of the windowless room. His men's voices echoed. If hoots weren't heard, Zack stayed safe somewhere amongst the plane's wiring. Feeling around, Cassy followed the shelves to the ground, fumbling over a bottle. Without her sight, the turbulence of the roaring engines, the men's slight whispers, and even the raspy breaths escaping her cracked lips, were more clearly heard. Too many bottles to count nudged into her as they made subtle shifts in the air. The darkness really did scare her over anything else they may have done. She plummeted into the depths of a chilly unknown.

What seemed to be hours ticked down before anyone brightened the small enclosure. It blinded her when the light switch flicked on. Cassy hunkered in a corner with her legs crossed, intently aware of Jonathon's movements as he creaked the solidly built door open. He closed the exit, half twisting to jeer at her. A black rope swung taut in his hands. She recognized the plan before he could squat next to her. From her position between the corner and Jonathon's military figure, Cassy's hands shot out to shove him away. Unable to fool around, Jonathon caught one of her hands and bent, flipping her onto the floor face first. Both wrists and her waist were tightly tied together as he knotted the two ends of the rope. Planted back into her original spot, Cassy grunted.

"If anyone, say, Zack, tries to cut you loose, this rope will release a gas which will knock them out instantly. You'll also fall unconscious, which honestly, is not a terrible price. In a couple hours, I'll untie you for supper."

"You can keep your rotten food."

"I assumed you would say that. However, if you don't eat, I will force it down your throat. We must keep you healthy. Death is an unthinkable option."

Cassy leaned forward to snarl at the man while struggling against the homemade ropes. They were durable and strong. An army man was the only one untying them.

Jonathon caressed her jawline. "Struggle all you like. I personally created these ropes. I've restrained men ten times your size without breaking a sweat. You have no choice but to endure it."

A cough formed when she held back a whimper. Jonathon stood and whistled his way out to seal her inside the blackness. Eventually, she helplessly ended her struggles, figuring that her energy was wasted on them. It was cold in the dark room, and as time went by, she lost track of the day and night.

It was some time before Cassy was startled at the sound of a nearby scratching across the floor. A grunt followed, which made her huddle closer into the cupboards and ask the person to go away. She squinted to find only a shadowy figure moving closer. Cracking bones popped next to her, and a hand landed on her trembling shoulder.

"Cassy?"

Zack's voice soothed her and then he fumbled to embrace her in the darkness.

Her lips wavered. "Zack... how did you get up here?"

"I found another crawl space."

His tender hug led down her back to graze the ropes restraining her. Recognition led him to sit next to her without an attempt to loosen the tight bondage. Cassy leaned her head against him, gently pressing up to his chest, unsure if he had any residual damage from the murder attempt. Averting the plummeting into the infinite abyss of despair, Zack tugged her closer to maintain a positive outlook.

She sobbed, "This is all my fault! I ruined your life. I wish I was never the heir."

Zack clenched his teeth with dislike of the words. "Stop blaming yourself. If you weren't the heir, we would be dead or still be at home, fighting about stupid shit until we seriously hurt one another. Good things came out of this, even if the bad seems to be prevalent." He kissed her forehead. "You rescued me, Cassy."

"I couldn't save you from those men..."

"You're not supposed to, Honey," Zack swooned. "Remember, I'm *your* protection. You don't ever worry about me. Just worry about being strong until we are rescued, and then we won't have anything to worry about any longer."

"When you..." she choked, "when you died, all I could see was relief. You wanted it all to end. Did I bring you back just to hurt you again?"

"Stop this, Cassy. You're making yourself sick. I wasn't relieved, but just as the bullet hit me, I realized that I was leaving those bastards. I was selfish because I *wanted* it to end, but I couldn't find a better way to do it rather than committing suicide."

"I've been trying to do that for the past week, Zack. It's not selfish at all," Cassy mumbled in honest admittance. "I even tried to get them to keep you alive and kill me. That would've been much more selfish on my part."

In the pitch blackness, Zack couldn't see her sunken cheeks, but he embraced her defeated form snuggly, encouraging her to remain brave. Both hands snaked up and down her back to let her know that he placed no blame upon her.

"Cassy, I love you and I'm glad that Victor and his men saw through that lie. Had they not, they would've killed you, I would've lost my chance to contact the FUA, and I would've never been able to see you again!"

"I love you with all my heart and I now see the truth behind my desperate actions. That's not how our paths were laid out. I was always destined to retrieve the diamonds. It's too bad that so many had to die for this."

Zack's grip quickly released when footsteps paced back and forth along the adjacent hall. Things shifted outside as the men hunted for the missing agent who had already settled on a plan to rescue the heir. His appearance confirmed their worries, and now the FUA surely was on their way. Zack stood next to his girlfriend for a short while, ready for the dangerous altercation that would occur between him and the men. Cassy rested her head back onto the bare wall beneath a shelf and allowed it to loll over when she fell asleep. Zack petted her head. He silently swore to never leave her side again.

Her sleep lengthened, giving Zack time to sneak back into the crawl space and give an exhausted yawn, then flick on his watch. The screen flashed brightly, blinding him.

"How much longer till you guys get close?" Zack questioned. "They found out I'm on the plane."

Mr. Edwards replied with a worried tone, "At least six more hours, and that strictly depends on us keeping on their tail. Their movements are definitely evident of them being cautious. They're changing their flight path. Have you encountered Victor personally?"

"I'm hidden for now. Victor's on the war path to find me. He even threatened Cassy with a knife."

"We will hurry, Zack. How is Cassandra doing? She's probably quite scared."

"I'd say. She's officially the heir and those diamonds are a force to be reckoned with." Zack stroked his face to stop his drooping eyes from falling further. "I can tell she's struggling with it, but she's finally sleeping. She still has some fight left in her."

"Keep her safe, Zackary, and get some rest yourself," the boss urged. "We may need your help during this raid. We've determined that we will need them to land."

The back of Zack's throat rumbled in a groan. "How the hell are we supposed to accomplish that?"

"Agent Rognas is working on getting a secure radio signal to the pilot. Since they've kept the pilot out of the loop, he may already be suspicious of them. If he learns he'll be charged as an accomplice to two kidnappings, he will likely land as soon as possible. I need you to be ready. When they land, you get the hell out of that plane."

Zack tentatively accepted the raid plan and flicked off the watch. He curled up his knees into his chest, balancing over a support beam. The past week flashed by in his memories. Rescuing Cassy felt impossible. He listened for Cassy to shift above him. *Cassy's hurting so much. She deserves to be home with her family, not fighting for her life against these bastards.* He closed his eyes to rest for a moment's time. *Cassy, I'm taking you home.*

•   •   •

Jonathon intruded on Cassy with a late dinner. He carried a tray in his grizzly hands. A loud grunt at her calmly sleeping form showed his dislike at his presence being ignored. The tray collapsed to the ground, spilling water onto the shadowed floor, and he snagged her shoulders to begin untying her. Cassy yelped at the startling arousal. As he undid the professional knots, she examined the shadows for Zack and listened for the hooting of the men that would signal finding him. Based on Jonathon's indifferent personality and the lack of celebration by the men, she assumed he hid back inside the crawl space.

Cassy rubbed away the indentations from the rope as Jonathon dropped the tray into her crossed lap. The small sandwich and water looked appetizing to Cassy, though she restrained herself from nibbling on it. She had to continue the trend of starvation, or they would notice her anticipation of an approaching saviour.

Jonathon growled. Squatting down and ripping apart the bread, he shoveled a bit into her mouth.

"You better eat, you brat, or I'll shove this entire sandwich down your throat and watch you choke on it."

She gagged a bit at the dry flavours of overcooked chicken, lettuce, and very little sauce when the sandwich was lodged inside her throat. Instinctively, her hands found the water glass, and she chugged back half of it to get down the choking food. Pleased his aggression was effective, Jonathon stroked her head and stood up.

"Good. Now, eat up."

The man shuffled out after retrieving a bottle of tan liquor from above her. Cassy moved the tray from her sight and huddled into another corner. She wasted another ten minutes before she heard a groan expose Zack's half-aware form moving beneath her. He illuminated the watch's face to lead him to Cassy. Bringing her close to his lean hip, he gave a gesture to prompt her to eat. Cassy shook her head but inclined her chin to invite him to have some.

He was famished, and appreciated the small meal. "Thanks," he said. With his fingers, he ripped apart the sandwich. "You're still not eating, huh?"

"I've got to stay strong until I return home or die. If something happens that lessens our chances, then I'm getting out of here somehow..."

Guiltily, Zack realistically understood that the FUA team was up against formidable foes. Even with the cards stacked against them, Zack kissed her forehead and clutched her hand.

"We are going home! It's ending here!" Zack announced.

He inhaled the sandwich, unable to savour it. The clock ticked away to Jonathon's unknown return to double-check that she ate. Zack snuck back into the cramped living space. Cassy paced in the darkness to waste time. Minutes crawled by, but no one arrived. Their stomping outside seemed distracted. Swears and grunts growled around, with Victor's being the most prominent. Something had thrown their precious plans for a loop, and it frustrated them.

Zack startled Cassy while she pressed her cheek into the cool floor to look through the crack beneath the door. He kneeled next to her. Satisfied that nobody would bother them, she welcomed his arms around her shoulders.

"Zack," she hopefully said, "if we get out, can we go on that date?"

His arms stiffened with pleasure at her optimism.

"Of course, we can!"

He tenderly rubbed her back and brought sanity into the overwhelming situation. Content, the two no longer cared if the men caught them. They found an ounce of happiness that would linger.

• • •

The plane swerved and tumbled them with the bottles into walls. Bottles hit them both, cracking open their skin and shattering around them. Her face grimaced in pain, but she contained the cry that threatened to erupt. Excitement fluttered as they understood the reason for the drastic fluctuation in altitude and sudden movement: the long-awaited rescue was coming to fruition.

The plane entered a dive, and Zack took hold of any permanent structure he could reach and clung to Cassy. He expected the landing to become rough and aggressive, which it quickly did. They heard the men scrambling to their seats. After fifteen minutes of turbulence and a rushed descent, the aircraft settled into silence. Mumbles were heard from outside as they released their seatbelts.

"Someone," Victor ordered, "go check on the girl. She probably got flung around that storage room. That damn pilot better have a good reason for this!"

Zack removed his ear from against the doorway as someone marched towards them. He ushered Cassy backwards to hide from the soon-to-open door.

"This isn't good, Cassy," he whispered. "When that door opens, you run… you head straight for that back entrance and hide."

Holding Cassy's trembling fingers, he patiently waited for a man to unlock the storage area. The plane rumbled with storming feet and shattering glass. A loud swear exploded from Jonathon's mouth before Zack and Cassy heard their saviour's orders.

"FUA Rescue Team! You're all under arrest!" Mr. Edwards' voice echoed.

The sound of scrambling feet exploded as the FUA swarmed inside and the men attempted to flee. Zack bent his knees, ready to be freed from the unending nightmare. At the moment the door slipped open, Zack froze. It was Victor. He gripped his trusted pistol that pointed in their faces.

Victor's features shadowed heavily at the sight of the supposedly dead agent protecting his assignment. He smoothly aimed the gun and pulled the trigger. The shot hit Zack squarely in the shoulder. The agent howled. Red-hot crimson blood seeped through his fingers. He struggled to subdue the pain and prepared for Victor's wrath, which came quickly. Victor stormed up to the wounded boy and cowering girl, shaking in fury.

"You should've stayed dead!" he hissed.

A punch struck Zack's stomach, which crumpled him into a ball. Cassy kneeled and attempted to assist her boyfriend before Victor ravaged him more. Victor kicked Cassy as punishment. Victor squeezed her cheeks and sealed her lips with his hand to prevent her from yelling at the agents rushing about. He seized Zack's hair to raise him from the ground.

"We're going on a trip; cooperation would be wise."

He hauled them down the hall towards the back entrance. Cassy hunted around. Agents were preoccupied with chasing the six fleeing men. It was mayhem of threats inside, while outside there towered a calm tropical rainforest that was being disturbed by the few men who had escaped the plane. None saw the leader slip from section to section with the two captives. The man pinched tighter as he escorted them straight off the plane.

Cassy desperately reached out a hand to hold herself within the plane's boundaries. If Victor dragged them off, she foresaw only a miserable hell. Victor swore at her. His grip viciously strained her muscles into an unnatural position. Her hand wept with thick blood as it slipped from the metal bracing.

Down the lowered steps, they fell onto dirt and were weighed down by the dense humidity of the tropical region. Cassy and Zack panicked as the foliage of the dense forest concealed them as they stumbled deeper within. Cassy's back pressed against Victor's chest while they tripped over roots and listened intently for pursuing agents. Zack fell behind. His legs put their brakes on to slow the speedy man down. Strands of hair were ripped out within Victor's fingertips.

The deeper they marched into the forest, the less likely the FUA would be to find the heir and her companion. For half an hour, the trek brought them over and under fallen, ancient trees and between vines so compactly overgrown that Victor was forced to slice them while controlling his two captives. Victor refused to give up on fleeing until he was officially out of harm's way with the precious teenage girl. Eventually, the thick foliage broke apart and a grand waterfall halted their movements. A cliff of multi-coloured rocks dropped down into a swirling pool beneath the chilly waterfall that cooled the air. Victor snagged Cassy into his hooked elbow and tossed Zack forward towards the cliff's range.

"Find a way across, or I'll hurt your girlfriend."

She cried out. The man cut her with his digging nails to get Zack to move faster. Barely reserving any brutality for later, Victor throttled Cassy around as though she were a rag doll begging to be assaulted. Zack fumbled along the cliffs and hunted for any plausible route across the plummeting waterfall. However, Victor wrenched the boy back by the hair in haste. Mr. Edwards appeared in front of the captives, defending his ground with his own gun pointed at Victor. The old FUA boss stepped vigilantly from the lush greenery.

"Let them go, Victor!" Mr. Edwards commanded.

Zack took advantage of Mr. Edwards' presence and swung his elbow back to strike Victor's unguarded chest. Victor huffed out an exasperated grunt and went to reach for Zack again. Cassy struggled and tripped him up, refusing to follow his orders. Zack went to wrench Cassy out of harm's way, but Victor dragged Cassy to block Mr. Edwards' raising gun and snuggly clung her to his waist. Zack scrambled back to lessen his threat to Victor's perturbed behaviour.

"There, take the boy. Now, you will let me and her pass."

A fast heart raced against her back. Cassy finally noticed unconcealed panic escape Victor. Mr. Edwards edged closer. The cool metal of Victor's gun pressed into her temple; she vaguely heard his threats. All that crossed her mind was that Mr. Edwards had come so close, and she wouldn't let it go to waste.

"Back away or I'll kill her."

His tense grip choked her. Mr. Edwards stepped slightly closer to find a vantage point.

The gun glistened in the sun. It blinded her. Determination fueled her adrenalin. She wouldn't allow this man to go any further unless he was arrested. Her fingers flung up and tightened on to the gun's butt and barrel for dear life. She couldn't afford to release it. Cassy used all her strength against his one hand to manoeuvre it to face him. If she were no longer a threat, the agents could rescue her. He grumbled in her ear about her annoyances. Neither one of them could afford to lose.

"Mr. Edwards, his threats are empty!" she screamed. "Stop him!"

Zack shuffled closer. More agents crept nearby. A blonde one, obviously in a powerful position, steadied his weapon, his blue eyes narrowed. He barked orders at the agents to surround the twosome. They weren't going further into the forest, and the canyon of wet cliffs was their only option.

Victor's gun shook, going back and forth between Cassy and Victor. Cassy felt Victor's rage increasing. If she was anything but the heir, he would've killed her already. Instead, he sacrificed the gun by tossing it away. Rather than using something with a trigger, his hand disappeared behind his back to extract a ready-to-use blade. It snuggly kissed her cheek.

"It will honestly be a shame to lose such a priceless artifact. Do you truly wish to lose the Egyptian Heir when she's within our grasps?"

"She won't die," Zack rebutted, "I won't let her."

The blade pinched Cassy. Weeping blood seared her cheek as he took a leisurely slice out of her.

Her eyes met Victor's. Her determination was beyond anything he'd seen before. She willed to survive his tyranny. The bloodied knife slid across the girl's throat, tickling her enough to shudder. Without any other options, her life was going to end.

"You're truly forcing my hand."

"Zack, Mr. Edwards, please… Kill him!"

Zack frowned at her tone. "Cassy, we'd hurt you. That's not how this will end," he insisted.

Cassy's cheeks became smeared with her blood as the blade lightly swiped across her open wound. His other hand wrapped around her waist.

"Don't be stupid, Victor!" Mr. Edwards reasoned. "We have your men and all the diamonds. You're in the middle of a jungle. There's no way we will allow you to go any further with her. Just let her go!"

Victor shrugged his shoulders, suddenly showing an excited expression. "Fine... I will just... let her go!"

Victor backed up effortlessly towards the ledge. Cassy skidded across the rocks; her eyes widened when she twirled to face Victor. The blade sliced her neck open slightly, but Victor's intentions concerned her more. Zack determined the movement's endgame and jumped into action in haste. Inches from grasping Cassy, his fingers slipped and missed her frantic reach. Shrieking, Cassy was flung off the rocky cliffs towards the pounding waters below.

"There, Zack! Let's see you save her this time!"

Zack never hesitated. He dove directly off the cliff, leaving Mr. Edwards to hurry to Victor who prepared to run off back into the jungle to disappear once more. The boss caught and tripped him to the ground and then twisted his wrists more than necessary as a satisfactory arrest handcuffed the criminal into submission.

"You'll pay if she dies," Mr. Edwards threatened.

"We shall see!"

• • •

Cassy twisted and flipped, gasping for air during the long drop. The icy, crystal-clear water impacted her hard, leaving everything in her world in pitch blackness.

Zack was close behind, diving feet first into the dark depths of the fresh water. The currents swept him up, swirling him around and disorienting him in the waterfall's pool. The water was paralyzing; however, his only goal was to rescue his assignment. He widened his eyes to find Cassy's whereabouts. He spied her sinking form no more than a few metres away, and swam towards it. He used his adrenalin to kick harder and outreach his hands to grab her before she drifted too far downstream. The moment his hands huddled her into his shivering, drenched chest, Zack waved an arm into the air to attract the team's attention. Each kick against the current was laboured, and he realized if they were swept past the waterfall's pool, both would drown. Hollering, he attempted to reach for the banks while struggling to hold Cassy's head above the splashing waves.

"Cassy," he choked, "I swear I'm not letting you go!"

Further downstream, he witnessed a heavenly gathering of agents briskly preparing to climb the rocks. A thick cord dangled down as a Rescue Agent prepared to leap off the lower cliff. Zack struggled to breathe as water pummeled him. He forcefully clung tightly to Cassy's lower waist. He outright refused to let her die when they came so close to returning home. The Rescue Agent dove with the cord whistling behind him. Swiftly, he swam outwards into the middle of the fast-moving stream and spread his arms in preparation for the impact of two people's weight. Catching the drifting twosome, the Rescue Agent grunted. With his signal given, the team that remained on the cliff tugged the cord and attempted to pull the three as close as possible to the cliff. Once rocks were able to be grasped, the Rescue Agent pulled out a piece of spare rope and tied Zack's torso onto the jagged stones jutting from the white-capped rapids.

"Listen carefully. I'm taking her first. I'll come back for you. You do not let go of this. This rope will only hold you for a couple minutes. Don't you dare pass out!"

Zack nodded and helped clip Cassy onto the agent's belt. The agent wrapped his arms around her waist and rose above Zack's head. Zack felt a twinge of guilt at his failures. He had allowed her to be seriously injured. Hindsight nagged him that he should've tucked her into the crawl space as soon as the plane landed and hidden there until the team rescued them. Had he done that, none of this would've happened. He had been an idiot, and without knowing her physical condition, he could only assume the worst.

Frostbite nipped at Zack's fingers. The chilled water soothed all the battle wounds across his body; however, it also tempted him to drift into a relaxed state of mind. The agents above worked tediously to rescue the two and Zack shook off the will to fall unconscious. The sensation of almost ending this horrific trial could not be satisfied until he sent Cassy safely home.

Again, the damp Rescue Agent dove far off the cliff and was dragged back to Zack's location. After he clipped Zack onto his belt, both were lifted from the water. The quick breeze swung them violently, whipping them against each other and the rocky ledges. Zack hated this sensation more than any other training he had gone through. He preferred to survive through his instincts, and yet, lately, his instincts regarding Cassy proved to be untrustworthy. He'd allowed so many unacceptable things to befall her.

The Rescue Agent unclipped Zack as they grew close enough for the other agents to wrench him up. Zack gaped when he landed on his wounded shoulder. Irritable, he was adamant that he was fine and searched for the heir. A moan of worry escaped him. She lay upon an emergency stretcher, smothered in blankets to keep her temperature up, and an agent monitored her breaths, which were shallow. She remained unconscious and unresponsive to Zack's wet caresses. Before he overreacted at the sight of her, agents ushered him to sit on a large boulder for a quick check up. Four agents gathered Cassy to haul her through the rainforest. Agents taped thick gauze against the wound and blankets fell across his shoulders. Once they determined that he was fit enough to stumble his way back, they allowed Zack to hurriedly catch up with the stretcher. Zack huddled in a blanket and tried to quickly regain his warmth. Catching up with Cassy, he tenderly brushed her face.

Gasping breaths escaped Cassy, and when fewer were taken, and at times, skipped, Zack begged the agents to stop and check on her. The first responder on the team hurriedly attached a manual breathing device over her face and began pumping air rhythmically into her weak lungs. Zack tossed his spare blanket over her.

The dreaded Boeing entered their field of view as the leading agents shifted a large, drooping vine. It was silent now. Zack did not see any more escaping criminals or the Rescue Team up in arms. The entire event had ended. Zack was able to feel the dazing sensation of freedom once more.

Regrettably, the Rescue Team agent directed that Cassy be returned to the Boeing that once imprisoned her. Zack restrained himself from snatching the stretcher and carrying her off. No matter the disdain directed at the plane, he knew the FUA required the larger plane to facilitate Cassy's medical needs. As they moved across the lush underbrush to the plane, Zack led the way. His sore shoulder throbbed in pain, and he embraced it. It reminded him of their sacrifices to get where they were now. Her damp clothes and dead weight seemed to heavily weigh upon the agents up the sloped ramp. They began moving her into the farthest bedroom, which Zack anticipated would give the doctor the best space to care for her.

Zack released her palm and stood back to watch Rescue Agent Rognas handcuff Jonathon behind his burly back. Pleased to see them finally in chains, Zack sneered towards the members of Victor's gang visible to him. Mr. Edwards took over tending to Jonathon and ordered Rescue Agent Rognas to alert the physician that Cassandra needed assistance. With a sigh, Mr. Edwards marched Jonathon away. Rognas touched Zack's shoulder.

"She's really hooked you, huh? I've never seen you care this much about an assignment since Tomas died."

Zack awed at the perceptive agent. "She took all of the bullshit I tossed at her in stride, and then she was able to weasel her way into my heart without any effort. She's a glistening light unlike any that I've ever seen..." Zack chuckled at his description of her. He swiped his hair with both hands and nudged the fellow agent with an elbow. "I fell in love with her, and even then, I couldn't prevent her from serious injury." Defeated, Zack bowed his head and whispered, "Mitchell, let me know what the doctor says. I can't go in there with her like this."

Agent Rognas inclined his head to the casual name used, and accepted Zack's friendly plea. "I can do that."

Agent Rognas took long strides to march down the hallway to patiently lean against a wall in wait for the diagnosis.

Zack went in search of Mr. Edwards down the nightmarish plane. His arm was becoming numb, which stubbornly made him admit that a doctor would be needed. He went around the corner into the recreation area, where Victor's men were all gathered on the plush couches and lightly bickered amongst themselves. Jason and Eric snarled at Austin. Buddy quivered in a corner like a snivelling dog, trying to keep strong amongst the men. Jonathon sucked in his cheeks, creating a gaunt look that made his round face more menacing. It was Victor who caught Zack's attention. Fury boiled within Zack after the initial shock of seeing Victor's sneer. Zack sank into an icy lake of emotions. Victor knew the results of his attack as the rumours of Cassy's condition were uttered around all six of the men.

"So, I killed her, huh?" announced Victor.

"No, she'll pull through. She's strong!"

Zack swung an enraged fist across Victor's sharp jaw. Victor spat blood out, welcoming the abuse without even a retort. Abandoning the group of men, Zack furiously listened to the comments shouted at him as he cowardly hid from the kidnappers, squatting in a corner of the cockpit.

Chapter 18

The doctor beckoned Agent Rognas forward. He rubbed his temples, wondering how it should be told. Finally, he asked, "How is Exacil holding up?"

"As suspected, based on Mr. Edwards' warnings. He's grown close to her, and her recent state is causing him to become distressed."

"Well, my diagnosis will probably not waver the worry."

Explaining Cassy's condition, the doctor covered his lips as though preventing the bad news from escaping. Agent Rognas shook his head in disbelief. The doctor finished, placed a hand upon Agent Rognas' broad shoulder, which towered above him, and returned to the room containing Cassy. Agent Rognas took a spare moment to massage his forehead before sighing and going en route to Zack.

He found him sitting in a far corner near the cock pit with his face covered to hide his solemn tears. Agent Rognas crouched low to touch his arm softly.

Zack spoke first. "What's wrong with Cassy?"

Zack rose as he stammered the words. Agent Rognas bowed his head before he followed Zack upwards. Protecting himself by folding his arms across his chest, Zack prepared for the worst.

"She has a few injuries, which we assume happened when the pilot landed. Glass was found in a few of her cuts, and while we searched the plane, we found broken alcohol bottles in a storage area." He rubbed his neck. "I guess she was locked inside there for awhile."

Zack gave a simple nod.

"This is hard to say... Those are the minor injuries, along with a cut on her hand and cheek." He bulldozed on to avoid watching Zack's trembling chin. "When she hit the water, she landed on her head... hard. She's alive... but..." he paused when Zack's eyes burned into him, "she's in a coma. The doctor doesn't expect her to become conscious. Her mind still functions, but it almost seems... off, I suppose. It's like she's stuck in a dream and can't leave."

"She's alive, though... She's in there, probably fighting." He inquired in a hushed tone, "Is there anything to do for her?" Zack acknowledged the answer before Agent Rognas shrugged and looked away. His frustration boiled over, and he hollered, "Cassy has to wake up!"

A sinking feeling erupted into Zack's gut. *She can't be gone... I won't let her give up after finally becoming free.* Hurrying his feet into a run, he ducked from agents that ordered him to visit the doctor. He heard Mr. Edwards' voice booming on the ramp. Zack's pace froze just outside of their field of view, and he listened to Victor and his pompous men waiting to be loaded in the opposite plane, which would fly them to their prisons until their trial. Unnerved by the men's closeness, Zack pressed his brakes. The men were caught, yet they were unconcerned. Mr. Edwards gave them their rights and then passed the men off to other agents. Victor mockingly bowed to the FUA Head. He had his proof of the heir. Nothing else mattered to him, not even being caught for the first time in his professional career.

Zack reversed to make his way to Cassy's resting place. To broach on a subject as sensitive as the one that weighed his heavy heart in front of Victor and his men would only gain him ridicule. His feet heavily shuffled down the corridor of the plane. He was within reach of Cassy, and the suffocating sensation that she was no longer awake terrified him. His hand settled upon the doorknob, just outside, and was unable to widen the entrance. Once he did, he had to face reality.

"Zackary," Mr. Edwards' voice startled him greatly, "have you not gone in to see her?"

"Not yet..."

"Cassandra's current condition is unfortunate, but the FUA will do whatever possible to make her comfortable. I trust Cassandra will fight this. Her mind needs to rejuvenate, but we can't honestly know if it will ever heal enough for her to awaken. Go see her, Zackary. Once we return to Saskatoon, you're returning home."

Zack backed up. "What? I'll be able to see her all I want."

Mr. Edwards' head shook. "You will return home and stay with your mother. You'll act like we haven't found her. If you visit too often, it will bring suspicion. Her brothers will become even more desperate to find her and will pester you until they do. You will no longer be permitted to be around her."

"No! I'm staying with her until she wakes up," Zack demanded.

"Zackary! Be reasonable. She could wake up in ten years! She might never wake up!" Mr. Edwards laid guilt on Zack. "Do you really believe your mother should suffer that much while she waits to hear from her only son?"

Zack steadied his gaze, regretting the options available to him. "Please!"

"Let me think about it… You must obey my orders, even if it's not what you like."

Zack agreed venomously at his boss.

"By the way," Mr. Edwards mumbled before allowing the boy to embrace his girlfriend, "Victor has been ranting about how he will come for her once she awakens. Do not engage with that man any longer. Victor is arrogant, and him knowing that his actions have debilitated you is a cherry on top of his sadism," he sternly said.

Mr. Edwards backtracked to ensure Victor and his men were sealed away on the other plane before they took off. The teenager edgily strode into Cassy's room. She lay flat on the same bed she cried upon the day before. Zack sank into a chair and held her tender hand. A heart monitor beeped overhead, seeming weak in between each beep. A breathing tube stretched through her mouth, and IV needles jabbed into her skin.

Zack disliked the solemn look. *Cassy, please, wake up.*

●　●　●

Hours later Zack woke up still holding Cassy's cooling fingers. He released them. Shakily, he stood and stretched to find an agent ordering him to see the doctor who was set up in the recreation area. Gauze and medical tools scattered across the table for the injured agent. Zack sank next to the doctor, lifted his shirt over his head, and prepared for him to prod inside his wounded shoulder. The bullet was removed and left a stinging ache. His arm was partially numb, but his worried eyes never left Cassy's resting place. The doctor stitched the wound and contained Zack's arm in a clean sling. Zack then, dazedly, returned to Cassy's side for another couple of hours until the doctor ushered him away.

Zack strolled along the plane before finding himself inside the dining room where Victor had tried to make Cassy doubt him. It was the same room where Zack had been transported while he slept and forced to watch Cassy be assaulted. Victor had listened to their conversations and drank his liquor throughout the duration of their flights. Now, the room became an area for the agents to socialize after a stressful raid had ended.

Zack had become solitary in the last few hours, losing his will to celebrate with the agents while Cassy's affliction lingered on.

Locking the outside world away, Zack grabbed a crystal glass. Thousands of shards exploded across the floor as he threw it across the dining room in rage. Grunting, he tugged at his thick hair and punched the door. Watching the clouds broken apart by the slicing wing, Zack sank down to the bench seat. His throat choked him. His eyes watered and depression overwhelmed him. He swiped the salty tears away. His entire emotional barrier crumbled to the ground. Not even when he realized he was about to die did he cry, and now, he lived, thanks to her, but the diamonds were useless without her. The miserable situation would continue until she found a way out of it.

He rested his arms against the table to support his head. *I should've avoided this assignment like the plague... I've seen assignments get hurt all the time...* Slamming the table, Zack wondered, *Why couldn't Obeko give me some power? I could help her. This is ridiculous! I'm here to protect her... I can't even do that right!*

A knock had him frantically wiping the tears and calming down the hysterical thoughts. He leaned against the doorway, questioning the person outside. It was Mr. Edwards. He spoke gently and calmly, awaiting Zack to slip the wooden barricade open and allow him in. When it happened, Mr. Edwards squeezed by and instantly went to the table to put his feet up.

"Zackary, would you like to talk?"

"NO!" Zack stated, ruder than intended.

"Okay. When we arrive in Saskatoon, Cassandra will be placed in the medical wing of the FUA. I wanted to warn you that she may remain there until we justify moving her into another hospital so her brothers may tend to her. That'll be six months down the line, if she doesn't awaken."

Zack slumped his shoulders when the man spoke bluntly. *Nobody expects her to wake up...* "What about those bastards? When will I be testifying?"

"Unfortunately for us, Victor is a deceptively cunning man."

Piercing eyes ensnared Mr. Edwards into a death glare.

"He wished to proceed to trial in the normal court system."

Zack growled, "But that means I won't be able to testify! They could get off because of this!"

"He manipulated the others into using this tactic, so they will individually go through the trial process. We will receive results as they come in. You can make a statement, but that's all we can do. If Cassandra were awake, she could've testified, since her ties are only as an assignment. I assure you that we will be placing our best lawyers on the prosecution so those men will lose the opportunity to abuse the system. We also will have Susan's death put onto them. Unfortunately, that is all we can do. If they are released, let's hope we can protect Cassandra if she ever wakes up."

"How did they find out about that loophole?"

Mr. Edwards rose and shrugged, accepting Zack's dislike for the chosen topic. "Obviously, he has been looking into ways to avoid heavy sentences for his crimes. Quite a few of the assignments and evidence found throughout the past three years won't do us any good because they picked this route. Those were FUA cases and will be hidden from the courts."

"Cassy's going to be attacked the moment she wakes up..."

"Let's hope not."

Excusing himself, Zack shuffled through the plane to prepare for a lonely night of sitting in solitude next to Cassy. He scooted a chair close, and then clutched her motionless hands.

He spoke aloud, "It's not right. Victor should be punished, not slapped on the wrist. No jury will see the real monster behind that deceiving face. He'll wink and act as a charming victim." He squeezed her fingers. "Cassy, just wake up so we can spend at least a few happy moments together."

A tall, broad shouldered, dirty blonde man randomly peeked in over the course of the flight. Zack noticed Agent Rognas keeping tabs on him. Not a word was spoken, but he would close the door securely to hide the broken boy. It took all Agent Rognas' might to hold back a sympathetic tone whenever Zack spoke to Cassy.

A day of travelling brought a pestering Mr. Edwards in. He stood near the foot of the bed and admired Zack's sunken form. Mr. Edwards pressed for information about the past week. Zack's testimony would help more than the little evidence found throughout the plane. It worried Mr. Edwards to ask so soon after the trying events, but with Zack's increasingly bottled-up emotions, they could lose the key facts they needed to win against the men's cleverly devised plot to overthrow the FUA.

Zack scooted his chair around to avoid having Cassy hear the story. It was a sad fate that Cassy, if she were to ever awaken, would now be stuck as being the heir forever.

• • •

The first sight of the FUA headquarters was refreshing. Zack made it home in one piece. Inside the entrance, agents swarmed him to congratulate him for finally ending this long-term assignment, but his focus was stuck on the sight of Cassy being rolled onto the elevator. She would be up on the third-floor medical wing waiting for him to join her. Sloughing off all his co-agents' words, he scooted to the stairs and darted upwards to reach her hospital room before even the doctor could begin setting up her breathing tubes and IV properly. Zack gave them space until the doctor permitted him to huddle next to her.

Days and nights swept by without notice while Zack took all his waking hours, which were long since he slept very little, to talk about anything that might interest Cassy. He spoke about stimulating happenings in the FUA and finally revealed as much about himself as possible. He wished she subconsciously heard him. The Zack he hoped to show was appearing, and there could be no more secrets.

In the mornings, he strolled into the humming room to find her as he left her. At nights he was sent out to sleep in the agent barracks. It broke his heart whenever he said goodnight without hearing a chirped response back.

Curious agents strolled by in groups when news of Zack denying any new assignments and becoming secluded spread. Hardly anyone saw him except during his short bathroom breaks and brief nibbles on dry food, leftover in the cafeteria, late at night. Agents walked by and slipped quick glances inside, wondering who could hold such power over a top agent. What they found brought tears to their eyes. Zack clutched her palm, kissed her cheeks repetitively, and whispered, "Cassy, please, wake up. I didn't mean to lose you."

This routine continued for a long two weeks. Nobody, except for the primary doctor, could command Zack to leave her. It took Mr. Edwards hauling in seven envelopes, five of them already opened, for Zack to pay any attention to him.

"Zackary," he solemnly said, "I have the results of the trials."

Six of the envelopes dropped onto Zack's lap. Zack released Cassy to shuffle through them all. He was outright nervous to learn the outcomes. The one left unopened was Victor's. It had the man's name typed neatly across it from the New York City FUA Branch.

"I need to hear what the others got before I read this."

Mr. Edwards bowed his head in anticipation of this. "I thought you might. Jason and Eric have earned themselves twenty-five years, which includes their previous four-year sentence. They have no chance at a parole hearing. Jonathon has twenty-one years, mainly because he was found as the main culprit for Susan's murder. He has a chance at parole in five years. If he has good behaviour, he will most likely be released. Since Buddy is the newest of the group, our lawyers were unable to pin too much of the original kidnappings on him, but they were able to charge him with impersonating a therapy professional. He'll be out in ten years or less, if he's got good behaviour. Austin was charged with possession of paraphernalia, having an arsenal of illegal weapons; with this and his assistance in hacking into government mainframes, he got fifteen years. Since we tested Cassandra's blood for drugs, he was charged with drugging a minor as well."

Unable to withstand the wait, and unpleased with the results of the others, Zack tore open the letter and trembled as the paper unfolded to learn of Victor's sentencing.

New York City Federal Undercover Agency
Correspondence
Victor R. Folgin v. New York State
Judge Keith M. Matters

- -

Victor Folgin has thus been tried and found guilty of six accounts of felonies against the State.

(1) 1st degree kidnapping with use of a dangerous weapon. Found guilty on two accounts and sentenced to four years.

(2) Assault with a deadly weapon. Found guilty on one account and sentenced to five years.

(3) The use of a firearm or electronic defense weapon against a victim. Found guilty on two accounts and sentenced to five years.

(4) Manslaughter 1st degree with a firearm. Victim Susan Ibe. Found guilty on one account and sentenced to six years.

End of Transcript
Agent Oliver Zoleak
New York City Federal Undercover Agency Head

Zack crumpled the letter, and then admired Cassy again. *Twenty years. That's all that monster got!*

"Zack?"

"Twenty years… That's it! He should rot in prison for the rest of his life for what he's done!" The initial shock of the failings of the court system vanished and anger sprouted. "That bastard isn't going away. He's on goddamn vacation, thinking of new ways to torture her!"

The crumpled letter was tossed, and Zack twisted to return to his girlfriend's diamond-shaped features that were pale in comparison to her usual brightly rouged cheeks.

"Be grateful that he will serve any time at all," Mr. Edwards muttered. "I spoke with a few agents keeping tabs on the trials. They were planning to let him walk. Quite a few of the jurors were being swayed by the men. We're lucky that none of them were. Cassandra being in a coma is already hard, but if Victor had gotten off, he'd move here and lurk about until she woke up. He could stroll around and there would be no reason for us to arrest him until he made a move."

"Only twenty years isn't long enough, not for everything he's done during the past three years alone."

Mr. Edwards pressed his hand onto Cassy's toes. He showed condolences at seeing her in this state.

"They left no evidence. They were extremely careful throughout the years. If we hadn't located Susan's body, and had your statement and evidence that they assaulted Cassandra, they may have all walked out of there free men. Obviously, the only thing that landed Victor into jail was Susan's murder, which he claimed was self-defence because she 'attacked' him while they were having sex. He pled guilty of kidnapping. I have no idea why he would. We assume Victor conned his way out of a hefty charge by pleading guilty. All of them received the bare minimal charges for their crimes."

The second unopened letter was shoved into Zack's face. Taking it, he eyed the letter with only his first name written in neat scroll and no return address.

"I recommend that you go for a stroll before reading this. You may not like the contents."

Zack gazed upon Cassy's closed, hazel eyes. His boss shifted to pat his shoulder, and then went to the door.

"She will still be there when you come back. Take a break." Mr. Edwards mumbled, "You need to clear your head and read it only if you're ready. Victor's going to attempt his mind games."

The man left and permitted the tears to burst out from Zack's brown, weary eyes. He sobbed for a long while. He couldn't hide it any longer. The stiffness in her arms, her blank expression, and her shallow breaths overwhelmed him. *Is this how Cassy felt when I was lying in that bloody sand?* Emotions of utter loneliness gagged his breaths into tiny gasps. *Have I lost her forever?* Guilt fluttered his stomach when he realized his selfishness. His mother had lost her husband and oldest son, and now had no idea that her only living family was secluding himself inside this dreary place. *Is it worth staying here? I could help Cassy's brothers through this and ease my mom's pain. Maybe Cassy will heal better by herself?*

He vaguely heard scratches against the floor as he shifted his chair back to stroll to the elevator. His mind was determined to finally resolve an unfinished issue. Zack's long index finger pounded the button to the ninth floor, where the Hazardous Goods Ward contained a force of unknown power. The elevator glided into the air, making his stomach nauseous. Leaning up against the glass, with his back turned on the people meandering beneath the overcast of the moon's gleam through the skylight, Zack crumpled the unread note into a tight wad. Something about the intimidating letter increased his anxiety. He couldn't yearn for something if there was always a looming shadow over her to shrink her into a corner.

A ding of the elevator alerted him that it soon would shift to a complete halt.

"Badge number and agent's name," the robotic voice demanded.

Absent mindedly, Zack responded, "Badge number Y-six-P-one-B-four, Zackary Exacil."

The doors widened, after which Zack edgily stepped out. His feet were the heaviness of concrete. He felt as if he might fall through the floor with the weight of them. Up in the Hazardous Goods Ward, there were no unlocked rooms. A solitary hallway led to a single storage unit, and four offices sat directly across from the elevator. Excluding the hallway, the floor was littered with sixteen secure rooms. Each one had a specific locking mechanism from low to high security and followed the railings in the center to protect agents from falling to the first floor. Zack went straight from the elevator and followed the railing. He passed specially equipped rooms on which he hadn't been briefed; each had blinking screens upon a podium for a ten-digit code to be inserted. The first few locked spaces had hazardous medical signs covering the main entrance and were sealed behind glass and steel. He always assumed that dangerous bioweapons were hidden in there, ones that were unpredictably made by the research lab and uncontainable. The next four were unused, with their screens blacked out. Zack turned right with the railing and went down two more enclosures before landing in front of his chosen destination.

This room had recently been remodeled. Unlike the previous ones, the steel entrance opened to reveal two separate doors once the fifteen-digit code had been typed into the tiny screen. One room was a small research facility with two computers set up to monitor the potent objects floating within the other chamber, which was on the left-hand side. It was completely sealed, and was set up for any type of reaction the diamonds may potentially have. Zack eyed the diamonds from his vantage point behind three-inch-thick, bulletproof glass which displayed them in all their glory. The seven diamonds each floated above individual mechanised pedestals which registered the energy transmitted from the diamonds and recorded it onto the computer system.

Zack stepped closer in long strides until he was able to reach the glass. Typically, the glass was meant to be a two-way mirror; viewing was only possible from the inside of the diamond's holding room, and yet it almost seemed like the diamonds were transmitting such high energy through the glass that concealing them was impossible. Until the two main researchers found a way to stop the diamonds' transmission, only privileged agents were permitted anywhere near this location.

The colours swirled vigorously, hypnotizing Zack into place. No sounds escaped his lips; rather, Zack trembled and fell onto weak knees in defeat. Accepting his fate, Zack unravelled the letter and slipped his finger inside the lip of the envelope to shred it open. He pulled out a short, neatly scrolled letter on crumpled paper. The man who wrote it had known what he wanted to say and how he would say it.

The letter began with dripping ridicule.

Dear Zackarass,

You better hope she never becomes conscious, because the moment she does, I will find any way in my power to escape this imprisonment you've landed me in. Cassandra will be my prisoner. I've already won. I only need to know where she is, and I'll wrench her away from that happy family and from you. No matter where the FUA tries to hide her, she will be mine.

Sincerely,

A Dear Friend

Zack's parched lips cracked when they trembled, holding back the cry of intolerable anger welling inside his chest. He sprang up and rounded on the gems happily bonded to their precious heir, no matter if she were in a coma or not. His cheeks flared and reddened. He landed several punches against the glass and split open his knuckles. Zack felt no pain and continued a rampage, tossing the letter and stomping on it.

"You haven't won, you son-of-a-bitch!" he howled. "You bastard!" Zack rushed at the glass and hit it again. He began barking at the diamonds, almost expecting a reply when he stated, "You did this to her! You made her the heir! Bring her back to me." Spittle sprayed over the glass before he slipped to the floor and huddled into a solemn ball. "You brought this hell… nothing you ever did was in her favour." He banged his head roughly into the windowsill. Blood trickled down his knuckles and smeared his jeans as he ran them up and down his thigh. He expressed his desperation in a gentle whimper. "Obeko, why won't you help her? You brought a beast in the form of a man to hurt her, and yet, you still do nothing."

The biggest enemy, the one he despised most, was Obeko. The Pharaoh had claimed the diamonds were meant to allow Cassy to perform miraculous things during her life, but had he asked her if she wished for this, he would've learned her inheritance was unwanted.

"Obeko, because of you, I've lost everything... I lost my brother, a normal life, and my girlfriend. That greedy bastard is laying in wait for her! He can easily come after her again! I just want you to tell me what to do!"

A comforting hand fell onto his shoulder. Jerking from the grip, a blurred image of a man standing above him had him almost believing Obeko heard his pleas and offered some help. However, the man in his clearing vision was a better man than Obeko could ever strive to be.

Agent Rognas stood next to him, staring at the diamonds, sorrowfully. Kneeling, he wrapped an arm around Zack's shoulders and set his agonized eyes upon him. Zack tried to wipe his tears away.

"Zack," he said tranquilly, "stop." He halted Zack's swiping hands and prompted him to let loose. "It's fine to cry. Just let it out. This pain will eventually go away, I swear."

"Mitchell, you don't understand... how I feel..." he hiccupped. "All of the expectations of me have fallen short. I failed beyond any measure. I was supposed to be another prodigy like Tomas. I was meant to stop Victor before he kidnapped her. Obeko even expected me to protect her until my last breath. I took my last breath, but then was returned only to enter hell! I'm a failure!"

Agent Rognas gave a grin. "Zack, quit worrying about what everyone thinks. You are Zackary Exacil. Don't worry about being like Tomas because, guess what, he made similar mistakes as you when he was young. He let his guard down before. Hell, he even *failed*!" The hand over Zack's shoulder nudged his cheek. "It wasn't your fault that Victor got her all the way there. Nobody expects a single agent to battle six specially trained men. The blame is to fall upon the FUA Board."

Zack frowned in dismay.

"Egyptian agents were at the tomb for four days. When news reached the Board of another theorised Egyptian Heir, they risked her life to ensure she would arrive there. They've been waiting for this opportunity ever since Bryce Éclair sought them out. They wanted the diamonds to be retrieved so they could control the heir and the diamonds. Mr. Edwards has been fighting tooth and nail to ensure that the diamonds and the heir remain in his custody. He officially won yesterday afternoon. If she wakes up, she'll be given the choice of training with the diamonds or having them sealed away here forever. It will be no one's choice except hers."

"Those corrupt bastards allowed her to be abused just so they could gain a rare opportunity over those useless diamonds!"

Agent Rognas nodded. "Zack, as long as she's here, Mr. Edwards will prevent them from ever laying a single greedy hand upon her. Given the circumstances, I think you have gone beyond your duty as an agent. You have sat with her all this time. That is, I think, the best protection she'll ever need. You proved that you would fight for her if, in the end, you can be with her. Your love will set her free, Zack." Agent Rognas stood tall and hauled Zack up with him. "Now, no more sour face. Let's go have a coffee. Mr. Edwards mentioned the sentencings have finally arrived. I'd like to hear it from you. Besides, it'll clear your head to talk about those bastards rotting in prison rather than dwelling on how they *might* escape."

Startled to hear that, Zack cocked his head to find the crumpled letter, half straightened out, in Agent Rognas' other hand.

They spent the rest of the night talking in soft tones over steaming cups of coffee. They lavished in memories of old assignments and Tomas' outgoing personality, Zack also relinquished a lot of his harboured worries. Once the first early birds interrupted their visit, Zack begged Agent Rognas to start meeting each night. Agent Rognas accepted pleasantly, and their visits became a trend which brought out the courage Zack needed to develop a smile again. The male became much more pleasant towards other agents and was found more often at dinner times.

Mr. Edwards visited and was impressed with Zack's improved mood, but always dreaded the day that Zack would be forced to go home. It became less stressful for the aging man when Zack started to consider that he might return home to ease Cassy's brothers' and his mother's sickly worry. Some days he looked at Cassy's face and was certain that he would leave at the end of the week, but then others, he found excuses to not leave her motionless form. However, his only saving grace from plummeting into the abyss of depression was Agent Rognas. No matter what Zack's mood, Agent Rognas remained a supportive friend.

The daily visits with Cassy and nightly ones with Agent Rognas stayed the same for days, which passed into a week and then into another.

Chapter 19

Cassy surveyed the everlasting crashing waves of the turquoise ocean. She finally saw the freedom of the men who stole away her life, yet, she was still trapped in this strange place. The fog rolled across the water, sprinkling the sunset with an eerie calmness that swept over the horizon in light pink and purple hues. She continued to wish to return home, but something halted her attempts to rise.

For a while longer, she watched the sunset. She was alone and scared. Slumping to the sandy ground, Cassy called out for someone to arouse her. Each dawn brought a known hand to touch hers, and she saw blurry images of her heroic boyfriend when her eyes flickered into the bright lights of Cassy's true sight. He spoke to her. She heard sections of what he said, learning all about the FUA and Zack's secretive personal life. At times, other gurgled voices surrounded him, to which he responded, sometimes angrily, sometimes relaxedly. Whenever she went to reply to his desperate cries, it didn't seem to reach him. He always left her with an unhappy goodbye.

The sun disappeared as the cool night sky settled into its rightful place. Her throat held a lump of sorrow coursing its way up from the pit of her stomach. Trapped within her own mind, time was infinite, and she lost track of it after three 'days'. It always ended up the same, no matter if she ran through the forest behind her or jumped into the water to swim for hours.

Cassy tossed a clump of sand into the glass-like water tickling at her toes. It was impossible to break free and rescue Zack from his self pity.

A strong hand swooped in and lifted her from the ground. This never happened before. When she spun to rip from the probable kidnapper snatching her away, she instead saw Obeko grinning above her.

"My dear heir, you still have many years to live. Leave this heinous place! It is not your time for eternal sleep."

He lifted her into the air and allowed her to float high into the darkening sky.

•   •   •

Cassy jolted into a state of panic as soon as the exterior smells of a hospital reached her nostrils. It nauseated her to the point of gagging. That's when she realized it wasn't the smell, but the tube that pumped air into her lungs against her own rhythm of breathing. No one was within the room, and it seemed odd that the hospital did not have the typical white-washed walls and curtained dividers separating other patients from herself. This one was completely sealed in, and reminded her of a bedroom. The panic overwhelmed her.

Oh god! she thought. *Victor got me again. We weren't saved at all!*

Cassy sprang into action. They were not going to take advantage of the diamonds. She snaked the breathing tube out of her throat as she tugged the hose. Her gag reflex reacted, tightening around it to make it tougher to slip out. Eventually it did, but after many revolting grunts. Her legs swung over the ledge of the bed and her bare feet met with the cool tiled flooring. They toppled under her weight as if they hadn't been used in weeks, and she collapsed. The IV burst out of her veins and prompted blood to spew out from the broken skin. She ignored the pain and ripped off the heart monitor attached to her finger. A loud screeching noise burst her long-unused eardrums. A swear erupted from her cracked lips as the alarm alerted whoever was outside. Using all of her might, Cassy crawled into a closed linen closet and listened to the people scurrying in. Three sets of footsteps clicked around.

It was a small woman in purple scrubs that located the quivering patient. Extending her hand out, she encouraged Cassy to grab it.

"Cassandra," a man said from behind the nurse, "it's alright. You're safe."

Cassy croaked low volume words. "Where's Zack? Did he make it out alright? Where's Victor and the others?"

The nurse cooed, "Cassandra, we will go grab Agent Exacil. Do you know where you are?"

Her matted hair swayed with her stiffly moving head as it shook. "You're in the FUA."

"Please," Cassy pleaded, "I want to see Zack!"

The doctor ushered her from the closet to fix up her wounds and adjust a new IV into her arm as they waited for Zack. The excitement exhausted her almost to the brink of fainting. Her tearing out the breathing tube left minimal damage to her throat tissue, but she still felt its rawness as the doctor calmed her down with a small dose of sedative.

Zack, a strange blonde male, and Mr. Edwards all barged in as she began to grow tired. The doctor urged them not to rile her up anymore, since she needed to recuperate from the excitement of her alarmed arousal. The blonde snuck back into the hallway with Mr. Edwards, both cheering in celebration. Zack snagged his typical chair and perched upon it. His hands snatched her freshly bandaged one, and he instantly smiled when her hand also curled around his. Cassy's heart raced in absolute serenity. Her eyes drooped heavily from the sedative, leaving her at the mercy of visions of the week she was held by those monsters. Rather than dizzily tolerating it, she rose her head, wanting to stay awake if possible until the too-good-to-be-true dream ended.

"Victor..."

"Lay down," Zack reassured. He pressed against her shoulder to settle her back to the pillow. "You don't need to worry about him. He's locked up in New York City."

"They're already in prison?" the hand with the IV rose to her forehead as she asked this. "How long have I been out?"

"A month and two weeks, give or take a few days."

"My brothers..." *They must be so worried!*

Zack took the hint before slipping her frantic hand out of his grip and sneaking to the doorway to call Mr. Edwards back inside. The old man bustled in with utter excitement, leaned in, and gave her a peck on the forehead. He was a good man, and saw a lot of his agents as his young charges, but the two before him had caused him to become the fatherly type. Cassy's eyes drooped more heavily, suppressing Zack's hidden eagerness to finally view a responsive girlfriend.

"Mr. Edwards, can I see my brothers? They're probably freaking out if it's been almost two months since I was taken."

"That is very true, Cassandra. However, we can't bring them here. You and Zackary will be transported to Royal University Hospital, where Dr. Carlisle will tag along and tend to you until you're strong enough to head home. Lucky for us, the FUA has its own wing. Zackary, since nobody knows of him being home—"

Cassy shrilled as loudly as possible, "Zack! You haven't seen your mother yet?"

"I had to wait... I couldn't leave you like that."

Zack's smile drooped and he was pinned in guilty displeasure as she tiredly scolded him. Mr. Edwards calmed the teenage girl before continuing.

"Cassandra, he is to pretend that he has been recently discharged. We have a backstory, but you need to play along with it. Alright?"

She nodded and the man praised her for understanding. Excusing himself, Mr. Edwards whispered something to Zack and then disappeared. Cassy rested again. Her mind was foggy. Safety had surrounded them, and Zack's pleasant deep voice talked away as she drifted back into a calm, dreamless sleep.

•   •   •

Michael poured a steaming cup of coffee and flipped through the newspaper. Brant left early in the morning to walk around the city, tacking up missing posters with Cassy's most recent picture on it. Vince restlessly slept upstairs. He had stayed up until three-thirty in the morning to browse international newspapers on the internet. If any of them mentioned a missing brunette girl, he was going to spot it. Michael ruffled his hair in distress as he checked the time. He was going to be starting his first week of work in a day after two months of personal leave. The man on the bracelet was unreachable, and the police were beginning to lose faith in finding her. The amber alert had been lifted four days previously, returning the Waters' lives back to a routine. Vince was drinking again, not as heavily, so he could be productive when he needed to be, but enough to numb everything around him. Brant had failed four finals and was now taking summer classes so he could graduate and enter a university in the following winter term. Michael wanted it all to end. He could handle the bickering between Cassy and himself, and preferred it to this.

The telephone abruptly rang, shaking the house with its loudness. Michael grumbled away from the table. Recently, consoling neighbours had been calling to give condolences to help ease the mourning. It irritated all three brothers. She was not dead. He outright refused that option. He would believe it only if they brought back her body. He slumped from the kitchen to the telephone next to the staircase on a taller coffee table.

"Hello?" he moaned.

"Good morning, Mr. Waters. It's Officer Grust," a woman's voice said.

Michael's stomach sank. They hadn't called him for quite a few days. Their last conversation had not been pleasant after she recommended to expect the worst after such a long time. Most kidnapped victims were not found alive after the first forty-eight hours, and she could only apologize as Michael stubbornly denied this outcome.

"Any news?"

"Well, Mr. Waters, I have some exceptional news! During a raid, the New York City police located two teenagers being held captive in a warehouse just outside the city. The girl was found unconscious, while the teenage boy was badly beaten and didn't speak a word about who either of them were until late last night when the girl finally awoke. We have just identified them as Zackary Exacil and Cassandra Waters. Early this morning they were transported back to Saskatoon to be admitted into Royal University Hospital. She is aware of her surroundings and has no memory loss."

Michael's grip tightened with every spoken word.

"We are sorry it took so long. They were found two weeks ago, but since they were not talking, we weren't able to identify them. The doctor has confirmed that she is strong enough for a visit, if you'd like to come."

His balance wavered from this small light at the end of the tunnel. "She's home… she's been found!"

"Mr. Waters, because I know you had some issues with Zackary Exacil beforehand, you should know that he saved Cassandra's life. He stayed with her the entire time and refused to leave her side until she woke up. He would sacrifice a lot for her."

"Is he at the hospital as well?"

"Yes, I believe his stay there will be short, since he is mostly healed."

Michael praised the officer's efforts before hanging up and darting up the steps to retrieve Vince. Each shake of his shoulders became progressively more aggressive, as Vince refused to rise from his half-pleasant dream. A moan of irritation escaped from him, and he swiped Michael's hands away. Michael stubbornly persisted, growing with anticipation to reach the hospital.

"Vince, get up!" he exclaimed. "We have to get to the hospital!"

"Why? Did something happen to Brant?" Vince rubbed his eyes, lolling his weary head around.

"Thank goodness, no! They found Cassy! She's there, waiting for us!"

Vince instantly jumped out of bed. Slipping into dirty clothes, he rushed out of the bedroom, tripped down the steps, and landed at the foyer before Michael had the chance to grab hold of his keys and cell phone.

"What about Brant? Will he meet us there?"

"I'm texting him now. He'll meet us at the front lobby of the hospital."

Both sprinted across the driveway in the fresh summer air to unexpectedly welcome back their sibling after a nightmarish stretch of time.

• • •

A new hospital environment came into focus. The brown walls had now become the typical white colour, and the hustle and bustle of doctors darting about, gurneys carrying patients, and people in wheelchairs aroused Cassy from the drug-induced sleep. A white lab coat billowed around the lean man she had seen at the FUA. He tapped the IV package to assure that it flowed properly. Cassy smiled back at his wispy "Good morning" and then curled into the blankets, feeling the chill of the hospital surrounding her. The doctor requested to do some vital checks and began fiddling with a stethoscope to check her heart rate. Cassy jerked lightly when the cold metal claimed the heat from her skin. She was quickly comforted by the hand of the beloved boy who had tolerated everything, even if it meant he might die.

"Zack!" she swooned.

"Hey, beautiful," said Zack, "how was your rest?"

Unlike in the FUA, where he had been dressed in a black cotton shirt and dark-washed jeans, he now had pajama pants and a partial hospital gown on to act as though he had been admitted in the hospital as well. Cassy clung to his palm, noticing that the small scratches on his face had healed and the bullet wound on his shoulder was covered in gauze, stitched up earlier in their rescue.

"Thank you, Zack..." she whispered.

"For what?"

"For being there this entire time... I heard you, in my sleep... You kept my mind alive. You sat next to me every day and held my hand. I even remember you asking a nurse to do my hair because you liked it better when it was pulled back." She rose her free hand to the less than perfect French braid tucked over one shoulder. "Swear to me that you will stop blaming yourself for what happened. It's not your fault, ever!"

"You heard it all?" Zack awed at her abilities to surprise him.

Cassy shrugged. "A lot is hazy, but what I do remember will remain in my heart forever. I love you!"

He leaned in to kiss her reddened lips. The long-awaited moment to feel them against his without being cold was too hard not to revel in. Unfortunately, their time alone was short lived, and a nurse burst inside to prevent the doctor or the couple from continuing their activities.

"Excuse me, Doctor, but there's two young men here to see Miss Waters. Will it be alright to bring them inside?"

The doctor raised an eyebrow. He was surprised the brothers were tolerant enough to wait when Cassy was a mere three metres away.

"I suppose Cassandra is up for a visit."

Cassy excitedly lifted herself into a seated position and clenched Zack's palm, half-expecting the deceiving cloud of happiness to fade just as the door opened. However, nothing of the sort happened. Rather, a grin from ear to ear spread across Michael's bearded features and he rushed in, warming her torso with his thick arms. They protected her like nothing had before. Michael pulled back to view her. He had awaited the sight of her and found no words to express his bubbling emotions. Vince shoved Michael away as his arms folded around her. Cassy smelt the scent of alcohol on his clothes, but it was not on his breath when he whispered "I love you." She sensed the kidnapping might have increased his drinking. Instead of questioning it, since it was an argument meant for another day, she cocked her head, waiting for a third hug.

"Where's Brant?"

"He got stuck in traffic. He'll be here soon."

Tension quickly grew when Michael noticed Zack awkwardly sitting beside Cassy, clinging to her bandaged palm. Cassy panicked that he might blame Zack for the kidnapping. However, what she saw in Michael was not hatred, but appreciation towards the young man.

"Zack," Michael barked. Tears brimmed his eyelids. Within seconds, Zack was lifted from his butt and into Michael's bear hug. "Thank you so much for protecting her. If it weren't for you, she'd be dead. She'll be alright now. I'm sorry for being an asshole. I should have trusted you. You were among the handful of people that didn't betray this family." He released. "You are welcome around her any time!"

Zack was taken aback and gaped at Michael. Finally, after all their arguments, Michael seemed to realize that there were worse people than the fifteen-year-old boy.

"Thanks, Michael." Zack added, "If it's alright with you, I'd like permission to officially take Cassy out for a date."

"Only if Cassy accepts."

Cassy giggled, "Of course I accept! I love my knight in shining armour!"

•   •   •

Brant drove in a frenzy to reach the hospital. Each swerved pass nearly sideswiped someone. At the hospital, he fumbled to pay for parking and then bulldozed his way inside to meet his brothers in the main lobby. The wait painfully increased when nobody was there to greet him. After twenty minutes of pacing, Brant finally decided to approach a receptionist for help. He tapped an anguish-filled finger when he spoke to the woman.

"Hey, I got a text from my brother saying to meet him here, but I don't see him. Is there possibly a Michael or Vince Waters that's been admitted in the past hour?"

"No one of those first names."

Brant was paralyzed in his stance. "By chance, is there a Cassandra Waters?"

"Yes, there is. She was transferred here just this morning from another facility."

"Which room is she in? She's my little sister!"

Brant halted in his fast-paced shifting once the woman announced her room number and backtracked to ask curiously about someone else. "Was there a young man, Zack Exacil, with her?"

"Yes. Both were safely transferred here."

He dashed up the steps two at a time. The elevator moved too slowly for the excitement dispelling his dread. He ran around nurses and patients once he reached the proper level. His feet slipped across the recently cleaned floor as people around him shouted to slow down. He just couldn't. Worriedly, he prayed that she was no longer in danger. Just outside the closed, windowed door, Brant took deep breaths in. Closing his eyes and releasing the feelings of astonishment, his palms shook against the silver handle. Twice he turned it, but never slipped it open, feeling as if he dreamt of something wonderful. He finally decided not to knock and barrelled inside. The sight he saw caused him to sigh in relief: Cassy sat up in her bed, bundled up in the thin flannel sheets and a hospital gown, her hair in a dishevelled French braid. The inconspicuous cuts along her arms and neck made him wince.

She twisted just in time to find Brant inches away and wrapping his arms around her.

"Oh, dear God, I'm so glad you're safe, Cassy!" He rubbed her cheek with the tip of his stubby thumb. "How did..."

Michael interrupted before Brant broached on a touchy subject, "The cops called me and alerted me that she had just awoken from a coma. She was found in New York City."

"What was she doing there?"

The eldest gave an honest shrug. "I have no idea. All I can say, is I have really grown to appreciate that Zack kid..."

Brant gaped and turned to Cassy's glistening features.

"You all heard that, right?" she cheered. "He can't deny it now! Zack's a keeper!"

Resting her head on Brant's knee, she was becoming worn out from all the delight on her first conscious day. The youngest brother jested about Michael's sudden acceptance of the troublemaker of a boy.

Brant queried, "What's changed your mind about him?"

"He kept her safe, and compared to those other men, he's a saint."

"Men plural? Who kidnapped her other than Buddy?"

Michael spoke in a gentle monotone to the resting sister. "She said, right before you came in, that *they* are in prison. She mentioned that Buddy's involvement was minimal compared to a few of the others. She refused to talk much about it."

"What about Zack? Have you seen him?"

"Yeah, you missed him. He was here but wanted to get a glass of water. I think he felt overwhelmed with us bawling like little babies."

Vince punched Brant's shoulder and mentioned, "Michael even apologized to him!"

Brant pet Cassy's silky hair and then called her name to check if she was awake. When no motion happened, except for a tiny exhale of dreaming air, he resituated Cassy onto her pillow.

"Jeez! Could your text be anymore vague? 'Something happened, meet at Royal University Hospital.' Then you don't even meet me at the lobby! I thought Vince had died or something!"

Michael sloughed off the accusations.

"I was in a rush. Besides, you did text that you were stuck in traffic. We got antsy and needed to make sure it wasn't a prank."

"This is definitely an unexpected surprise."

Cassy slept passively under the watchful eyes of her brothers and the FUA agents scouring the hospital for threats.

• • •

With a grimace smeared across his face, Zack's hand halted just outside the hospital room. He heard the brothers whispering in a monotone, and no Cassy piped in with her delicate, sweet voice. He assumed the strain to keep awake took its toll on her. Zack's nerve to sit with her brothers while she slept slipped away quickly. Besides, if he interrupted them at this point, they would berate him with questions he wished not to answer. Abruptly turning to return to the cafeteria, Zack met Mr. Edwards' solid chest.

"Sorry, sir."

Mr. Edwards snoopily peeked into the window. He raised an eyebrow in questioning. Zack's intent to leave offended Mr. Edwards. He hoped that Zack had gotten over the petty battles with the brothers. Zack shook his head back and forth, tensing his jaw.

"Michael actually apologized and everything... it's just..." he mumbled into his collarbone when his head dropped down, "I can't see her sleep anymore. I want to wait until she's up."

Mr. Edwards nudged Zack's chin in jest. "See, I told you you'd get sick of her lying there day after day."

Finishing up with the task of checking on the Egyptian Heir, Mr. Edwards began his stroll back to the elevators.

"Sir," Zack interrupted, "how long do you think we have until news reaches them?"

Zack couldn't remove the letter from his thoughts. *Victor is ready to break out. He's going to come for her! I can't become emotionally flustered again. This will mean life or death for her.*

"Relish in this small victory," Mr. Edwards replied. When Zack's hypersensitivity to the letter was shown, Mr. Edwards heaved in a large sigh. "Zackary, I have agents on high alert for when the news does reach them. The New York FUA will monitor it for the following six months. Those men won't be escaping."

"Jason and Eric escaped, and they aren't even specialized in evading punishment."

"Look inside that room." Mr. Edwards pointed through the small, wire crisscrossed window. "You see that family? They are welcoming their baby sister home after two months of being separated. This is a victory. You need to erase the fear for the time being and join them. Michael accepted you. Take it while you can, because one day, our small victory may become hell again." Encouraging Zack to go inside, the boss added, "If anything ever happens with those men, you will be the first to know. For now, no more serious Agent Exacil. Be her boyfriend and fret not."

It was then that Zack's heart fluttered at the echo of heeled shoes. He heard someone bustling around, calling out for help in finding her son. Zack and Mr. Edwards both spun to find a blonde, long-haired woman in a grey skirted suit and black heels bustling about in panic. Her blue eyes glistened when she began to conclude someone played a nasty trick on her. That was when she halted, looking at the far end of the hallway. Zack wore pajama bottoms underneath a gown, which hid most of the battle wounds scarring his torso. His socked feet took off and reached his mother before she could even react. Her frail arms trembled against him in astonishment.

"Zackary! Oh, my sweet, sweet boy! I'm sorry it took so long. They couldn't get a hold of me because I was in court!"

Zack winced when she pressed tightly on the bullet wound. It was mostly healed, and yet a tenderness still lingered. She gasped, pulling down the gown to check on him. The gauze was clean and hid the stitches that would be removed in three weeks. An infection had spread, since Zack had refused to treat it properly.

A whirlwind of concerned inquiries spewed out of her as she fiddled with his upper torso to check on him in a motherly way. Zack needed her to stop, so he tugged her in a tight embrace.

"What happened to you, Honey?"

"Mom, I'm fine. I swear. Cassy is the only one who needs to be in the hospital right now. I just can't be released until you sign some papers."

"Where is Cassandra?" Zack's mother had been told about the classmate kidnapped along with Zack. "The officer said that she just woke up from a coma. Is she seriously injured?"

"Nah, she'll be alright." Zack looked towards the room. "She's in there with her brothers right now, sleeping. We'll visit her later."

"I would like to talk to them. They really did all they could to find you two when all I could do was cry."

"I bet you did all that you could, Mom, given the circumstance." His height over his mother had him looking down on her reddened eyes, which were usually prim and proper. "Mom, want to sign those papers and then go to the cafeteria and have a drink? I wouldn't mind sticking around until Cassy wakes up."

She muttered a simple yes and then searched around for the strange man who seemed to be an acquaintance of her son. "Your friend may come as well."

Embarrassingly for her, Mr. Edwards had already snuck passed the two, under the watchful eye of Zack, and entered the dinging elevator before he was questioned any further. Zack's personal life and secret life were separated by the unspoken rule that they must never clash.

Patting her startled back, Zack escorted his elated mother to the ward clerk for the paperwork.

●　●　●

Cassy's bandaged hand laced into Zack's while he lounged in the cushioned chair, lolling off to sleep. The brothers' exhilaration evaporated into exhaustion as the long-awaited day drained them. They had to restrain themselves from questioning the twosome too vigorously on the events of the past two months. Zack declined several times, and Cassy shrugged honestly in response to questions about the time they were gone before Michael and Brant began to mention other things. Mrs. Exacil stayed awhile, introducing herself to the Waters family and then hugging Cassy, which was the only way she could empathise with the horrors both teenagers had faced. Once the warm welcome was relinquished, Zack offered to go home with his mother. She, however, declined, and told him to stay with Cassy for a bit longer. As visiting hours ended, Michael and the brothers whispered their love and left the sister with cheer written across her bright cheeks.

The moment the returned teenagers had the room to themselves, Zack longingly kissed her and then sank into the chair to become comfortable. The doctor permitted him to stay if he wished.

She patted his hand, wondering what her life would turn out to be. "Nothing's going to be the same..."

His head leaned backwards on the chair's back, and he mumbled, "No, it's not."

She widened her eyes as she realized with clarity that the diamonds sealed her fate. As Zack fell asleep, she considered the possibilities of what would be expected of her. She stretched her legs underneath the blankets and accepted the role as the Egyptian Heir.

"I hope, Obeko, that you will help me fix this miserable world!" the heir demanded. "I wish it!"

CPSIA information can be obtained
at www.ICGtesting.com
Printed in the USA
BVHW070205231021
619501BV00003B/10